CROWNS OF FATE

THE BROKEN PROPHECY BOOK 3

ANNA APPLEGATE

HELEN DOMICO

CONTENT NOTES

This book contains content that some readers may find triggering such as:

On-Page Violence
Threats of Violence
Torture
Grief
Death
Mental Health Struggles (Anxiety, Panic Attacks)
Profanity
Open-Door Intimate Scenes

Read with Care <3

DEDICATION

To you, our readers: You are stronger than the darkness within you.

And to **KPop Demon Hunters**: Thank you for being our soundtrack while working on this book.
Jinu—we're down on our knees, please be our idol.

BROOKMERE
BROHAM
LARKSLARY
UPPINGTON
ELLEVALE
LOGAN LAKE
VALEFORD
STARHAVE
ROME
SOUTHERN FORESTS
DEMARVA
BRIARTOWN
HEMLOCK
CRIMSON FOREST
CANYON CITY
MOUNT LEGION
FIRESTONE
MYSTHAVEN
RIDGEMONT
ATHERIA
N

SHADOWS OF RUIN RECAP

- Lana has been kidnapped by the king-murdering marriage trials contender, Kade, and taken to the Forgotten Kingdom, also known as Mysthaven, a world that shouldn't exist. We are immediately introduced to Kade's friends Raya and Jax.

- Lana tries to escape back to Brookmere on more than one occasion while they are traveling toward Kade's home. But in true magic-less princess fashion, she is no match for the Shadow Daddy and is stopped at every turn.

- Poor Ian is trapped in the dungeons in Brookmere, being tortured at every possible moment by evil Andras, who has taken over the palace at Ellevail. The queen is locked away, and Andras's mind magic is hard at work convincing anyone and everyone of his lies. But he's not the only one entering people's minds. Raya slips into Ian's mind while he's being tortured, establishing a connection to Brookmere that Ian is anything but thrilled about.

- Back in Mysthaven, we learn that not only is the king horrifically evil and spent years torturing Kade, but he is also Kade's father. Meaning Kade is a prince!
- King Dargan enacts the Festival of Swords and the Blood Oath. Lana is called to fight during the festival and must make the oath herself. But she stands her ground and reveals her true identity.
- Kade, in a stupid attempt to keep Lana safe from his father, acts like a giant jerk during a ball but quickly realizes he can't keep it up. He makes it up to her by having his shadows give Lana the best birthday present. (Have you read the bonus scene yet, from the shadows' POV? If not, run to our website now… You do not want to miss this.)
- Back in Brookmere, with the help of Kalliah, Corbin, Leif, and Hale, Ian is able to escape the dungeons. However, Andras's plans proved sinister. He let them escape so Ian would eventually return Lana to him. While letting them go, Andras killed Queen Roxana, Lana's last remaining parent. Leif sacrifices himself to give everyone time to escape Ellevail. Is he alive? Only time will tell… Regardless, Kalliah is heartbroken.
- Finally, Ian, Kalliah, and Corbin are reunited with Lana, Kade, Storm, Jax, and Raya. Lana learns about her mother's fate. Ian punches Kade. Raya and Ian are so standoffish toward each other, it's uncomfortable. Jax is just sitting back enjoying the show and constantly munching on apples (you'd think he was a horse shifter instead of a panther).
- The group ventures to Lana's birth parents' home in Valeford to look for something hidden that she'll need to win this war. The house was left as is, blood still smeared on the wall, but the grave site is

preserved. Lana discovers a mysterious hidden dagger, and a suspicious note reveals that the item they were seeking, a journal, has been hidden.

- Poor sweet Hale betrays Ian and the crew and leads Lana straight into Andras's hands. A battle ensues. Hale saves Lana and dies telling her about how much he loves her. Meanwhile, Andras flees the minute it seems like he won't win, taunting everyone instead of returning Lana to Ellevail.
- Lana and company return to the Knotted Willow, their base of operations, to regroup. Vivienne is there, spouting more crazy absurdities. Lana starts to believe in herself, and they know they have to separate again to defeat Kade's father and gather an army to fight Andras. Ian, Corbin, and Kalliah remain in Brookmere to build an army with all of their allies through the Hidden Henchman. Lana, Kade, Jax, Storm, and Raya return to Mysthaven to speak with Cassandra to find out more.
- Lana and Kade learn an additional prophecy from Cassandra, revealing that the seer has a mate… and he's the epitome of evil. But nothing goes to plan. Storm is kidnapped, Raya is under Dargan's spell, and Lana accidentally unleashes Thames, the thousand-year-old sorcerer desperate to take over the world who has been the source of the darkness, trapped in the void.
- And worse yet? Thames overpowered Kade.
- And all he could do was tell Lana to run…

Buckle up…it's about to be a battle of good and evil.
For Atheria, we fight.

PROLOGUE
CASSANDRA, PRESENT DAY

A thousand years of running from fate should have prepared me for this moment.

A thousand years of waiting, of only hearing part of a prophecy that I knew would determine whether Atheria will rise again or fall forever.

A thousand years without the sister I had sacrificed everything for.

Yet at the beginning of the end of the Fates' plans, I couldn't run fast enough.

Fleeing the halls of this palace—this prison—became my singular focus as the earth trembled beneath my feet. *I knew.* One did not need to be a seer or a sorceress to know the gates of hell had been opened and evil now poured into our world.

Thames.

Every bone in my body rejected his presence as the tendrils of his power, of *our* power, permeated the cracks within the walls. Whispers of promises once sung, an unrequited love, searched desperately for me, attempting to trap me in his grasp. A thousand years of pain enduring the bond I wish could be severed.

The crimes I'd committed in the name of unconditional

love for my mate were unfathomable. The years I spent tormented at the agony and evil in this world, the very evil I helped make far too powerful, haunted me. Some nights, it dragged me into a place deeper than the lowest bowels of the earth. Into void lands and utter darkness.

But I had righted my wrongs. I turned to something far more powerful than the dark magic on which Thames thrived: true love and sacrifice. Together, the two provided me with enough power to create a prison, trapping Thames in the void. I would not fall into his hands again.

The dark palace, nestled among the mountains of rock, lurked behind me as I mounted the chestnut stallion, already saddled in the stables. A calling pulled me forward as we made our way through the rocky terrain of Mount Legion. While it had been hundreds of years since I'd left the palace grounds, it did not matter.

The Fates' unrelenting insistence lured me away from my home. It waged a war against the inexplicable urge to return to my mate. The strength it took to deny my bond threatened to knock me off my horse. I growled, holding in the scream building inside of me at the tension. I'd resisted *his* callings for a thousand years. The summons of a seer, though, *must* be obeyed. Ignoring the Fates was impossible, and even if I managed to, it could lead to dire consequences. A burden those chosen must bear.

"Faster, Phoenix." Urging my stallion to move quicker, we navigated the dusty terrain, through forests of leafless trees. Intertwined branches lay bare in the eerie tunnels the landscape created, carving our path forward.

Beads of sweat dripped down my back as the setting sun shone the last of its rays on our perilous journey.

Where exactly the Fates wanted me to be remained unclear, but I knew we traveled toward destiny, a thread pulling me to my eventual end.

The winds warmed my cheeks the longer we traveled,

lulling me into a false sense of security, begging me to rest along with the rhythm of my horse, despite the frantic speed. When my eyes pleaded to close, I forced them open. I would not let my body betray me now.

Hours passed. The sun moved across the sky, creating shadows of my figure on the dry paths. How much farther would it take to answer the Fates' call?

Phoenix faltered more than once, until eventually, neither of us could travel any farther. My beautiful stallion collapsed upon the dirt, panting for air as I fell sideways off his back.

"We are safe. You did well." I whispered reassurances to the steed, even if I knew we would never truly be safe while Thames roamed this plane. But for now, we had to rest. Just long enough for me to be able to heal the aching hooves of my companion.

The powers I shouldn't have, ones that have been lost to the history books of old, allowed me to conjure the water deep within the ground to pool atop, granting my steed much relief.

Whispering the words of my long-forgotten ancestors, I opened my hands before me, summoning water for me to drink as well. I pushed past the exhaustion engulfing me, making my hands shake. Gulping down the cool liquid soothed the fire burning my lungs. My strength returned slowly, with every sip, and with every bite of the chewy fruit I found hidden in the saddle bags.

I closed my eyes, just for a moment to rest my weary soul, though I didn't deserve it. The first time I ever slept peacefully occurred when that little prince healed in my quarters overnight after his father whipped him bloody. He didn't know I lingered next to the bed in the late hours of night, soaking in his innocence as he recovered. He reminded me my power could be used for good. He reminded me, even with my evil past, there might still be hope if I could get him to his future.

His destiny had been determined by the Fates themselves.

When my eyes peeled open, the last rays of light were

disappearing on the horizon. A caw echoed in the distance and reminded me we weren't alone in this world. We had to press forward. I jerked my body up and dug down deep to find the will to continue.

Rubbing the neck of the horse, light emitted from the tips of my fingers, healing the unimaginable aching muscles of my friend.

"Just a little bit more," I whispered, gently rubbing his mane. "We must keep going."

He nuzzled my palm and huffed a breath in agreement.

"Let's ride."

The tendril of Fates calling grew louder and threatened to explode as we reached a jagged, rocky line in the ground. The mist, which once lay impenetrable over the void holding Thames in its grasp, had disappeared. In its place lay a colorless river of debris, soil, and deadened ground. The land completely and utterly drained of life. Thames had infested his prison exactly as he planned to infest the world—with death and destruction.

A shiver skated over my sweat-slicked skin as we crossed the threshold into the area where the void once stood. One careful step at a time, we wandered into the foreign land. More caws echoed in the sky. An alert to the world that something was coming.

The wings of a voidling created a shadow as it passed ahead, flying in the opposite direction I rode. Its monstrous scales glittered in the sunlight, but the beast ignored me completely.

A stray breeze danced across the dusty ground, pressing against my back and pushing me forward.

My heart pounded, thudding with both anticipation and fear. I knew where the Fates were leading me now. I felt her. Closer than she'd been in a thousand years.

Would she forgive me for what I'd done? For the pain I'd caused us both? While she knew why I cast this horrible spell, while she agreed it must be done—after all these years, would she still love me, even if I didn't deserve it?

My heart raced, erratic, panicked. It had been so long. I pushed Phoenix forward as his careful steps turned into a frantic gallop toward the only person who loved me through every evil deed. The person whom I'd sacrificed it all to protect.

I didn't do it alone. A thousand years ago, Evelyn, Queen of Brookmere, Jasper, King of Mysthaven, and I may have each sacrificed everything to save our world, but selfishly, I'd done it to ensure Thames could never reach *her*.

On too many occasions he kept me from her presence. When he threatened her life to ensure I remained his and only his, I knew the time had come.

I surged through the landscape before me, urging Phoenix to jump over the dead bramble and decaying ground, searching as the string luring me onward tightened.

Suddenly there, where the world should've ended had the curse still been in place, stood my sister.

Relief overtook every one of my senses, seeing her face-to-face again. My beautiful, strong sister. Her face tilted toward the sun, arms reaching for the sky, eyes closed in apparent reverence.

I stopped just a few lengths before her. Dismounting, I fell into a heap, my legs giving out beneath me, my body yearning to run to her before I even had my footing. But still, I rose, racing for her. Her eyes opened, and when her gaze met mine, her arms fell to her sides.

"Cassandra," she whispered. Her wiry grey hair stood on end, begging to be tamed.

Fear, longing, anguish, love—all stuck in my throat, unsure of how to make amends for our past, yet frantic to wrap her in a hug and reassure myself she was truly here.

Smiling, I thought about reaching for her but paused, coming to a halt and swallowing down the part of me that so desperately wanted to touch her. "Vivienne. You look terrible," I joked.

She scoffed, and her mouth, open in shock, morphed into a smile spreading across her face as she took me in. I didn't miss the pain glistening in her eyes. "A thousand years will do that to someone."

Lightning cracked above us, splitting the sky open, as rain spilled instantaneously. The ground making up the void drank in the water like a starved Fae.

A gust of wind followed, whipping around us, weaving through our hair and clothes. I felt it everywhere, embracing me in its tendrils.

Whispers, faint at first, carried toward Vivienne and me until it was not only the wind itself surrounding us, but the Fates' words as well.

Void of magic, a heroine born,
Destiny calls, though faint and torn.
Many will come from across the land,
Yet only the strongest will win her hand.
With lover's touch, she shall ignite,
Without it, perish from the kingdom's blight.

Vivienne's hand found mine and when we intertwined our fingers, the words continued, this time familiar ones that rang in my ears since I'd first heard the prophecy.

Rebels rise where darkness lies,
Not one but two must break the ties.
Across the void, a queen you must seek,
Trust freely given, for one alone proves too weak.
Though evil will free and be bound no more,
Fate still awaits one final war.

The rain soaked through my clothes, plastering my hair across my face as the storm continued to crescendo until it hit a deafening peak. I stepped up to my sister, grabbing her. The moment we embraced, a surge of power passed between us, claiming our bodies for itself.

This was where we were supposed to be.

Nature demanded it.

The Fates commanded it.

All at once the wind stopped, the rain ceased, and an eerie long-awaited finality settled over me.

With gazes locked, Vivienne and I spoke in unison the words flowing in my mind. Revealing together the final piece of the puzzle to rid the dark magic plaguing our lands all these years by my own hand.

Banish all ties to darkness with light,
If any remains, so will this plight.
In the end, a willing sacrifice of life
Will trigger events to cease this strife.
For the loss of love will heal what's torn
And allow this world to be reborn.

CHAPTER 1
LANA

My grip on Onyx's reins tensed as I doubled over, fighting back the nausea and pain that had become a near constant companion on this hellish escape.

Sweat beaded against my forehead as the ache pulsed somewhere deeper than any physical wound could travel.

Images flashed in my mind. Kade. *My Kade.* Crawling across the stone floor to get to me instead of paying attention to Thames materializing into this world.

"I love you, Illiana."

I whimpered, not from my own pain, but from imagining what Kade was going through.

A strong hand wrapped around my own.

But it wasn't the hand I wanted.

Still, a now familiar heat flickered across my tight grip, urging it to loosen.

I inhaled through my nose, sharp, staccato sounds as I fought the torrent of emotions flooding me. Ones of pain. Of frustration. Of anger.

My name is Illiana Dresden, the rightful Queen of Brookmere, and I am stronger than the darkness threatening to overtake our world.

I managed to inhale one steady breath. Then another.

The warmth traveled upward from my hand, dulling the pain enough to allow me to sit straighter. I glanced at the man beside me, who wore the same haunted emotion distorting all of our features.

At first Storm reassured me Kade would be all right, but after a day and a half of lending his strength, even his began to wane.

I closed my eyes before pressing my knees into Kade's horse to urge him onward.

A day and a half. That was all it had been since we escaped the palace at Mount Legion. Since Kade killed his father. Since I accidentally released Thames back into our world.

Since Kade had been overtaken with the darkness.

I rubbed my chest, despite knowing the aches were not something that could be magicked away. Only one thing would soothe this and he wasn't here.

I will not lose him.

After being told mates hadn't existed in a thousand years, I learned not only that they did, but that I had found mine. Only to have him immediately ripped from my fingers. The bond connecting Kade and myself as mates stirred with a vengeance in my soul, reacting violently to my rage and demanding I return to his side.

Wiping the sweat from my brow, I pushed past the jabbing pain in my chest, refusing to succumb to it, as we rode under the cover of night. All it would take was one misstep for me to give in and run back to Kade's side.

Something else rumbled angrily, right alongside the gnawing pain. Something foreign and itching to consume me.

My magic.

I possessed magic.

Years of torture produced not one single drop of power, and yet it all came down to a prophecy I never believed in.

With lover's touch she shall ignite. My mate ignited it. Kade unleashed it.

I had to return to him but not yet. Not when he'd given us time to run, even if it was the last thing I wanted. With distance from Thames, we would devise a plan.

We would save him.

Through a complicated network of passageways, we traveled toward a secret safe house. One unbeknownst to Kade, formed while he was competing in the marriage trials for my hand; Jax and Raya had been anything but idle while left behind in Mysthaven.

Storm rode beside me, stress lining his features. Most of his injuries sustained from Dargan's torture were healed enough, but deep purple and blue bruises still marred his arms. His nose sat at an unnatural angle where one of the guards broke it. In due time he would heal himself, or we would find a healer to expedite the process. We had no idea what battles lay ahead of us, so it seemed pointless to waste energy on such a menial task. All of us needed to be fully rested if we had any hope of making it out alive.

"We have to find Cassandra." Anger laced my tone as I finally broke the silence. Pent-up energy coiled and simmered below the surface of my skin, eager to be let free. "She knows too much and has told us far too little. She needs to tell us everything. No more riddles, no more 'what the fates will allow' bullshit. All of it."

When no one responded to my outburst, I snapped more forcefully. "We need to know."

"It's not much farther," Jax murmured, ignoring my outrage, as he once again adjusted Raya's semiconscious body in the saddle to keep her from falling. "We can talk when we know it's safe."

"Nowhere is safe, Jax." The indignation in my tone left nothing to the imagination. "Now that Thames is free, the dark ones will continue to spread. Andras has already overtaken Brookmere, no doubt with Casimir by his side, spreading evil across the kingdom. We're going to be fighting on all fronts, completely blind."

I ran a hand over my neck, breathing deeply, trying to calm my racing heart. To stop from screaming at everyone that we should go back to save Kade and forget everything else. "We at least have to warn Ian and the others. They are working on building an army, but they aren't prepared for the absolute hell that has been unleashed with Thames's release. If Raya was coherent enough…she could speak to Ian."

Jax's eyes narrowed on me. I didn't think him capable of delivering such malice to anyone, let alone me. "When Raya is awake and responsive, we will see if she even feels up to talking to Ian," Jax stated bluntly, "but *only* after we give her time to rest. We don't know what she will be like when she finally comes around."

"Lana isn't suggesting we do it this instant, brother," Storm said, placating his friend's unusual anger. "While we wait, we can come up with a plan. A realistic plan that doesn't get us all killed."

I took a moment to breathe in through my nose and held it, slowly releasing the air as a distraction before I said something I would regret.

A pained groan escaped Raya's lips and her body jerked in Jax's arms. We halted, stopping completely as our worried gazes rested on her. Jax wouldn't let her go, not since carrying her out of the palace. In all fairness, I hadn't made it easy for Storm to haul me out either.

We'd hoped Raya would've been able to heal herself, especially now, since Dargan's death meant she'd escaped his control. Unfortunately, she hadn't managed to stay awake for more than a handful of minutes during our journey. None of us knew the lasting damage of mind manipulation, or how Raya would recover after what she had endured. The longer she remained unconscious, the more our fear grew.

"Ia—" Raya coughed, unable to finish even one word. She didn't talk anymore, but her head rolled from side to side as she fought to sit upright in Jax's grasp.

Jax murmured in her ear as he slowed his horse. "You're okay. You're safe."

Did she say Ian? I couldn't help but wonder if they'd been able to speak, even in her semiconscious state. It seemed absurd to think they could, but Fates, I had magic, so right now, anything seemed possible.

Jax's brows furrowed as Raya laid the back of her head on his chest, her breathing shallow and erratic. He shook his head at Storm in some sort of silent communication I couldn't understand.

"We're almost there," Jax said. "We probably only have about thirty minutes left until we reach Canyon City. The safe house is on the outskirts. We need to stop and see if she'll drink something."

Storm looked around us, giving Jax a sharp nod in agreement.

With the horses settled and nibbling on dried pieces of grass, I grabbed a canteen and a small piece of bread from a folded satchel on the side of Storm's horse as he moved to help Raya down.

Jax propped up a sack from his own horse and helped Storm lean her against it. He brushed the damp braids from her neck, just as Ian would've done for me. Jax's loyalty to his friend shone through with every action.

Hurrying, I twisted off the top and handed him the canteen. He tilted it to her lips. Most of it spurted out of her mouth when another cough racked her body.

"Come on, Raya, you need to do this," he murmured.

She refused to look at him but drank a few sips.

My mind reeled at how broken she must be feeling, the anguish of her friends seeing her so vulnerable. I'd seen those looks on my friends too many times throughout the years.

Jax stood and stepped to the side, Storm following his lead.

"We have to get somewhere where she can lie down," Jax croaked. "She needs rest. Somewhere she isn't being jostled around constantly."

I hadn't known Jax for long, but the lack of playfulness in his gaze, in his tone, threatened to snap the minor amount of sanity I clung to.

Everything was going to shit.

"It's not much farther, we can let her rest for a few minutes," Storm conceded.

I kneeled in front of Raya, examining how much water was left in the canteen. "Do you want anything else? More water?"

She turned her head away from me.

"Raya?" I asked, reaching out toward her, but she tensed, jerking away from me like I was going to hurt her.

I swallowed, leaning back on my heels. "You need to get your strength back, we can't do this without you," I said. "We have to get in touch with Ian—"

At his name, Raya hissed, a pained sound that, based on her widening eyes, she didn't mean to make.

I reached for her arm, but she pulled away again, toppling over with the movement.

Jax ran over, lifting her from the ground. "I said after she had time to rest, Lana."

"I was trying to help, I wasn't pushing," I argued.

He pulled her body closer, and Raya's expression looked so hurt, my heart broke. What was she going through? What tormented her so much that she couldn't stand looking at us?

"I'm sorry." I stepped back.

Jax scowled, storming off back toward the horses.

Yeah, *everything* was shit.

The bond between Kade and I tightened, so much so I

glanced behind me, swearing I'd see his shadows beckoning for me, desperate for my touch.

But there was nothing there.

"Run, Little Rebel. Please don't let me catch you."

We left him. *I* left him.

I stared out across the reddish terrain, glowing in the setting sun. I took one step, then another, fully facing the direction we'd come from, my resolve to leave him wavering. Turning back like this lessened the pain. It had to be the right thing to do. Besides, turning back meant I could be with him, and those shadows that I longed to feel again just to reassure me he was safe.

Storm shouted my name, but I ignored him. Everything would be all right if I could just get to Kade. My light could help him, and he'd be free.

"Lana, you can't," Storm yelled, and in my trance-like confusion, he had moved and somehow stood in front of me.

I shoved him, needing to run. That agitated power inside of me simmered beneath the surface, urging me onward.

"Lana," Storm shouted, this time so close to my ear I flinched. His arms folded around me before I could move, holding me back from my escape.

I blinked a few times and my body slackened. I stared down at my trembling hands, clawing at his still-bruised arm.

"Fates," I yanked my hands away, guilt coursing through me.

I hadn't even registered what I'd been doing. Storm was right. This power inside of me, though, refused to listen to logic as it writhed, begging to be set free. All I could do was shake my head before a tear fell down my face.

"Look at me," Storm whispered.

I raised my head, turning to face him, as I met his gaze. It wasn't just my eyes exuding desperation and exhaustion, but his as well.

"We *will* get Kade back," he said firmly. "We will win this war. You will see your mate again. I will be with my brother again. But for now, we have to get somewhere safe."

My gaze dropped, feeling as heavy as my heart. "It feels so wrong leaving him there with that kind of evil. The real Monster of Mysthaven. What if when we finally come up with a plan, he is too far gone to be saved? What if I've lost my mate before I've even had a chance to tell him that I know? That I love—" I choked on my words.

Storm took my hands in his. "In the short amount of time we've known each other, I have seen you fight for your people. Save them time and time again. I have no doubt in my mind that you will save Kade, save your people, and hopefully, save our world." He chuckled dryly. "I'd expect nothing less from the Queen of Brookmere, let alone Kade's mate. Fates help us once the world has been restored. You two will be unbearable."

I couldn't help the smile peeking through my distress. "You act as if Kade and I are incapable of acting with proper decorum." I sighed, but before I could continue, Storm spoke once more.

"For all of us, my future queen. Let us give ourselves the best shot at you leading not just Brookmere, but all of Atheria." He squeezed my hand one more time before walking away toward Jax and Raya.

I looked at the horizon again, inhaling the dry, gritty air before allowing Storm's words to settle. He was right. I could do this.

Thankfully, I didn't have to do it alone.

"I will see you soon," I vowed my promise into the breeze, as if it could carry my words straight to Kade. "And I'll hold my dagger to your throat until you swear to me you'll never do something so reckless again."

I returned to Onyx, brushing a hand over his mane before mounting him for the final stretch of today's journey. Storm pressed his hand to Raya's arm. "Hold on just a bit longer, my friend. We will get you the help you need."

Raya took a deep breath, coherent enough that Jax relaxed his grip around her waist slightly, and with a nod of his head, we were back on track.

The sun dipped below the skyline as we crested the last hill and entered one of the side streets of Canyon City.

I couldn't help but remember what had happened the last time I was here. The Fae who had been "murdered" by Kade's shadows. This time when we entered, we tried to escape death, not be the ones *supposedly* causing it.

Lanterns illuminated the dimming night sky around the strangely quiet city. An anxious energy filled the air as we made our way down the alleyway toward the center of town. A sole scream echoed in the silence. Instantly, my heart raced, triggering my defenses. Reaching down, I brushed my fingers over the dagger resting on my thigh, preparing to unsheathe it if need be.

Out of the corner of my eye, a woman in tattered robes ran toward us but stopped short to hide between some barrels.

"Opal?" Jax said.

Even from here I saw her shake her head and bring a finger to her mouth.

"What the hell?" Storm questioned, dismounting from his horse and staring around the far too empty streets.

"Well now," a booming voice echoed through the square. A Guardian appeared, rounding a corner and twirling a sword in his hand. "What do we have here?"

CHAPTER 2
LANA

Storm straightened, approaching the cocky Guardian. "You, what's your name?"

A smile spread over his lips as he let out a shrill whistle. Voices and boots thudded behind him until four more Guardians appeared.

He stepped around Storm, ignoring him completely. "Why is it you lot think you can break curfew?"

Curfew?

"I would stand down if I were you," Jax warned, his arm clutched around Raya as the two remained atop his horse.

The Guardians laughed haughtily, without a care in the world. Did they not recognize Storm, Jax, or Raya as fellow Guardians?

"I said who—" Storm's question abruptly halted as a blade whipped toward his neck, laying against the skin. His eyes flared with shock at the Guardian's impertinence.

"We're the ones who will be asking the questions here." The man licked his lips and pushed the knife harder against Storm's neck. "So, let's try this again. Why are you out past curfew? Tell us now, or, well…" He chuckled. "Die."

"I am one of the elite Guardians." Storm grunted through

gritted teeth. "You will step down and let us pass. We are on official business for King Dargan."

The group of Guardians snickered. "You, one of King Dargan's elite Guardians? Don't recognize you at all. Seems to me you be tellin' lies."

A low growl rumbled from Jax, but if they heard it, they ignored the sound to continue their taunting.

"Yeah," another soldier jeered from behind. "There is no way you pathetic lot are part of the elite. Doubt you could pass the Blood Oath even if you tried. You smell of traitors."

One by one the Guardians drew their blades, their smiles unnaturally cruel, twitching with similar tics, while their icy stares sent a chill down my spine.

"Dark ones." My voice shook as I realized. The movements, the gleam in their eyes. They were Guardians turned by the king. "Storm—"

"I know." He grimaced, blade still at his throat.

I almost couldn't breathe. *Not again.* I didn't want to fight so soon after what we'd been through. I barely had the energy to have a conversation, let alone take on another group of Fae brimming with Thames's darkness.

"You will be punished for your disobedience." Storm glared deep into his attacker's eyes, daring him to make a move.

"Oh, you think so, eh?" the man at Storm's throat dared. "I run this town now. You see, I have it on good authority— the king is dead."

My heart stuttered. *Impossible.*

"The king, dead?" Jax cocked an eyebrow, steadying his anxious mare. "Who's telling lies now?"

One of the men from the group behind their leader strode forward. "Hear that, Samuel?" he snarled. "They claim to be the king's elite and don't even know the truth." The man twirled his blade in a circle before pointing it toward Jax and Raya. "He is dead, and Thames rules this land now. Pledge your loyalty or you can perish like the rest of the dissidents." The man used his own sword to pull up his sleeve, revealing an inky black mark.

The wavy line that looked like an eye cast in a circle—I recognized it instantly. It was the same mark on Hale's arm. The same tattoo branded on Andras.

The mark of the dark ones who *willingly* turned. These men were not ones turned by force. No, these Guardians were infected by choice.

Thames had been free for less than two days, and if these Guardians were telling the truth, he'd already overtaken at least one major city in Mysthaven. How had Thames accomplished that so quickly?

I fought to keep down the bile rising in my throat. The power and control Thames already wielded would bring the world to its knees and he scarcely had to try.

Samuel glared at the man beside him. "Idiot, shut your mouth."

The slight distraction was all Storm needed. He raised his hands, shooting balls of fire toward the men before him.

Screams erupted in the alley as a few of them burned, falling to the ground as their clothes ignited. Those still standing surged forward, swords drawn.

I shared a quick, passing glance with Jax. He repositioned himself and whispered something to Raya. I saw her head nod gently once. She wouldn't be able to fight; she could hardly keep herself upright. But we needed her to if we had any hope of making it out of this alleyway alive.

Jax leapt from his horse and partially shifted into his panther form. One of his hands formed into sharpened claws, yet he appeared Fae-like everywhere else.

The control he had over his shifts left me reeling. *If only Ian could see this.*

A shout drew my attention back to the fray. Samuel, unfazed by his shirt catching fire, swirled his hands in front of him in a sweeping motion, conjuring the air around him into a tornado. The magic lifted the dirt from the alley into the air and dropped it over his body, completely snuffing out the flames.

Maniacal laughter left his lips as he pointed at Storm. "You're mine."

Storm conjured another wave of fire and threw it at Samuel, but the Guardian's air magic pushed the flame out of his way.

I reached to my thigh, yanking out the blade, and went to jump from Onyx's back, but hesitated when I heard Raya whimper to my right. Her body slumped forward. "Fuck," she hissed.

She looked so defeated. Conflicted, I watched Storm and Jax battle the evil Guardians, but I knew the most vulnerable person here was Raya. I had to protect her. Jax and Storm would never forgive me if something else happened to her. I would never forgive myself.

Fates, Kade would never forgive any of us if we weren't all alive and well when he returned.

I refused to lose another person I loved.

Moving toward Raya, I positioned Onyx between her and the fight before me.

Jax fought two men, swords and claws clashing in the night. Another Guardian, still on fire, hadn't regained control as he rolled on the ground trying to put out the flames overtaking him. Samuel flung his arm toward his fellow Guardian and doused him in dirt, just as he had done for himself earlier.

In the blink of an eye, he was back on his feet. His lip curled as vines shot out from the ground around him. Thick, thorny branches crept toward Storm's ankles. I cried out to warn him, but the vines lurched faster than my shout and he fell flat on his face, taken by surprise.

A flurry of emotions bubbled beneath the surface of my

skin. I had a duty to protect Raya, but I couldn't lose Jax or Storm to the dark ones either. A flicker warmed inside of me.

I had magic. I knew deep down it was there, but calling it the way the others could didn't feel natural for me. The flicker from earlier was all there was, nothing more.

Come on, I pleaded internally.

I looked at Raya, her eyes glistened as her mouth opened. Jerking my attention forward, I noticed another group of dark ones stalking toward us from an alley away from the others.

We were utterly surrounded.

"Run, Lana," she rasped, her voice gravelly. "Leave me and run. You must get to the others. To warn them."

"I will not leave you here to die. To be infected with their darkness," I barked back. "Can you stay on your horse?"

"I don't deserve to be saved," she cried out. "Go!"

My heart raced faster at the certainty in her voice, simultaneously breaking for Raya at seeing her so vulnerable. I'd have to deal with her words later—right now I had to fight. I would protect my friends.

Leaping from Onyx, I grabbed the other blade from my boot. The white dagger I'd found hidden in my parents' coffin hummed in my grasp the second my hand wrapped around the hilt.

Pushing down the fear at how vastly outnumbered I was, I readied myself against the four Guardians closing in on me.

One ran forward, as the others jeered and taunted. At least they weren't attacking all at once…yet.

The Guardian fought arrogantly, unaware I could possibly know how to wield a dagger. I sliced it across her forearm, and she laughed. "Little pretty wants to play."

I yelled in frustration, ducking low before stabbing her in the gut. The smile fell from her face as a cloud of darkness exploded out of her in a shadowy burst. She collapsed to the ground.

The other three watched, their eyes widening in horror

before narrowing, prepared to engage me without further hesitation.

"Tits and daggers. Storm!" I yelled over my shoulder above the commotion. "Might need some help over here."

One of the Guardians shouted Samuel's name.

As if in slow motion, the scene unfurled before me. Storm had taken down Samuel and was fighting with Jax against the three remaining Guardians, but that didn't include the group headed my way. Raya struggled behind me to get her dagger out of its sheath.

My resolve strengthened. I wouldn't fail. Two more steps and one of the remaining Guardians would be within fighting distance.

When the dark one swung his blade in my direction, I was ready. Crossing my daggers, I formed an *X*, and the attackers' blade landed in the middle, allowing me to push him off balance.

Grinning, he attacked once more. Parry after parry, I deflected his blows, not allowing him to gain any footing. But another joined the fight, and my strength wavered after so little rest on the road.

My hope faltered. In the past, Storm and Jax could take out dark ones with ease, but these ones were stronger. Quicker, somehow.

Panic pooled deep in my belly as we continued our fight. The hopelessness threatened to take over, pushing me near a full-blown panic attack, back to a place I'd worked too hard to overcome.

My breathing shortened, becoming shallower with each passing millisecond.

Worthless.

Counting my steps to ground myself, I continued my frenzied dance, letting my rage fuel me forward. I'd done so much to overcome these panic attacks, and here I was, yet again.

Andras's voice had no place here. Not anymore. I knew myself—knew the truth. *I am not worthless.*

The dark one in front of me hissed as his block missed its mark and my dagger sliced into his thigh.

I am Illiana Dresden.

I am worthy.

And I have a magic my enemies should fear. The flicker from earlier pooled in my stomach, wild, untamed.

I would not lose another friend to such evil.

These new friends made up some of the only family I had left since Thames and his darkness took everything from me. He took my parents, my birth parents, Elisabeth, Hale.

No. *No*, I would not allow another death by his hand, or his minions.

The power inside of me seethed, angry, filled with vengeance and fury. It pushed through every part of me until I screamed, losing all control.

Blinding white light exploded out of my body. I stabbed my attacker straight through the heart.

A seeping cloud of black mist left his body as he collapsed, another dark one eliminated.

Then, silence.

I trembled, looking around at the bodies strewn on the ground—all of the remaining Guardians. Stumbling to the side, energy zapped out of me, like the light had taken my last bit of strength with it.

"Lana," Storm said, breathless as he ran toward me. He reached out his hand but quickly yanked it back. A small burst of light shot onto the ground next to his feet and he jumped out of the way.

"I'm sorry," I whimpered. "I don't think it will hurt you, but I don't know if I can control it right now."

"Take a deep breath," he said softly.

I fell to my knees, body shaking uncontrollably. This time when Storm reached for me, he didn't hesitate.

"Magic takes time to understand. You haven't trained it yet," he murmured. "But you will. We will help you."

Storm's magic drained into me and, pulling from a depth inside of me I didn't know I possessed, I rose to my feet.

"I'm okay," I reassured. "I'm all right."

Jax stood in front of me, a tired smile gracing his lips. "There she is." He winked.

"I could say the same to you."

"I'm sorry," he said, pulling me into a hug.

I nodded against him.

"Raya is my family. With her this injured, and Kade gone, I lost myself for a minute," he whispered. Then he stepped back, with a contrite look. "We're going to get through this. Come on," he urged. Some of the lightness in him returned, like he needed a victory, even a small one, to remind himself of who he was. "The safe house is a few more miles."

"Jax," a voice cried out, and a woman ran toward us. Opal. She must have hidden herself well during the fight; she looked uninjured.

She paused in front of us. "You cannot stay here. These Guardians are different, vicious. There will be more."

"When did this happen?" Storm asked.

Opal ran her hands over her arms, adjusting her worn shawl. "A day ago, they flooded the streets and took control. They established a curfew last night and killed a few Fae in the square for the fun of it."

Storm's jaw clenched. Jax reached forward, grabbing Opal by the shoulder gently. "If more come, you will obey. We're working on a way to get rid of them. Trust me."

She swatted his chest. "I always do, to my detriment, I'm sure."

Jax grinned, walking back to his horse and Raya, who shakily fumbled her attempts to put away her sword. She seemed more alert, but the distant look in her eyes remained.

"Can you bring food to the safe house?" he asked.

"Tomorrow," he added when he saw Opal nervously look around. "Whenever curfew is lifted."

"Of course," Opal replied. "Be safe. And for the love of the Fates fix this."

Jax saluted, then mounted his horse behind Raya, Storm following the motion onto his own.

I climbed onto Onyx, running a hand over his mane. The insistent tug stirred, calling me back toward Mount Legion again. This time, I didn't look over my shoulder. I had to move. Forward.

We made our way through Canyon City, passing tightly shut windows and doors. In just a few days' time, the bustling city turned into a place of fear. It broke my heart to see Mysthaven fall into such disarray. I could only hope Ellevail was holding up better than this, even if it was under Andras's thumb. Deep down, my stomach churned because I knew it was wishful thinking, and I used that fear to drive me forward.

We remained on high alert, silent as we took in our surroundings. Even the slightest sound made me jump, wary of potential attackers.

Raya regained enough strength to hold onto Jax's arm, allowing him to focus as we rode. But she didn't look back to meet my lingering gaze.

At the opposite end of the city, Jax held up a hand, halting our progress. He inched his horse forward, ensuring the surroundings were safe.

After a few minutes, the silence stretching on, he gestured to continue. The farther we moved away from the city center, the sparser the houses and structures became until jagged terrain stretched around us more than civilization.

A small home appeared alone in the distance.

"Let's ride. Better to hurry than risk anyone spotting us," Jax ordered.

We obeyed, cantering off the road and across the

unmarked land. The wind swept around us, stirring up the dust lining the streets.

As we got closer, I could see a stone wall surrounding the two-story home, covered in thorns. An iron gate creaked as it swung open in the wind.

Jax dismounted outside of it, ushering us to follow.

"How many are supposed to be here?" I rubbed my arms to brush off the unease crawling over me.

Jax glanced over his shoulder, a furrow marring his brow. "Should be at least thirty at a time before they move on to the next location."

Thirty Fae would certainly make a noise of some kind, right? They definitely wouldn't have left a gate unlocked, hanging open if they were trying to hide.

The yard lay empty.

The front door of the home was closed. Two pots of pink flowers sat cheerfully on either side, almost welcoming.

Jax raised his hand, knocking at the door.

Still, we were met with quiet.

His shoulders tensed, and I shifted uncomfortably. Something felt wrong.

Jax turned the knob and the door opened, yielding to his gentle touch.

He shuddered a breath as we stared into the home.

The safe house was empty. Not a single Fae in sight.

CHAPTER 3
KADE

My vision blurred to black, consuming me in unending night as I walked silently down the steps outside the palace.

The lack of sight didn't deter me. My feet confidently carried me down the well-memorized path toward the courtyard. I'd stood there so many times before. As predator and as prey.

A pinch in my chest flared to life, aching as it had so many times before. An invisible force tugged me, halting my steps. The hesitation lasted barely a second before the suffocating darkness curled around my dead heart, snuffing out the calling before I could give the feeling a second thought.

My master summoned me forward, tightening his hold on the swirling darkness within me, urging me on.

The shadows in my vision parted, revealing Thames standing in the middle of the courtyard. Darkness hovered around him like an aura of absolute power. The slight breeze shifted wide, as if even nature feared venturing too close to him. Not a single strand of his mahogany hair lay out of place, erasing the greasy black-looking locks I'd seen on him when he first returned to this world. His restored, eerily perfect porcelain skin made him appear more like a marble statue than Fae. His thin lips twitched, drawing up slightly, holding a triumphant gleam in his eyes, as I descended the stairs.

My chest tightened as a small swirl of my own magic desperately fought back against him in the internal battle wearing me down day by day.

Our new majestic king curled a finger toward himself, summoning me to his side. I obeyed without hesitation and kneeled before him. Thames's Guardians had been gathering the citizens of Mysthaven to pledge their fealty to him. My public display of loyalty exhausted me as the days went on for reasons I did not understand.

I forced my head to remain bowed low, waiting for his approval. Just as I had waited for my father's approval time and time again.

"Rise, my monster." Thames's voice lost the grittiness he first had when he emerged from the void. Now it echoed loudly around the mountains with a charismatic lilt.

Obeying without a second thought, I rose, taking my place at his side. Waiting for his next command like the obedient servant I'd become.

Yet my magic still tried to fight his orders. My shadows clawed at my mind against my wishes, aching for me to hold onto *something* I couldn't remember.

Peering beyond the line of guardians on bent knees before us, citizens stood in clusters, waiting for today's show. Concern lined their brows, etched into their tired faces.

Though they were crowded around the gates as usual, the typically rambunctious attendees remained silent. Unlike the wild circus my father allowed, Thames ruled with an iron fist, serving swift punishment for any and all who dared to cross him.

Or perhaps he'd spread so much of his darkness, there weren't any uninfected citizens left in Mount Legion to protest his rule.

How long had it been since Thames released me from the burden of the crown? Only two days? It seemed like a lifetime. The amount of instant chaos he created had thrust Mysthaven into darkness, as if he'd merely flipped a switch and his new, more powerful world arose.

"My Guardians. My fighters. My people. I stand before you a humble servant. A ruler, fair and just," Thames bellowed to the crowd. His obsidian crown glistened in the afternoon sun.

Shadows leaked from my fingertips, responding to his presence, dancing a dangerous line with the darkness thrumming within, as if speaking to me.

Listen. Fight.

My body jerked, twitching. Momentarily.

Return to the light.

Closing my eyes, I didn't fight back like I had before the exhaustion set in. Were they speaking? A vice tightened around them, but they shouted, louder now.

Return to her.

Shaking my head, I aimed to rid myself of these futile treasonous thoughts. My attention returned to the task at hand.

"I will restore our land," Thames shouted. "Restore all of Atheria to its former glory. Our world will no longer be bound by this curse to remain separate. We will be one kingdom again. We can take back the fertile land that always should've been ours."

A few Fae in the crowd cheered wildly, pushing their way to the front, while others whispered in confusion.

Rumors spread fast, thanks to the army of dark ones he and my father created. They took to the streets, to cities and towns, whispering about the powerful new king who'd been trapped by the evil rulers of Brookmere. That they'd used dark magic to divide our lands and keep the riches and power all to themselves. Leaving us with nothing but death and despair.

Thames positioned himself as Mysthaven's savior while promising to infuse our people with more power.

"Pledge your allegiance to me, and together, we will conquer all. I will take back what is rightfully ours. You will have power greater than you could ever imagine. Power that will allow us to rule over all of Atheria once more." Thames's smile spread across his face, a twitch in his lip.

Despite being trapped for a thousand years, stuck in the mist of the void, his body returned to this world unharmed. His magic hummed, almost palpable in the humid afternoon air. His time in the void hadn't weakened him. Instead, it was as though the more the darkness spread, even in the last couple of days, the stronger he became. As if it fed his very soul.

I shifted uncomfortably. My shadows stretched, clenching inside of me as they demanded I follow this inexplicable pull past the palace walls.

Go. Run.

My shadows had never spoken to me before, and it was unlikely they were doing so now. Perhaps, it was a test from my king, one I wouldn't fail.

Our mate needs us.

The dark power coursing through my veins ebbed and I gasped. Pain pulsed past the darkness as memories of rose-gold hair flooded me. But it hurt. A tether inside of me, freeing itself from the darkness, pulled taught.

Yes. Listen.

Thames's head snapped in my direction as his eyes met mine, narrowing. Just like that, the pain ceased. The darkness took control once more, soothing the tension inside my chest. The voice I thought I'd heard silenced instantly. Thames smiled as if he knew he'd saved me, before returning his gaze to the crowd.

I was a good and loyal servant. I would stand by Thames's side and play the villain I was created to be. This was what was best for our people.

"Now, Guardians of Mysthaven. Stand before your rightful king and reveal your loyalty to me."

The first Guardian approached, pulling up the sleeve of his tunic to reveal his inky mark. An eye encased in a wavy line. The brand of those who accepted the darkness willingly into their bodies. Giving up their very soul for power and the promise of *more*.

"Tyson Rivbane, Your Grace." Bowing his head low, he continued to hold his arm before Thames.

"With blood may you reign." Thames nodded and I signaled for Tyson to begin a line to my right.

I lost count of those standing beside me, succumbing to the black clouding my vision. Names and faces blurred together, growing hazy as time passed.

"Your Grace, I can explain," a panicked voice trembled.

The commotion from the crowd and the Guardian's words snapped me back to the courtyard.

Shaking on his knees, a Guardian exposed his arm to Thames. A pathetic hand-drawn design lay visible on his skin.

Thames took three steps toward the man before spitting at his feet. "Your words mean nothing. You dare kneel before me with a mockery of my brand? Not an ounce of loyalty to your king. No wonder Mysthaven has fallen to pieces since I've been gone."

An anxious energy hummed, setting my skin ablaze. A sinister feeling, drowning out the pain, raced excitedly through me.

Our time had come to unleash what we were made for. Death.

Fight it.

The voice was back. But weak. Why would I fight my king?

"Your insubordination will not be tolerated," Thames hissed at the man before turning to me, beckoning me to him. "End him."

I bowed my head. "As you wish it."

"No, Prince Kade, no," the Guardian pleaded. "I accept! I pledge myself to you, Thames."

Thames jerked wildly back around to face the man. "You dare speak my name. I do not give second chances. Your cowardice has no place in my army. You will pay the price for your failure, and you will die."

I commanded my shadows forward, even as they fought me. My magic had battled me before, but never like this. This was like dragging a leaden ball through the sand. They refused to budge.

I snarled. *You will listen to me, shadows. You are mine to command.*

A dam burst inside of me along with a lingering shadowy voice.

We will regret this.

Reluctantly, my shadows crept along the stone path, covering the man's mouth, his screams lost to my power.

Whipping my hand around, the shadows twisted, snapping his neck. His body fell to the ground, the *thud* of his head on the stone echoing into the silence surrounding the crowd.

It took all my energy to reel the shadows back to my side, their anger palpable in my being. They vehemently hated what just happened, but I didn't have time to decipher what it meant.

I was a harbinger of death, waiting for my next order to kill. Created to ensure the king's wishes were executed.

As the line of pledging Guardians thinned, the army of loyalists grew. The dark buzz of energy growing among the courtyard radiated outward, as those who had accepted the call of darkness twitched excitedly before its citizens.

Not many resisted our king's call. Those who refused to turn died. Which meant when two more Guardians showed their brandless skin, they met their demise by my shadows as well. Each death at my hands caused Thames's smile to grow. My swift justice pleased him.

I raised my head, noticing the last Guardian now kneeling. Without hesitation, he revealed his arm. It bore no mark.

Thames reared back in anger. "You dare kneel so arrogantly before me," he seethed. "Let this be a warning to all those who are thinking the same. Those unloyal to the crown will be dealt with by the Monster of Mysthaven, but those traitors who attempt to infiltrate my ranks… Well, there is a special punishment for that level of disloyalty."

"I have no regrets. You are a usurper. You've poisoned people, and call it loyalty," the Guardian shouted, rising and drawing his blade. "Prince Kade is the true king!"

He speaks the truth. Listen.

Thames snapped his fingers, and a wooden contraption materialized, summoned by his power. Four Guardians moved from the shadows toward the man, who looked wholly unafraid.

I tilted my head, scrutinizing him. How could he not fear what was about to happen?

Because he knows the truth. As do you. Fight. Back.

"*There is nothing to fight,*" I said, attempting to silence the treacherous shadows.

The man fought feverishly, but when more loyal Guardians joined the fray, he was easily overpowered. They grasped him by his hands and feet, tying him to the device until the traitor hung suspended by ropes and chains.

"Not so brave now, are we?" Thames sneered. "Kade, show him what happens to those who dare to trick me."

"Kade, you are our rightful king," the man pleaded. "You are better than him."

His words stirred that thing inside of me again. One day, whatever plagued me would come to an end, and I wouldn't have to fight my magic.

The darkness took over, unrelenting in its need for death and destruction. The shadow sword formed in my hand.

No, run, fight.

Thames passed by me, waving his hand at the traitor. "Make it memorable," he whispered in my ear before he turned, walking up the stairs back toward the palace. He crossed his arms, watching from a perch higher than everyone else. Removed from the violence yet observing the pandemonium he created.

I shook my head to get the noise out that was swimming in my brain as I approached the man. In his fight against the contraption, others took their chance to cut him with their own blades. Blood dripped from his wounds, wetting the ground before me.

I raised my shadow sword and slowly, deliberately, dragged the tip of the blade down the center of the man's chest, snagging a loose thread, and his tunic slowly fell to the ground on a whisper of a breeze.

"He can't control you if you fight him. Whatever has happened, you are stronger. I saw you, I've seen you save people."

I snarled. "That was before I saw the truth."

"No!" the man entreated.

A delirious laughter escaped my lips, one I didn't recognize as I dragged the sword back up the man. I pierced his skin at the top of his sternum, twisting the blade, only to drag it down once more. Back and forth.

The cuts should've been cleaner. My shadow sword felt dull, barely cutting the skin beneath it.

"Obey!" I yelled to my shadows.

To anyone else, they would believe I was screaming at the man, but I knew better.

The man's breathing slowed. He raised his head, his entire body trembling. "You can defeat him. I believe in you. More will fight."

I snarled and my shadows flared as if in agreement with the traitor in front of me. I stabbed my sword through the man's stomach. The blunt way my shadows molded couldn't withstand the force I threw behind my weight. Blood gurgled in his mouth, dripping from the edges of his lips. "We would've fought by your side."

I raised my arm, refusing to answer his words, and waved my shadows away, drawing my steel blade instead. With one slice, I gutted the man, as he finally gave in to the pain and screamed my name. His chest opened, body sagging, his intestines falling out as the blood pooled beneath him.

To make it memorable, to make absolutely certain no one else disobeyed our king, I swung at his head, letting it fall, rolling across the stones before it hit my boot.

Grabbing the dead man's head by his hair, I walked the souvenir up to Thames, holding it proudly above my head for everyone to see.

"Well done," Thames praised before he bellowed to the crowd once more. "With blood may you reign."

"With blood may you reign," they echoed back in unison.

Thames waved his hand in the air, signaling to the crowd that the events for the day had ceased. Upon his dismissal, they dispersed.

Blood ran down my arm, soaking every inch of my body. Before I could take a step to the side to dispose of the head, Thames grabbed me by my arm.

"Do you think I don't notice your hesitation at my commands?" he hissed.

I frowned. "I don't hesitate, my king."

"You do." He gripped harder and his touch burned. "You will be fully mine soon enough. Your shadows may fight me now, but they won't be able to for much longer. It won't be long before the darkness completely takes over." He chuckled as he released me from his grasp, wiping the blood on his hand across my face. "It's just a matter of time."

CHAPTER 4
IAN

The crisp breeze of the morning air glided between my speckled feathers as I soared above the rolling hills of Brookmere's lush landscape.

Flying had always been an escape. Not being bound by the confines of one's own two feet allowed me to observe our world in a way so few ever would.

But as I made my fifth pass over where the border between Brookmere and Mysthaven used to be, the hope I'd been clinging to find Lana dwindled. It suffocated the sense of freedom flying usually provided.

Fates, I'd even be happy to see Kade at this point, but I couldn't give up hope. It'd only been two days since she left.

She had to come. Had to be safe.

Soaring over the land, the illusion of the sea had disappeared, instead revealing the cracked earth. This new kingdom appeared so different than our own. A clear divide of death and decay between the verdant fields of Brookmere versus the reddish dirt of Mysthaven.

My feathers shook as a shiver tore down my spine. A dark energy simmered in my veins, biding its time, just waiting to be unleashed. It took all my energy to ignore its call.

Slowly, I descended closer to the ground as an ache burned in my chest. It writhed, pulsating slightly each time I drew close to the void to search for Lana and the others.

I must get to *her*.

I squawked, signaling to my friends on the ground. I'd take one more pass.

Riding the warmer winds of the updraft, I flew until the trees became specks and the moisture trapped in the clouds formed droplets on my feathers as I passed through.

Speed was one of my biggest strengths as a hawk. I could travel hundreds of miles in a single day if I really pushed myself. Fortunately, today I only needed to patrol a ten-mile stretch of this newfound border.

I dug deeper this time, searching not just the miles of land but inside my head as well. I'd spent my time between panicking for Lana's safety and frantically trying to reach Raya.

Raya, of all people.

I didn't even know if it was possible for our connection to work for me to call to her.

The last time I saw her, she entered my mind broken and screaming, and a small part of me almost died in fear. Fear for her. For Lana.

Yet there was nothing I could do to help.

Some hours I would have sworn she almost appeared, lingering on the outskirts of my mind. I could feel her presence almost there. So close I swore I might touch her if I wanted to.

Grasping on to that feeling, I tried to clear my mind and call to her once more.

Raya? Are you there?

Silence. Nothing but damn silence. A pain sharpened in my chest, not knowing if her absence meant she hadn't survived.

I wanted so desperately not to care if she responded to

my communication attempts, but it bothered me in a way I didn't understand. Especially since I didn't even know if I could get through to her in the first place, or if it only worked one way.

Maybe it was merely my protectiveness for Lana. She couldn't handle losing another friend, and if there was anything I could do to stop that from happening, I would.

That was all it was.

Besides, I'd had enough of this waiting.

Waiting for news, for Lana, for *her*.

I screeched, that dark energy pulsing in my chest as I angrily flew straight down toward the ground, barreling into a nosedive at breakneck speed. My wings lay tucked tight to my side as I spiraled closer to the ground.

I didn't slow down, daring to get as close to the lush blades of grass as possible.

"Ian Stronholm, you stop that this instant," Kalliah screamed as I finally pulled out of my dive. Shifting back into my Fae form, I somersaulted my way across the open field before coming to a stop. Sprawled out on the ground, I lay panting, catching my breath as the adrenaline coursing through me tried to slow down. I had to pick several sticks out of my tunic as they poked my side from my fall.

Kalliah stomped her way toward me. "You could have killed yourself," she seethed. "We have enough to worry about without you trying to prove"—Kalliah waved her hands in the air—"whatever that was."

Pushing myself up on my elbows, I glared at her. "Aren't you tired of waiting to see if Lana is all right? If she's alive?" I stood and brushed the dirt off my pants. "The world literally exploded. The barrier to Mysthaven is gone, and what? We are just sitting here, hoping she'll show up?" I ran a hand through my hair, worry building into a festering anger threatening to drive me mad. "*Something* happened. We have to find them."

Taking out my frustrations on Kalliah wouldn't do any of us good. I closed my eyes and inhaled. "I won't keep waiting."

Turning abruptly, I stormed back toward the Knotted Willow where Corbin stood, leaning against the front door.

"Do not walk away from me," Kalliah shouted.

Immediately, Corbin pushed off the door, coming toward us.

"We cannot just go running off into this unknown land and hope that we find her." Kalliah jogged to keep up with my pace, reaching out and grabbing my arm to stop me. "We know nothing about Mysthaven, Ian. We have to stay here. This is where she will come."

"What's going on over here?" Corbin folded his arms across his chest. His brows furrowed, as his gaze shifted between Kalliah and me.

Kalliah positioned herself between us and took a deep breath before continuing. "Ian wants to go flying off into the unknown to try to find Lana." Her eyes narrowed in my direction. "Even though he's a brilliant captain who knows that is the least helpful thing to do right now."

Logically, I knew she was right. Why, then, did this entire thing feel so wrong?

"You know we can't do that." Corbin sighed heavily. "I know you're worried. I am too. But what good are we to her if we don't follow the instructions she left for us? She is our queen, and she gave us an order."

My blood boiled as uncontrolled rage welled deep in my belly. We'd always been a team, but a clear divide in ideology started to form.

"She needs us." I rammed my finger into Corbin's chest, articulating each word.

Corbin grimaced. "She needs us to trust her."

I shoved him, unable to grasp my sanity. A small part of me knew I was spiraling. I wasn't fully myself, slowly losing my grip on reality and fighting bouts of rage.

"Ian." Kalliah gasped. "What are you doing?"

She moved to stand next to Corbin, mimicking his stance. "We stick to the plan. We get Lan an army and wait for her to return. *That* is what you can do. We've never let her down before and I sure as Fates am not going to start now."

My whole body twitched, darkness clouded my vision. Hate, vile and bitter, swelled up in my throat, burning like fire. "Who are you to say what I can and cannot do? You're a lady's maid, Kalliah." Striding forward, I stood directly in front of her. "Who died and made you queen?" I exploded in a fury unlike anything I'd ever felt before.

Kalliah's jaw dropped, and she took a step back in shock.

"You dare speak of the fallen like that again, and you won't live to tell the tale, Ian Stronholm." Corbin flicked out his wrist, and thorny vines shot out from the ground, separating me from them.

He grabbed Kalliah's hand, turning back toward the Knotted Willow, and they walked away, leaving his thorny barrier standing between us.

Corbin had never spoken to me that way before. In fact, he'd never spoken to anyone that way before. The burst of magic and sternness from him shattered the anger latched onto me, loosening it to a place where I could wrestle it back into submission.

What the hell had I just done? And said?

Shaking my head, I tried to rid myself of this inexplicable feeling of doom. What was happening to me?

"Kalliah, wait," I shouted, dodging around the vines as a few thorns ripped at my pants, scratching my legs when I tore them free. "Wait."

She'd taken three more paces before she finally faced me, a tear slipping down her cheek.

"I'm sorry." I grasped her hand, bringing it to my chest. "I'm so sorry."

She pulled her hand from my hold.

"I don't know what came over me," I continued. "Something happened to me when I was in the dungeons with Andras." I swallowed, then whispered, "Anger or hate is just festering inside of me, and I don't know how to stop it."

Kalliah murmured something to Corbin, and he took off inside the inn without sparing me another glance.

"I know you've been hurt. Tortured. Nothing will make that okay," she said. "I'm here, Ian. If and when you're ready to talk, I am always here. But don't forget, I want my best friend back too. I want to storm Ellevail and ensure Leif is alive and breathing." Her voice trembled as she wrapped her arms around herself. "If you ever speak to me that way again —" She choked on her words.

She didn't need to say anything else. We had been friends long enough for the rest of that sentence to linger unspoken between us with complete understanding.

We wouldn't survive this if I let myself act this way, if I hurt those around me because I was hurting.

At least I hoped that was all this was.

I reached out my hand. An offering.

Hesitantly, she intertwined her fingers with mine and squeezed. "We can't turn on each other."

I kissed her head. "Never again."

Together we walked in silence into the inn.

An hour later, I held two trays of food in my hands, climbing the stairs to Vivienne's room. She had disappeared soon after the earthquake, only to return with a woman wearing the same wild look in her eyes. Ever since, the two had been locked away together, refusing to leave Vivienne's quarters. Fates only knew what was going on there.

There were endless questions we wanted to ask, but had not yet been afforded an opportunity to speak with them.

Kalliah attempted to eavesdrop on their conversation last night, but the doorway had been magicked to block the sound from within.

I had questions of my own that went unanswered. Like where had Vivienne gone? Who was the stranger now holing up with us? Did the woman know Lana?

The only way we knew the two were even remotely okay was because their food trays returned empty after each meal. Lana already felt so much guilt for how she'd treated Vivienne throughout the years, she would want us to give her the space to be at peace.

So none of us pushed, allowing them the time they apparently needed.

Gently knocking on their door, I murmured, "Lunch is here." I waited only a moment before bending over to leave the trays of cheese, bread, and jam on the floor like we had each been doing the past few mealtimes.

Just as I regained my full height, Vivienne's door flung open, and she grabbed my arm. "Ian."

Startled, I flinched but didn't jump back, forcing myself to remain calm. "Vivienne, are you okay? Can I get you something?"

"Have you not heeded the words of your queens?" Her once wild, wiry hair lay smooth in ringlets against her shoulders. The color in her cheeks had returned, her eyes clear of that eerie white usually present when she received some sort of vision. She looked almost sane.

Staring into her eyes, I searched for a hint of context, any sort of clue as to what she could be implying. "Of course I obey my queen, Vivienne. I—"

She released my arm and whipped her finger in front of my face, stopping me. "Not one but two queens gave you a command, Captain. You have a critical role to play in this war. Or have you forgotten so quickly of the vows you made to your queens?"

I almost didn't know what to say. Vivienne never spoke so bluntly or called me out for my actions. How she even knew of any vows I'd made, I'd never know—probably didn't want to know. That was two people in one day putting me in my place.

Standing straighter, I replied, "I always honor my vows."

Vivienne stared at me. Not backing down, finger still raised. She sighed and moved to cup my cheek, nodding like she wanted me to say something else.

I watched her, seeing her take in parts of me that I wasn't sure I knew I was sharing. Until finally, taking a deep breath, I whispered what I had been too afraid to say out loud these last few days. "I'm afraid I've lost her."

Vivienne shifted on her feet as the white-haired woman approached behind her, laying a hand on her shoulder. Tilting her chin, Vivienne looked me in the eyes. "The only thing worthy of your fear is never finding out what could be. You must do your part and trust the Fates if we hope to survive. Be the leader your father died knowing you'd be. Be the captain not one, but two queens entrusted with their lives." She patted my cheek once.

"I can't leave without knowing she's safe," I confessed.

Vivienne smiled at me. "Be the man Lana chose as her closest confidant and friend. The one stronger than any darkness. Let her return to the army she commanded you to obtain."

Without another word, she somehow managed to move the trays in the room and close the door before I could even blink.

Vivienne was right. I needed to be the man my father raised me to be. The man I'd vowed to be for Queen Roxana. The man Lana, my best friend, my *queen*, needed me to be.

Determined and with a newfound sense of purpose, I practically ran down the stairs and back into the dining area of the inn, where I had last seen my friends.

Kalliah and Corbin sat at a small wooden table, eating their rabbit stew in silence. Their bodies hunched and tired. The toll of the unknown weighing heavy on their shoulders. We wouldn't sit around any longer. We couldn't.

"We move out tomorrow, Corbin," I said. "Tomorrow we begin building an army for our queen."

CHAPTER 5
LANA

With the safe house empty, we didn't dare linger for longer than necessary.

We agreed to rest for the remainder of the evening, even if it was only for a few hours.

Besides, Raya still hadn't fully recovered, a fact worrying us as each hour passed.

Jax settled Raya in an upstairs room, hovering over her like a worried mother hen. Storm and I slept on couches downstairs, just in case anyone decided to appear. I don't think he ever truly slept though.

My mind refused to stop spiraling so I could rest. I replayed the moments in Mount Legion, unable to let go of the simple mistake I'd made trying to protect the amulet. How could I have been so foolish as to let my blood touch it?

How different would things have been if I had taken just a moment to think?

No.

If I let these thoughts consume me, I'd live forever in pain. I could not belittle myself anymore. What was done had been done and none of us could afford to look backward. We had overcome greater odds before as a unit. We would do so again.

Together, we'd find a way to get Kade back and keep both of our kingdoms safe.

Only once in these few hours did the desperate *tug* of wanting to be close to Kade have me reaching for the door handle to leave the safe house and return to his side. The devastating weight of missing him pressed against my chest, even though it had only been a few days. I badly craved the warmth and weight of his shadows. Their sweet smell of faded rainstorms and crisp morning air.

The sting of burning metal met my fingertips and I yelped, suddenly realizing I had reached for the doorknob. Storm grunted from his blankets a few feet away. "Serves you right."

"I'm sorry," I whispered, but he didn't answer. He didn't have to.

With Storm's magic sealing me into the house, I finally allowed exhaustion to win, and my eyes closed before I even hit the makeshift bed.

It felt like only minutes passed before Storm shook me awake. I found him and Jax sitting in the living room of the abandoned home, waiting for me. Raya hadn't appeared yet.

True to her word, Opal left two baskets of food on the step shortly after sunrise. I hadn't realized how hungry I was until we devoured the bread and cheese in mere minutes. My stomach growled, begging for more. We planned to save the dried sticks of meat for later, but we each snuck a piece when we thought the others weren't looking.

Jax managed to find several apples and other small pieces of fruit in a storage cabinet. They were still fresh, so the refugees who were once here couldn't have left too long ago.

"Where would they have gone?" I voiced the concern we were all feeling.

Jax shrugged as Storm sighed, running a hand over his face. "Maybe the quake scared them and they went to the next safe house."

"We should keep going. They can't travel quickly with the children and elderly, and they'd most likely go to the safe house closest to the void," Raya said as she entered the sitting area. The color had almost returned to her cheeks this morning, and her voice had returned to its usual timbre. She walked with a little more confidence, even placing a hand on my shoulder in silent greeting before sitting next to Storm.

"I'm glad you're okay," I whispered to her as she passed.

"We have another three-hour ride before we get to the next safe house," Jax started, before biting into his apple. "They've set up a small encampment. Make sure your weapons are accessible, just in case something is amiss. Does everyone understand? We don't know what will be waiting for us."

Storm stood and nodded. "Keep close together and your magic at the ready." Turning to me, he said, "Except you. Do not use your magic unless it is absolutely necessary."

Tits and daggers.

If my look could shoot blades, it would. I started to speak but was promptly cut off. "You still do not know how to use it properly, and until we've had time to train you, it could be more of a danger than an asset. Fates know we don't need you destroying anything more than necessary with your light."

I crossed my arms and let out an exasperated grunt. "I'm pretty sure that untrained magic saved your ass last night."

"Be that as it may, Princess—" Jax started.

"Queen," I countered with a wink I knew he'd be proud of.

He chuckled, and the nervousness I felt finally started to ease now that we were getting back to ourselves again. "Fine, Your Most Esteemed Royalness. Let's try not to die just yet, okay?"

"It would be my greatest honor not to die on your watch." I rolled my eyes and leaned down, touching my toes, stretching my legs. It would be another hard ride, and my muscles already ached.

Storm retrieved the horses, who had rested in the stable behind the house all night. Onyx rubbed his nose against my shoulder, huffing a breath of hot air in my face. "Well hello to you too."

Stroking down the neck of the creature soothed the anxious energy thrumming within me.

With everyone mounted on their respective horses, Jax turned to face us again, Raya seated in front of him once more. "Ready?"

After a nod from each of us, we left.

Guilt pooled low in my belly as the city structures disappeared behind us, fading into barren land. I prayed to the Fates the citizens of Canyon City would remain unharmed by the crazed dark ones threatening them. Just another reminder that we needed to make this right. That more than *our* lives depended on figuring out a way to destroy Thames and the reign of darkness ravaged upon us.

We would be back and ensure Opal was repaid for her kindness, not only yesterday, but for everything she had done to help protect those threatened in Mysthaven. We would repay all those who dared to stand against Thames, and Kade's father as well. Atheria would be reunited and stronger than ever before.

We rode silently except for the hooves beating on the land, the only sound in the miles stretching around us. I watched Raya and Jax as they took the lead. Raya sat straighter, her slim braids plaited tightly down her back. With her strength returning, I felt more inclined to ask her to contact Ian again once we stopped at the safe house. We had to let them know as soon as possible that we were all right.

The passage of time seemed never-ending as the landscape around us didn't change. Wide dusty crimson dirt pathways, spiky green plants, and the same wind-shaped trees were seen for miles. It was a wonder Jax even knew which direction to go, everything looked so similar.

An eerie feeling of dread suddenly permeated the air. Breathing became more difficult, the desire to return to Kade multiplied tenfold. I swallowed the lump in my throat fighting what my body knew was right. The others must have felt the change, too, because Jax slowed us to a walk. A tension grew, so thick we were practically swimming through it.

"Shh," I cooed at Onyx, leaning down and stroking his mane. "We'll be okay, sweet boy. Almost there."

Jax sniffed the air, using his shifter abilities to discern what the change might be. He looked back at us and shook his head from side to side before he continued cautiously down a narrower path lined with bramble bushes.

"The safe house is just on the other side of this—"

A cry in the distance cut Jax off.

We all halted, searching around for a sign of what might be coming. Storm pulled his sword out.

Another cry reverberated around us, a scream of absolute terror. Something or someone was in distress, and it was coming from the direction we were traveling.

Bolting from their spot, Jax and Raya took off at breakneck speed. Storm and I followed fast on their heels.

The number of shouts and shrieks echoed louder the closer we got. Anxiety crept into my veins as my heart beat so hard, I could hear it pounding in my ears. My hands trembled in anticipation of what we were about to see.

Coming through the final pathway of leafless trees, we all stopped abruptly.

The dark ones were everywhere, attacking innocent civilians who scattered through an encampment surrounding a larger stone home. The enemy hunted them down with reckless abandon. Fear and anguish laced the air.

Jax leapt from his saddle and shifted into his panther form, bounding toward the battle ahead. Storm hurled hand-sized balls of fire across the morning sky, targeting the backs of the dark ones. A distraction for Jax to take them out while their clothes began to blaze.

Raya repositioned herself in the saddle, and I called out her name. She turned, looking at me with a steadiness I hadn't seen from her since before Dargan's demise.

"I'll be okay," she said to me. "Whatever happens, take care of yourself and get to the void."

"You will not do anything reckless," I ordered, as if she'd ever listen to a command I'd give her.

"If anyone should have to sacrifice themselves, it should be me for the pain I've caused." Her eyes lowered in shame.

I steered Onyx closer toward her. "For what it's worth, Raya, I really like you." I drew my dagger from the sheath at my thigh. "But I never took you for a martyr. Where's that badass take-no-shit warrior I admired so much? Haven't you figured out you're so much more than what Dargan did to you?"

Her eyes filled with determination and she tightened her grip on the reins.

"We're in this together. I refuse to allow you to believe you're anything other than worthy. Now let's go save your people."

A genuine smile graced her lips. "For what it's worth, Lana," she said, nodding, "I might actually like you too."

Approaching the battle before us felt almost normal now that I knew what we faced. As if a piece of who I could be settled into place each time I pulled my blade. It served as a stark reminder of how quickly life had changed these past few months.

Rolling my shoulders back once, I readied myself, picking my first target: a dark one tearing violently into the siding of a large tent as people inside screamed.

Asshole.

Grabbing Onyx's reins in one hand, I grasped my dagger

in the other. Crouching low in the saddle, my faithful friend steered us straight toward the dark one, and I slashed the crazed Fae's side as we rode by. She fell, twitching and bleeding out on torn pieces of leather she'd cut from the tent. Raya quickly followed me into the fray.

She sliced the arm of her own dark one, and I circled around and finished him.

"Storm," Jax yelled as he shifted back into his Fae form, swords twirling in both of his hands, slaughtering those before him. "The safe house." He grunted as he sliced through the neck of one of his attackers. "There are children in there."

Children.

My stomach dropped. In no world would I allow harm to come to those sweet innocent children. The Fates themselves would have to pry these daggers from my cold dead hands if they thought I wouldn't fight for those who could not fight for themselves.

"Raya." I motioned for her to follow. "We need to get there. We must protect those kids."

Nodding, she whipped her horse around. This battle seemed to give her strength, as if danger fueled her recovery. She was coming back to us. The Raya we knew.

We rode side by side, taking down all those who tried to stop us. Fireballs laced the sky, and Jax's roars, mixed with cries for help, echoed across the small-town square as he destroyed the dark ones.

Storm ran, weaving through various-sized tents toward the safe house, standing centered among everything. Dark ones infiltrated the area from all sides, ducking behind too many of the tents to count. The overcrowding made it nearly impossible to track them all.

As we cleared the last inside row of tents, both Raya and I halted, staring at the amount of people fighting around the house. Storm and Jax were nowhere to be seen, but a small group of dark ones had already made it to the door of the house.

"In here. This must be the spot," one of the dark ones yelled.

They tried to crash into the door but bounced off the wooden entrance as if magically repelled. But they were not deterred. Again they attempted to break in the door and cross the threshold but were stopped short.

Storm met the small group and engaged in a three-on-one dance as Raya and I raced toward him, desperate to catch up.

"Come out, come out, children." The dark one laughed as the *clang* of swords rang throughout the air. "We know you're in there."

"I won't let you take any of them," Storm raged. Sweat dripped down his face as fire and sword fought once more.

The dark one cackled, as two more swept in behind him. "Children are the easiest bait. So easy to manipulate. To mold into the perfect solider of darkness."

Storm stabbed him straight through the heart. "We will defeat the darkness, and your time will come to an end. Faster than you think."

Around him, others fought the dark ones with fervor. I had no idea if they possessed training or not, but they were here. Battling valiantly for their lives.

Raya and I leapt from our horses and engaged the two dark ones who had replaced the fallen, lying dead thanks to Storm.

Raya was a skilled fighter, even on her worst days. She glided through the air with a poise and grace most would never accomplish. Her enemies never stood a chance.

My attacker appeared unfazed by her change in position. He parried; I blocked. I struck; he struck back.

"Aren't you tired?" I asked between pants. "Living with this evil inside of you?"

His brow raised as his blade clashed with mine. "Are you

not tired of being nothing? You could join us, you know. You could have power and status. Things you could never even dream of. All you have to do is say yes."

"I would never," I hissed.

Our swords clanged together once more as a voice behind me yelled, "The barrier is down, get the children!"

Shifting my eyes to the right was all the dark one needed before he twirled his sword around and dislodged my dagger from my hand. The blade bounced off of a rock and ricocheted out of arm's reach.

Ian would be ashamed, and my heart dropped low in my belly. I knew better than to take my eyes off my opponent. Innocent lives were at stake, and I'd made a foolish error. It was a mistake like this that would get me killed. Avoiding using the white dagger that might trigger my magic, I took a deep breath and placed my balled fists in front of my face for protection.

But the dark one charged past me as I avoided his final strike. With the magical barrier that seemed to protect the house broken, the dark ones still standing ran directly to the building. We followed, chasing them down.

If they breached the safe house and grabbed the children, I'd be out of options. Preparing, I grabbed the white dagger stored in my boot. I'd have to pray the Fates let me use it without detonating with uncontrollable magic.

The dagger warmed at my touch, reminding me it contained more secrets yet to be discovered. It was sharp and ready, and so was I.

Jax and Storm had already entered the building and were standing their ground, fighting those trying to make their way inside.

One of the few dark ones left, who hadn't made his way up to the door, turned and watched me approach. He licked his lips in feral anticipation. "Any last words before you meet the Fates?"

"The Fates already know my wishes, no need to bore them with anything else."

As the dark one rushed at me, a vine shot up from the ground, tripping and felling him. A young boy darted behind me, his hands held out toward the man.

"Well done," I told him.

"I don't think a few vines will keep him down, miss."

I didn't hesitate—my dagger found the Fae's chest. A dark wisp of smoke left his wound as the muscles in his face relaxed. "Thank you."

He looked content.

I expected to see anger or fear etched into the dark one's features as he fell, but relief? *No*, that didn't make sense. Or did it? Something scratched the back of my brain.

I turned to the boy. "Find somewhere safe to hide."

"No need. That was the last one."

"What?" I turned, running inside the house to discover the rest of the dark ones lay dead just inside.

The battle was over.

Jax approached from an area partitioned with large sheets of leather, signaling to Storm.

"Is everyone okay?" I panted, exhausted not only physically from battle but mentally as well.

"Safe," Storm replied, adjusting his disheveled tunic.

Raya appeared next to Storm. Color filled her cheeks, and she had a pep in her step that wasn't there before.

"Who would have thought a good fight would bring you back?"

She shrugged. "Good distraction."

"Raya—" I started to ask her about her words earlier, about the fact that she told me she didn't deserve to live before. The weight of what she carried from Mount Legion was evident in how withdrawn she was becoming. Before I could remind her of her worth, people began thanking us.

Walking out of the house, Fae appeared with

wheelbarrows, already cleaning up the makeshift paths circling from the house through the tents. Their efficiency astounded me. They worked together so flawlessly both in the battle, eager to protect each other, and after, while picking up the remains.

A profound sense of determination skated over me as the wind blew, pebbling my skin at its touch. Until now, nature hadn't revealed itself to me here in Mysthaven, but here it was, finally making its presence known.

These people were all my responsibility. It wasn't just those in Brookmere, but in Mysthaven as well. The Hidden Henchman had been a persona to protect and serve all of my people, but now, I didn't need her. I was a queen. I could do whatever and save whomever I wanted, however I pleased.

I would make a difference in this world.

After helping for about an hour, Storm brought water over to Raya and me. Raya sat, collapsing slightly as she moved to the ground, spilling her water.

"There's so many people here," I said, looking ahead toward the still-bustling encampment.

Storm chugged some of his own water before answering. "Last time Kade and I were here to take people across the void, there were only a handful of additional tents set up." He sighed, hanging his head. "They're a bigger target now with so many. We should have tried to do a run as soon as we came back."

I touched his arm. "This is not your fault. You've given them hope and kept them alive. They seem to have figured out how to fight back on their own too."

He grunted, though I knew he didn't accept what I'd said.

"Where's Jax?" Raya asked from behind us, her breathing becoming more shallow.

Perhaps she wasn't as healed as we all thought. The momentary rush of adrenaline vanished, revealing her still healing body. Her shoulder slumped forward, and she fell to the ground.

"Lana!" A shout came from behind us.

Ignoring the call, I rushed to Raya's side, rolling her onto her back. She remained breathing but did not respond as I shook her shoulders.

Jax sprinted toward us, completely out of breath. "I went to check the perimeter." He slicked back his hair with his hand, removing the strands from his eyes. "The void—Shit," he muttered, seeing Raya's limp body.

"Quick, we need to help her," I begged.

Storm rushed to her side, kneeling and cradled her head in his hands "She will live. She's done this before. She just needs a moment."

Jax inhaled sharply, assessing Raya's injuries before returning his gaze to mine. "Lana, the void."

"What about it?" I asked, distressed not only for my friend's well-being but for the worry etching Jax's brows.

He raised his gaze to me, shaking his head.

"The void is gone."

CHAPTER 6
KADE

The screaming of the Fae trapped in the dungeons served as a reminder that Thames held no room for mercy.

"Turn willingly and you can be free, or"—he leaned into a Fae who had resisted arrest earlier in the day,—"fight me, and I'll make you mine, whether you like it or not. Either way you *will* submit."

The man spit in Thames's face.

He's fighting more than you are.

The obnoxious voice I attributed to my own magic seethed at me. I flipped the black-tipped dagger in my hand, unbothered by their antics.

You don't know what you're talking about, I argued.

In retribution, the fucking things pulsed inside of me, and when they did, that spark in my core flared.

Lana loves you. Our mate is out there. Start fighting back.

I stopped tossing the blade in my hand, drowning out the sounds of Thames's final offer toward the unrelenting man.

Lana.

Thinking her name made the light grow, pounding through the murky darkness filling me from the inside out.

A small, useless section of my mind flared to life. My subconscious screaming alongside the will of my shadows. For her.

Now hold on to that.

"Kade," Thames barked. His scrutinizing eyes scanned me as he leaned against the wall, arms folded, beside the man bound and chained. Could he see the inner demons I battled?

I approached, malice spreading once more through my veins as the man jerked against his restraints. Blood dripped from his wrists as the chains dug mercilessly into the skin from his futile attempts to escape.

"Show our guest how painful the darkness can be when it's resisted," Thames instructed. "Slowly."

"My pleasure," I rasped, swirling the blade in my hand.

My shadows strained against the evil inside of me as I stabbed the black-tipped edge into the man's gut. I reveled slicing through the layers of skin. Technically all it takes is one little cut for someone to be infected. That's what those willingly accepting the darkness received—a slit on their thigh, somewhere fleshy. The marking appeared immediately along their arm, designating them as belonging to Thames. It was easy and agony free. For the most part.

Those who fought secured a much worse treatment. If need be, Thames healed them, aiding whatever magic they possessed after I cut into their skin. Killing them did us no good. We had to ensure our army of dark ones survived no matter the cost.

I knew Thames derived greater joy from those who resisted, so I played my part. Each dark one I infected shrouded my own mind in more of the murkiness. Each stab, each thrust of the knife fueled the beast within to drown out the pesky magic reminding me of my past.

Nothing from that time was here now anyway. That Kade was gone.

No. She's waiting for you, you fool.

The forceful tone took me by surprise, enough to make me still my blade. Instead of noticing it as hesitation, Thames grinned at the man who'd started screaming.

"Now, now, enough of all that noise." Thames rolled his neck from side to side before leaning down. "You've done well, lasted longer than I expected, but I can't have this taking so long. Since you clearly won't choose loyalty to someone stronger than you, someone willing to give you, a mere lesser Fae, the chance of power beyond your wildest dreams, I will give you a different choice. I am a *gracious* king after all."

Thames looked over his shoulder, smiling at me. I knew what he wanted: my attention. An audience. A puppet to feed his ego.

You know this is wrong.

My shadows released themselves inside me again, letting that ball of perfect light show momentarily. A warmth crashed over me like a wave, burning my insides like fire. Suddenly, I realized what my shadows had been doing all along.

Fates, no. What was I doing? *Lana.* The pain in my chest, the light. It was all Lana. I'd succumbed to the darkness instead of fighting for her.

The scene in front of me finally registered, forcing images in my mind of every death at my hands since Thames took over.

Every damned one.

I stepped back slightly, swallowing down the growing chasm of guilt while plastering a cruel smile on my face. My mind reeled, knowing I had to hide my thoughts lest Thames take notice of my change in demeanor. His power tightened in response to the light peeking through from the bond, but my shadows fought back, unyielding.

Now do you see?

My magic not only fought the darkness inside of me, but it wrapped itself around that tether to Lana. Protecting it.

I must do the same.

"I can throw you into the volcano in Firestone—after my army tortures you. Though brutal, your death will enhance my weapon there." My attention caught on his words, and I tried not to show too much interest. "Or…my monster's shadows can kill you here." Thames had no intention of letting the man go without turning him. This scare tactic had worked on plenty of Fae for the past few hours. Although his mention of the weapon was a new addition.

Thames leaned in, a repulsive sneer on his face as he hissed at the man. "The choice is yours."

The prisoner held on to his conviction, refusing to turn. I had to admire him for his fortitude. Though the evil inside me relished the disobedience for what it would get to do, I couldn't stop the sense of pride at the man's strength.

"Volcano," the man spat. "And I'll be sure every single one of your minions gets infected with the *truth* before they destroy me."

Thames chuckled and glanced my way, ignoring the man momentarily. "One good thing your weak father did before I returned was beginning my creation at Firestone." He turned back to the man, a bored sort of indifference falling over his face. "There is nothing but darkness there, I've ensured it."

It took more of my willpower than I cared to admit to stay standing. I gritted my teeth, as Thames's darkness and my shadows battled for dominance.

My mind shifted between knowing Thames could bring us the power we deserve, and remembering he was the villain of our story. That he'd hurt the people I loved.

The light in my chest flared. The brave man in front of me deserved better. A feeling of resolve washed over me as the shadows agreed and choked the darkness.

I tucked away the curiosity at Thames's volcano project and focused, unleashing my shadows quickly, and snapped the man's neck before he even realized what was happening. The deafening *crack* echoed in the damp cell, and the warrior's body hung limp seconds later.

I shoved as much of myself into that space of light as I could, locking it down and praying Lana would forgive me.

Fates, let me be able to forgive myself too.

Thames jerked his attention toward me, but instead of anger, there was an eerie glint in his eyes.

Guilt gnawed at me as my spirit faltered and deflated.

"Ah, there's my pet," Thames chuckled. "I underestimated your thirst for blood."

I bowed my head, trying to hide the relief and indecision warring for control.

The inexplicable pain at what I'd done on top of worrying about Lana nearly had me doubling over. She had to be safe. Storm and the others would protect her.

Thames approached me, patting my cheek with pride.

His magic flared inside of me, but I held on to thoughts of Lana. My mate. How could I have forgotten my mate? I clung to my love for her, letting the tether to her burn through his influx of darkness.

"Apologies, my king. It has been a few hours since my last kill. I simply wanted to make this one memorable."

Thames's laughter bounced around us off the walls, the wailing in the dungeons ceasing at the wicked sound. "It happens to the best of us."

Too quickly his eyes narrowed, and he snatched the blackened dagger from my hand and stabbed it into my thigh.

Gritting my teeth, I swallowed down the pained noise attempting to escape my throat.

He leaned in. "Even *you* must be reminded who's in control here." He twisted the blade, and I couldn't stop the sharp inhale through my nose.

His darkness surged inside of me, more powerful than before.

No! my shadows yelled as they hurried to protect Lana's light.

That negative emotion, the unexpected influx of Thames's magic and the blade was all the darkness needed to fight back against my advantage.

More in tune with my magic, I felt my shadows firmly close around my bond with Lana, protecting it fiercely. Only, their focus on the most important part of me left me with nothing to battle the evil.

I slipped inside my mind again, losing myself as a vengeful force eliminated my doubts.

Thames looked at me with a sense of pride.

I did that—made him proud. I would ensure his vision was brought to life. Loyalty. Unlike the traitors down here.

"I think you're ready," he said, clasping a hand on my shoulder as he removed the blade from my thigh. A blade I barely felt now with Thames's power radiating through me, stronger than any wound.

"It's time."

"Time?" I asked.

That sinister grin returned to his face, his eyes turning pitch black as he pulled me close. "There's a problem we must eliminate. Bring me"—he leaned in, whispering the next words with disgust in my ear—"your mate."

CHAPTER 7
IAN

Determination settled deep into my core as I soared with the humid northern winds toward Broham.

My ability to fly a hundred miles in a day was finally being put to good use. Even as Captain of the Guard, I was rarely afforded the freedom to fly so far on any given day. My duties to Lana had been important then, just as they were now.

I stretched my wings, relishing their power. I would rally any and all who were willing to fight for our freedom.

With Kalliah, Corbin, and I all in agreement, we divvied up our respective tasks. Corbin would head west toward Valeford, searching there for those the Hidden Henchman had aided. They'd spent years rebuilding from the destruction dark ones had delivered to their doorsteps. Corbin would continue on small day trips to any other villages within a few hours' travel of the Knotted Willow until I returned.

"I will not let her down, nor you, my friend," Corbin had said as he'd mounted his mare, then rode through the fields toward Valeford.

Kalliah grasped me in a tight hug before I left. "We'll all

be together soon and finish this," she whispered into my ear before releasing me.

Kalliah had remained behind at the Knotted Willow to organize those who came, answering the call to stand with their rightful queen. She would assist with setting up camps and training schedules based on the skill level of those arriving.

She was also tasked with keeping an eye on Vivienne and Cassandra. Who knew if they'd emerge, let alone eat a few meals without one of us leaving food. Besides, William flat out refused to be left alone to tend to the two women at his inn. "There's something not right about their magic and I don't have any time for that kind of crazy," he grumbled, before Kalliah reassured him she had it handled.

My path took me northeast. There were many villages on the northern borders of our realm. Growing up, I'd traveled this way a few times with my father and remembered they were known for swordsman competitions. We'd done fewer drops for them due to their distance, but we weren't ignoring any potential allies. The knowledge that Ryland, one of the contenders from the marriage trials and an excellent swordsman, may have returned to his home, helped too. If I could find him, he may help convince others to join our cause. Assuming he agreed and wasn't already working for Andras.

My wings beat faster; I would visit as many villages as possible over the next few days. So much could change in such a short period of time, we didn't feel it wise to be apart for too long in case we needed to pivot our strategies. There were a hundred things that had to be done, including getting all of our new allies settled at camp. We didn't have many resources, so we would have to make do with what people brought with them. William could only provide so much for so long, and we had no idea when this war would end.

Stretching my neck, I grimaced. *Ugh, there's so much to work out.*

I prayed to the Fates we wouldn't encounter any dark ones, or worse, Andras, as we gathered everyone together. Who knew what lies that despicable Fae was spinning.

Anger burned through my entire body thinking about Andras. The death of Queen Roxana and the callous way he'd murdered her still weighed heavy on my heart. I hadn't needed Vivienne's reminder of my solemn vow to her. It replayed in my head constantly.

"Keep her on her path."

"Don't lose hope."

I almost let myself drown in fear, but I'd made a promise to both my queens. I made a promise to my best friend, and I would not break it just because I was afraid.

Being in the air soothed my aching soul and allowed my brain to disassociate from the weight of the world. The trauma I'd endured. The deaths I'd witnessed. The flight gave me time to prepare for what was to come and chase away the darkness crowding my mind.

Something lingered inside of me from the dungeons with Andras. Something cold and wicked. Shifting and flying almost eliminated the remnants that had become overwhelming as of late.

Hours passed and I savored the sweet sound of nothing. Nothing but sun, air, and the wind beneath my wings. I spun, twirling, and flapped my wings harder, letting the rejuvenation from the flight speed me forward. I paused when a familiar sensation clouded my mind. A feeling meaning I wasn't completely alone.

Raya was here.

"Ian?"

Her voice held none of the confidence and irritation it normally did, but nonetheless the relief of hearing her again made my heart skip a beat. Letting the moment pass, a feeling of dread oozed over me, making my wings feel like lead in the sky.

Raya. I swallowed, breathing her name once before letting out the onslaught of questions. *Are you all right?*

She interrupted. *"Where are you?"*

What happened? Where are you? Why were you bloody when you came to me before? I inhaled, pausing momentarily as I tried to rein in the chaotic thoughts coming from somewhere inside me other than my mind. *Is Lana safe?*

Raya didn't respond. I knew she hadn't left, but she didn't speak. I couldn't picture her either. She remained a distant shadowy figure.

Is. She. Safe? Raya. Please don't make me ask you again.

"She's safe." Her answer was short, her voice practically dead. What happened to her? Anger and fear churned, washing away the brief moment of relief, even after hearing Lana was safe. Raya hadn't answered any questions about herself.

A tug in my chest emerged and settled. Heavy. Worry and unease wrapped itself around the ball. What in the Fates names was wrong with me?

What's wrong? What happened?

"Nothing, I just—"

Raya, tell me right now. What is going on? Are you hurt? Is someone else? My wings stiffened, my body freezing waiting for her answer. An uncomfortable acidic taste grew stronger with every passing second of silence. Her heartbreak seeped into my mind, pounding in my own chest.

A deep sense of shame washed over me. But it didn't stem from my own thoughts or feelings. It came from Raya. The guilt tasted sour on my tongue.

Something had happened. I knew, as if it were my own feelings, Raya was not all right, she just clearly didn't want to talk about it right now, so I wouldn't push her.

Where is Kade? Are you on your way back to Brookmere? Did you get the answers we need?

She paused, like she'd sucked in a breath and couldn't let it go.

Raya—

"We're almost back. We'll see you soon, Ian."

No. Raya, you can't just leave me. I need answers.

Raya hesitated only briefly before she left the recesses of my mind, and I was empty once more.

Even though this woman infuriated me most of the time, I hated when she disappeared, severing our connection. This time when she left, it was like she took a part of me with her. A fragment I didn't even realize was missing before she invaded my very soul.

This time especially, it felt like more than mind magic at play. As if something bigger entwined around us that opened her emotions to me and not just a mental connection. I shook off thoughts of the infuriating Fae. Perhaps her particular form of magic worked in mysterious ways. If she refused to give me answers, I didn't need to spend time thinking about her.

At least, I could try not to.

The first village on my route appeared below, aiding me with a much-needed break. Swooping down, I landed just off the main road and shifted back into my Fae form.

Cautiously, I made my way toward the center square and turned to the first person I found, a woman with a young baby swaddled to her chest. She eyed me warily.

Holding up my hands, I approached calmly. "Excuse me, miss, I'm looking for Caden Blaine."

Caden had previously made two requests to the Hidden Henchman, and both times asked how he could help our cause. He'd be the perfect person to help me rally any others in the village.

She nodded once, glancing over her shoulder toward the busy village square, but an elderly woman down the road called her name. She stumbled a few steps back as if scared.

Instead of pestering her further, I smiled in thanks and strode farther into the village.

The Fae moved with purpose, and though the sounds of conversation filled the air, they were cautious of my presence. I shifted through buyers, hagglers, and beggars, searching for a familiar face. When I landed in the middle of the square, I tapped a man on the arm.

"Excuse me, do you know Caden Blaine?"

The man hmphed. "Just came from him. There." He pointed to the left side of the square where a small crowd gathered.

I watched, lingering momentarily to observe Caden writing down requests from the people who shouted at him. Hay, wood, salt… Their needs were endless. He ducked behind the door of a small shop and returned carrying bags, divvying them up among the people.

Not a single person provided any sort of payment.

I approached once the main group dispersed from his storefront.

"I'm sorry, friend, I'm low on everything, what with the Hidden Henchman disappearing, but—" He dropped his clipboard as soon as he made eye contact with me, bowing his head.

"Well, that's completely unnecessary," I grinned.

"Captain." He nodded. "What can I do for you? I—I'm not sure what we—"

"Take a breath." I clasped his shoulders, trying to alleviate his anxiousness with my smile. "I need your help."

"My help?" the man squeaked. His floppy brown hair fell on his face, and I was reminded how boyish eighteen-year-olds could look. I remembered his first visit to us when he was merely sixteen. His persistence in helping his neighbors made my chest swell with pride that Brookmere had citizens like him. It was a shame the darkness had forced him to grow up so quickly, erasing his childhood in an instant.

Just like it had for Lana. And me.

"Inside?" he beckoned, but I shook my head.

"Here, I don't mind being overheard." I took a deep breath. "I know you worked with the Hidden Henchman twice," I started.

Caden nodded.

"I know the Hidden Henchman gave you an extra five hundred gold coins at each delivery. Looks like you've put that to good use."

"I tried, Captain. But if you don't mind me asking…" He trailed off, eyes darting around. "How did you know about that?"

I couldn't help my grin. This would be the first person I revealed our identity to, besides Kade and Storm, who didn't count. "I coordinated both of the drops on behalf of the Hidden Henchman."

Caden's eyes widened. "What?" he gasped. "You? But sir, you're the Captain of the Guard. That means…" He lowered his voice. "You know the Hidden Henchman's identity."

Nodding, I pulled him close. "The Hidden Henchman is Princess Illiana Dresden."

Caden frowned, pulling away. "The princess?"

"Should be queen now, but yes, which is why I need your help."

Caden stared at me, wide-eyed with disbelief as I told him about Lana, the trials, and the aftermath of what happened at Ellevail. He knew some of it, rumors further exasperated by the bounty Andras put on Lana's head.

"People have been traveling from border villages, desperate to escape the darkness. Some say the princess fled and let evil rule." He stammered, "But she's…she's okay?"

"She will be. If we can recruit people willing to help her take back Ellevail. Take back Brookmere."

Caden inhaled. "I would fight for Brookmere and the princess without knowing her role as the Hidden Henchman.

Her identity only makes me even more willing to help her. She's the reason half of our village didn't starve last winter, the very reason so many of us survived. She's the reason I could give my people a chance." He puffed out his chest, looking me in the eyes. "What can I do to help?"

"I'm going to need the crowd's attention and your support. They may need to hear this news from someone they trust."

"It's yours," Caden said. He ran into the shop, grabbing a bell, and immediately started clanging it. "Town square! Town square, now. Everyone, grab your neighbors."

Watching him take charge, I took a moment to thank the Fates that we had people like Caden. It might not be easy to raise an army, but this scrawny eighteen-year-old Fae certainly gave me hope.

Twenty short minutes later, Caden gave me a nod as he pushed his way through the crowded square into the center, standing next to me as the Fae circled us. The stench of musty clothes and sweat-drenched workers amid the humid air accosted my senses. But here they were. Almost an entire village. Waiting.

I raised my chin. "My name is Ian Stronholm, and up until a few weeks ago, I was Captain of the Guard at Ellevail."

A few murmurs hummed through the crowd. Andras may have formally stripped me of my title, but when the former Captain of the Guard says he has a story to tell, people tend to listen.

"Caden tells me rumors have been circulating, but I want you to hear the truth from me. The marriage trials for our Princess Illiana Dresden were interrupted when the king's royal advisor, Andras Braumlyn, allowed dark Fae into the final trial with the intent of capturing the king and harming the princess."

Gasps and louder murmurs increased around me.

"The princess was removed from the palace against her will for her own safety." Kade Blackthorn fucking owed me for not outing him to everyone for kidnapping her. "Ellevail fell. The king was killed. I was imprisoned and saw firsthand the damage Andras sought to enact. I escaped thanks to Queen Roxana, who sacrificed herself so we could get to the princess." I took a moment to breathe, grounding myself in the here and now as I spoke of our queen. A knot formed in my chest as I remembered the queen's brave face. She'd been the only mother figure I'd ever known, and she'd been brutally taken from me. More importantly, taken from Lana. From all of Brookmere.

"We must find a way to work together to defeat Andras and the darkness spreading across our land. It's our only hope of survival."

I paced, slightly antsy as the crowd took in my words.

"Before she became the rightful queen, when Illiana and I were still in Ellevail, we established a network for the people of Brookmere. Your queen saw her people suffering and refused to accept it. She created a secret identity you may have heard of—the Hidden Henchman—and worked tirelessly to ensure she aided those who required help. Many of you benefited personally, exactly as she hoped."

A woman in front of me brought a hand to her mouth, shock etching her features. Caden stepped forward and rubbed her arm.

"Brookmere is facing its darkest hour, and Illiana has sent those who are loyal to the crown, the true crown, to rally our people. We can't take back Ellevail and defeat the plague on our land alone." I made sure to meet everyone's gazes as they heard my message. I prayed they heard my desperation and how much we needed them. "We're asking for help from anyone willing to do so. We have set up a small camp near the border, and your queen requests that if you wish to join her, you do so quickly. For Brookmere."

"The borders are where the darkness thrives," someone shouted.

"We will fight to protect you, just as you do Brookmere. I won't lie and say this will be easy, but we will train and provide weapons for those who are willing. For as long as we possibly can. We will work to reclaim our land together."

Caden took in a sharp breath. "I will go." He brushed a stray strand of hair behind his ear. "Our queen kept me from starving. Kept all of us alive through her generosity and asked for nothing in return. If I can help return Brookmere to its rightful ruler and keep it safe, healed from this plague on our lands, I will do it. I will take whoever is willing to where Captain Stronholm tells me."

A group of Fae to my right jostled through the crowd. "We will go with Caden."

A chorus of shouts and cries of others rang out, people echoing their agreement and willingness to fight.

"I may have greased their ears a bit when I told them to come to the square," Caden whispered to me.

I laughed, staring with pride at the young man.

The woman Caden had reassured during my talk approached me, touching my arm gently. "My son was starving to death. One of the dark ones overtook his father, and I—" She stopped, tears spilling down her face. "I protected my son and myself from what he'd become." Her voice trembled before she cleared it. "Caden brought the food the Hidden Henchman provided and coin to help us survive. He healed, as did I. Only because of what my queen gave. I can't fight, but I can sew. Cook. Some other things. Will you take those of us wishing to repay our queen in ways without a sword?"

I placed my hand over hers. "We're honored to have any help we can get. There will be many who need assistance, but perhaps you should stay for your son."

She smiled at me. "He was the first boy who volunteered after Caden. So, Captain." She straightened, raising her gaze to meet mine in a confident way. "Looks like I'll be joining too."

I raised my voice again for the crowd. "Those willing to fight, bring whatever weapons and resources you have and meet at the Knotted Willow outside of Demarva. I'll provide Caden with directions. Training begins as soon as you arrive."

A small child ran to my side, pulling on my tunic to offer me a cup of water, which I gulped down. I needed to continue.

"Thank you, my friend." I patted the child on the head, returning the empty glass, before he ran back to the safety of his mother's side.

Caden approached, and I quickly relayed everything he needed to know to get to the Knotted Willow.

"I must go; there are others to recruit. Be strong. We're lucky to have you," I said. "Brookmere is lucky to have you."

My pulse quickened, and I couldn't help but smile. If every town was half as helpful as this one was, we may just have a shot. Their enthusiasm for defending their country strengthened the bit of hope in my chest.

I clapped my hand on his shoulder and stepped back, ready to shift and take flight, off to find the next group of recruits.

A flush stained his cheeks as he bowed his head. "May nature guide you, Captain."

***

Two days later my energy dwindled. Flying, shifting, telling the same tale to any who would listen drained all my reserves. I rested for only a few hours at a time, scared I would never make it back in time to begin training our recruits.

Andras surely would have heard whispers of what Corbin, Kalliah, and I were doing. Someone would have said something by now, which meant we needed to ready ourselves for battle. One we were wholly unprepared for.

Raya had yet to return. I told myself my anger at her absence was due to the unknown of what occurred in Mysthaven and not being sure that Lana was truly all right, instead of the other option. It had to be. Because what was really burning inside of me, an ache I couldn't name, didn't belong when it came to her.

She intruded in my mind and left as she pleased, deciding when I was worthy of her time. Withholding any knowledge she may have.

Stop being pathetic.

A heaviness settled in my bones, and with the dark clouds lingering ahead, it did nothing to help my spiral of emotions. We were doomed.

I would lead these civilians into battle, and all would be slaughtered. Each village had farmers, lesser Fae, people who had never trained or fought a day in their life. Yet somehow, we were going to fight off those as powerful as the dark ones?

I shook my head in my hawk form as a haze crept over my vision.

Was there a point to moving ahead with this plan? We could live and submit to terror or die trying. The options seemed insurmountable.

Dew collected on my feathers as I flew through a low-hanging cloud, and I stretched out my talons.

Black spots circled my vision, or perhaps the storm clouds had been closer than I thought, waiting to dump a deluge of rain upon our lands.

Thunder cracked and lightning streaked through the sky. *Great, just great.*

A storm of this magnitude would severely inhibit my flying capabilities. I would be forced to take shelter, waiting for it to pass.

Which meant losing precious time.

My final destination on this journey was only a few more hours away. But I'd never make it with this overwhelming sense of dread weighing me down along with the impending storm.

You're better than this, I told myself. This thing inside of me had been calmed as I witnessed the response from our citizens rising up and declaring their loyalty to Lana. But now, facing down fears and managing the weight of exhaustion, it slipped through the cracks, breaking free once more.

Gliding through the end of the cloud, a high-pitched *clang* attracted my attention to the land beneath me.

A skirmish waged far below.

Flapping my wings harder, I dove toward the fight. I tumbled gracelessly onto the ground, shifting into my Fae form slower than usual. Exhaustion inhibiting the full use of my magic.

I pushed myself up onto my feet and drew my sword from its sheath before examining the fight around me. A group of dark ones fought a small caravan of civilians. Their carriages of goods lay tipped over off the small dirt pathway.

Fight with your brothers. The menacing thought crossed my mind as my grip tightened around my blade. Anger danced in my veins as I ran toward the skirmish, impatient for release.

Rain fell from the sky in sheets. Thunder cracked. The storm turned the sky dark as night.

The dirt pathway quickly turned muddy, and my boots squelched as I entered the fight.

I gravitated toward the dark one closest to me, the same darkened spots clouding my vision, but as I swung toward the civilian, I had to catch myself. Shaking my head forcefully, I shoved the darkest thoughts out and focused on the battle that lay before me.

What is happening to me?

Quickly sidestepping, I maneuvered my sword toward the

dark one and sliced through his stomach in one swing. He crumpled to the ground.

The Fae he battled grabbed the fallen dark one's sword as he thanked me, running to aid a friend. Turning, I too ran to help with the nearest fight.

Slowly, the number of dark ones dwindled, the Fae citizens reigning victorious.

The sounds of crashing swords behind me alerted me that victory hadn't been won just yet. The clang of individual swords clashing became more prominent as the surrounding battles ended. Fae uninjured in the skirmish assisted those less fortunate, tending to their wounds.

My limbs ached and body protested, but I sprinted toward the dwindling fight.

This time I crashed the hilt of my sword down upon the nape of the dark one's neck in a surprise attack. The Fae he battled slammed his dagger into the dark one's heart without hesitation.

As our gazes met, and my eyes widened in surprise. The very person I was flying to see stood in front of me.

Ryland chuckled, as he shoved at my shoulder, panting, hair slicked with rain and blood against his face. "Fancy meeting you here, Ian Stronholm."

CHAPTER 8
LANA

The shock of seeing the barren land without its creepy mist left me breathless.

I'd seen the dead grey earth when we crossed the void before, but for some reason my mind made me believe it was the mist making it so desolate. Staring at the lifeless stretch of land made me sick.

"It's so much worse than before," I murmured.

Storm grunted his agreement. "It's as if Thames destroyed it even more once he broke free."

I shivered, the wind caressing me as if urging me through the dead land back to where nature thrived in Brookmere. Nature had always spoke to me, and I wondered if that would only grow in my role as queen. The thought sobered my already anxious mind.

We forged across the mistless void, eyes on the skies and ears open for the terrifying creatures that lurked inside.

"I wonder where the voidlings went?" Jax asked, unable to hide the strain in his voice.

"Scared?" I smirked in his direction.

"Of beasts confined to deadlands for a thousand years? Absolutely I am."

I laughed at his confession as we ushered the horses forward.

The moment Onyx's hooves touched Brookmere, the wind pushed at our backs, urging us away from the void and completely onto Brookmere's soil. My eyes widened.

Storm shook his head. "That's quite a welcome."

I blew out a breath. Emotion welled in my throat as we continued ahead into my home. Not just my home, but my kingdom. A kingdom that needed me to be strong even as the pain of what I'd endured suffocated me.

As the Knotted Willow came into view an hour later, my heart leapt with the unfettered joy of being back with those I loved most.

Almost all of them. *Almost.*

Raya slipped in and out of consciousness our entire journey from the void, making us all anxious to find her a healer once we returned. Whatever evil still lurked inside of her refused to let go.

The leaves of the willow tree next to the inn swayed in the gentle morning breeze. A picturesque moment despite our uneasiness.

We cantered toward the stables and Corbin appeared from around the corner, ready for us. A profound sense of relief appeared across his face as he waved us toward him.

Corbin assisted me off Onyx and grabbed the reins as he bowed his head. "Welcome back, Your Majesty."

I rolled my eyes, and he chuckled, knowing his unwillingness to address me by anything other than my royal title would always get under my skin. "It's good to see you, Corbin." I pulled him into a hug. "We need a healer—Raya is not doing well."

Jax dismounted, holding Raya in his arms as Storm grabbed the reins of his horse. "Go, I'll help Corbin with the horses while you get her inside."

Raya murmured incoherently, trying to push out of Jax's arms and stand on her own.

"Stop being stubborn," Jax insisted, assisting her despite her protests.

"Go," Corbin urged, taking the reins from Storm. "She needs you. I have others who can help me with this." Corbin took control of all three horses as he called for a young stable boy to assist him so we could get Raya inside.

"Thank you."

Corbin nodded in return before leaving with all the horses in tow, the stable boy running to meet him.

Upon entering the inn, Jax quickly sat Raya down at one of the tables and went to find a glass of water. Storm sat by her side as she held her head in her hands.

"Raya, I am going to find William and get you a healer," I told her. "Just hang on a little longer."

"Thank you, Lana," she whispered as her head nodded forward. "I felt fine earlier. I'm not sure what happened. It's like the moment I think I'm back to normal, something grabs ahold of me and brings me back down."

"You fought well today." Storm rubbed her back. "But you shouldn't have had to. We need to get you rested and ready for what is to come."

I laid my hand on Raya's shoulder and turned to go in search of William, but a movement out of the corner of my eye caught my attention.

Cassandra descended the staircase.

Utter rage overtook my entire body, filling every crack and crevice of my soul. "You."

I lunged toward her. A blast of light left my fingertips before I even knew what happened. I lost complete control, my light exploding toward the woman I believed responsible for losing Kade.

If she had been more honest with us, more forthcoming, he might be here.

Cassandra held up a hand, splitting my light so it diverted it around her and crashed into the stairwell wall behind her, leaving a singed mark on the stone.

Storm stopped me before I could get any closer to her, grabbing me by my middle.

"Don't you stop me, Storm," I screamed. "She knows. She knows what's happening and is keeping secrets." I pivoted back to face the seer. "You spoke in riddles, not giving us an ounce of direction. Do you see what happened to us? Do you see who is missing? Who was *taken*. This is your fault."

Another blast of light left my palm, again without me even trying. Storm jumped away from me as it careened into a chair next to the stairs. "Lana, calm down."

I turned to him. "Calm down? You want me to calm down? Her evil mate is free, trying to destroy our very world, and you want me to calm down?" I shook my head incredulously. "Oh no, not while *my mate* is out there, with only the Fates knowing what is happening to him."

Cassandra appeared unbothered by my outrage. The lack of reaction to my words about Kade seemed so unlike the caring woman I'd met those few short weeks ago. "I'm glad you finally realized he is your mate. One less thing for me to worry about." She finally finished coming down the stairs and stood before me. "But you may want to get all that in check." She pointed to the incinerated chair before looking me up and down.

This woman was unbelievable. Who did she think she was, acting like she was so unaffected by it all. She cared for us, she loved Kade. I know she did. This wasn't the same Cassandra who'd healed me at Mount Legion.

"This is your fault," I said, pointing at her. "You did this."

Cassandra faltered for one moment, a flash of guilt, before steeling herself back into this new hardened version. "You touched the amulet. As did Kade. What's meant to pass did. No use being upset over it," she retorted.

I screamed, grabbing for her, only for Storm to wrap his arms around me again.

"Lana, it will do us no good if you cannot have a productive conversation," he whispered to me.

I closed my eyes and took several deep breaths, slowing my breathing and my racing heart. Tears flooded my eyes at how angry I felt, and I hated it. Hated the reaction that would let her know how much her actions got to me.

Several moments passed before I opened my eyes, letting some of the rage dissipate enough for rationality to return. Unclenching my fists, I nodded at Storm. I could behave. My anger must have visibly simmered to an appropriate enough level because he felt comfortable to release me from his grasp.

"You have not fulfilled your destiny," Cassandra said as she met my gaze. She moved across the room toward the bar top. Kalliah appeared, and she gasped. "Lana." Hurriedly, she set the cup of tea she carried down on a table by Cassandra and ran toward me.

I choked back a sob, sweeping her into a hug.

"We were so worried," she said, pulling back and looking me up and down. "Ian is travelling to gather your army." She squeezed my arm before letting go.

I swallowed down some of the anxious energy I'd felt seeing her again. Once I put eyes on Ian things would be better. Then we'd find a way to Kade and I'd know everyone I loved was here. Safe. I adjusted my tunic, my gaze shifting back to Cassandra. In order for us to get Kade back though we needed answers. Giving myself a moment, one steadying breath, I faced the seer again, refraining from cursing her for good. "What else aren't you telling us? There must be more about the prophecies you can share. You must have seen something else."

Her eyes narrowed in my direction as she sipped the tea. "You do not ask the right questions."

Frustration didn't even begin to come close to how I felt at the way she continued to act. I clenched my jaw tight to keep from spewing hateful comments. Storm stayed close to my side, ready to intervene again if necessary.

Before I could fire back a retort, Jax finally returned, trailing behind a flustered William. "What is all the racket going on in here? I leave for two minutes and there's screaming. Sounds like absolute pandemonium, and you know I never want to miss a fight."

Somehow Jax had found another damn apple, and bit into its juicy red skin.

"Do you ever stop?" I huffed, rolling my eyes.

"Me? Never." He winked at me before moving to Raya, who still sat slumped in her chair.

"A healer can be here in twenty minutes." William grunted. "We've just sent your stable hand to fetch her. Room three on the left is clean. You can meet with her in there."

Cassandra had turned her back to the room, slowly making her way toward the stairs, clearly trying to escape unnoticed.

"Cassandra, we are not done here," I yelled, trying not to get riled up all over again. "Don't you walk away from me."

Raya's head lifted and she looked around the room, her expression hopeful that her pain would be over soon. She took a deep breath and anchored herself against the table for support before she tried to stand slowly. Her body swayed and she leaned so far right, Jax had to catch her. He delicately placed her limp body on the floor. Grabbing a towel thrown over a nearby chair and lifting her head to form a pillow.

"You should be more worried about your friend here than me," Cassandra snapped. "Can't you see she is unwell?" Gathering her skirt, she hurried to Raya's side. She leaned down and placed her hand on Raya's forehead, and the seer's eyes widened. "No ordinary healer can manage this."

My throat constricted and I froze. Jax, Storm, and I all exchanged a look. William threw his hands up, leaving the room muttering to himself about the constant headaches we'd caused.

"Move, move, out of my way," Cassandra growled, waving for us to take a few steps back from Raya's body. She sat by Raya's head, hovering her hands over our friend's forehead as she chanted something unrecognizable.

We sat in silence as Cassandra used her magic on Raya. The minutes crept by, stretching into endless time. Still, Cassandra sat entranced over Raya's body.

Small beams of a green-hued light floated over her.

Raya gasped loudly and tried to sit up. "What did you do?"

"Now, now, dear, lie back down. You've not been well," Cassandra instructed in a soothing tone. "Your mind has been riddled with torture over the years, and what you did in the end to fight Dargan? Well, it will take some time for your body to return to normal."

Raya shivered and reached for Cassandra's arm. "Thank you," she whispered.

"Storm, dear," Cassandra said, looking at him. "Take her upstairs to rest. I will continue healing her mind and body there soon."

Storm and Jax helped Raya stand and assisted her up the stairs.

They left me standing with Cassandra, the version of her I recognized. "Thank you for healing her."

She peered at me. "There is much work still to be done, but she should be feeling better soon. You are not the only one who will need her."

Just like that, she shifted back into her unwelcome new facade. Her cryptic words made it hard not to go back to being pissed instead of grateful. "Me and you have unfinished business, Cassandra." I ripped the white dagger from its sheath and slammed it down on the table next to us. "Now, before you go anywhere else, tell me what you know about this dagger. And I mean everything."

A shuffle of steps echoed behind me and a whisper of a breeze grazed the back of my neck.

"It's not my sister you need for that," Vivienne said, a half-smile gracing her lips. "It's me."

CHAPTER 9

LANA

"Vivienne." My heart pounded in my chest. "Sister?"

She nodded her head. "The better-looking one."

I looked at the seer I'd been around my entire life, really looked at her, and internally scolded myself for not putting it together myself. Of course they were sisters—the resemblance was uncanny.

I blinked, shaking my head. "What do you mean, it's you?"

She sighed, pulling out a chair before sitting and patting the empty one next to her. "Come, child. We have much to discuss. Let my sister help your friend while we speak." Cassandra nodded and disappeared up the stairs, not waiting a moment longer.

Vivienne and I were alone, something I generally avoided for any length of time, but I couldn't recall her ever being so lucid and clear-minded. There were so many things I wanted to say to her after the revelations of how she'd saved my life when I was a baby. My questions would have to wait though; I needed *this* information now.

"Illiana, for so long your bloodline has prepared for this.

To know it's finally time brings me excitement and fear." The pained smile gracing her lips sent my stomach into knots. It didn't bode well for our conversation to start in such a manner. After everything we'd already discovered, the truths about to be revealed would likely break me yet again. I wasn't sure how much more my heart could take.

Vivienne reached for me and clasped my hand. I turned to face her in the chair, our knees touching in the cramped space. Patiently, I waited for her to speak.

"Please know, everything I am about to tell you, I did for the good of Brookmere. What I thought was the right choice for our people to protect them from evil." Her eyes wandered, lost in thought. "The Fates demanded my actions, sending visions until I became lost in myself. I heeded their warnings, even though it doesn't seem like every choice led me down the right path."

My heart pounded in my ears, and I pulled my hands from her grasp to wipe the beads of sweat from my palms on my pants. "Go on, Vivienne. I'm listening."

Taking a deep breath, a shiver ripped through her shoulders, and she began. "That dagger you have in your hand was buried with your parents, your biological parents."

"I know." I shook my head. "I found them. My father—well, the king—told me in a letter. I know all about how you saved my life that night in Valeford." The note never left my person. I kept it in my pocket, too afraid for someone else to find it. Too afraid to lose the last piece I had of my father. I could feel the worn parchment poking my leg in my pocket.

A silent stream of tears fell down Vivienne's face. "That night," she sighed. "It changed the course of our lands forever. Such a terrible, terrible night. That was the night your prophecy came to be, but the Fates warned us. Danger lay ahead. I had to protect everyone. I had to protect you."

All I could do was whisper, "What did you do, Vivienne?"

She paused, wiping the remaining tears from her face. Collecting herself for a moment before continuing. "I couldn't risk this information getting in the hands of those not deemed worthy. I didn't know if the dark ones were aware of Thames and his potential plans." She narrowed her gaze. "You're looking for the journal? If you found the dagger, then you know it's missing."

"You took it?" Despite already knowing the answer, my stomach still dropped.

She nodded once. "To protect it for when you were ready. When you found your light."

"Where is it? Where do I find it?" I grasped both of her hands in mine, not caring my palms were still sweaty. "This could help save our kingdom. You have to tell me."

"The last place anyone would look. Where all manner of beasts lie in wait."

I frowned. "Beasts?" Then it dawned on me. "The Southern Forest? But those rumors are bedtime stories," I murmured, almost to myself. But were they? We'd seen a strox when we met Ian and the others before heading to Valeford.

She nodded. "I do not know the journal's significance, only that it must be something great. The journal is locked and will only open for your bloodline. I didn't dare anger the Fates by reading what was not intended for my eyes."

"So, we need to leave—"

A gust of wind slammed the inn door open with a bang, causing both Vivienne and me to flinch in our seats. A small group of grumpy-looking Fae trudged in, surveying the empty room.

"You wouldn't happen to know where we could find the Hidden Henchman, would you?" He stroked his beard as he spoke, the fiery tendrils of copper hair coiled into perfect curls.

I stood, tentatively walking toward the men. "I guess it

depends on whose asking." Placing my hands on my hips, I brushed the hilt of my dagger, hidden in its sheath at my thigh.

"Some shifty type of fella said the Henchman was looking for an army." The man looked back at his companions and chuckled. "And well, me and my friends here are itchin' for a fight. Pay back to those ugly bastards for what they did to my farm a few months ago."

My heart soared. My friends had done it. Ian had done it. Fae were coming to fight for their kingdom. We would not be fighting alone.

His words caught up to my mind, diminishing the excitement. "What they did to your farm?"

The man eyed me warily. "You been living under a rock, girl?"

I cocked an eyebrow and a woman stepped forward from the group, shoving the man out of her way. "For Fates' sake, Angus, leave her alone." She turned to me. "The old royal advisor, Andras, has been spreading his evil throughout Brookmere. You join his army, or you're punished. Most have been leaving people without a way to survive, burning crops, fields—anything to make us rely on him."

I sucked in a sharp breath, rage boiling in my veins along with a crackle of magic shooting down my arm. My people were being hunted and left destitute.

"What he needs an army for, Fates only know."

"Rumor has it that the border was fake. That another land exists, and they're coming," the man huffed. "Which brings us back to needing to find the Hidden Henchman. He's raising a resistance, and we want to fight with him to protect our home."

The flame inside of me flared with hope. Thames and Andras were creating an army by force and coercion, but we were creating one of love for our kingdom.

If I could obtain some answers, alongside building an

army, we might have a chance of surviving and living to see Brookmere and Mysthaven united into Atheria again.

"Does she look familiar?" A Fae standing behind the man and woman whispered to him.

My lips twitched into a small smile as I took a step forward and held out my hand. "Welcome, friend." He eyed it as a frown spread over his face but stuck out his own hand to shake mine in return. "You might know me best as Princess Illiana Dresden."

The Fae fell to their knees, murmuring and stuttering.

I held up my hands. "There's no need for that, especially since we'll be fighting side by side."

"Your Majesty?" The man looked up, face wrinkled in confusion.

"I'm no man, but I am the Hidden Henchman. Seems only right I should thank you personally for answering my call."

As the afternoon went on, more and more Fae appeared on the Knotted Willow's doorsteps. Some came prepared with wagons carrying supplies, while others came with only what they could carry on their backs.

Behind the inn lay a large grassy field. Earth Fae constructed small enclosures for the new arrivals. Groups of them stood together, using their magic to raise the earth into small hills and then carve out the inside to create hut-like structures built into the field itself. They left grass growing on top of the homes, which allowed the structures to blend into the surroundings. What once lay flat and open now looked more like rolling hills. A brilliant idea from Corbin to protect our citizens—no, our warriors—from anything flying overhead.

To the left in an adjacent field, other earth Fae constructed gardens, sowing the plots of land to harvest fruits and vegetables for the growing number of people. William had traveled to order supplies for the inn and picked up a few plants as well to make sure we could carry on as arrivals showed up.

To the right, a group of metal wielders began construction on a makeshift forge. Fae built a covered structure with plenty of ventilation for more than one metal wielder to forge weapons in. We would need so many more than we had in order to arm everyone for the battle to come. Storm had already agreed to help each morning to stoke the fires.

Corbin walked over, standing next to me as he looked on, overseeing it all. "This is incredible," I whispered as the awe of what the Fae were accomplishing overtook me.

"They've been adapting and working together to build these structures all on their own," Corbin said, crossing his arms. He looked on proudly.

I nudged my shoulder into his. "With some guidance from you."

He shook his head. "Honestly, once we set up a team of leaders for each area, they ran with it. They're teaching each other different ways to use their magic. Expanding their abilities. Then working on projects together, figuring out ways to make their magic last longer."

I couldn't stop the grin as pride swelled in my chest.

It didn't matter in what direction I looked, every Fae, both man and woman, worked together to create a space for our army to build, grow, and thrive. They'd traveled for miles, away from their homes and families, to fight for our kingdom. To fight for all our freedom.

Nobility in Ellevail would scoff and look down on most of the Fae here as unimportant. Yet I knew better. These were the people our kingdom relied on. The Fae allowing our kingdom to flourish. I'd always known it, feeling more comfortable in the lesser Fae parts of Ellevail than among nobility. All this did was solidify that knowledge.

I sighed. "They're considered lesser Fae, yet they're so much greater than the nobles flicking their wrists around, showing off parlor tricks."

Corbin turned, standing in front of me, and placed his hands on my shoulders. "You see them. You always have."

I met my friend's determined gaze as he continued. "You ran through the palace as a princess, greeting the lesser Fae by name. Those living in the lower parts of Ellevail know you better than most of the nobles combined. When you take your place on the throne, you will change everything. These people will be seen because of you."

I smiled. "Thank you for reminding me. For always saying what I need to hear."

He nodded once and moved to stand next to me again as we watched our people.

When we won this war, things would change. The division and insinuation that these Fae were lesser in any way with all that they accomplished would cease. We would live as one people.

While I should have been feeling scared or nervous because of everything to come, I couldn't help but feel such an overwhelming sense of calm. I was honored so many had answered my request. I would not let them down.

Two children ran around a small patch of flowers at the base of a tree by the forest's edge.

"How do you think my garden is holding up?" I asked wistfully.

Corbin glanced over at me as a grin appeared on his face. "I too learned tricks with my magic," he said. "If the flowers have died or withered, the soil will remember them. It's a sort of protection spell."

My jaw dropped. "How?"

He shrugged. "Self-taught."

I shook my head in amazement. "So all the flowers you've created, we can bring them back year after year."

He nodded. "Yes. Or change them. Whatever you'd like."

I threw my arms around him, feeling him tense slightly beneath me. He was, after all, the most formal of everyone. But I didn't care. "You're amazing, Corbin. Thank you for always being here."

"There's nowhere else I'd rather be, my queen."

I let go, sighing. "When we finish this and get home, I think we should share some of your beautiful creations. I've been hoarding your talent all to myself."

Kalliah bumped into me from behind, surprising both of us with her appearance. "Tommy would love a huge garden outside the pub. Especially having to take care of it after his patrons vomit in it."

I shoved her right back. "I bet Tommy would adore the shit out of some roses."

Corbin chuckled beside me. "Make a list of what you want to dream up next, my queen. We'll have much to do once you return home."

My smile spread as I allowed myself to dream about what life would be like after all of this.

As I continued to take a moment to admire everything, Jax, Raya, and Storm walked up from behind us. Raya looked brighter and healthier. She had a noticeable energy about her that had been missing since our escape from Mysthaven. Her eyes shone, looking clear for the first time since our battle at Mount Legion. She carried her sword over her shoulder as if ready to enter battle right this moment. Whatever Cassandra had done clearly helped.

"I have to admit, I'm impressed," Storm murmured. "Looks like the Hidden Henchman crew came through after all."

Turning, I smiled. "Brookmere helps their own. Just you wait, we'll double this in the next few days. I just know it."

Jax threw his arm around my shoulder. "You know, Queeny, if you need a general for your army, I've always thought I'd be an excellent choice." He waved his hand in front of our faces. "General Jax Wilder. It's got a nice ring to it, right?"

"Jax, you barely held our operation together while Kade and I were gone," Storm chided. "You think you can lead a whole army? My friend, think again."

Jax furrowed his brow. "I would say I did just fine while you were off gallivanting at the marriage trials, which, by the way, I will forever be upset I wasn't invited to participate in."

Raya snickered. "Do I really need to remind you about what actually happened when they were gone? You may have succeeded in running routes, establishing a new safe house—"

"A feat of epic proportions, mind you," Jax jumped in.

"However," Raya continued, "I seem to remember being the responsible one every damn day. Waking you up every morning, forcing you to train, ensuring you didn't slip into a sullen fit that we were left behind."

"You are no fun, Raya." Jax pouted before returning his attention to me. "How about master sparer? Commander of shifters? Trainer extraordinaire?"

"Speaking of, we do need to start training soon." Storm crossed his arms. "We need to assess everyone's skills and place them into battalions. When Ian returns, we can start the assessments." He turned to face me. "And you need to start training your magic as well."

Kalliah's eyes shot wide open as she gasped. "Did you say magic?"

Grinning, the warmth of my magic tingled. "He sure did and, get this—Kade's my mate."

Kalliah rested a hand on her hip as she faced me, ignoring everyone else. "I'm listening."

"The two go hand-in-hand really. When I finally accepted Kade as my mate, my light exploded out of me. I've used it a couple of times, but I don't really have any control over it yet." I shrugged. "Turns out there was something to the prophecy after all."

"Fates help us." Kalliah ran a hand over her face, but then she paused. "So, you're saying there's a chance? A chance your new unprecedented magic can get us out of this mess?"

I couldn't help but chuckle. "I'm saying there's a chance."

Storm interrupted our moment, coughing to get our attention. "Look, as fun as this all may be, you can't afford to have any more outbursts and incinerate us all. You need to be trained by someone who can get your magic under control."

I sighed, knowing it was true. Unless my emotions ran high, I couldn't even call on my magic. "But who can do that? I don't know anyone who has ever had light magic like this, have you?"

"No, we haven't, but light and fire feel like they could be similar." Storm created a ball of fire in his hand before blowing it out. "I'll train you for now until we can figure out something else. At the very least, I can teach you the basics of feeling for your magic."

"Apparently we're tabling the discussion about my promotion," Jax huffed.

"Jax, come on. If you were '*trainer extraordinaire,*' Lana would get injured somehow and Kade and his shadows would literally kill you," Raya said, waving at Jax to come to her. "Let's go see if anyone needs help. Or maybe someone wants to spar for fun."

At the mention of Kade's name, my heart dropped.

"Come on, Lana." Storm grabbed my hand and gave it a squeeze before I could even think. "Let's go train for a bit. It always helps me when I am upset."

I waved to the others as they dispersed in various directions. Storm and I walked the few minutes in silence to an empty area just north of the inn. It was a small space, on the other side of a hill, away from the rest of the Fae bustling in the fields. No one would see us practicing here, for which I was thankful. I didn't need an audience watching me fail at using my magic before we even started this battle.

Storm had me sit crossed-legged in the swaying grasses, and he did the same. "Let's start with the basics. Can you feel the well of power in your body? Is there a place it has settled?"

My eyes slid closed, and I reached, anxious to grab on to any bit of magic wanting to make itself known. The only thing I felt inside my chest was an ache in the space connecting me to Kade.

I gritted my teeth, trying again, this time attempting to ignore that cavernous emptiness. I came up short. Frustrated, I opened my eyes to meet Storm's gaze. "No, I feel nothing. Nothing at all." I rubbed my chest as if it could lessen the pain throbbing inside. "My magic just happens to show itself when I am overly emotional in some way or if someone is threatened. But I can't feel it inside of me."

Storm reached out and grabbed my hand. "We have been practicing for our entire lives, but your magic appeared only a week ago. It is not surprising you're struggling." He released my hand and lifted his palm in front of his face. A tiny flame floated above his hand, no larger than a pebble. "For me, I focus my mind and reach down in my core. Breathing deeply used to help me pinpoint where it settled. Jax says his magic lives in his heart, encompassing all of it. He yanks his power from there. Once you find your 'well,' that place it feels like your magic rests, it will be easier to access."

Storm's gentle and patient approach to talking me through how to access my magic was in stark contrast to the way Andras tried to torture it out of me. What would have happened if he had actually succeeded?

"While your magic is beautiful, Lana, it would be normal to have some negative emotions tied to it," Storm whispered.

I swallowed. "I was just thinking about Andras."

Storm stayed quiet, allowing me space to process.

"If I'd been able to bring it up back then, would Ian have been spared? Would we have had an easier childhood, free of the things that haunt us both now? He became a target for Andras because of my deficiency."

"Stop," Storm said firmly. "You are not, and were never, deficient. Fate determined when your light would show. Your magic pouring out of you in that moment saved us all. As for Ian, I promise you he wouldn't change a thing about you or your past because none of it was your fault."

My lip trembled at his words. I didn't realize how much resentment I had for my magic. There hadn't been time to really process it thoroughly.

"Our magic is a part of us. I wish we had the luxury of time to let you work through your feelings about it, but we don't. Only you can come to terms with that and build the connection to your light."

Storm was right. Holding on to anger over my repressed magic did no one any good. In fact, it gave Andras the power back that I'd worked so hard to take away from him. I wouldn't go back to that place of helplessness. Too much time had passed. Too much was dependent on me learning to harness this power now that I had it.

"Close your eyes again. This time, start with your mind. Clear your thoughts so we can invite your magic to simply be here with you. Just be calm."

I opened one eye and shot him a look.

Storm rolled his eyes. "Just try it, okay?"

I wasn't good at calm, but I would try.

Storm continued, speaking softly. "Okay, after you've cleared your mind, I want you to relax every part of your body, limb by limb. Start with your toes, up your legs, and so forth. Notice how each part of you feels. Does any area feel different?"

Breathing in and out, I tried Storm's method, but with my

guard down and logic slipping away, every part of me demanded I run toward Mysthaven. All my mind could think of was Kade.

The part of me that felt different was the ache in my chest where my tether to him lay quiet. Every moment of every day that we had been apart, my soul longed to be near him. Even for a second, just to ensure he was all right. It hurt so much, I had to physically restrain myself from leaving. Digging my nails into my thighs, I forced the pain to ground me here. My head dropped.

"I miss him so much." A tear rolled down my cheek and I let it fall onto the leather of my boot. The droplet stuck to the end of my woven lace before falling onto the ground. "What if he's not okay? What if he can't be saved?"

Storm reached over and pulled me into a hug as the tears flowed faster and harder. "I know, Lana. I miss him too."

"I feel like I should be able to harness this ache, this anger at what's happening to him, and instead I'm floundering. What use am I if I just sit here sad?"

"You aren't sitting here floundering. You're demanding answers from the crazy seer sisters." He smiled. "You're softening William to the hordes of Fae coming in to train. You're moving forward each day. But that doesn't mean you stop needing Kade."

"When did you get so wise?" I raised an eyebrow at him.

"If Kade knew you were suffering on your own and I didn't do everything to help, he'd have my head. You know that, right?" Storm chuckled dryly. "Besides, you also mean something to me, Lana. You forget you'll be my queen too. And my family."

I couldn't form words at his declaration. So instead, we sat there silently, and Storm held me as I wept. For the first time I truly had the chance to let all of my emotions out. Too much had happened in such a short period of time. It would take me years to work through the trauma of the last few months, but letting myself grieve for a minute helped. Eventually, I pulled away, and when Storm wiped the last remaining tear from my face, I felt lighter.

"If anyone can save him, it'll be you," Storm reassured.

I nodded, sitting up straight again. "Let's try to coax my magic out one more time. That way I can kick Kade's ass when we see him next."

CHAPTER 10
LANA

Weak.

Pathetic.

You left him.

A tug at my ankles jerked me awake from my nightmare. Sweat beaded on my brow, and my brown short-sleeved tunic stuck to my skin.

The room remained pitch dark, the moon hidden behind clouds, suffocating any light that should've entered through the window.

Andras's words from my youth twisted in my dreams. Instead of being in the dungeon, I stood watching Ian burn *and* Kade get swallowed up by Thames's evil shadows. All the while hearing Andras's vitriol about how useless I was as a princess.

The sensation of calming, cool peace swirled around my legs before I jumped at the tug. Sitting up in bed, I glanced down toward my feet and gasped.

Twirling around my ankles in a familiar inky pattern were Kade's shadows. A sob escaped my lips as I brought my hand to my throat. I was still dreaming. I had to be.

"Hurry."

I froze.

"Hurry, mate."

The light in my chest sparked, flaring to life, flowing out of me, intertwining with the shadows. They swirled together in what I could only describe as bliss. With what little I knew of my magic, it felt at home.

"He needs you."

Without a second thought, I jumped from the bed and grabbed the closest pair of pants I could find. As they had done in Mysthaven, the shadows swirled around me, leading me on an unknown path. I tiptoed barefoot to the door and cracked it open. The shadows muffled the creak of the old inn. A cursory glance over the hall assured me everyone remained behind their doors, unaware of my actions. No one heard me.

I slipped into the hall. The black tendrils of Kade's shadows shimmered as my light followed its trail, guiding me through the night. My body trembled with anticipation. Was Kade really here? He had to be if his shadows were, but something must be wrong if they called me instead of him coming himself.

I crept down the stairs, my hands shaking on the railing, praying to the Fates I didn't make any noise. I wanted to run. To bolt through the door and find him.

"Patience. You must not be caught."

I twisted the doorknob to the front of the inn and slipped out into the night. A slight chill hung in the air, as a tentative feeling of dread crawled up my spine. Kade was nowhere to be seen, but his shadows trailed forward.

They swirled around the outskirts of the camp. All the tents remained dark, with the only light coming from the dying embers of their fires. Our army slept, but the shadows hid me from the watchful eyes of those standing guard. The shadows would never betray our position, but I couldn't help the discomfort of deceiving those around me by sneaking out.

Still, I followed.

The wind brushed at my skin, delicate but steady. The sounds of nature surrounded me as I followed Kade's shadows. They stopped a few times as we made our way into the woods, as if straining and pulling taut, but it only lasted a few seconds.

"Help him."

My body tensed with the urgency of the words his shadows poured into me. I ran my hand along the dagger at my thigh that I'd taken to sleeping with, just in case.

Please let him be all right, I begged the Fates.

The shadows led me into the woods, eerie in the faint moonlight. Sensing my unease, they reassured me to follow every few steps. My light flared among the shadows when we entered the tree line, allowing me to see a short path in front of me.

Now you decide to come out? I thought, frustrated my magic refused to show itself for all the times I'd recently worked with Storm.

"Kade?" I called out in a half whisper, straining my voice with the choked rasp as the ache in my chest grew until it burned. "Kade?"

I trailed the shadows farther into the forest, and the dread I felt earlier doubled. Beyond my own steps, the forest was silent. Not a rustle of an animal skittering about or an insect buzzing in the night. Even the wind halted this far in, refusing to follow me any deeper. The stagnant air thickened around us.

In a single breath, the shadows stopped. Instead of remaining in their trail-like shape, they tightened around me, pooling at my feet.

"Kade?" I called out louder.

A low, throaty laugh echoed around me. "You shouldn't have come here alone, Little Rebel."

He was here.

"Is that—Is it really you?" I stumbled over my words.

I turned around in a circle, searching for him through the dark. If I could see him with my own eyes, I could reassure myself he was actually here. No matter what happened to him, we would figure everything out.

An outline materialized from between two trees, hidden as much by his shadows as I was, as they continued to grow around my calves and up my legs.

"I told you no matter where you flee, my shadows would find you, did I not?" Finally, his face came into view, but the smile on it didn't look like Kade's. Not *my* Kade at least.

My heart didn't listen to the warning in my mind as I ran, lunging toward him, desperate to throw my arms around his neck and relieve the restless bond inside of me. We were together again.

But I never made it to his arms.

Kade's hand shot out, grabbing me around my throat and keeping me from him. "He'll be thrilled to know how easy you made this."

I gasped, unable to inhale a deep enough breath as I choked. "Kade?"

His grip didn't quite cut off my air supply, but it tightened even more at my question.

He pulled me toward him and ran his nose along my jawline. "Oh, Little Rebel. To be fair, I did tell you to run."

I shuddered, unable to help reveling in his touch while warning bells sounded in my head, alerting me that I was far from safe right now. Fear radiated throughout my body hearing his deep, menacing chuckle.

"No." I struggled as his grip tightened painfully.

Without warning, his shadows forcefully wrapped around me, jerking me away from his grasp to form a protective barrier between us.

I fell to my knees, gasping as my light infused the magical

wall, wrapping itself around the shadows until it illuminated Kade's face.

Seeing him clearer stole my remaining breath, while tears flowed freely down my face, an endless waterfall of emotion. He looked tired. Defeated and so worn down.

But he was there. Still mine. I didn't care what darkness thrummed in his veins. We were stronger than anything else. It may have taken me too long to realize it, but he was mine.

My. Mate.

I would be damned if this was how our story ended.

"Kade, this isn't you," I said firmly, rising from the dirt ground to stand. "Whatever Thames has done to you, you can fight it."

He laughed, tipping his head back. "Thames made me stronger."

"You are more than his darkness," I said. His shadows stopped me as I tried to take a step forward. Kade lowered his gaze, glaring at his shadows in disgust. They trembled, shaking almost violently before slipping away from me altogether.

The shadows retreated from their protective position around me, and sucked back into Kade so fast, I barely registered what happened. He stalked forward and gripped my neck once more. His thumb aligned with the column of my throat. "Off we go."

I struggled against his hold. "Please," I said softly, placing my hands over his. "Please fight for us."

His dark eyes momentarily flashed to grey, and he ripped his hands away from my neck, crying out in pain.

"Run."

I reached for him, staggering on my feet as I took in his hunched-over form. "I can help you," I insisted.

"Run," he roared, as he clutched his head in agony.

I obeyed, his shadows escaping his hold to shove me forward.

My bare feet pounded against the forest floor. Twigs poked at my soles, slicing into them and against my legs. Dipping low, I ducked beneath some low-hanging branches but nicked my legs on the thorny brush. I sucked in a sharp breath as I sprinted away from Kade.

Deeper and deeper into the woods I ran, my pulse pounding, nearly unable to see a path in front of me. My heart raced as the darkness of the woods closed in around me, but I had to lead him away from the camp. Away from the inn. If the others heard him or knew we were out here, they'd see him like this. I couldn't be sure someone wouldn't get hurt with him in this state.

Or worse.

I wouldn't let that happen.

"Faster."

His shadows urged me onward. My light brightened inside of me in response, my skin glowing.

"No, he'll see you," I hissed. Not a good time to have zero control over my magic.

The trees parted into a small clearing, and I looked around.

"Your fleeing is pointless, Little Rebel," Kade shouted with the dark edge to his voice. He was too close. "You know I'll catch you."

I ran to the left, ducking under an old fallen tree as the bark scraped down my back. I let out a pained hiss but didn't let it stop me.

"Where can I go?" I asked the shadows.

They didn't respond this time, and my light panicked as I felt them slip away.

Shit. Shit. Shit.

A growl reverberated around me, and Kade's body slammed into me, sending me flying to the side.

I screamed as my body skidded across the ground, scraped by sticks and rocks along the forest floor.

"Got you," he grunted, attempting to roll on top of me. "And now? I think I'll devour you."

I lifted my knees, kicking out at him as hard as I could, taking him by surprise. I jerked to the side, pulling my dagger from my thigh as I scrambled to stand.

Kade chuckled as he looked up at me from his knees. "You know I've never seen your blade as a threat? Especially not now."

"You should," I said, moving to circle him. He jumped to his feet in one fluid movement, ushering his shadows toward me.

They gripped me, but my determination to save the man I loved in the deepest marrow of my soul remained steady. My light surged out of me, entwining with them until they fell back.

"No." His lip curled as he watched my magic break his connection to his shadows.

I gripped the blade tighter. My body glowed, brightening the space around us in anticipation of his next move. Kade's eyes narrowed as they blackened.

This time he raised his hands and even more shadows poured out of him, intent on reaching me. They wrapped around my arms and pinned them to my sides. Kade knocked into me again, taking me to the ground and straddling me. He tipped his head back, laughing as the shadows released their hold now that their master had me firmly beneath him.

Still, I fought.

"I always did love your spirit. You should know he'll enjoy breaking it."

I shouted in his face, furious at the darkness inside of him and the words it allowed him to say with no remorse.

Let me out.

I swear my light screamed, bursting to escape while speaking to me exactly like Kade's shadows did.

I lashed out, wiggling my arms from underneath his

thighs, aiming to slap some sense into him. Something. Anything to bring him back to reality. "You will submit to my darkness. Submit to me as the Monster of Mysthaven. The alternative is not an option."

"What alternative?" I spit at him.

He tightened his thighs around my body and pinned my arms above my head. "Thames will kill you." He hardly looked as if it bothered him.

Seeing him so far gone that even the thought of Thames hurting me didn't faze him broke a part of me.

Touch him. Need to touch him.

That voice, softer than the voice of Kade's shadows, echoed in my mind again.

"He can't have me," I seethed, throwing my head forward. Kade jerked back out of the way, loosening his grip just enough that I twisted one of my arms from his hold. "And he can't have *you*."

I thrust my hand forward against his chest as light exploded from my open palm. Kade's eyes widened, and his body slackened above me. His grip relaxed enough for me to yank my other arm free. Immediately, I brought my hand to his face.

"Come back to me, mate," I commanded, my voice infused with magic in a way I'd never heard before.

His hands fisted into the dirt on either side of my face as he leaned down and snarled as if the beast inside of him craved another shot at me. I wavered as a wave of light escaped from me and wrapped around him so quickly, it made me dizzy.

The space around us detonated with light, encompassing us. I brushed my thumb across his cheek.

"He can't have you," I repeated again, a tear falling down my cheek.

I watched the black fade from Kade's eyes as the light twirled around him.

A breath shuddered out of his body, and my light faded. Kade finally took stock of his surroundings and let out a garbled sound while lifting a hand to my face.

"Mate," he whispered reverently.

A whimper escaped my lips as relief and love bubbled to the surface hearing him say the word for the first time. Kade's gaze morphed from awestruck love to absolute horror.

"Illiana, I—" He closed his eyes, and a tremor coursed through his body. He moved to get up, to pull away from me.

"Let me go, Little Rebel," he said. "You have to let me go."

CHAPTER 11

KADE

Lana's light soaked into my soul and filled every dark corner, expanding and cascading over me like nothing I'd ever felt before.

I shuddered, trembling with concentration as I latched on to my shadows and let them force the remaining darkness down, deep enough to cage.

Together, we'd done it. Lana had succeeded at the hardest part: breaking through the black. Enough for us to shove down the evil so that I could take control again.

But it didn't matter.

The peace only she brought me, the utterly consuming obsession and love for her hadn't been enough to stop me from hurting her.

Fuck.

I hurt her. Again.

I moved to stand, but my Little Rebel clutched my shirt, not bothering to hide the frantic look in her eyes.

"No, Kade," she sobbed, tugging at my tunic. "Not again."

Helpless against her, I froze, this time shaking for a different reason. I lowered my hand to her neck, gently

113

running my fingertips over where I'd gripped her too tightly. "He infected me with more of this darkness. More of his power. I'm not safe. I don't know how long I have until it returns."

I may have control now, but things had changed. The darkness lingered, only contained by my shadows.

"You're safe with me," she argued.

I rubbed her skin tenderly, caressing her with the tips of my fingers. "I wouldn't be able to live with myself if I did something to you. Fuck, Lana, I've already hurt you too many times. I can't let it happen again."

"You fought it. You came back." She cupped my cheek but didn't release her other hand from the white-knuckled grip she had on my clothes. "He can't have you. I refuse to let him take you, whether by force or from your guilt."

I shook my head at the resolve on her face. Her light skin was scratched from running into branches through the woods. A few scrapes almost looked healed. Because my mate had unlocked her magic.

Fates, I'd been so proud of her, in awe of her at that moment back in the king's study.

Now, watching her use her light to save me mended some of the broken pieces of my soul that had shattered from knowing what I'd done under Thames's influence.

Streaks of light hovered around my arms, curling around my wrists like they'd hold me here alongside her.

I was a fool to think I could leave her. Even death wouldn't keep me from her now.

"Your light seems as bossy as my shadows." I smiled down at her, hoping my renewed devotion and amazement were clear. I'd thought she was a powerful force, unmatched, even without magic, but now, with the fearsome way she wielded her light—Fates, she was a reckoning.

"It refuses to let the darkness claim you," she said. "Just as I do."

The world around us halted. Those perfect blue eyes stared into mine, glistening with unshed tears as she stroked a thumb across my cheek.

"Say it again," I whispered.

A slow smile spread over her face as a tear fell from the corner of her eye. "Mate."

I leaned forward, kissing away the tear. I didn't stop. Each one caused me pain, and an overwhelming urge to erase her sadness and fears tore at me. I had to ease all of it.

"Again," I said against her skin.

She cried out and threw her arms around my neck. I shifted and pulled her against me. Leaning back, I dragged her up and she immediately wrapped her legs around me. I settled her on top of me as I kneeled on the ground.

"You're mine. You're mine and you're here," she sobbed against me as I clung to her. Every word breathed life into me, reforming my entire being.

I ran my hand through her hair, gently tugging on it to pull her face from my neck. "And you, Little Rebel." My voice shook with raw emotion. "You are my *everything*."

"So we're agreed." She sniffed. "You aren't leaving, or telling me to run."

I sighed, closing my eyes. My heart thudded in my chest, and that tether to Lana thickened, expanding as I held her, relishing in her physical contact. Though I knew the darkness remained inside of me, believing I could leave her now was foolish. "I suppose I can't defy my queen."

"No, you may not." She leaned forward, brushing her lips against mine. This time when she pulled away from the soft kiss, she met my gaze with a burning light reflected in her eyes. "I love you, Kade."

Every fragile piece of resolve I had conjured up snapped at her declaration, and I pulled her to me, claiming her lips as if they were the key to my survival. Fates, it felt like they fucking were.

"I love you," I panted against her mouth. "I love you so fucking much."

She laughed, a beautiful sound filled with relief and hope. She shifted in my lap, kissing me just as fiercely while pressing her body into mine.

I groaned. "Careful, or you'll shatter the last remaining strand I have on my control."

"Consider it shattered," she argued. "Right now."

Her hands trailed down my neck, tracing over my chest and stomach. Her smile reappeared before she returned to kissing me. Gripping her hair in my hand, I inhaled everything about her. Her scent, her whimpers—all of it was mine.

Mine.

"Fucking Fates." I rose on my knees, holding her in place while she loosened her thighs and allowed her hands to trail lower, unfastening my belt and pants as they fell to the ground.

I brought my hand around from her perfect ass, skimming it up her thigh as she shivered beneath me. Running my fingers over the top of her pants, feeling the heat from between her thighs, set my skin ablaze.

I groaned and tugged her pants down, both of us shifting and maneuvering, only breaking our kiss once until she was bare.

"So wet for me, aren't you?" I traced my fingers around her clit before pressing one into her.

Lana threw her head back. "Always for you."

I laughed, leaving a trail of kisses down her neck.

"Harder."

"You are so demanding." I nipped at her neck this time, gently biting her.

"Clearly, you aren't understanding how much I need you."

I tsked. "I know exactly how much you need me. I know exactly how much I need you too, but I want this to last. It's the first time I'm taking you since you learned I'm your mate.

And despite being in the woods, I will take my time with you."

She paused grinding on my fingers and looked at me. "Since I learned? You mean since we learned."

I shook my head, slipping a second finger inside of her and making her shudder. I ran my thumb over her clit, moving in and out as I watched her. "I knew long before you, love. You just needed time to catch up."

She whimpered as her hands gradually made their way down my chest and wrapped themselves around my hardened cock.

She stroked the entire length of my shaft once, while I stared into her hungry eyes. She licked her lips, and I knew holding out was done.

"Take me, Illiana." I slid inside of her, both of us groaning.

She moaned. "I missed you." She tilted her hips, moving faster until I gripped her tightly, stopping her mid thrust.

"Slower," I begged. "Please, Little Rebel. Slow. Let me feel you stretching around me. I want to feel every part of this."

She obeyed, slowing her pace against me. I trailed kisses over her collarbone before licking up her neck. Lana shuddered, clinging onto my shoulders and marking me with her nails.

I took one of her hands from my shoulder and pressed it to the center of my chest. Right where I knew our bond rested. "I feel you everywhere, in every part of me," I said, not stopping the slow, deliberate thrusts inside of her. "But I feel you most of all right here. Your soul is here."

She let out a strangled sound. "Don't ever leave me again, Kade. Never."

"If I had to go, never doubt that I'd find you again. I'd hunt down the Fates themselves and demand they return me to you." I gripped her hips and plunged into her harder, sheathing myself fully as she tilted her head back.

Fire lit in my chest as the tether between us tightened and wove into a nearly tangible thing, so much larger than it had been before.

"Kade," she whispered. "I feel it."

"I know," I said with a strained voice. "I know." I chanted it over and over as we both devolved into panting, moaning messes.

She tightened around me, hot and wanting, and as I slammed her down on my length one more time. She shattered, coming undone. The sound of her delicious orgasm sent me over the edge as I emptied everything I had inside of her.

She fell forward onto my chest, breathless and sweaty.

I lifted her hair from her neck and slid my hand there to hold her close. I never wanted to leave, even if we were in the middle of the damn forest.

She pressed her lips to my chest after a few minutes of silence except for our thudding hearts and heavy breathing.

"We should go back," I whispered against her hair before kissing the top of her head.

She nodded. "Only if you promise to do that again."

I laughed, lifting her from my lap. Grabbing her pants, I slipped them on her, reverently kissing her thighs as I slid them to her waist.

I rose, adjusting my own clothing, but stopped, frozen at the sight before me. My shadows spanned around Lana and the soft glow from my skin told me her light was wrapped around me. Between us, our magic lay intertwined.

"Apparently our magic wants each other too." Lana snorted, noticing their movements as well.

Ours. All of her is ours.

"I know," I said out loud both to her statement and my shadows. "My shadows talk to me."

Lana blinked, staring with surprise. A sly grin spread

across her lips before she laughed, the sound warming me again. "I know, they talk to me too."

"What?" I stared at her, feeling the furrow in my brow forming. "They talk to you? They just started talking to me."

"No, I think they've been talking for a while. Maybe you were ignoring them or just couldn't hear them."

An indignant feeling rushed through me. Evidently, she was right.

I grasped her hand in mine, kissing her knuckles. "All right, know-it-all. Catch me up on what's happening. You have until we're at the inn, before your mouth is occupied with something far more interesting."

CHAPTER 12
LANA

"I don't want to leave this room," I whispered against Kade's chest.

His arms wrapped around me. Here, nestled under the covers, we were shielded from the weight of the world. No Thames. No war. No prophecies.

Kade rolled me over, cradling my face in his hands. "One more minute."

I grinned; this was about the twentieth time he'd said that.

He took one of my rose-gold strands, curling it around his finger before leaning down and kissing the tip of my nose.

My hands roamed up and down his back, over the horrific marks of his past.

Even though his father had died by his hand, some pain couldn't be erased. The scars would forever be a reminder of his tortured past, but I would always strive to remind him of his inner strength. That his father failed to turn him into a monster.

A slight tremor coursed through Kade at my touch, and I savored every second of it. Relished in the power between us that had grown since being together last night.

"I love you," he said as he gazed at me tenderly.

I kissed him, pulling him close to me as our mating bond surged with delight in my chest. "I love you," I whispered against his lips.

Kade rolled over until he kneeled behind me, kissing my back. My magic healed my injuries quickly last night, but it hadn't helped Kade manage the guilt he felt at having caused them during our "adventure" in the woods.

"Never again," he said. "Never again will I succumb to the darkness and hurt you, Illiana. It may still be here, inside of me, but I will fight it every breath of every day."

"You have more than made up for it." I winked over my shoulder.

He grasped my chin in his fingers. "I swear it. I'll die before anything like that happens again."

"It won't come to that." I turned, facing him so I could touch his face. "What happened with Thames? What did he do while you were trapped there?"

Kade's shoulders slumped, and he closed his eyes. I rubbed my thumb along his cheek, tracing the lines of his face.

"I killed too many people in his name," Kade said, his voice shattered by pain. "I don't deserve your love, Lana. I don't deserve it."

My heart crumbled under the weight of his tortured words. I leaned forward, kissing his forehead. "You do deserve it. You were trapped by his darkness."

"It's my darkness. It's lingering," he sighed, pulling away from me. "Fighting me constantly to take control. When I think about what happened, what I've done, the darkness gets stronger."

I refused to let him bury his pain and continue feeling alone, instead wrapping my arms around his neck. "You don't have to talk to me about any of it now. But just know I'm here when you're ready. We can carry the pain together. You will never suffer in silence again. Not from Dargan. Not from Thames."

He met my gaze, shifting me to the side, and kissing me briefly. "I know I'm not alone. I wasn't alone with Thames either."

I frowned and he leaned over the bed, reaching into the pocket of his pants. He pulled out the necklace he'd given me for my birthday. His mother's necklace.

"Every night I remained in Mysthaven, I slept in your room. Even when fully consumed by the darkness, my shadows led me there. To lay where you once did, even if it had only been for a short period of time. I saw this left on the nightstand and grabbed it. Keeping it with me." He swept my hair behind my ear. "Even when my mind lost hope, you were here." He pressed a hand to his chest. "You will *always* be here. Saving me from the darkness."

My lip trembled as I took the necklace, running my fingers over it before I clutched it in my hand.

Kade traced my lips with his thumb before rising from the bed. He ran his fingers through my hair, combing out the knots we'd created together. "Now let's go before I never let you out of this bed."

Exiting our sanctuary, we walked hand in hand down the stairs toward the tavern. Kade smiled at me when he caught my gaze. Our hearts were full, our bond and bodies satiated. It was as though something had clicked into place when I first admitted what he was to me during our battle at Mount Legion. But last night, it fused together, unbreakable. I touched my chest with my free hand.

Hope flickered, enticing and expanding. If I could bring Kade back from the darkness lurking beneath his skin, maybe there was a way we could defeat Thames and the evil plaguing our lands.

Before we took the last few steps down the stairs and

walked into the main tavern room, I stopped, pulling on Kade's hand. "Are you ready for this?"

He kissed the top of my head. "Ready as I'll ever be. Come on, let's go cause chaos." He threw me a wink before continuing down to greet everyone.

He stood at the bottom of the stairs, sending shadowy tendrils toward Jax, Raya, and Storm, who all sat together eating their breakfast. As his shadows poked Raya's ankle, she dropped her spoon into her porridge and let out a yelp, splashing the food all over Storm's arm.

"What in the actual fuck?" Jax laughed as he bit into another apple. He looked up and his grin morphed into shock as he dropped the fruit, which clattered to his plate.

Storm shoved his chair back, turning toward us immediately. His shoulders sagged in relief as he looked Kade over. When he met my gaze, we shared an unspoken sentiment. We'd both missed him, and the relief in his eyes reflected back in mine. I gave him a soft smile as he exhaled sharply.

Raya jumped up from her chair, knocking it over as she ran to Kade. "You're okay?" The pained expression on her face was riddled with a combination of guilt and relief.

She moved to kneel before him, but Kade reached out, grabbing her arm and wrapping her in a hug. "I'm okay."

Raya pushed herself back. "I'm so sorry. Everything is my fault." She wrung her hands with a nervous energy so unlike the hardened warrior she portrayed. "I couldn't fight him. I hurt you. I hurt Storm. I hurt Lana. I don't know how to fix what I've done."

Even without knowing Raya for long, I knew this was not a side seen by most. The guilt caused by the events at Mount Legion had weighed heavily on her this entire time. While none of us would ever blame her for what happened, she needed to know that *Kade* did not blame her.

"Raya." He grabbed her hands. "You are not at fault for

anything. There is nothing to apologize for and I will not have you thinking otherwise. As someone who is intimately aware of what it's like to be controlled by another, you are a true warrior for fighting as hard as you did. As you can see, all of us are in one piece. We're together again."

Raya bowed her head and stepped back, wrapping her arms around herself. Hopefully with his forgiveness, she could stop destroying herself for things she had no control over.

Storm came forward to greet Kade. The two embraced momentarily, clapping each other on the back. "Happy to see you again, brother." Storm smiled.

"It's good to see you too." Kade pulled him in again. "Thank you for keeping her safe."

Storm cleared his throat and took a step back, coming to stand on the other side of me. I rested my head on his shoulder, knowing if anyone understood what the separation was like, it was him.

Kade positioned himself to speak to all of us. "Thank you for everything you all have done to keep each other safe. To keep Lana safe. I will be forever grateful."

A warm tingle skittered down my arms. I would never grow tired of looking at this man and knowing he was mine.

Jax approached Kade and playfully punched him in the shoulder. "Enough of the mushy stuff." He waggled his brows. "How did you escape?"

Kade motioned for all of us to sit at the table as he pulled an extra chair over for me. I didn't miss how he moved it to be practically on top of his own.

Possessive mate of mine.

"Thames is worse than we even imagined." His expression turned sour.

"Just what I wanted to hear," Jax moaned, a disgruntled look overtook his features.

Kade shot him a look. "He has taken over Mysthaven and placed himself as ruler and is creating an army of dark ones.

While we knew that's what he was doing through my father's confession, I think it's much more than just an army. There's something happening at Firestone."

An army of dark ones was terrifying enough to deal with, but the thought of Thames having some sort of secret up his sleeve sent chills up my spine.

"What is Firestone?" I asked.

Kade's hand came to rest on my leg. "It's a volcano in Mysthaven. It hasn't erupted in our history, or at least that I'm aware of, but the place is still avoided by most."

"By all," Jax corrected, clearing his throat. "Unless you have a death wish."

Storm's eyes narrowed. "I wonder what he's hiding?" he mused, steering back to the conversation at hand.

Kade's head dropped slightly. "I don't know. I was never given access to that information. The last time he forced me to torture a so-called 'traitor' in the dungeons, he mentioned if the Fae wouldn't turn willingly, he could choose between dying by my hand or being used to feed his weapon at Firestone."

The haunted look in Kade's eyes broke my heart. He'd need time to process whatever Thames had forced him to do. All he ever wanted was to escape the monster his father created him to be, and here he was, forced to be it once more. One day, when this atrocity was behind us, he would never have to be the Monster of Mysthaven again.

"That volcano always did creep me out." Raya shivered. "Nothing good can come from this. A weapon of any kind is bad, but something created by a sorcerer as powerful as Thames could have more implications than we can fathom."

Storm folded his arms across his chest. "We'll just add it to the growing list of questions we need to answer."

The door to the Knotted Willow slammed open, and a warm breeze whispered across my back, urging me to turn around.

A tall frame filled the doorway, light shining around him and through his blond hair in beams. He looked like an avenging angel.

"Ian!" I shouted, jumping up. I tried to move past Raya, who sat stiffly in her chair and didn't make space for me to pass. I didn't wait for her to move as I shoved her chair to the side so I could run to my oldest friend.

He wrapped his arms around me. "Fates, Lan. It's so good to see you."

"I was worried about you," I said into his neck, not releasing him. Too many times we'd been separated, and I'd faced the thought of not seeing him again. I hated it.

He pulled away, inhaling deeply. "Just happy we're together again."

I ushered him into the room, closing the door behind me, while he greeted those closest to him. He even gave Kade a warmer acknowledgment than I'd imagined. Though that was probably because he didn't know what had happened in Mysthaven.

Ian stepped in front of Raya. His hand twitched at his side, and he slowly brought it toward hers. Raya took a small step away. "Glad you're back," she whispered before turning around and moving away. His gaze followed her, lingering for a second too long until he closed his eyes. I frowned, looking between the two of them. I would've thought he and Raya would be on friendlier terms, considering she could talk to Ian in her mind.

"Drink," William huffed, shoving a glass of water into Ian's hands.

Kalliah appeared from behind the bar door, carrying platters of food in both hands. Her face lit up as soon as she saw Ian and then quickly turned to shock upon seeing Kade. Her eyes kept dancing between the two, clearly unable to decide which story she wanted to hear first.

Before we even had time to celebrate our reunion, the inn

door swung open once more. Ryland Lockbane strode through, removing his hat with a flourish as a wide grin spread across his face. "I heard you were in need of a swordsman."

My entire body stiffened. *No.*

Ryland had been in the hallway with Casimir. They'd been conspiring about something. Casimir most likely had been trying to convince him to work with Andras against Brookmere.

He couldn't be here. If Ryland was here, then surely Andras was not far behind the traitorous contender.

"No," I seethed before pointing at Ryland. "You're a traitor."

Kade immediately sent his shadows to the man, shoving his back against the wall and forming a shadow hand wrapping around Ryland's throat. He sputtered for air, a confused expression on his face.

"Lan." Ian hurried to my side.

I ignored him. "I saw you working with Casimir that night." Seeing Kade's shadows hold him in place allowed me to feel a bit of boldness. I wasn't the same woman who'd felt trapped in a panic attack in that hallway anymore. Not at all. "How dare you come here with Ian?"

Turning to Ian, I shook my head. "We can't trust him. If he was working with Casimir before, then he is working with Andras now. I will not allow anyone into our group unless they can be trusted with complete certainty, and Ryland Lockbane is not one of those people."

Ryland's face turned from red to blue, and Storm and Jax rushed to Kade's side. "Whoa, whoa there, brother," Storm said, working alongside Jax to calm Kade and the angering shadows. "Let him speak."

"If my queen says he is not to be trusted," Kade seethed, a dangerous expression flashing across his face, "then I can't be held responsible for what my shadows do or don't do."

Ian shouted, "Stop, he's on our side." Shoving past me, he

knocked into Kade's back, forcing him to stumble for a moment, which loosened his shadow grip, but not completely. "Kade, let him go."

Hearing Ian vouch for Ryland made me pause.

"He was with Casimir so many times in the trials. I gave him the benefit of the doubt then, but I refuse to be caught off guard again, Ian," I warned, imploring him to see reason.

"Hear him out," Ian requested.

I knew Ian wouldn't ask me to listen if I was in danger. I worried my bottom lip for a second, then nodded once in Kade's direction. Slowly the shadows receded, dropping Ryland to the floor and leaving him gasping for air.

"You better start speaking," I ordered. "I will not have everything we've done so far be ruined by a spy." My heart ached thinking about Hale and everything he'd sacrificed. Even with his devotion and loyalty, he'd put all of us through hell. Ultimately, it was not a risk I was willing to take again. Especially not with someone who didn't have the same history with me.

Ryland wheezed, heaving down gulps of air while on his hands and knees. Once he finally caught his breath enough to speak, Ryland pushed himself up onto his feet, brushing the dirt off his pants. "Some welcome this was, Ian. I thought the Hidden Henchman was desperate for help."

"The Hidden Henchman doesn't need help from those who give their loyalty to evil, mind-controlling mad men." I crossed my arms over my chest, battling my anger unsuccessfully. "Ryland, you have two minutes. Convince me or I can't be held responsible for what happens to you."

He took a few steps toward me and bowed, lower than one normally would for royalty. "First, I just want to say how sorry I am for the loss of your mother and father. Brookmere lost two exceptional leaders, and I can't even imagine how you must be feeling. I am forever grateful for their love and generosity throughout the years. They always treated us well."

Ryland placed a hand over his heart. "May nature guide them."

"Thank you." I nodded, swallowing down the grief threatening to break me once more. "Continue."

He took a deep breath. "I never worked with Casimir. He tried to recruit me to help him with some crazy plan of his. Fates, he even threatened me a few times, but we Broham Fae cannot be coerced. Our loyalty to Brookmere is unmatched. I turned him down time and time again."

"And yet you never reported his scheming," I snarled.

Ryland hung his head. "I truly thought it was ramblings of a delusional Fae. Yes, his threats hit their mark, but I didn't think he was truly capable of what happened. After the third trial, when Ellevail fell into the hands of Andras's minions, I escaped back home to ensure my people were taken care of." His brow furrowed. "I wasn't so certain, with my unwillingness to help, if we wouldn't face some sort of retaliation." His voice lowered. "And I will not have my people suffer because I refused to stand on the side of evil."

My initial anger dissipated slightly. It sounded convincing, like he'd done everything he could to protect his people, just as I would hope a city leader would, but I still needed to be sure. "Do you pledge your loyalty to me, Ryland Lockbane? Do you swear upon the Fates themselves you will fight for Brookmere and all of its citizens? Will you follow any and all directions given to you by me or those in this room?"

Ryland surveyed all of the Fae before him before dropping to one knee. "Queen Illiana, I swear on the Fates, my sword remains true to Brookmere and to any citizen who calls it home. I pledge myself to protect Brookmere. I pledge myself to you."

I took a moment, scanning the faces of my friends and trying to read their expressions. Ian subtly nodded his head in agreement.

"Fine, you can stay." I extended my hand out to his, and

he shook it with fervor before I pulled him close. "You will be watched. Carefully," I said, my voice leaving no room to question on how serious I was. "The moment you cross us, you die by my hand or Kade's shadows. Whichever is faster. Understood?"

"Understood." Ryland gulped.

Ian coughed to break the tension. "Well, now that's all taken care of. Ryland, why don't you get the rest of your people settled. I'm sure there are some earth Fae out back who can help build shelters while we prepare."

He nodded and left before any of us could change our minds.

Jax giggled in the back of the room. "He looked like he was about to piss himself."

Raya sighed loudly. "You are a child, Jax."

He threw an apple core at Raya's head, but Ian smacked it away before it could reach her. Ian glanced over at her, but she immediately averted her gaze. I narrowed my eyes, wondering what in the Fates was going on.

I turned to Kade. "We have the most chaotic friends."

He chuckled in return, before grabbing my hand and pulling me close to his side. He whispered in my ear, "And I wouldn't have it any other way."

Vivienne appeared from behind the bar, clapping her hands slowly. "Well done, Illiana. Your parents would be proud."

Red colored my cheeks. I wasn't sure I had ever spoken to someone with such conviction before, save for Andras and King Dargan. Vivienne was right. My parents would be proud. I was proud of me. "Thank you, Vivienne. That means a lot."

She stepped forward, standing close to me before opening her arms wide. "Now, let's discuss taking back your kingdom, my queen."

CHAPTER 13
LANA

"So, even though Kade killed his evil father, we don't just have Andras left," Ian said, rubbing his forehead with his eyes closed. "We have a thousand-year-old, powerful, evil psycho to kill too?"

I slumped in my chair. "Accurate," I sighed.

Kade's hand squeezed my leg underneath the table, comforting me despite the panic rising in my throat at how much we had to face still.

We'd finally gotten around to explaining who Thames was as we tried to figure out how to fight a war against Andras and this new evil.

To save Atheria.

"So," Kade said, looking around at the group. "That brings us back to what we should handle first."

Each person brought something slightly different to the table. Whether it was a desire to protect a certain village, or training the new army, or growing the necessary food to feed everyone, the requirements of what we needed to do kept expanding at a dizzying rate. No one could agree on what our highest priorities should be.

"We need to take back Ellevail," Kalliah said again, for

the third time in the last ten minutes. "We need to find Leif. Plus, Andras needs to die, preferably a heinous death."

Ian and Storm simultaneously let out exasperated sighs. Storm turned to Kalliah. "How do you expect us to do that when we haven't even trained anyone yet? We need time to prepare and cultivate an army. We can't go in there as a ragtag group of misfits hoping for the best." He spoke like a true strategist. Calculated. "Andras will die, but we need to try to minimize our losses in the process."

"I agree it needs to be done sooner rather than later. Nothing good can happen by evil living in our home, but Storm is right." Ian passed a glass of water to Kalliah. "Training the army has to be our first priority, and unfortunately, that takes time." He reached for Kalliah's hand. "We will ensure Leif is safe. We all want that, but we can't storm Ellevail without a solid plan."

"If this were any of you, we'd be breaking down the gates," Kalliah said. Her voice squeaked, but she clenched her jaw, anguish melting into fury. "I can't believe we aren't making him a priority after he sacrificed himself to buy us time to escape."

I leaned forward, reaching for my friend's hand. "Kalliah—"

"No." She abruptly rose from her chair. With a shaky breath, she turned, heading toward the front door. "I'll help elsewhere. Just let me know when you decide our friend's life is important again."

I collapsed back into the chair, closing my eyes. "She's right," I whispered.

"Yes, she is," Ian said, rubbing his forehead. "But it doesn't change the fact that we have zero eyes inside Ellevail right now. There's no way of knowing where he is or what situation we'd be walking into. It's a fool's errand until we can do this effectively."

Kade's shadows wrapped around my legs, crawling all the

way up toward my waist, as if they knew I needed comfort. We had no clue whether Leif was okay, and as much as it pained me, it was killing Kalliah.

"It's the same reason you couldn't return for me, Little Rebel."

I jerked my head toward him and examined the compassion and warmth lining his features.

"So, training it is," I sighed. We had farmers, builders, remote village Fae, and young men and women arriving daily now. None of them were soldiers or knew how to do more than a few defensive moves. "At least for you all," I finished.

Storm and Ian exchanged a look. "For us?" Storm questioned.

Raya snickered, smiling for the first time since we'd sat down. She'd remained unusually quiet throughout this discussion. I could only wonder what she was thinking and feeling right now. She'd been excluded from any type of strategic planning sessions for so long, it must be surreal for her to finally sit at the table and be able to fully participate in the conversation.

"I need to find the journal," I announced. "It feels like the missing piece to this puzzle—maybe it will contain information about the dagger too. Vivienne wouldn't have allowed the journal to remain hidden for so long if it wasn't important."

I knew the dagger had a part to play, I just hoped it would be enough.

Ian scowled at me and his eyes darkened. "The only problem is that we don't know where the journal is located." He stood and started pacing among the tables. Every few steps I could have sworn his entire body twitched. Almost like a spasm. "And even if we did know where it was hidden, we'd be leaving our people here while we went gallivanting around Brookmere."

"I do know where it is though." I swallowed hard as all

eyes fixated on me. "The Southern Forest," I whispered, almost wishing Ian wouldn't hear and react the way I knew he would.

"Absolutely not," Ian growled, his glare practically shooting daggers in my direction.

Jax frowned, ignoring Ian's outburst. "The home to that terrifying flying creature… What did you call it, a strox?"

I nodded. "The very same."

Slapping his hand on his knee, Jax looked Kade straight in the eye. "Count me out. You all have fun with the nightmare beasts." Kade cocked a brow at Jax. "What? I've had my fair share of evil creatures to deal with while you were gone. I'm just saying."

"Scaredy cat," Storm teased, and Jax hissed in response.

"Your taunts don't even bother me anymore. I'll take them over flying creatures." He overexaggerated a shiver and then bowed his head at Ian. "Except you of course, Captain."

"I'm needed for training the army." Storm kicked Jax's leg under the table. "*You* are going."

Jax's mouth hung open for a moment before closing it and furrowing his brows. "I'm telling William to pack me mead," He grumbled. "Lots of mead."

"So we split up." Kade rose and stood next to where Ian now paced. "I will take Lana to find the journal with Jax. Meanwhile, Ian, Storm, and Raya will stay here and start training the army."

Ian's jaw clenched with fury. "Absolutely not. If you think for one moment I'm going to let you take Illiana on some secret mission," he chuckled sarcastically, "you are profoundly mistaken. Every time I leave her with you, something terrible happens."

I tapped my finger on the table, glaring at him. Fighting would get us nowhere. I would think, after everything we'd been through, Fae male bullshit would be the last thing on their minds.

Apparently not.

Kade scoffed. "I'd die before letting anything happen to her."

Tension filled the room, thick and heavy as it pressed in around us. Ian scowled. "Says the man infected with the darkness. Who let her get kidnapped on, what—two separate occasions? Who knows what you've done under Thames's control? No thank you." He stalked to Kade and shoved his finger in his chest, twitching slightly. "I'll be taking care of *my* queen."

Ian's distorted features forced me out of my chair, heart racing as shock drove me to stand suddenly. The anger and hatred on his face weren't like him at all.

"Ian," I said quietly, terrified of what he was feeling to make him act out like this while simultaneously wanting him to snap out of it.

Shadows slowly billowed around Kade's legs, ready and waiting to pounce. As Kade slowly approached Ian, his eyes widened as a sly smile formed on his face. "I'm the one infected by darkness? How are *you* feeling Ian?"

My attention shifted fully to Ian.

"What does that mean?" I asked, only to be ignored as the two stared each other down.

William yelled from across the room, "If you're going to fight, you better do it outside. I'm not fixing anymore broken chairs."

"Gladly," Ian and Kade replied in unison.

These men were incorrigible. "Tits and daggers. You two are absolutely ridiculous. No one is fighting right now. We don't have time for this."

My words fell on deaf ears. Ian and Kade were outside before I could even finish my sentence. Ian rolled his sleeves up, ready to take on Kade and his shadows.

"Yeah, fight," Jax exclaimed, clapping his hands together once. "Fates, I wish I had a snack for this." His gaze shifted around the room, eyes widening at a tray of nuts on the bar top. He ran toward it, taking the whole bowl before racing outside to watch the brawl.

I followed behind, hoping someone would stop this nonsense. No such luck. Ian and Kade were circling each other, taunting, each waiting for the other to make a move.

Kalliah had been standing with a group of Fae just outside of the inn, but the minute she locked eyes on Kade and Ian, she ran over to me, scanning my worried expression, "Kade won't actually hurt him, and neither will Ian. Let them duke it out for a minute. Maybe it'll break up some of the tension brewing between them."

I rolled my eyes. I couldn't believe this was the kind of behavior the two men I loved the most resorted to. They may feel the need to choose violence, but I wouldn't let them actually hurt each other.

"You can feel it calling, can't you, Ian," Kade taunted. "Tell me, are you feeling angry? Do you feel out of control?"

Ian remained in a defensive position, hands up protecting his face as he mirrored Kade's movements. "Angry? Of course I'm angry. The world has gone to complete shit. Look at the mess we're in."

Kade chuckled, like this was a game. His shadows remained dancing at his feet. "Tsk, tsk, now you know that's not what I mean. You haven't admitted it yet, have you?" Kade shuffled forward and threw a jab at Ian's chest. "Afraid?"

Ian ducked and blocked the jab with his forearm. "I'm not afraid of anything."

I tried to step forward into their make-believe ring but was quickly pulled back by Jax and Storm. "Hey, stop that. Someone's going to get hurt." I ripped my arm out of Storm's loose grasp. "Kade, come on. Ian, this is stupid. Stop fighting."

They continued to ignore me.

The two carried on circling each other and taking small hits. They teased each other, both holding back, just waiting for the other to make a mistake.

Ian threw a jab-cross, aiming directly at Kade's jaw. To his credit, his shadows held back and didn't attack. They let Kade take the hit. His lower lip split open, and a small rivulet of blood formed on the skin. "I know you owe me a few of those," Kade said, wiping the blood from his face and then shaking it from his fingertips. "If you want to hit me to deal with it, fine, but you need to talk about it."

Ian's lip curled. "I don't know what you mean." He shouted the last few words.

My body tensed, frozen as I observed the exchange. A sickening dread filled me.

Kade took a step toward Ian, hands out in a placating way. "Out of anyone, you know I would understand. You can talk to me."

"Fuck all the way off," Ian shouted, sprinting toward Kade in a flurry of fists and rage.

Kade let him get in another hit before his shadows snapped forward. "Listen to me—"

"No," Ian said so coldly, my skin crawled.

"Ian—" I stepped forward, desperate to reach my best friend and understand what he was going through.

Kade's demeanor shifted and he chuckled, again smiling at me. "Don't worry, Illiana. This will be over shortly. I promise not to hurt him as long as he tells the truth."

Truth? What would Ian need to be telling the truth about? More importantly, how would Kade know something about Ian that I didn't?

"I am telling the truth," Ian spat. "I have nothing to discuss with the likes of you."

Ian punched again. Kade sidestepped and slammed a fist into Ian's side. Then Kade swept his leg out and clipped Ian's ankles, causing him to fall backward. "If you don't get it under control soon, it will be too much. The darkness. It will grow and fester. You won't be able to escape it."

Kade's shadows pinned Ian to the ground as he writhed beneath their grasp. "You're infected with the darkness, admit it. I can see it in your eyes. I can see it in the way your body moves. He got to you too." Kade held him there for a moment as Ian panted on the ground before releasing him. He stepped back, giving Ian room to compose himself once more.

"How fucking dare you," Ian seethed, scrambling to get off of his back and onto his feet.

"Your body—it twitches, just like the dark ones." Kade's shadows lifted Ian's shirt. "And I bet if we look over here, you're going to have a scar. Just like Illiana. Just like me." Kade lifted his own shirt to reveal the angry-looking scar on his side. "You and I are one and the same." Ian's eyes went wide and he stopped fighting the shadows, wiping the sweat off his brow. "The only difference is I've been living with this for years. I know how to control it. Do you?"

My heart dropped. "Ian?" I could barely breathe through the accusation.

Ian, my untouchable nothing-can-break-him best friend, infected with the darkness. Scarred from what? Andras? Just like me. I choked back a sob. I couldn't let Thames and his evil take another one of my friends.

"Ian, is it true?" Raya whispered, her face pale and eyes wide.

His head moved on a swivel, looking at everyone watching him. "I—I...I don't know." His head slumped forward. "When I was in the dungeon, Andras stabbed me with a dagger coated in a black liquid. It looked like the same blade he used to attack Lana all those years ago."

"Why didn't you tell me sooner?" I ran to him, pulling him into the biggest hug. "We would have helped you."

I may not fully understand my magic, but I did know whatever light I possessed helped with the darkness. I would make sure to eradicate it from Ian however I had to. Just as I would figure it out for Kade. Ian had suffered far too much on my behalf to endure this.

He straightened himself and took a step back. "I'm sorry. I recognized the liquid from when he hurt you, but I didn't understand the implications of it. I'm just so angry all the time. I bit Kalliah's and Corbin's heads off the other day for no reason at all, just because I couldn't control it. Since we've been back together, I haven't felt as angry and thought perhaps it was a fluke."

I grabbed Ian's hands, and mine glowed briefly as we touched. "Does it feel better now? Whenever Kade has his outbursts, my touch always helps him. I think it has something to do with my light magic."

He opened his mouth to speak and stopped, eyes widening in shock. "I feel it. That's— How? I feel the darkness retreating within me. It's not gone, but it's manageable. Thank you, Lana." He squeezed my hands, smiling, but then a look crossed his face I couldn't quite decipher. "Wait, did you just say light magic?"

Jax, Storm, and Raya all chuckled.

"Hah, yes. Well, surprise!" I said sheepishly. "Turns out I have some sort of light magic that helps to destroy darkness. I don't really know how to use it yet, but I did kill a bunch of dark ones in a minor freak-out. So…yeah. Turns out this magicless princess isn't so magicless anymore." I raised my shoulders.

Storm called from the side, "It's pretty incredible. She's got some work to do, but she'll get there."

Ian shook his head. "You leave for a week to go to a forgotten kingdom for answers about a prophecy and come back with magic. What next?"

I glanced over to Kade, who was already staring at me. The smile from him sent shivers up my spine, and suddenly, I wanted everyone to know exactly what he meant to me.

"Well…" I held my breath for a minute, looking back to Ian. "Mates exist again."

Ian's eyebrows shot up as his mouth opened. His immediate reaction wasn't to balk at my words though. Instead, his gaze flitted to Raya, and he frowned, then shook his head, looking back at me. I cocked an eyebrow, rethinking how many times I'd caught his eyes lingering on her.

"Mates?" he asked. He opened and closed his mouth a few times. "How did you find that out?"

I picked at my nails, sending my nervous energy somewhere besides my voice. After his fight with Kade, I wasn't sure how my news would be received. Steeling myself, I answered. "Kade is my mate."

Ian inhaled slowly, not reacting at all. He blinked a few times until a smile crept across his face. He took a step toward me, then another before wrapping me in a hug.

He was accepting this, accepting us. I glanced over at Kade, who grinned so warmly I felt it heating my skin like sunlight.

Ian pulled away, looking at me, and laughed. "Well," he said. "I shouldn't be surprised that you would be the one to find a mate." Taking my hands in his, he didn't break eye contact. "I am so happy for you, Lan. A mate and magic." He chuckled, shaking his head again.

I grinned up at him, grateful that the foreign look of rage on him had dissipated and instead, joy shone through. "I know. I'm still trying to wrap my head around it too, but like always, we'll figure it out together. Now can you and Kade get your shit settled so we can actually make a plan to get to the Southern Forest?"

Kade walked over to Ian and extended his hand surrounded by shadows. "Truce?"

Ian cocked an eyebrow before reluctantly sighing and shaking Kade's hand. "Truce. Not sure I have a choice if my best friend is your mate," he added. "As long as I'm coming with you to the Southern Forest, we're good."

Kade looked at me. "Of course," I answered immediately.

Ian gave me a soft smile before rubbing the back of his neck. "What do we do about what's inside of us then?"

Kade sighed. "That's what we need to figure out. In the meantime, control is easier around Lana and her light, but I don't mind sucker punching you when it flares either."

"Prick," Ian muttered under his breath, but I didn't miss the small smile tugging at his lips as he tried to hold it back.

Though everyone made their way back toward the inn, Kalliah hesitated, staring out in the direction of Ellevail.

I looped my arm in hers, resting my head on her shoulder. "I worry for him too," I said. "I swear to you, I do. But even then, I know it's nothing compared to how you feel."

"I spent so long pushing him away. Wanting something but being too scared to grab it," she said softly. "And now?"

I wrapped my arms around her fully as she let out a sob, turning in toward my body. "If he's gone, I'll never forgive myself. What he did, not even thinking twice in that moment —I can't breathe thinking about it sometimes."

I ran my hand over her hair, whispering words of reassurance. "We're going to get him back. We just need to make sure we can get to him *and* get him out so that he's never in that position again. The moment we can accomplish that, he'll be back with us. He'll be home with you."

She nodded, pulling away as she regained her composure. "Is that an official proclamation from our queen?"

I smiled, taking both of her hands in mine. "As my first official one, I had to make it good."

Kalliah took one more breath, looking toward home before returning to the inn beside me, hand in hand.

"Thank you for everything," I said to one of the Fae hammering away at a stack of weapons in our forge. "Make sure to let Raya know if you run out of anything."

The man bowed his head. "We've got everything we need, Your Majesty."

Though time was a luxury we weren't sure we had, I wanted to personally thank as many of the Fae I could who'd answered my call for help. I needed my people to know how grateful I was for their time, energy, and willingness to fight for our kingdoms before I disappeared again on our journey to the Southern Forest.

My father and mother would have loved to have seen so many of their constituents persevering toward a common goal: peace. I wondered, not for the first time, if they'd be proud of me.

So many stories were shared with me about how the king and queen had helped them throughout the years. Tales I'd never heard before. While in the last few years I had stepped up as the Hidden Henchman, thinking my father had done nothing, it was evident that for a long time he had been there for his people. I couldn't help but wonder if Andras's mind magic had convinced him to stop so the dark ones could grow their numbers.

"Once, the king sent a healer to my home when my daughter was gravely ill. Without her aid, my daughter would have died from infection. She saved her." The man cleared his throat, visibly upset as he recalled the tale. My heart clenched, but not merely with grief. I was grateful that others would remember not only my father, but Elisabeth too, just as I did. Bowing low, he returned to growing the grain needed to make bread.

An older woman recalled a time when the queen invited her to tea after learning she'd discovered a new kind of flower. "We talked for hours in her garden about flowers and other plants. It was the most genuine afternoon. She truly appreciated our conversation and made me feel like my contributions to our kingdom, no matter how small, mattered. I will never forget how she spent so many hours with me, as if we were friends instead of ruler and commoner."

Storm and Ian worked alongside the Fae here, taking stock of the weapons inventory we had amassed over the last few days. Fortunately for us, so many brought their own with more to share. The metal wielders worked overtime to create weaponry with vast options of blades, knowing the inevitable was upon us.

"You can never have enough weapons, Your Majesty," a burly metal wielder named Carl told me earlier this morning. "Better to have five weapons per person than no weapons per person. Just in case you drop one. That's what I always say."

None of them complained about the tight living conditions or long hours. Not one. Pride swelled to new heights within my heart. My people were worth fighting for, no matter how dark things became. They were worth it.

Every time I thought I had finished meeting with everyone, more would appear. The endless stream of support for fighting this evil, for standing up for our world against those who threatened to destroy our very way of life, reaffirmed what I needed to do.

We would not be able to continue to amass the number of people we were without going unnoticed for much longer. Andras would come for us. Thames would not be far behind.

The time had come.

To face the darkest beasts of this world.

To find the journal I prayed held all the answers to our questions.

The time had come to go to the Southern Forest.

CHAPTER 14
KADE

Our party moved quickly and quietly through the lush hills of Brookmere as we traveled to the Southern Forest.

Ian led the pack with Lana and me in the middle, while Jax took up the rear. We planned to use Raya and Ian's connection to send back any information if necessary.

Keeping Lana safe throughout this journey and doing as little as possible to attract attention was my only goal.

Lana remained hopeful all her questions would be answered when we found her mother's journal. *If* we found the journal.

Ian called back, "About an hour longer, then we'll stop. There's a grove that should provide us ample protection for the night."

I gave Ian a curt nod in response. The less noise the better.

So far, the dark ones had kept their distance since I'd arrived in Brookmere. But there was still a pull, a tug to return to Mysthaven and comply with the orders given to me by Thames.

Logically, I knew if I remained in my right mind, I would

never give Lana over to him, but what if the darkness took over? Would I be able to resist his calling? Would I ever be able to rid this disease from my body? Lana's light worked now, but I couldn't help but wonder what we would do if the darkness overpowered her magic.

Perhaps this journal would have an idea of how to rid the darkness and evil from not only the land but from Fae as well. She had her theories that the blade had removed the darkness from the dark ones she'd used it on. However, without any solid proof, we weren't sure. At this point, I should just let her use that dagger on me a few times to test it. I wouldn't mind being at the end of her blade again. Fates, she was beautiful when her eyes lit with fire.

I snaked my shadows sideways to curl around Lana. Since I'd opened myself up to them, especially after the memorable birthday activity in my mother's garden, I could feel her through them as if it were my hands caressing her skin. The comfort for me to be able to touch her, to know she was beside me, engulfed me with security and reassured our mate bond more than I could say. I wondered if it would always be this way, if I'd always need her touch.

We want to be with her magic, my shadows whined. *Let it out.*

Powerful shadow magic *whined*.

I rolled my eyes. *I almost wish I didn't hear you for how much you've begged to be with her magic.*

You beg to touch her. We want what's ours too.

Patience. She needs to learn how to reach it herself.

They sighed—at least I think sigh is the right word—and settled for covering more of her body. She looked down before raising an eyebrow in my direction.

I shrugged. "I have no control," I mouthed.

The sun's golden glow disappeared beyond the horizon as we approached the grove. A small opening surrounded by beautiful birch trees and a trickling stream lay a few yards away. I had to give it to Ian; I couldn't have picked a better campsite.

With the help of William and the other cooks now at the Knotted Willow, we'd packed a hearty stew for dinner tonight. The vegetables simmered over our fire in a perfect mix of rich broth and brown gravy as Ian and Jax shifted to hunt for small game to add.

Lana stood in front of the pot warming our stew, lost in her thoughts. I wrapped an arm around her from behind. "It feels like a lifetime since I've been alone with you," I whispered into her ear.

She turned and slipped her arms around my waist, staring up into my eyes. "When all is said and done, we're going to lock ourselves in a room for a week."

I laughed, loving the sound that had been so rare before her. I kissed the top of her head. "Anything you want, Little Rebel."

The pot crackled, simmering too hot, and Lana pulled away. She sat next to the fire, stirring the cooking stew as she gazed beyond the trees. "Do you think we can do it?"

"Do what? Defeat Thames?" I sat next to her and grabbed her hand. "It's going to be hard, but I know we can. We have no choice. For the good of our world, we must succeed."

She leaned her head on my shoulder, shuddering slightly. "I hope so. It all just feels like *so much*."

Jax trotted toward the fire, still in his panther form with a hare in his mouth, while Ian flew down with another in his beak. The shifters returned to their Fae form as they settled onto nearby rocks to skin their catches.

"Show-offs," Lana grinned at the two of them.

Jax bowed deeply toward her. "I live to serve, my queen."

Silence enveloped us as Jax and Ian tended to the fresh game, and Lana stirred our meal occasionally. I focused all my attention on her, rubbing my thumb on her arm, leg, wherever was easiest to reach.

"You know, Ian, have you ever tried partial-shifting?" Jax asked.

Ian looked perplexed as he added the cut-up hare to the stew to cook. "Partial-shift? I always thought it was kind of an all or nothing thing."

I chuckled. "We absolutely do not need a Jax 2.0."

Lana snorted, covering her mouth.

I twirled a loose strand of her hair in my hand. "He loves to play this game where he only shifts certain parts of his body. You'll be sitting there and all of a sudden there's a panther tail in your face or a claw running down your back."

Lana smirked. "Jax, you are something else."

"Thank you." He winked and added his hare as well.

Ian sat next to the fire, looking perplexed. "I never even thought to attempt to partially shift certain parts of my body." He raked his hands through his hair and proceeded to tie half of it up in a bun. "I'm going to have to try this."

He muttered to himself, concentrating very hard, probably trying to shift certain parts of his body. Jax may be out there sometimes and give me relentless shit for anything and everything he possibly could, but if there was something Jax had mastered, it was partial-shifting.

Jax tilted his head back, laughing. "You aren't meant to look like you're in pain." He stirred the stew once more before setting the utensil down. "About another thirty minutes and this should be ready. In the meantime, Ian," Jax said, turning to him. "Let me help you before you rupture a blood vessel and your face stays that way forever."

Lana watched Ian and Jax walk off away from the fire before she scooched herself closer to my side and laid her head on my shoulder again. "How are you coping?" She stroked my arm. "With the darkness? I haven't seen your eyes shift recently."

I took stock of my body. My magic swirled within me,

searching for the dark bits of evil that had been forced into me for years. But it was hard to find. Lana's light made an appearance, peeking out and glowing around her as it mixed playfully with my shadows. The darkest evil retreated to whatever nook and cranny it could find to hide.

"When I'm with you, when your magic mixes with mine, it's not so bad. It's manageable." I stroked her hair, wanting to reassure her despite my own fears of what might happen. "It's as if your light doesn't allow the darkness to surface."

She looked up at me, smiling. Happy. "I will keep my hands on you forever if it's what is needed to keep the darkness at bay." She paused for a moment, and I could practically see the thoughts whirling through her mind. "But we need to find a way to banish it completely. I will not rest until you are free from his grasp."

I clasped her hand in mine, kissing her knuckles one by one. "I'm just happy to be here with you. When Thames had total control over me, I didn't remember any of this. The sensation of our bond remained, but my shadows concealed it, protecting it from Thames, and from me." I shivered. The physical ache at not remembering the details of this incredible woman would haunt me forever. "Once I regained some of my mind again, I didn't know how I'd get back to you. It's been a long time since I felt this clear-headed and free for any length of time." I stood, brushing the dirt off my knees. "Now come on. Let's see if we can figure out how to get your magic to listen to you."

Jax shouted from where he and Ian trained. "Lana appears to only be able to produce her magic in times of extreme need or fear. Storm has tried to work with her for a few weeks now, but nothing. She also gave quite a show in Canyon City when she thought Storm was in danger." Jax brought a hand to his chest. "It was a sight to behold. Dangerous as fuck for all of us."

Lana jumped up and turned to sneer at Jax. "My light doesn't hurt the people I care about. But keep talking, and I might convince it otherwise."

In true Jax fashion, he smiled instead of cowering at the sharp words.

Lana turned to me. "I've been thinking about my magic and how it erupted."

She paced back and forth. "I thought the first time my magic ever showed itself was in Mysthaven, when we were fighting the king, but now I'm not sure if that's true. It came out in small moments before then. At least, I think it did."

Ian apparently decided to ditch his partial-shifting efforts and moved closer with Jax, listening intently to his best friend. I pushed down the irrational jealousy at how much longer he had been in her life. Knowing it was the mate bond and not my true thoughts, I took a deep breath, focusing on Lana again.

We stood next to each other in a line, watching Lana work through her thoughts. She continued pacing, then stopped and turned to us. "The first time my light appeared was right after you saved me in the hallway from Casimir. Right after we kissed." The blush rising on her cheeks made me grin. Fates, I loved this woman, and knowing us connecting physically for the first time had brought out her magic went straight to my head.

"I believe it came out again when Elisabeth was dying in my arms and I wanted to heal her." She swallowed, steeling herself. "Kade was there. Next, when my father was dying, and Kade was there again." She twisted her braided hair in her fingers. "And finally, it seemed to flare briefly at the Festival of Swords."

I stood up straighter and connected her thoughts. "So what you're saying is that *I'm* to thank for your magic?"

She scowled, clearly unimpressed by my joke, and continued processing. "Those were just small flickers of my light revealing itself. But what allowed it to finally break free?"

Jax and I looked at each other, while Ian put his hands up in the air, indicating he had no idea. Jax replied, "When we were battling Dargan. When Kade was in danger?"

She shook her head no, and now we were all confused. "That was *when* it happened, but it's not *why* it happened."

The three of us stared quizzically at Lana as she stared right back at us, like we should know what she was thinking.

"My magic came to be when I accepted Kade as my mate. When I made that realization and accepted it to be true, my whole body filled with light that exploded out of me. Clearly something about my magic is tied to Kade, since my prophecy stated, 'with lover's touch she shall ignite'."

Chuckling, Ian came and placed both of his hands on Lana's shoulders. "The prophecy isn't so bad now, huh? Mates haven't existed for over a thousand years, and yet the one person who still believed in them ended up finding her mate *and* getting one-of-a-kind magic."

"I told you they still existed." Lana stuck out her tongue at Ian and moved to stand before me. "So I think I need you to be the one to help me."

I tucked a wisp of hair that broke free from her braid behind her ear. "Of course I'll help you." Tilting my head to the side, I asked, "How about you give us some space, guys?"

Ian and Jax nodded in agreement and moved back to the campfire. Jax took over tending the stew.

My focus shifted back to Lana, and my shadows pooled at my feet. They seemed happy, giddy. They couldn't wait for Lana to be near them once more. As if those mere moments where she paced alone were too much separation. They swirled around her ankles and circled their way up her legs. She grasped my hands and the shadows continued up both of our bodies.

"Where is your magic, Little Rebel?"

Lana closed her eyes, and I could feel the beads of sweat forming on her palms. The shadows continued growing around us, creating a cocoon.

"Focus on wherever that feeling of home resides. Somewhere that light stems from."

Her brows furrowed. "That's what Storm said."

I huffed as she gripped my hands tighter. "Well, at least I know he gave you good advice."

My shadows around us swirled faster, practically pleading for Lana's magic to come out.

Please, come play with us. We promise not to hurt you. Come out, light. We've been missing you for so long. We must be one again.

Slowly, and with hesitancy, a glow emitted from Lana's entire body. The shadows became frenzied with their excitement, filling every crevasse within me. I could barely contain the anxious energy thrumming through me at their anticipation.

Lana's eyes grew wide. "It's working." She couldn't stand still, and she hopped back and forth on her restless legs as more and more of her light magic radiated out of her. Together, swirling in perfect harmony with my shadows, Lana's light shone brighter, reaching beyond her frame.

Suddenly it disappeared and Lana looked over her shoulder toward Ian.

"What is it?" I asked.

She worried her lip between her teeth. "My magic was always inside of me. If I had found a way to harness it sooner, Ian could have been spared so much."

"What?" I took her chin between my fingers.

She clenched her fists. "I'm angry," she admitted. "Angry that it didn't help him. Help us with Andras. Now it's out and I should be ecstatic, not weighed down with guilt. Sometimes, I wish it hadn't come. Then I wouldn't have to live with knowing I should have been able to do more back then." She inhaled sharply before finally meeting my gaze. If she expected to find reproach there, she'd be wrong. Instead, I softened toward her, feeling my shoulders slump as I took in this beautiful, selfless woman.

"No, Lana. If Ian heard that, he'd correct you immediately too. For some reason your magic was trapped. Yet even so, it protected you from the darkness Andras wanted to inflict on you." I brought my fingers up to her side to where her scar lay, tracing it over her clothes. My shadows continued to caress her even as I pulled my hand away. "Your magic came when it was ready. When *you* were ready for it."

She unclenched her fists slowly.

"Fighting against your magic will prolong discovering your strength."

My shadows flared. *Like you did.*

I released her chin from my grasp. "Are you ready to try again? Try to accept that your magic was limited, but now it's here to help you. Help Ian. Fates, help all of us."

She nodded, a new resolve dawning on her features.

"Now, my shadows and I may help you by being there, but each of those moments you remember were times when you pulled yourself together from the depths of emotional despair. They were moments that could have paralyzed you, and instead you fought through them."

She searched my eyes and let out a small sob. "When I accepted you were my mate, I also…" Her lip trembled, and I brought my hand to rest at the base of her neck, running my thumb along her jawline. "I told myself I was worthy. That I was worthy without magic. I accepted it."

"Ah, see? Not just me, Little Rebel. It's you. Now try again."

Lana closed her eyes and inhaled slowly. "I am worthy of this light," she whispered.

I squeezed her hands in mine and let her focus. The light flared quicker than before, and this time, my shadows didn't have a chance to coax anything out of her. She exploded with light, shining even as she opened her eyes and smiled at me.

She let go of my hands, and even though the light faded enough to see her clearly, her smile remained as she jumped into my embrace, wrapping her arms around my neck.

"I knew you could do it." I set her down and kissed her cheek. "You never needed magic to be worthy. You were a force before this, but now? My love, you are the light to my dark. The good to my evil. And nothing and no one will ever stand in your way again."

A faint smile appeared on her lips. "Thank you."

My shadows weren't ready for Lana's magic to recede.

Please stay. We've gone too long without you.

"Soon," Lana whispered back to them.

She really could hear my shadows. Maybe her light would speak to me too one day.

The intimacy of the moment shattered as Jax yelled, "Come eat."

Lana practically floated back toward the campfire with her head held high. Even in the twilight of the evening, she glowed. My shadows and I would follow her and her light to the ends of Atheria.

The morning arrived too quickly, but as soon as the first rays of sunlight peeked through the trees, we were up and dismantling our campsite. Last night, Lana lay restless for hours next to me until my shadows helped settle her magic. Now that it had freely come to the surface, it didn't seem to want to return to any kind of dormant state.

While it may take years to understand the full extent of what her light magic could do, I knew she could call on it and it would answer. Her fear about Ian's reaction to her magic appearing, broke a small part of me. They'd spent years under

Andras's thumb, suffering, enduring endless hours of torture. While I was no stranger to torture myself, the thought of my mate repeatedly hurt multiplied my rage and need for vengeance tenfold.

I trotted behind Ian, just like yesterday, as we made our way closer to the border of the Southern Forest. Lana rode beside me, and I couldn't stop glancing over at her, needing to reassure myself that she was here, and we were still together.

The ride to the Southern Forest only took a few hours. As the tree line came into view, the caws of a strox could be heard echoing in the distance. I'd never forget the sound of the beast from the third and final trial. Ian put up his fist in the air, signaling for us to stop.

"From here on out we are in uncharted territory. No one has entered the Southern Forest before and lived to tell the tale. Weapons out and be on alert," Ian instructed. "Should anything happen, our priority has to be getting Lana out and to safety."

I rolled my eyes, saluting Ian. "Aye aye, Captain."

Lana's huff of exasperation told me that the reminder of us placing her as the priority pissed her off.

I shot her as stern of a look as I could. "Ian is right. No taking any unnecessary risks. We find the journal and get the hell out of here. I, for one, don't want to be some beast's breakfast this morning."

"Second that," Jax quipped. "Mysthaven may have had voidlings, but your creatures are horrifying, Lana." His whole body shivered. "I can't believe I drew the short straw on coming along just because Storm is a more patient trainer."

"You would have had everyone sitting around, listening to ridiculous stories instead of training," Lana said, wrinkling her nose at him.

"Focus," Ian commanded.

I summoned a shadow sword as Lana pulled out the white dagger, turning it in her hand as we entered the forest. The blade glowed the second we passed the tree line, humming slightly in Lana's hand.

"I'm going to guess that means we're on the right path," she whispered.

A shadow passed above us, its cry indicated we weren't alone.

I tilted my head back and watched three strox circling above us. Their midnight-blue feathers glittered in the morning light above the canopy of trees. If even one of them decided to attack, our party wouldn't last long, but three? I pushed down the urge to tug Lana onto my horse and ride out of here.

The intense need to keep her safe would hinder her if I didn't get it under control. She was more than capable. If only this bond would listen.

We know how that feels, my shadows said wryly.

As we slowly edged our way farther into the forest, it became clear why Fae didn't return after entering. Beady eyes peered out from fallen logs, and a hiss permeated the air around us.

There was a charge in the forest as five creatures slithered out from their hiding spots.

"Razorven," Lana choked out.

"More make-believe nightmares?" Jax was the only one to answer her.

The creatures' shining red eyes and the black hairs standing along the spines of their white bodies were enough to make me want to flee. That was before seeing their slitted tongues whipping through the air.

One of them hissed, its tongue snapping out before it moved closer, the others following, echoing the terrifying hissing noise until I almost had to cover my ears. We waited, unmoving to see if the creatures would leave us alone.

The shrill cry from earlier sounded again, only this time, it was much closer.

One of the strox landed with a thud to the side of us, and a razorven tilted its head, as if ready to watch the entertainment.

Two more thuds sounded behind me, and I stiffened atop my horse.

Just like that, we were surrounded, with absolutely zero chance of making it out alive.

CHAPTER 15

LANA

Fuck. Fuck. *Fuck.*

The only thing that could make this any worse was if Thames himself showed up.

"We should turn around," Ian whispered. "We can't win against five razorven *and* three strox. It's suicide."

"We can do this," I whispered back angrily. "We don't leave here without the journal. We need those answers."

Kade glanced at me, then nodded once. I made eye contact with Ian next, then Jax. All were in agreement, albeit reluctantly, and readying themselves to attack.

Slowly, the beasts crept forward, taking their time while they assessed their prey. Their tongues flicking out, licking their lips as they made their way toward us.

A thought tingled in my mind. "Kade?" I flexed my hands. "Want to try something crazy?"

He looked down to where I pooled my light in my palms. This time it felt easier, like every time I called on my magic, it became more a part of me. The connection to it strengthened with each use. I wasn't quite sure how it worked when my magic exploded out of me, but Kade's shadows were almost like a faucet, pouring from him when he used them. I imagined my own magic working in the same way. Breathing deeply, I searched for the connection to my well of light and let the warmth spread over my body.

"Strox first, then razorven," I suggested. "I think the strox are the deadlier opponents."

"You think?" Jax asked, shaking his head. "Fingers crossed, I guess."

I cursed under my breath, trying to remember anything I could from the nightmarish children's tales that might help us. "Don't touch the razorvens spines," I shivered. "They're poisonous."

"Fates above, anything else?" Jax's voice hitched. "Just so we're clear, I'll be sitting out next time, princess."

"Get behind me," Kade ordered Ian and Jax, refocusing us. He stepped forward, holding his hands out toward mine while his shadows pooled around him. I put my hands up, hoping my light magic infused with his shadows like I wanted.

Slowly, our magics collided, the shadows and light swirled together, creating a force strong enough to momentarily hold back the strox from advancing any farther. I gasped, staring in awe at the shield-like blockade. It didn't last long though, as strox flew forward and a crack appeared in our magical barrier.

My light waned, blinking out.

"Lana," Kade shouted.

I reached for my magic again, the energy draining from me too quickly, but I pushed harder. One of the strox was almost directly in front of me when light and shadows collided again. This time, their intertwined magical barrier held, withstanding the force of the strox relentlessly pushing against it. After a minute or two, the strox cawed in anger and returned to the sky, flying south, deeper into the forest.

"Yes," I shouted. Our magic was stronger together, but my light magic flickered again.

A few of the razorven in front of us hissed, retreating

slightly as the onslaught of magic cascaded over the area. A magical shower of light and shadows fell from the sky, fizzling after an extraordinary display of magic.

"Whoa," Jax whispered, his tone almost reverent.

We repositioned ourselves, preparing our weapons for combat against the razorven. Using my magic like this depleted me, and I was unprepared for how much energy it took to wield this much power. Everyone made it look so simple, like breathing, just an automatic extension of their bodies. I didn't have time to think about it though—we had more creatures to battle, and I couldn't give up now.

Jax shifted, roaring in defiance as he lunged forward, attacking the closest razorven. Kade followed, running toward the battle. Meanwhile, a trail of shadows slinked up my leg and onto my chest, forming the shadow armor I'd worn once before. I flipped my dagger in my hand and moved to follow the others when a caw echoed around us. One that sounded eerily close to my head.

I froze, unable to move. Slowly, I looked behind me to come face-to-face with five strox. The beasts had returned—with reinforcements. They lowered their snouts, breathing a foul-smelling stench in my direction. I felt the shadows harden against my chest, turning more solid as the beasts narrowed their deadly gaze at me. Their eyes gleamed with malice as they slowly approached me.

Kade and Jax both were in the middle of battling razorven on the edge of the clearing, but Ian came running to my side.

"Great," he muttered. "How did that *not* work to scare them away."

"Looks like our magic slowed them down, intimidated them maybe, but didn't harm them," I replied, eyeing the giant birds. Their feathers flared, and they clicked their beaks angrily as they crept toward us.

"I thought my battle with these creatures during the

marriage trials would be a once-in a-lifetime event, but lucky for us, I get to do it again. Better move fast." Ian looked over at me. "Together?"

I nodded, pushing away my fear. There was no place for it here. "Together."

We charged forward, blades at the ready to fight the ancient battle birds. The strox were undeniably agile on their feet. A talon swiped at my side but bounced off the shadow armor fortifying my chest. My breath lodged in my throat, the impact of the attack knocking me off balance. The strox swiped at my outstretched hand, and its talon scraped across my palm. Blood oozed from the cut.

I grimaced, trying to push the pain from my mind. Jumping to my feet, I lunged forward, aiming my dagger at the bird's chest, only to fall sideways as a wing knocked me over.

"Lana!" Kade called out.

Shadows crawled over the forest floor, and my light answered in response. Together, like extensions of my own arms, they held the strox at bay, while I moved to drive my blade into its side. I raised my dagger to deliver the killing blow.

"Stop!" The sweet sound of a female voice echoed through the forest, bouncing off trees, amplified and booming around us. "No more."

A billowy figure, shimmered brilliantly against the dark forest, emerging from behind the strox. Instantly, the beasts stopped their attack, bowed their heads, and retreated to stand beside the figure. The razorven's hissing ceased as they too approached the figure in white.

"Is that..." Ian started as Jax quickly shifted back to his Fae form.

"A spirit?" he asked, finishing Ian's thought.

I blinked, still clutching the dagger. Kade moved to my

side, out of breath from his own battle, his sword still clutched in his hand.

"There's no need for those." The woman gestured toward our weapons. She made her way forward, her feet appearing to hover above the ground, as she moved gracefully through the forest.

Her words did nothing to placate the feeling that the beasts would attack us again. None of us put our weapons away.

When she stopped in front of our group, I stared at her in awe. Her hair fell in soft curls around her shoulders, but it was the color that startled me.

Rose gold.

Exactly like mine.

"Who are you?" I breathed out the question more than demanding it, my eyes widened in shock.

She smiled and reached her hand toward me.

"I wouldn't do that," Kade growled, raising his sword as shadows shot out before us, creating a barrier. Ian and Jax moved in closer, ready to fight our way out if necessary.

Instead of the spirit being offended, she smiled at Kade before raising an eyebrow. "I mean your mate no harm."

Goose bumps skittered across my arms in anticipation.

Surprise flickered across his face before he caught himself, narrowing his eyes as they filled with distrust. "*My mate* asked you a question."

The spirit laughed, her face appearing genuinely joyful while her bright eyes danced. "Is he always like this?" She moved through the shadow wall with ease and reached forward, touching the side of Kade's face.

He sucked in a sharp breath and froze in place, almost as if captivated by the strangeness of this spirit touching him. How had she gotten through the shadows? My pulse quickened, trying to wrap my head around who stood before us.

"You look so much like my Jasper." She patted his face once and pulled her hand away. "I'll finally get to see him soon, now that you're here."

"Who is Jasper?" Ian whispered to Jax behind me.

Kade's brow furrowed. "Jasper Blackthorn?" he asked.

The spirit nodded. "My name is Evelyn Everhart." Her gaze flicked toward me. "The first Queen of Brookmere but, I suppose more importantly, your quite a few times great-grandmother."

I swayed on my feet, silence falling around us. My heart rate skyrocketed. How was it possible the spirit of our first queen haunted the Southern Forest? And why?

"Wait," Jax gasped, breaking the silence. I turned to look at him, his lips curled in a confused expression. "If your Jasper is our Jasper and you're Lana's great-great-great-grandmother, then you two…" He pointed between Kade and me, eyebrows raised. "Did you not check a family tree?"

Evelyn's melodic laugher hit my ears and I jumped, noticing she now stood directly by my side.

Seconds later, she glided toward one of the strox standing guard, the creature's beady eyes observing the entire interaction. She reached out her hand and the deadly bird eagerly lowered its head. Evelyn ran her hand up and down its beak and the creature purred.

"What in the Fates' names is going on?" Ian said under his breath, absolute shock at what was happening clear in his tone.

"The animals here listen to me. They protect our line," she replied softly.

"It didn't feel like protection a few minutes ago," I argued. "Pretty sure they wanted to grind our bones into their next meal."

Evelyn tilted her head as she moved her hand from the strox's beak to its neck, scratching under its feathers. "It assumed you were here to harm me and reacted accordingly.

They understand now, and never again will one cause you harm."

"Wait," Ian interjected. "During the battle at Ellevail, the strox attacked us. I had to fight one with my own sword and barely made it out alive."

She ran a hand down the bird's neck as the creature nuzzled into her. A strox cozied up to this woman like a pet. I blinked several times, wondering if I was actually seeing the scene before me correctly. "Like I said, it was protecting our line. If you acted as if they were there to harm you, they will defend themselves against such attacks. Nothing is as it appears at first glance."

Ian gave her an incredulous glare, muttering to himself, "Unbelievable."

"Come," she said, finally pulling away. "We have much to discuss."

I hesitated, unsure of what to think anymore, and looked at the others, wondering if they were just as confused. "Hopefully one of the things we'll discuss is if we're related?" I whispered under my breath to Kade.

Kade grimaced. "There's no way, Little Rebel. We're mates."

"Might want to make sure," Jax mumbled, his brow furrowed like he had no idea what to think.

Ian stared, facing forward with a look of bewilderment.

I moved first, leading the way. Together, we followed Evelyn. The razorven skittered away, but the strox she had pet earlier walked elegantly to the side of our group. I was too scared to ask Evelyn questions as we moved to our destination, just in case the strox changed its mind. Kade's hand slipped in mine and squeezed reassuringly as we allowed ourselves to be escorted deeper into the forest.

We walked for what felt like a mile until we arrived at another small clearing, a path of flowers and moss leading to a semicircle of rocks. Evelyn clasped her hands in front of her and turned to face us.

"You may be seated." She pointed to the rock formations around us. "Not you, my dear," she clarified, stopping me. "You step forward here."

Tentatively, I let go of Kade's hand, and when he didn't loosen his grip, I nodded, indicating it was okay. He took a deep breath and eventually let go, allowing me to move before Evelyn.

"Payment must be made. A sacrifice in blood."

Why was everything always in blood? "Fine," I sighed, just wanting to get this over with so we could move on to obtaining answers.

The white dagger hummed on my side, practically trembling in its sheath to be free. I cut my palm, just like the others had during Mysthaven's Blood Oath, and let my blood drip onto the forest floor at Evelyn's feet.

The droplets sizzled as they landed against the mossy surface.

"Did I pass?" I asked, raising an eyebrow when Evelyn didn't answer.

Smiling, Evelyn raised her hand. "Let's see." She snapped her finger once, and a worn leather journal appeared in her palm. She stepped toward me, holding it out. "I believe you're here for this?"

"My mother's journal." I stared at the book in Evelyn's hand. Hope and fear collided, within me as I beheld what might be the final piece of information we needed to win against Thames.

She clicked her tongue. "This is not just your mother's journal. Every woman in our line has written in it and been tasked with keeping it safe. All leading to this very moment."

I frowned, watching her as my confusion grew. "What moment is that?"

"For the light to destroy Thames's darkness for good."

CHAPTER 16

LANA

"So, you know about Thames, then?" Kade asked standing slightly behind me.

I scarcely remembered to breathe.

"Know about Thames?" Evelyn laughed indignantly. "Whose sacrifice do you think trapped him?"

I glanced at the others, who stared at the spirit just as perplexed as I was. Evelyn huffed as I shrugged in confusion.

"The original sacrifice?" Kade asked.

"Well, I suppose I need to start at the beginning." She rubbed her forehead as a small smile spread over her lips. "Come, sit, and I will tell you all how it truly began."

Evelyn glided in front of us and I joined the others, settling onto the rock formations. Kade never left my side, choosing to stand beside me as I crossed my legs, getting comfortable for whatever story was about to be told.

"Ready?" Evelyn asked and we all agreed. "Good. Now, Brookmere celebrates me as the queen who stood alone, whose king wasn't worthy of mention, correct?"

I nodded.

"Pishposh. Jasper Blackthorn was my king. My mate."

Jax coughed, covering up a wheeze. "This is about to get really uncomfortable for you two."

I glared at him. Kade, exasperated by Jax's antics, sent a shadow to cover his mouth. Ian didn't bother trying to hide his chuckle but regained his composure quickly, wanting to avoid a shadow gag.

"We ruled in a time when magic flourished, rejuvenating the land and blessing all who lived here in Atheria. A few years into our reign, we began having trouble with magic wielders utilizing their gifts in dark ways. Greed for power corrupted them, darkening their souls. They plagued our land, stealing and destroying everything in their path. We were able to defeat most of them, but one grew stronger than the others."

"Thames," I said quietly.

"Yes. And Thames's mate was the only sorceress in the land." Evelyn glanced toward Kade. "You know Cassandra more as a healer, but the way she wielded magic, in addition to her spellwork, was unparalleled. We've never seen another Fae with the ability to perform half the magic she possessed. Defeating Thames was impossible enough, but the two of them together? They were unmatched.

"We fought them on three separate occasions, barely escaping with our lives each time. We feared there was no way to stop Thames's evil from spreading and eventually throwing all of Atheria into darkness. Vivienne came to us heartbroken at losing her sister to Thames, and told us of a prophecy. The Fates foretold a path would open for us to hold Thames at bay until they granted the world what it needed to defeat him." She pursed her lips. "One week later, Cassandra appeared at my doorstep. Thames's power scared her, and she realized she'd gone to a place she couldn't come back from. She'd had a vision that she refused to tell us about, but it led her to turn on her mate."

"But mates are supposed to be sacred. It's supposed to be

forever." My mind reeled, it was almost too much to take in. "How can one go against their mate?"

"Do not think it was easy. Cassandra lived in pain. I'm sure she still carries that burden even now. She created an amulet, one that would serve as a gateway to lock Thames in the middle of our world." She swallowed as despair creased her features. "Cassandra knew a sacrifice was necessary, one of immense magnitude. It wasn't until Vivienne returned with another prophecy that we finally understood. This particular prophecy changed our lives forever."

As Evelyn spoke, she slumped forward, her arms wrapping around herself. I couldn't help but want to comfort my ancestor. I could feel the pain radiating in her words. I stood from my seat and took a step toward her. She gave me a kind smile, though it didn't meet her eyes, and put her hand in the air, indicating for me to sit back down. Tentatively, I returned, desperate to hear more.

"When the Fates finally divulged the sacrifice needed, it left us heartbroken." A tear fell down her ghostly face. "Our bond as mates had to be sacrificed. It was the purest, strongest thing we could think of. To save our world, Jasper and I sacrificed our bond, and the magic created from that allowed Cassandra to trap Thames in the void, splitting the world apart forever into two. Everything we'd worked for to create a united kingdom vanished because of one power-hungry Fae. Jasper and I were cursed to live and rule our kingdoms alone. Forever forced apart by the void holding Thames's soul."

She looked up toward the sky, the sun shining on her face as she closed her eyes. "No Fae from Brookmere remembered the rest of the world. But I remembered, as did Jasper. As I understand it, he was able to fortify the magic inside of the gem with his own, ensuring Thames remained bound to the void after our sacrifice. Jasper needed an heir to continue his line, and his responsibility to keep Thames bound. His heir was born a century later. At the end of Jasper's days, he revealed all to his son and sacrificed his remaining magic and life to the gem, powering it to fortify the necklace protecting us all.

"I continued the family line out of obligation but never remarried, which is why Brookmere thinks it had no king during my reign. In a way it didn't, but my mate was the bravest man there ever was. We were separated by the cruel hand the Fates dealt us."

Evelyn silenced all of us with her story, even Jax. The shadows retreated back to Kade's side, no longer needing to keep Jax quiet.

"I knew a sacrifice was made, but I didn't know the extent of what it was," Kade murmured as he wrapped an arm around my shoulders.

If someone asked me to give up our bond, I didn't know if I could. We only just discovered we were mates, and leaving him behind once had already been enough to almost destroy me. Losing him forever? I wasn't sure I possessed the strength or the courage to make such a decision.

"I kept the secret, taking it to my grave, except for writing it down in a journal I left behind for my daughter. A secret passed down to protect our kingdoms should the darkness ever threaten to rise again. But that's not all we passed down." She held out her hand. "You found my dagger."

I pulled it out again to find it glowing. Even once transferred to Evelyn's hand, it illuminated the space around us.

She smiled, twirling it. "I designed this. I even gave it a name: Apollo."

I stared at her, captivated. What hadn't this woman accomplished in her time?

"I took our idea of Jasper's amulet and worked it into a weapon for the women in our line. In the journal, I explained that I imbued the dagger with my magic to call on as they needed. The idea being that when the one who the Fates blessed with light appeared, this would be a powerful weapon to cast out the darkness."

"Cast out the darkness?" Something scratched at the back of my brain, begging for more.

She nodded. "It should, in theory. None of us possessed the power to test the dagger's capabilities to destroy the darkness inside of someone, allowing them to return to their normal Fae state. The power contained within should amplify the light. I hadn't expected the line to continue with this tradition as it did. My brilliant daughter figured that out." She sighed, running a hand over Apollo. "Magic, fortified and continually strengthened over a thousand years, is pretty powerful."

"It only took these two idiots' bloods to break the amulet by touching it," Jax scoffed. "Let's hope something so simple won't destroy *this* weapon."

"Jax," Kade growled.

He shrugged. "Just thinking out loud."

I couldn't help but wonder the same though. "Do I have to kill someone to eliminate the darkness completely? I've seen a 'mist' come out of the dark ones I've killed with it. It looked like the darkness evaporated out of their body, but I've never tried it on someone who still lived."

She shook her head. "That certainly wouldn't make the most sense to kill everyone with darkness." She chuckled. "Cutting them, breaking the skin—something to release the darkness with the dagger should be all you need to do. Again, in theory."

"Right." I nodded. Unease settled in my belly. I hadn't had to kill the fae I battled in order to free them.

Kade's shadows rubbed my back, as if sensing my guilt.

The strox with us stepped forward, nudging Evelyn's hand until she laughed and pet its neck.

"Why do they listen to you?" I asked.

She cocked her head to the side, watching me, and

ushered me forward. Taking my hand in hers, she gently placed it on the strox's neck beside hers.

I refused to let the audible hitch in Kade's breath break my focus on surviving my contact with the beast, with whom I absolutely refused to make eye contact.

"When we sacrificed our mating bond, these beasts appeared. The strox. Born from pain. They recognize that in me, but you have also already endured so much. They recognize that pain in you too, Illiana."

Feeling braver, I brushed my fingers along the strox's neck and it shivered, making a content sound.

My body trembled slightly at what I was doing, but it also felt incredible. Touching a beast of fairy-tale stories.

"They will answer to you when I'm gone. They're loyal to our line."

"And the razorven?" I asked.

"Not as open to being pet, with the poisonous barbs and all." She grinned. "Every creature of our nightmares appeared from some great pain and sacrifice. Remember that. They all belong to this world, and they will aid you, if you let them."

I shook my head, not sure I could imagine an army of razorven and strox coming into the final battle with Thames.

"So you've been waiting all this time to reveal our true history and the purpose of the dagger? And now what?"

"There is a final prophecy that has been spoken. Thames will continue to exist unless all the darkness is destroyed. All of it. Somehow you must find a way to eliminate any and all of the darkness remaining."

I tamped down my rage hearing another prophecy existed that the seers hadn't mentioned and focused instead on the impossible task of eradicating *all* of the darkness. "It's everywhere though." I gaped at her, looking at Kade. His face tightened, forehead creasing as his features hardened. What Evelyn said would be nearly impossible.

"Yes, it is, and it will continue to grow. You will find a way to destroy it all. Every tie to Thames must be gone. Do you hear me?"

"Yes, I—"

"Time runs short," she said. Though her words were urgent, a smile shone on her face so brightly, it was as if she glowed from the inside. "It's time to see my mate. We've been apart since our sacrifice, but my life force remained here." She waved a hand around the forest. "Bound to empower the one foretold to save us all. Now that my role here is complete, I will get to see him again in whatever comes next." She cupped my cheeks. "You are the one, Illiana. I sensed it just as Jasper and I sensed what needed to happen to allow Atheria a chance."

"What if you're wrong?" I twisted my hands in front of me, my breath shaky.

She smiled, taking them in hers. "I'm never wrong, certainly not anymore." She winked as she handed me the journal. "You were given a mate whose magic strengthens your own. You will need to rely on those you love for what's to come. It won't be easy. The loss you will feel may shatter you, but this world will be reborn. Just know, it is you who will save Atheria. Defeat Thames. Bring light to our land and heal what's been torn."

She started fading away, but I wasn't ready. There were too many questions still unanswered, and a small part of me wanted to cling to her, the only person in my family left, even if she was just a spirit. To keep her here, so that it wasn't time for the end to come. Not knowing what I'd lose felt too great a burden to bear.

"I'm not ready," I called out, rising to chase the beams of light coming from her as she disappeared farther into the sun's golden glow.

"Read the journal and remember." Her body almost faded out entirely. But I heard the echo of her words loudly surrounding us. "You are Illiana Dresden, and you are stronger than any darkness."

With that, she vanished.

I fell to my knees, letting the weight of all Evelyn told us lay heavy on me.

Kade kneeled as well. Then Ian, followed by Jax. My chosen family. The ones who supported me, loved me, even if I hadn't known some of them for very long. Time meant nothing, it was their presence that would give me strength.

"We're all meant to be here, beside you Lan," Ian said. "The things you will face will be met by all of us. Never on your own." He grabbed my hand, kissing it before bringing it to his chest.

"I know," I whispered.

Jax gripped my shoulder and squeezed. "Also, we learned that the two of you are definitely not related by blood. Which is a definite bonus we didn't know we needed."

"What is wrong with you," I laughed, feeling lighter from his antics, just like always.

His knowing smile confirmed he did these things on purpose.

"So…" He heaved out a heavy sigh. "Should we head home to tell the others we've got an epic job ahead of us, and if we don't get rid of all of the darkness that's infected half our world, Thames will live on in evil infamy?"

It wasn't hard to convince Kade to let me ride with him back to camp.

While my horse followed, loosely tied to Onyx, I cautiously opened the journal, unlacing the thin leather ties.

My fingers quivered as I ran them over the binding of the well-worn journal. My mother had touched this, written in it. All of my ancestors pouring information in for me to find one day. Me being some kind of chosen one still seemed outrageous, but my light magic, the prophecies—I had no choice but to believe it.

Instead of starting at the beginning, I immediately flipped to the back. My mother's words would be the last in the book, and I had to read them. I wanted to know her, even if it was only this small piece of her.

I flipped a few blank pages and froze when I saw elegant handwriting. The last entry was only one page.

From the Hand of Fallon:

There's a sickness in our land, festering. Each day I feel it growing, shifting closer. Seb woke me from a nightmare last night. There had been blood everywhere. Hauntingly angry faces surrounded me as I weakened on the floor of our home.

It wasn't real, and yet…I can't help but know my time here is coming to an end. The Fates are at work, as much as I hate their cruelty for placing the future in Illiana's hands. Since this journal will be passed to her, I write to you now, my beautiful girl.

I gasped, chest tightening through the tears blurring my vision as I continued reading.

You will face a world that doesn't understand why you are magicless, but I know you will rise above. You are who Atheria has been waiting for. I know that I won't be here to see you shine, but know that I already see the woman you'll become. I swear when you were born, the sunlight streamed through the bedroom in a halo around you—ask Alister, he was there— and we all fell in love with you immediately. But be warned, he'll cry telling the story.

Wherever you are in your life when you read this, know that you were loved. Truly, unconditionally loved. I am proud of you. If my time has come and I'm not with you, know that I have convinced the Fates and whoever lies beyond to watch every step of your life. Rise up, my heart, and shine. I love you.

I wrapped my arms around my stomach, holding myself together. My entire body physically hurt, aching at the thought that my mother knew she wouldn't live. I reread the words again, clinging to them like a lifeline.

"Lana?" Kade asked, his shadows covering my arms, holding me tightly to him.

"She wrote to me," I whispered. "She thought she might not survive and wrote to me."

He brushed my hair back, kissing my head. "She loved you so much."

I nodded before sitting up straighter, flipping to another page. I read as we rode on, devouring words from my mother. About how she poured her magic into the white dagger. She was easy to love with a humor I knew my friends would have adored. I adored it.

I paused, coming to an entry where I saw the name Stronholm.

Alister and Victor have ganged up on me now, deciding for the safety of Illiana that Seb and I should stay in Valeford. Alister says he's getting a bad feeling about something inside the palace walls.

Though I wouldn't mind raising our baby somewhere more secluded and keeping her to ourselves, the fact that a decision is being made for me makes me want to rebel. Once a big brother, always a big brother I suppose.

Alister has gone as far as to tell me that when she's of age, he's relieving dear Captain Stronholm from his duties guarding the king and placing him in charge of Illiana. Victor didn't even balk. Probably because his son was born a few weeks before Illiana and he'll be able to keep an eye on both that way, assuming Ian follows in his footsteps. Little does he know, Vivienne whispered to me that they were fated to love one another fiercely, though not romantically. She had a vision of the two of them. Flashes of their life together. The Stronholms are the most loyal friends, even with Victor siding with Alister. It doesn't surprise me at all. But knowing such love lies ahead of Illiana warms my heart.

At least in Valeford I'll be able to teach her about our history without prying eyes and ears. She'll be prepared for whatever is to come.

"Ian," I choked out.

He pulled his horse up parallel to Onyx. I looked over at my friend "My mother wrote about your father. How he and the king were her friends. Actually—here, just read it."

I handed the journal to Ian. Kade sent his shadows to the reins, leading Ian's horse for him. The gesture burrowed under my skin, relaxing my tense body from the emotions of reading my mother's words.

A few moments later, Ian looked up at me with glassy eyes. "Vivienne foresaw our friendship."

I nodded.

He shook his head, handing the journal back to me. "Thank you for sharing it with me."

My lip trembled, and I leaned over, squeezing his hand.

The campsite came into view and I laced up the journal. I held it to my chest, knowing it contained my history. I looked up at the sky, wondering if my mother had indeed convinced the Fates to watch me from beyond. Maybe she was with her brother, watching me even now. I closed me eyes. "I succeeded," I whispered upward, hoping the king, the father I'd known could hear somehow. "I found the journal, like you requested."

Kade didn't comment, but his embrace tightened,

soothing and steady. I'd succeeded in my father's final request to find the journal.

I ran my thumb along the spine of the journal. With it, I'd unlock the secrets of the white dagger and what to expect from my power. Armed with that information, I'd make sure Thames was destroyed.

Once and for all.

CHAPTER 17

IAN

As soon as we returned to camp, the four of us spent an hour discussing whether we should try to use the dagger—Apollo—to rid the darkness from Kade and me here or back at the inn.

There was something to be said for trying this crazy experiment away from the others in case something terrible happened. Kade's biggest concern was a valid one: What if the darkness tried to fight back?

What if I tried to fight back against Lana and hurt her?

No. I wouldn't think about what *could* happen if this seemingly haphazard plan went to absolute shit. If Queen Evelyn said it would work, I had to hold on to the hope that it would.

I would be lying if I said there wasn't a small part of me that worried what my life would look like if I had to live with the darkness forever. What kind of life would that leave me?

I shuddered as soon as the thought entered my mind. Queen Evelyn made it clear no darkness could remain if we wanted to defeat Thames. The only options were remove the darkness, or have no life at all.

Jax stood leaning against a tree in the clearing, observing and ready to shift if necessary.

Lana took a step toward me, the white dagger in hand. She trembled ever so slightly as she approached. "Are you ready?"

Tilting my head to the side, I placed my hands on my hips. "Normally, I'm the one taking care of you, not the other way around. Perhaps Kade should be the one to do it. We know he wants to after all."

Lana gave me an incredulous look. "Well, he doesn't have light magic, so you're stuck with me."

All I could do was sigh in response. There was no talking this stubborn queen out of anything she wanted to do, especially if she thought it would help me. I wouldn't let this darkness flare inside of me and lash out at her. "Come on, let's get this over with."

"Good luck, sucker!" Jax called out from the sidelines. "You know, I was just starting to like you too. Such a shame."

Lana glared at him. "Careful, Jax, I might just call in a strox or two for a panther snack if you don't zip it."

Jax's eyes widened for a moment in feigned shock before playfully growling and swiping a panther paw in the air in a mock attack.

Lana rolled her eyes. "Moving on. Shall we?" She reached her hand out to mine. "Ian, just in case this doesn't work, I need you to know it changes nothing. You are my best friend. You have been my best friend since we were children, and no amount of darkness running through your veins will ever change that. I love you." She squeezed my hand and smiled at me reassuringly. "But I'm confident it *will* work."

"I love you too, Lan." I wrapped her in a hug and held her for a moment longer than usual. Anticipation collided with fear at whatever would happen next. I closed my eyes, inhaling slowly before squeezing her once and letting go. "Do your worst, Your Majesty."

Kade moved to stand behind me, his shadows pooled at his feet, ready to act if needed. With our differences set aside, we already made a pact that it would be up to him to protect Lana no matter what in case this experiment went horribly wrong.

I took off my shirt and turned to my side as the unhealed scars of my torture were exposed to the woman closest to me. Lana swallowed uncomfortably, and I swore I heard a low whistle from Jax. Rolling my shoulders, I tried to ignore their reactions. I couldn't look Lan in the eye right now though, or the wall I erected during my time in Brookmere's dungeons might break.

"I know we talked about my arm or leg or something." I cleared my throat and shrugged. "But I don't know, something about where he infected me seems like it might work better."

Lana warily took a step closer and placed her hand on my chest. "I will kill him for what he did to you." She gently touched the scars, saving the biggest for last.

I swallowed a lump in my throat at Lana's inspection. "It's no more than what he did to you," I said softly.

She looked up at me, shaking her head. She sniffed, eyes misting.

"I'm okay," I reassured her. Part of me didn't know if that was true. The time in the dungeons haunted my dreams still. I'd had my own nightmares from our time as kids with Andras, but now, they were accompanied by my most recent torture. Though I'd never admit that to Lan. She had weathered so much torture as a child herself.

"We've got this," she said. "Here we go."

I nodded, picking up on Kade breathing heavily behind me. I wondered if he was as worried as I was about all of this, or if his concern was merely for Lana.

"Three, two," Lana counted, and before she got to one, she made the tiniest cut on my side, not even big enough to draw a drop of blood.

I held my breath as we waited.

Nothing happened. No release of a magical dark mist, no cry in agony, nothing. Kade just stared at me blankly. My heart dropped.

"So much for what ghost lady said," Jax quipped.

Lana whipped her head around so fast and stormed over to him.

"Wait." Jax held up his hands in front of her. "I'll give you one hit. Just not to my gorgeous face."

She smacked him on the side of his head as he laughed.

Returning my attention to Lana, who had huffed her way back in front of me, I looked her straight in the eye. "You are going to have to cut me more than that, it seems, if this is going to work."

She hesitated for a moment. "I just don't want to hurt you any more than you already have been."

Her pain shone in her eyes. I knew I would have a hard time doing the same to her, if the roles were reversed.

"Lana, you could never hurt me. Nothing you could do would ever hurt me. I want you to do this—no, I need you to do this. This is not torture. You are not Andras." I cupped her cheeks, tilting her head so she had to look at me. "This is saving my life."

Kade chimed in from behind, "Lana, you can do this. It's just a cut. Even if it doesn't get rid of the darkness, he will heal before we've even made it back to the inn."

Lana straightened her body and gripped the dagger tighter in her hand. She closed her eyes and whispered something inaudible before opening them again, determination etched into her brows.

This time when she placed Apollo against my skin, I looked down and a soft glow of light emitted from her fingertips. The blade seemed to hum as she sliced into my scar, deeper this time, until blood flowed freely down my side.

I inhaled, surprised as a dark mist left my body in coiled

strands. I felt a weight dragging uncomfortably through my body from my extremities as it cascaded through me and out of the cut on my side.

Gasps echoed around me as Kade's shadows swirled at my feet, waiting to pounce. My head tilted back, and I let the sun's rays warm my face.

I fell to my knees as tendrils smoked from my side, slowing. Freedom.

I immediately felt lighter, happier. The evil plaguing my body was gone. I knew all the darkness was out of me just from the way I felt in complete control of myself again. The lingering anger and rage diffused, gone with the evil it entered with.

I leaned forward on my hands, breathing through the relief, as I realized how much the darkness had consumed me. How exhausting fighting this internal battle had been.

Even Kade's shadows seemed to be happy with the outcome as they swirled between my legs before returning to Kade.

"Ian?" Lana whispered, kneeling down beside me.

I grinned at her before jumping to pick her up and twirling her around. "You've done it. I'm free. Lan, it's gone."

Her face beamed, radiating pure joy. "I can't believe it worked. Oh, Ian. I am so happy for you." She returned the dagger to its sheath and proceeded to dance around the clearing, reveling in the achievement. "We can save everyone. No one forced to turn has to endure it anymore."

The joy in this moment was endless. "Well, you live to see another day," Jax chuckled. "Guess we'll have to see who the better shifter is after all."

Even through his teasing, I knew it came from a good place. Jax wasn't mean-spirited, he just didn't like to take life too seriously unless he had to. He'd make a wonderful addition to the palace if he stuck around when all this came to an end.

Lana returned from her celebratory dance, and the excitement in her eyes made me feel like we were unstoppable. We could do anything together, just as we'd always done.

The cut on my side had already healed as I put my shirt back on, covering the rest of my scars.

"Kade, come on, let me save you too," Lana ordered, beckoning him over. "If it worked for Ian, it will work for you." She grabbed the side of his tunic and tried to untuck it from his pants.

"Whoa, Lana." Kade took a step back. "Save that for when we're in private." He bopped his finger on the tip of her nose.

"I'm going to vomit," Jax muttered under his breath.

"Besides, you'll never be able to reach this over my head anyway." Kade winked at Lana before discarding his shirt off to the side.

I moved to stand behind Kade, just like he had done for me. Although, I at least was much more confident that nothing would go wrong now, since it had been successful already.

Lana wasted no time and removed Apollo from its sheath once more, gripping it tightly. Her hand trembled as she looked from it back to Kade. His gaze never strayed from her, his face softening the longer he stared. He brought a hand up to her arm.

"Are you ready?" she asked him. The slight tremor in her voice was impossible to miss.

Kade smiled at her. "If anything could rid this darkness from me, it was always going to be you."

Lana blew out a steadier breath this time, nodding at his words. She looked down at the dagger and the same soft glow of light filled her palm. She sliced into Kade's side, and he didn't even flinch.

We watched, but this time, no inky black mist left his body.

"Do it again. Deeper this time, love," Kade said, his voice

low but reassuring as he spoke to Lana. "I've been infected for years compared to the few times Ian has. I may need more than one cut."

Frowning, Lana's hand trembled slightly as she sliced into Kade again.

"Again," Kade directed.

Still nothing.

I swallowed down the pain of watching Lana cut time and again, the desperation growing in her movements. My heart ached as her body tensed, and her face fell.

After the fifth cut to his body, Lana's head dropped as she let Apollo fall from her hand. She took a step back, staring in horror at the blood pouring down Kade's side.

Barely a whisper of darkness floated away on a breeze after leaving his body, nowhere close to the density of the mist that left mine.

It hadn't worked.

"I'm so sorry, Kade." I stepped back, away from the two of them as Kade approached her.

Lana's expression was frozen in horror and her body trembled as she wrapped her arms around herself. The moment, once filled with triumph, was no longer the joyous occasion from just a few minutes ago.

A heaviness settled in my chest. This was my best friend's mate, and the one thing that should have rid the darkness from inside of him didn't work. So what did that mean for eliminating all darkness to destroy Thames? What did that mean for the two of them?

I walked toward Jax, who stared with a look on his face that told me his thoughts weren't too far from my own.

Glancing over my shoulder back at them, I watched Kade comfort Lan.

"Don't worry, Little Rebel," Kade assured her, rubbing his hands up and down her arms. "This is not the end. We'll find another way."

After the events of the day, we weren't prepared to begin the journey back to the inn. Exhaustion, both mental and physical, hit the four of us hard. Jax went out to hunt for dinner, and returned quickly with several rabbits, his face ashen.

"The strox decided to 'help,' if you will," he said as he sat by the fire, skinning our soon-to-be meal. He refused to answer any other questions about his encounter, and we reluctantly let it go—for now. I was very curious as to how a strox helped catch rabbits. Especially for Jax, who was the most terrified of the beasts out of all of us.

Perhaps another day Jax would tell the tale.

"I'm heading to bed," Lana announced after we finished our meals and made plans to return to the inn at first light. Her mood hadn't improved much despite Jax trying to rile her up and Kade comforting her. But she had smiled a few times, which I counted as a win. "Kade?" She reached out her hand, and he didn't bother looking at us before picking her up and carrying her in his arms to their makeshift tent.

It brought me so much peace that she'd found someone who made her laugh and accepted our friendship without jealousy. And even with today not ending the way any of us expected, he was still able to make her smile. It was everything I ever could have wanted for her.

"I'm not carrying you to your tent," Jax said, stretching as he rose from the fire. "Don't bother asking, little birdie." Jax headed toward his own tent for the evening and left me to sit by the fire alone, to take the first watch of the evening. I didn't mind. About a hundred different thoughts flowed through my head, all of which would keep me awake anyway.

While we'd learned so much today and knew what we needed to do in order to win this war, it didn't help ease the dread of all that was left to be done.

A battle to be fought, innocent lives to be lost, and a hope and a prayer to the Fates we would all make it out relatively unscathed.

A cool breeze swirled around me, calming my anxious energy. Nature soothed me, reminding me I was not alone in this fight. Ever since we were kids, nature had played a role in our lives. I'd heed its presence as reassurance.

"Ian?" A whisper of that sultry feminine voice I'd come to know as well as my own entered my head.

My lingering anxiety disappeared altogether the minute Raya's voice entered my mind.

Yes? I couldn't help my smile as I dragged the word out, said only in my mind.

"Did you find the journal?"

Mmm… Well, hello to you too.

Raya sighed and an image of her appeared before me in my mind. She stood in an inky expanse as endless as the night. This hadn't happened since she'd appeared to me screaming and bloodied. Before I knew they were safe during their time in Mysthaven. I pushed that thought down, unable to breathe thinking about the moment she materialized in my mind, battered and sobbing.

Instead, I wondered if I could be in a physical form. Squeezing my eyes shut, I imagined myself walking toward her, and suddenly my body manifested. A version of myself within myself. *Does this mean we're both physically here in our minds?*

"Apparently so." She stalked toward me in this empty expanse. *"Let me ask again, did you find the journal?"*

Of course we did, I replied, as I thought about reaching for her hand. Could we touch? *We may have even gotten some reinforcements.*

"What the hell is that supposed to mean?"

I reached for her, nudging a finger under her chin playfully. *Wouldn't you like to know?*

Gasping, I realized I could *feel* her skin in a fuzzy kind of way. She wasn't completely solid, but it didn't feel like touching a cloud, instead lingering somewhere in-between.

Raya frowned, but I wasn't able to focus on that like I should have. The simple act of touching her froze me in place. The smile I wore faded as an overwhelming sensation rushed through my body, rewiring my very essence. Fates, this was something stronger than I'd ever experienced before. A small bright tether inside my chest snapped into place, lining up every emotion I had regarding Raya.

I'd fought against what this thing between us was previously, the annoying attraction, my inability to admit that having her closer always felt better. But now? Now there was no way I'd fight this any longer.

The way I craved this woman I hardly knew made no sense. An overwhelming urge to run to her in the physical realm and wrap myself in her dark, rich skin while I ran my hands through those braids overtook me. The way they swung with the beat of her hips when she moved. It drove me mad in a way I couldn't explain.

"You are insufferable. As this is the only way for any of us to remain in communication, I am forced to be the liaison between our two groups."

I stared at her cocked eyebrow, and I swear I was a fucking goner. *Don't worry, we'll be back tomorrow.* My hand twitched, daring to brush my finger against hers, touching her hand and tracing my thumb along her wrist. Raya jumped back, surprised by the second, lingering touch.

"What are you doing?"

Don't you think it's odd that you can mind-speak to me when you've never been able to do it with anyone except for King Dargan?

"I—uhm—haven't tested that theory." Her breathing hitched, and her chest rising and falling increased.

Don't you think it's strange that we can now see each other while we are mind-speaking? I stepped closer and reached out my hand to her, praying she would take it. Just one more touch might calm my racing heart. *Don't you feel it?*

She didn't take my hand, but she didn't move away either. She left me in limbo. There was still hope.

"Feel what? You have been nothing but rude to me since I was forced to enter your mind. I feel nothing for you except you are Lana's friend, and against all of my better judgment, she's grown on me over the last few weeks. I wouldn't do anything to hurt her after the kindness she has shown me."

I grinned at how Raya hated that others were entering her life who loved her. She was about to have to add me to that list. *She does that. It's hard not to love her. But that's not what I'm talking about, Raya, and you know it. There is something between us. Something that neither of us has ever felt before.*

"Don't you say it," she whispered. Her eyes darted around like she wanted to escape, but I knew if she truly wanted to leave, she could cut me off and disappear. She'd done it before.

I stepped even farther into her space and cradled her cheek in my hand. An electric jolt passed over my entire body and exited my fingertips into Raya. Her gaze flickered between my hand and my face, confused as to what had just happened between us.

See? I cupped the other side of her face. *We are something. The Fates themselves know it to be true.*

"I know nothing of the Fates or their wishes." She stepped back out of my grasp. *"But whatever it is you're thinking might be happening—it can't be. They don't exist anymore."*

I couldn't help but chuckle. *Except we do know it to be true. Look at Kade and Lana.*

Raya stormed off farther into the abyss of my mind, but I couldn't let her leave yet. I wasn't ready for her to go. *Raya, come back.* I ran after her and caught up to her in mere moments. I stopped just past her, so she faced me. *Don't leave. Just talk to me.*

"There is no talking to you. Not when you've got these crazy ideas in your idiot head. Now get out of my way, or I'll make you."

Is that a threat? I couldn't help my smirk. My smile had always worked in the past whenever I'd tried to woo a lady. I was always told it was one of my best qualities. I had a feeling things would be harder with Raya, and Fates, I'd do anything to win her heart.

"Hah, you have no idea." Without warning, she dropped and swiped her leg out, knocking me off balance.

As I fell to the ground, I grabbed the tunic of her shirt, bringing her down to the imaginary floor. Raya landed on top of me and proceeded to try to punch my side. I blocked her attack with my forearms and wrapped my left leg around the outside of hers. Grabbing her arm, I brought her body close to mine and thrusted my hips up, flipping her over, so I sat on top of her.

She lay there panting. *"Let. Me. Go."*

Leaning down, I brushed a few loose strands of hair out of her face and whispered in her ear. *You can try to fight this all you want, Raya, but I'll be here waiting when you're ready to admit it. Whether in my mind or Brookmere, or Mysthaven, or in Atheria now, I will always choose you.*

Shock and then indignation crossed her face, before she disappeared from beneath me, leaving me alone in the chamber of my mind specifically carved out for her.

With my heart racing and anxious butterflies filling my stomach, I left my mind and returned to the crackling fire at the campsite. Breathing in the smoky air grounded me in reality as the stars twinkled above.

I was totally screwed. Raya was mine. I would do whatever it took to win her trust and get her to admit what this was.

I'd found my mate and I'd prove to her that the Fates got it right with us.

For as long as it took.

CHAPTER 18

LANA

We arrived back at the Knotted Willow the next afternoon, just in time to make dinner with the rest of camp.

A perfect opportunity to find out what had happened while we were gone, even if it had only been for a few days.

Riding up to the inn and surrounding campgrounds took my breath away. It was a true work of art for these Fae to have constructed such a well thought out and efficient site in such a short amount of time.

We quickly dropped off the horses at the stable and made our way to the main dining hall in the tavern. The army ate outside, surrounding their individual campfires or at long tables they'd constructed themselves, but thankfully William allowed our group to eat inside so we could plan away from the others. Or perhaps he was still too wary of Vivienne and Cassandra and didn't want to be alone with the seers and their magic any longer.

Settling around the back table of the tavern, Storm, Kalliah, Raya, and Corbin joined us with plates of food in hand. Kalliah even managed to find a carafe of wine, which paired perfectly with the tomato-sauced noodles piled on our plates.

As we all shoveled in the delicious meal, the questions were endless about what we'd learned. Kalliah's eyes remained wide the entire time as her gaze split between me and Jax, who continued his habit of exaggerating every minor detail.

"You should have seen it," Jax explained, his hands in the air. "There were about twenty strox flying in the air, attacking us from every angle and that was before the fifty razorven lined up like a battalion, ready to eat us for breakfast."

Corbin raised his brow and studied Jax. His face practically screamed *you've got to be kidding me.*

Determined to convince everyone at the table, Jax continued, "But you know, my super shifter abilities kept them at bay." He blew on his nails. "These paws are lethal."

"Right, Jax," Ian mocked. "Definitely how it all happened."

"I can't believe you found the journal," Kalliah murmured as she took a small sip of the earthy liquid. "And you battled a strox? Sounds like an adventure I'm glad I wasn't a part of."

Jax leaned forward across the table, "Oh beautiful, I would've protected you." He winked, lifting her hand and kissing it. "You have nothing to fear when I'm around."

Kalliah rolled her eyes, taking her hand back before she continued to swirl the long noodles around her fork, ignoring Jax's shameless attempt at flirting.

"You know the man she's not-so-secretly in love with for the last three years is likely being held hostage somewhere, right?" Ian asked.

Jax shrugged. "I could save him too." He grabbed the bowl of noodles from the middle of the table and proceeded to serve himself another giant helping.

Kalliah blinked at Jax a few times before shaking her head and returning to her food.

Despite the hunger pains I'd felt earlier, I couldn't help but stop what I was doing. There was something Evelyn said that I couldn't wrap my head around. My head rested on my palm as my fingers tapped my brow.

"Tell me what's going through that head of yours, Little Rebel." Kade nudged my side as I sat there in silence.

Pausing, I lifted my head to look at him and the others at the table. "How are we possibly going to destroy all the darkness? We'd have to know where every dark one is, the location of every place Thames has infected. It feels impossible."

Kade shifted in his seat, turning to face me, and placed his hand over mine. "Impossible? Never. With you, anything is possible." He smiled, and I couldn't help but smile back. "Just look at you now, you've got magic after all."

It still amazed me that after twenty-three years, after years of torture and suffering, I could finally say I had magic. There was no more hoping and praying. No more hiding in plain sight, terrified to be discovered.

I was a true Fae. An heir to the royal throne of Brookmere. I would be queen.

And I had magic.

I couldn't help but feel every step was just a little bit lighter. Every sound crisper. My vision even felt clearer. The cut I'd gotten yesterday during our battle, and the one from slicing my palm, had both already healed.

I was never one to believe in the prophecies by our seer, but perhaps I should've heeded more of her words over the years.

As if they knew I was thinking about them and this Fates-forsaken prophecy, Vivienne and Cassandra descended the stairwell and joined us at the table.

"Did you discover what you needed to learn?" Vivienne asked casually as she placed her hands in her lap. "Did you meet someone along the way?"

"You could have warned us," Jax tried to shout through a mouthful of noodles. "We almost died."

"Oh right, Mr. Super Shifter," Kalliah mocked. "I thought you *totally had it?*"

Raya snickered. "I knew I liked you, Kalliah."

Cassandra and Vivienne stared at each other, chuckled, and Cassandra turned to Jax. "Yet here you are, still alive to tell the tale. Honestly Jax, when did you lose your sense of adventure? One would think you've reverted to the teenage Fae I caught hiding in the stables after being chased by a simple fox."

Jax slammed his fist on the table, and strands of his black hair fell into his eyes. "First of all, that thing was rabid and trying to eat me. Second of all, I wasn't hiding." He crossed his arms in disgust.

I dropped my fork, throwing my head back to laugh as the others joined in around me.

Cassandra waved her hand at Jax, dismissing his antics before returning her attention to me.

Vivienne also looked my way and began reciting. "Void of magic, a heroine born, destiny calls, though faint and torn. Many will come from across the land, yet only the strongest will win her hand. With lover's touch, she shall ignite, without it perish from the kingdom's blight."

Everyone's attention shifted to focus directly on the seers, utensils and drink suddenly laid down on the table.

Cassandra took over speaking Kade's prophecy. "Rebels rise where darkness lies, not one but two must break the ties. Across the void, a queen you must seek, trust freely given, for one alone proves too weak. Though evil will free and be bound no more, Fate still awaits one final war."

"Yes, we know the prophecies," Kade began. "Lana is a queen from across the void, and we will work together to fight the darkness. Clearly, we have a war to fight." He ran his hands through his hair, sweeping it straight back. "We're in love. I don't think there is anything we don't know at this point."

"Tsk tsk." Cassandra stood and held out her hand to Vivienne, who joined her next to the table. Together they began speaking in unison. "Banish all ties to darkness with light, if any remains, so will this plight. In the end, a willing sacrifice of life, will trigger events to cease this strife. For the loss of love will heal what's torn, and allow this world to be reborn."

Silence.

Complete and utter silence filled the room.

While Vivienne and Cassandra looked pleased with themselves, a third prophecy was not what we expected to hear from them right now. Not that I ever knew what to expect, but another prophecy? I had no words.

"How long have you had this prophecy?" Kade growled.

Cassandra and Vivienne released each other's hands and sat back in their respective seats. "Not long. The Fates only deemed us worthy of this knowledge a few weeks ago. As sisters reunited, and the worlds collided, the Fates showed themselves once more."

I rose, quickly walked over to the bar area, and found a piece of parchment and a writing utensil to copy the third prophecy. "Say it again but slower." I needed time to process this information, and here, out in the open, I wasn't sure my heart could handle what was foretold. I returned to my seat, ready to capture everything.

They spoke the prophecy again as a chill ran over my arms. Evelyn had spoken of loss to come, as did the prophecy. None of this was coincidence, and the doom echoing from Evelyn's words was confirmed now. I rubbed my chest as if it could protect my heart somehow. The dread pooling in my belly solidified into something hard. I poured myself a hefty helping of wine to calm my racing nerves, throwing it back, enjoying the burning sensation that distracted me from my helpless thoughts.

The front door whipped open, and a slender Fae male quickly entered, closing the door behind him in a hurry. The young man stood panting for a moment before saying, "Colonel Storm, news from Ellevail."

Storm stood, grabbing a glass of water, and proceeded to hand it to the winded Fae. "Here, first take a drink, Kristopher, then your report."

"Colonel Storm?" Jax muttered begrudgingly. "We leave for three days, and he's promoted himself to a colonel? Unbelievable." I felt Kalliah kick Jax under the table before he yelped, and I couldn't help but giggle. Rising, I went to stand by Storm. As queen, I would hear any information about my country, but especially Ellevail. My home.

"What mission could you have possibly orchestrated in less than three days' time?" Ian asked, turning in his chair to face us.

"We found a few smaller shifters willing to try to sneak into Ellevail to investigate what was happening. I dispatched them only a few hours after you left."

"That's why he's promoted." Kade grinned at Jax.

"I call captain, then, since I battled a strox, you know."

"Will you hush," Kalliah said, her words accented by another thud.

Jax leaned in toward her. "I will keep that leg in my lap if you kick me again, gorgeous."

Kristopher gladly gulped down the glass of water, before standing at attention once more. "Your Majesty." The man bowed.

"None of that, especially not right now. Kristopher, was it?" I smiled at the man who appeared much younger than he had when he'd first flung open the doors.

"Ye—Yes, Your Majesty. It's an honor."

I nodded at him, encouraging him to continue.

"The mission was successful. We were able to infiltrate Ellevail and the surrounding area, especially the outskirts where the lesser Fae reside. The closer we got to the palace itself, the harder it became. The dark ones were everywhere, patrolling the streets as efficiently as the royal guard. The Fae we saw were either living in fear, running from a store back to their homes, avoiding contact, or have pledged their support to Andras as king."

The anger inside of me simmered to a slow boil. "How dare he."

"Continue," Storm demanded.

Gulping, Kristopher continued, "There was one slight mishap." Storm remained quiet as Kristopher prepared himself to speak once more. "Joseph was caught—"

"He was *what?*" Storm seethed.

"Wait, it's okay, Colonel," Kristopher pleaded. "It ended up being a good thing."

I could hear my heart pounding in my chest. The anger mixed with sudden fear for those who willingly risked their lives for this mission made the palms of my hands sweat.

"What happened to him?" I asked, trying to portray a collected version of myself.

Kristopher glanced between Storm and me, unsure of where to look. "You see, the Fae who apprehended Joseph turned out to be on our side. A tavern owner. Tom, I believe is his name?"

"Tommy Solomon?" I asked at the same time Ian did. "The owner of Dukes Pub?" I pressed.

It would be truly fitting if Tommy was out there kidnapping my men off the street.

Kristopher's eyes lit up. "Yes, that's the one." He began speaking even faster, his nervous energy seeking a way to be released, "He too is building a resistance. He wants to help. Dukes Pub has become a sort of meeting place for those willing to fight against Andras and the dark ones. You just have to know the password. While we were there, we met several Fae who were ready to fight, and their next meeting is soon. Joseph stayed behind to serve as a point person on the inside. They want him to learn what they're doing so that when we come, we can concoct a better plan together."

Storm stepped forward. "And I assume you know the password, Kristopher?"

He stood straighter, returning to a solider-like position, which he had lost momentarily in his excitement. "Of course, Colonel. It's tambourine marching band."

Raya cackled from behind us. "You know, after all of this is said and done, I might decide to stay here in Brookmere, just to go to the infamous Dukes Pub for a night of debauchery. Every time this place gets brought up, it just gets better and better."

Ian leaned forward in his chair. "I'd be happy to escort you there. I happen to be friends with the owner." He winked, which made Raya blush. I narrowed my eyes at them looking for a tell as to what was happening there. I'd have to dig into that development later.

Ian settled back into his chair, allowing Storm and Kristopher to continue talking.

I knew it was hard for Ian to allow Storm to handle the army while we were gone. He had always loved being in control. He needed it after our childhood, and he'd worked damn hard to earn the right to it. But it impressed me how willingly he gave it up to be a part of this team. Our team. He truly understood what it meant to be a leader.

"Thank you, Kristopher. If that is all, you are dismissed," Storm dictated. "Get some dinner—you are off duty for the next twelve hours along with the rest of those on the mission. Be sure to advise your superior accordingly."

Kristopher saluted and left, but not before bowing his head.

Kade came to stand with us and put his arm around

Storm. "Three days and you've built a command structure, rotating schedules, and Fates know what else."

"Ian and I planned it together before he left," Storm said, nodding toward Ian. "I simply had to put it into action."

I would never have been able to accomplish any of that on my own. "We're lucky to have both of you," I said, hoping they knew how much I believed that.

Ian stood, glass of wine in hand as he paced around the room, deep in thought. "I think it's time we take back our city."

"With this unexpected insider knowledge, I'm leaning toward agreeing with you," Kade added.

I nodded too, taking in a slow, deep breath to calm both the excitement at thinking of home, and the fear of what a siege could mean.

"You're right, it is time to return home." I lifted my chin, holding it higher. "And it's time for Andras to die."

CHAPTER 19
IAN

A stinging bolt of light struck my side, and I whipped my head around to throw my best glare at Lana.

"I swear to the Fates, Lan, we're lucky you didn't have magic all those years." I rubbed my eyes, then smacked at my cheeks to wake up, especially since she'd tagged me with her magic more than once already.

"I need to practice aiming," she said innocently, lifting a shoulder. "Besides, your mind is somewhere else, Ian. It'll help you stay focused."

I inhaled slowly, rolling my eyes at her.

Three days of endless scheming had led us to a plan that gave us a fair amount of confidence. One mostly concocted by Storm and me. While he might not have spent nearly as much time in Ellevail as I had, to have someone else versed in the art of battle planning proved immensely helpful.

I couldn't stop the smile remembering how exasperated Storm had become at Kade poking holes in our plans. He was doubtful of everything, mainly because he knew we shouldn't underestimate Thames and his power. That and the bond between him and Lana had him practically feral over her safety, leading to even more hesitation.

Storm and I fell into devising our strategy with ease. "We will have to use your network of connections as captain and Lana's role as Hidden Henchman to make this work," he murmured. "Moving an entire barely trained army without being noticed is a task unlike any other I've ever had to accomplish."

Kade sighed louder than he needed to. "If we don't move them, we'll draw too much attention to ourselves and put the women and children here at risk."

I'd agreed with Storm on the difficulties moving our army, but there was no turning back. We had to hope for the best. Though Kade's grumbling irked me, he had a point. Staying here was more dangerous each day we remained. We needed to relocate our forces away from the Fae here who couldn't fight. Or they would have fled to us for nothing.

Even when our plan settled into place, it took an inconceivable amount of convincing for Kade to let me take Lana into the city by ourselves. Kade's shadows were needed with the army. His ability to hide them with his shadows as the sun began to rise would obscure their movements around the forest. He'd also be able to protect them if they came across their first battles with dark ones. But that meant, staying behind while Lana stayed with me.

Leaving in the middle of the night allowed us to move the fastest while shielded by the night sky. With the "evil beasts" like the razorven no longer an issue, more of the Fae felt comfortable moving under the cover of darkness.

The army would follow behind us, moving slower as one unit, commanded by Kade, with Storm and Raya each leading a battalion.

As soon as night fell, Lana and I prepared two horses to ride hard toward Eomer Forest.

Before we left, Kade threatened me within an inch of my life. Should one hair of Lana's perfectly rose-gold hair be out of place by the time we reconnected, his shadows would have the pleasure of wreaking havoc on my soul. I laughed at him this time. I would never let anything happen to Lana after everything we'd been through. Kade knew it too, but I'd let him have the last word. I felt like I owed him one for helping me realize darkness had been inside of me.

He was still an asshole. Just an asshole I'd tolerate.

Even William saw us off as the clock struck midnight. "I'm finally going to get my peace and quiet again. Thank the Fates." While I knew he barely seemed to put up with us, I couldn't help but notice the extra hug he gave Lana and that he'd slipped something into her cloak pocket when he thought none of us were looking.

Vivienne and Cassandra were nowhere to be seen to wish us well, or say goodbye. Maybe it was better not knowing what the seers were doing.

Lana and I left galloping toward our destination ahead of the army.

About a mile ago, we'd left our trusty steeds and walked the rest of the way. We didn't want to attract any more attention than necessary, the closer we got to town. Kalliah and Corbin would retrieve the horses as part of Raya's battalion before meeting us in Eomer Forest at one of the Hidden Henchman drop spots.

"It feels like old times," Lana whispered excitedly, snapping my attention back to her as she ran from tree to tree in the early morning hours. Her cloak billowed behind her as she moved. "It's like being the Hidden Henchman all over again."

I looked at Lana, and the moonlight exposed the tremor in her hand, shaking with nervous energy. "Only this time, we want to find Andras and not avoid him at all costs." She grinned.

I couldn't help but return her smile. Working together with Lana by my side again just felt right. Knowing that this would be the end of Andras, made it even better. "Remember when he almost caught us after our first drop? I swore he saw us enter through the back kitchen door."

She laughed. "Thank goodness for Lucien. He really came through and saved the day by knocking over the stack of dishes. We made it just in time to hide in the pantry."

"I told you he understands us." Ducking under a branch as we trudged farther through Eomer Forest, I swiped the leaves out of my face. "He came to me in the dungeons."

Lana stopped and faced me. I hadn't talked much about that time yet. I knew eventually I could, with her. I didn't want to burden her, but if anyone would understand, it was her. I swallowed the lump in my throat, rising at the memories. I hated how weak my time there made me feel.

She reached for my hand. "I don't know what I would have done if I'd lost you."

I squeezed once. "You won't have to find out." I let go, retraining my focus on the forest around us.

Lana sighed. "I miss that pugron." She paused and her face fell. "And Leif. Do you think we'll find him alive?"

I ran a hand through my hair, worried about our friend. I wasn't sure why Andras would keep him alive, but I'd refused to accept anything but his survival.

"He's stronger than you think. He survived Lucinda chasing him around the palace kitchens all these years after all." I smiled, wanting to break the dread that festered if I thought about him for too long.

Lana smiled, but it didn't meet her eyes. "I swear if Andras harmed him in any way, I'll make sure he suffers even more than what I already have in mind."

"Do *not* do anything crazy. We stick to the plan." I grabbed her arm and forced her to look me straight in my blue eyes as a warm breeze wrapped around us. Nature agreed. "Lan, I need you to promise me." I knew her. If anyone was at risk, even that pugron, she'd act without thinking. "If something goes horribly wrong, you get out. We will regroup and come back to fight another day, understood?"

Lana's jaw clenched. "There is no failing. This happens now. Andras will die by my hand. Ellevail will stand again. We will not lose, Ian. Not if we're together."

I waited a beat, knowing I couldn't force her to listen. I admired how much she'd grown though, in strength, in courage. A queen stood before me, forged from pain.

"Okay." I nodded once. "For the record, I've added Lucien to our 'must save' list after he comforted me in those dark moments. I will be forever grateful for that little pugron."

Her eyes lightened before I signaled for her to continue as we made our way through the trees.

My mind spun, and when going over the plan for the hundredth time made my head throb, I finally settled, allowing myself to think about Raya.

My mate.

She'd scarcely looked at me once I'd returned from the Southern Forest. Between planning with Storm and the few hours of sleep here and there, there wasn't much time to pull her aside and talk. The few moments I did have, she made sure she was nowhere to be found.

She avoided me, dodging the very necessary conversation we urgently needed to have. When the knowledge had snapped into place that she was mine, my mate, it reshaped everything inside of me. There would be no one else. I'd assumed she had felt it happen too.

But what if she didn't? What would I do if she never felt the same?

"Lan?" We were almost to the open wildflower field we'd crossed so many times before during Hidden Henchman meetings in the forest. "Would you have chosen Kade if we had gotten to the end of the marriage trials?"

"Yes," she said without hesitation, "I think I've always known we were connected in some way on a deeper level.

There was an undeniable pull toward him, unlike anything I'd ever felt before. Clearly, now we know why."

"To think, you were right about mates all along," I teased, brushing against her shoulder. "I should have believed you from the start. We could have spent far less time arguing about love matches and mates and more time training."

Lana huffed. "You loved reminding me it was the last possible thing that could ever happen to any of us in our lifetime. Ever." She smirked before her brow raised in suspicion. "What are you getting at here?"

I drummed my fingers against my thigh, shifting my weight, unsure of how to continue.

"Ian?"

I ran a hand along the back of my neck. Fates, saying it to Lan would make it real. "I feel that. Sometimes." I swallowed. "No, that's not true. All the time now."

"Feel what?" she pressed.

"A pull."

A smile spread over her face. "I'm going to need more than that."

I knew she absolutely did *not* need more information than that.

"I know you and Kade have your mate thing going, but perhaps I might have found mine too."

I'd only said it in my head, but once the words escaped my lips—fuck, it felt so right.

Thinking of Raya sent a warmth into my heart. The second I'd touched her in my mind, I longed to be closer to her. Even though I knew she barely wanted to be in my presence—she'd made that much abundantly clear—the desperate need to be near her, to just breathe the same air as her, was enough to break my concentration more times than I could count.

Lana grinned and drew me into a hug. "Maybe when this

is all over, we can finally live the lives we always dreamed of. We just have to make it out alive first."

"You know who I'm talking about?"

This time, instead of hugging me, she slugged my arm. "Everyone would know who you mean. Come on, Ian. She can only appear in your mind. That alone is obvious enough. Besides, the tension is so thick, you've made everyone around you nauseous."

"Don't even start with me on tension, with you and Kade eye-fucking every minute of the day," I grumbled.

Lana gasped, holding a hand to her chest in mock outrage. "Not *every* minute."

The tree line ended and we stopped, halting our progression. Once we crossed the field ahead we'd be close to our well-used hidden entrance into Ellevail. "We're getting closer. We've got to make it to Dukes Pub by daybreak without being seen, even if the likelihood of us not running into a dark one is slim. Which means we have about an hour left if our plan is going to work. Are you ready?"

Lana took my hand, squeezing it once before she donned her hood, hiding her hair. "It really is like old times."

Moving silently through the fields, we ran in tandem. Even with the likelihood of failure and death, in this moment I could see Lana free. Running, her arms out beside her, feeling the flowers as she passed, I watched in awe as they leaned into her. How we thought she didn't have magic with nature's responses to her was beyond me. We'd all been idiots.

A slim ray of sunlight peeked over the horizon, and a warm breeze swirled around us, guiding us forward.

We approached the concealed stone grate on the outer wall of the city, and the energy in the air shifted. The warmth disappeared, replaced by a dark, foreboding chill, despite it being the middle of summer.

The grass surrounding the outer wall appeared dead, straw-like and void of its lush green color. The usual morning sounds of birds chirping was nonexistent. Instead, we were met with silence, and goose bumps ran up my forearms.

Lana turned to me as we crouched by the steel grate that would let us into the city. "It's like there's no more life left in Ellevail," she whispered. "You can feel it, right?"

I nodded, quietly yanking away the metal bars. "I can. Andras has ruined our city." I slid through the tunnel, checking outside before beckoning her forward. The street was deserted. Noiseless. "We will restore Ellevail and Brookmere to the way it should be."

Grabbing my hand, she squeezed it. "Atheria."

I nodded. "Right. That will take getting used to."

We continued making our way through the outer limits of Ellevail, keeping to the shadows as we had done so many times before.

Sweat broke out over my skin. We were home. Yet the memories of my last time here threatened to overcome me. I faltered, leaning against a wall. My breathing hitched, unable to get a deep enough breath.

"Ian?" Lana asked, bringing a hand to my chest. "What's wrong."

I shook my head. "Just need a second."

Her face softened and she leaned in to me, resting her head on my shoulder. "You're not there anymore," she whispered, wrapping her arms around me. "You're here, with me. Real as roses."

I squeezed my eyes shut. "Real as roses," I repeated. There had been too many times we'd brought each other out of the dark. If we could do this, succeed in this war, I prayed we never had to endure this pain again.

"You will heal," she said softly. "And I'll be beside you every step of the way, just as you have always been beside me."

I rested my head on hers for a moment and took a steadying breath, as if that could rid me of the memories.

There would be time for working through the nightmares of the dungeon, but for now, we had to press on.

We rounded a corner, halting abruptly as a lone dark one limped into a side alley, headed away from us. An agitated energy thrummed in my veins, waiting to be set free. Seeing the twitching creature on our streets infuriated me. This darkness didn't belong here, or anywhere for that matter, but seeing it permeating the city we called home made it worse somehow.

Lana put a hand on my arm. "He's alone. Let me use Apollo first to see if he can be saved."

I frowned, hating that idea immediately since it added more risk to our plans. "It could draw too much attention."

She settled a stern look at me. "I have to try," she hissed.

Drawing my blade, I stalked our prey, prepared to engage the second after Lana cut him if need be. We used the shadows of dawn to our advantage and crept alongside our target. Lana jumped, grabbing his arm and raked her blade down its length.

The man sharply sucked air through his teeth as the inky-black darkness seeped from him in waves. He blinked a few times before his nostrils flared, rage contorting his face. He shoved forward against Lana.

Not wasting a moment, I thrust my sword into his back, tearing clear through his stomach. He hit the ground before he could even mutter a sound.

Lana stared at the man so long I almost intervened. But then she sighed, looking up and meeting my gaze. "Not everyone can be saved," she said. "One down."

"A hundred or so more to go." I wiped my blade on the seam of my pants.

As we continued to move through the city, the view turned my stomach. Lana remained silent as her eyes darted around, taking in our surroundings. Even in the early hours of the morning, it was strange that not a single soul milled about, preparing for the day. Windows remained tightly closed, homes were dark, and the flowers sitting in window boxes, usually bright and vibrant, appeared withered and dead.

We'd prepared to enter the city as it woke, sneaking through the lower levels filled with Fae getting ready for their days. We hadn't expected to find eerie silence.

A child peeked through a window and met my gaze. Her eyes widened with terror as she watched Lana's cloaked figure next to me. She quickly shut the curtain and disappeared out of sight.

Our people were living in fear.

Everything King Alister and Queen Roxana did for the Fae to build a community, to protect them, encourage them, had crumbled. Lana's breathing stuttered, and I took her hand in mine, knowing she was fighting to hold back tears. Her home, which was once so full of life, had been destroyed, fading away under Andras's reign.

I had worked with these Fae every day. They were my people too. Fae whom I'd sworn to protect when I took my vows as captain. The resolve to finish this with Andras burned in the deepest recesses of my body. I would not let them down —our people deserved better than this.

"We're here," Lana whispered, as we stopped in front of the door to Dukes Pub. She knocked three times, pausing a second between each one as our informant had instructed. The hook above the door normally holding the establishment's sign lay bare.

A makeshift peephole slid open, and a wide eye pressed against it from the other side. "Password?" a gruff voice sounded from behind the door.

"Tambourine mar-marching band?" Lana stuttered, a hint of skepticism in her voice.

The peephole slammed shut without another word from the burly sounding man.

Lana and I stared at each other for a moment in confusion. "Do you think we got it wrong?" she asked.

Suddenly, we heard locks turning before the door cracked open, one chain lock remaining in place.

"Name?" the man with the gravelly voice asked. The small sliver we could see of him gave nothing away as to his identity. A wound stretched under his eye, red and raw, still healing. Whoever he was, he clearly didn't have strong healing magic.

"Ian Stronholm, former Captain of the Royal Guard." I pulled Lana back. I would rather give my name in case this didn't work. Lana could at least have a chance to escape and Andras would only be able to guess if she were truly here or not.

"And your friend?" he growled.

Lana looked at me as we hesitated, but only for a moment. She nodded, then raised her chin like the queen she was born to be. "Illiana Dresden. Rightful ruler of Brookmere. If you are a friend, you will let us in, and quickly so we can get off the street before we are seen."

The door slammed shut in our faces, and we were left wondering if we were being met with friend or foe. The chain slid on the other side of the door, and slowly, it swung open. We were ushered into the bar before the door closed shut once more. The man locked the handful of bolts and chains before turning to us.

He stared at Lana, who remained cloaked. After a few moments, she took the hood off.

The man stumbled back a step and bowed. "Your Majesty." He rose hastily, limping toward the back. "Take a seat, I'll get Tommy."

Lana nodded and sat at one of the nearby tables. "Thank you, sir."

He let out a chuff, but I saw the grin on his face. Lana had a way of making people feel seen.

"He probably hasn't been called 'sir' ever," I chuckled. "You flustered him."

I stood beside Lana, ready just in case this was a trap. Looking down at her, I noticed she left her hand on her thigh, right on the hilt of the dagger in its sheath. She was prepared for a potential fight. I'd taught her well.

Two minutes later, Tommy Soloman appeared from around a corner. "I miss the days when breaking tables was the biggest problem you caused me, but now"—he paused surveying Lana and me—" look at you."

"I—" Lana started.

Tommy shook his head. "Doing the king and queen so proud." He bowed his head low. "What can I do to help serve the crown, Your Majesty?"

I could see the muscles in Lana's shoulders relax as she exhaled a large breath. "I heard you've started up a resistance." She smiled at the barkeeper. "I'm hoping perhaps we could work together to take back our kingdom."

A crash in the kitchen caused all of our attention to immediately shift to high alert. I positioned myself in front of Lana, sword drawn. I would take no chances when it came to her safety. Not when we were so close.

"Not again," Tommy muttered.

A second clang of a metal container being dropped sounded, and a figure appeared in the kitchen doorway, just beyond the bar.

I dropped my sword in disbelief. My eyes had to be playing tricks on me.

The man before me had his sleeves rolled to his elbows and flour spilled all the way down his pants.

"Leif?" I practically whispered at the sight of my friend.

Lana jumped from her seat and ran toward him. "Oh, Leif." She threw her arms around his neck. "You're alive. You're all right?" she asked, squeezing him so tightly I didn't know if he could answer.

When she pulled away, she shoved him as she cried and laughed all at the same time. "I'm so angry you risked yourself, but you saved them all." She wrapped her arms around him again. "I am so happy to see you."

Embracing her back just as enthusiastically, Leif held on to her, chuckling. "And I would do it a thousand times over, Your Highness. I'm relieved you're safe."

I stepped forward, grinning as my own eyes welled. "You're okay," I said under my breath, like I needed to reassure myself. "You're alive." I forcefully blew out a breath, hardly believing he stood before me uninjured.

Leif untangled himself from Lana and held out his hand. I grabbed it, tugging him closer, and froze.

My smile fell as fear tightened my chest and my stomach dropped. I let go of Leif's hand, reaching for Lana. "Lana, get back."

She turned to me and then looked back at Leif, whose arms returned to his side. He frowned at me. "Ian?"

I pulled Lana behind me before gripping Leif's arm and shoving his sleeve up higher.

What should have been a moment of joy and gratitude lay ruined in an instant.

"No," Lana whimpered. Her expression transformed from shock and confusion to one of pure outrage. Though it was impossible to hide the despair there too.

Her voice shook, tinged with anger and pain. "You had better have a damn good reason for that mark on your arm."

As she spoke, her eyes rested firmly on Leif's arm and the black mark designating him as a dark one.

CHAPTER 20

LANA

"Why, Leif?" My voice trembled along with the flurry of emotions coursing through my veins.

Anger. Hurt. Devastation. I'd lost another friend to this evil, and I wasn't sure how many tears I had left to cry. These losses were too many.

"No! Wait, Lana, I can explain." Leif took a step forward only for Ian to pull out his blade and hold it against his friend's throat.

I didn't miss the way his hand trembled as he clutched his weapon harder. The way he tried to keep his voice calm and steady, but instead it came out uneven. "Do not come near her."

I lowered my hand to Apollo, now resting on my thigh, feeling the cool hilt between my fingers. I'd purge Leif of the darkness haunting his body. He couldn't be trapped like this. Ian couldn't handle losing someone else. Fates knew I couldn't either after losing both sets of parents, and Elisabeth. And Kalliah—I couldn't even think about the devastation she'd endure knowing he stayed behind and turned into the very evil we were trying to destroy.

Leif put his hands up in the air in surrender. "Hold on, just watch," he said, lowering his arm.

I inched forward, earning a glare from Ian as I unsheathed my dagger. His eyes widened before nodding once, understanding my intentions.

Leif produced a cloth from his pocket and rubbed hard at the dark one's mark on his arm. I watched the ink faintly smudge.

"It's not real?" I gasped, hope filling my voice.

Leif grinned as Ian tentatively lowered his weapon.

"Of course it's not real," Leif retorted. "I just came up with a way to fuck with them. One that allows me to get around as I please to get the information I need. It took a long time to get it right and be able to pass for a real one, but I finally figured it out." He shoved the cloth back into his pocket and started mumbling to himself, "Going to take forever to fix that."

My whole body relaxed as the tension released from my shoulders. I rubbed my neck to work out the last bit of ache in my muscles. Where were those damn shadows when I needed them?

"That's—" Ian paused, shaking his head before he laughed. "Ingenious."

Leif bowed his head, flourishing his hand dramatically. "Thank you, Captain."

Ian finally put his sword away and pulled Leif in for a hug. "Fates, I'm glad you're safe. I really didn't want to have to hurt one of my friends."

Leif opened his mouth to say something, but a shout interrupted him.

"Boy," Tommy roared as he stormed back into the main area. "I told you to stay out of my kitchen. You're a magnet for disaster."

"A magnet you adore though, right?" Leif asked.

Tommy huffed and pinched the bridge of his nose. "If you weren't such an integral part of this resistance, I'd have kicked you out the first time you thudded through my door."

"How did you end up here?" I asked, as Leif brushed flour from his pants.

"You're cleaning that up," Tommy grumbled, as he grabbed a rag and swirled it around a set of glassware drying on the bar top.

"I've heard all of your infamous stories from Dukes Pub. I figured if that old grump let you both in time and time again, he might accept me too." Leif shrugged. He turned fully toward me, reaching for my arm. "Is—is Kalliah with you?"

My breath caught in my throat. "She's travelling with the others and missing you, if you can believe that."

"Never." His blush told me otherwise. "Anyway, we've been trying to update Joseph so he can help, but I'm assuming if you're here, we're tight on time?"

I nodded.

"Our army will be hidden from sight until we're ready." Ian transformed, shifting into captain mode, getting down to business. "We just need to know whatever details you have about access points and what locations are most heavily guarded."

"It's like planning for the Hidden Henchman all over again." Leif rubbed his hands together excitedly.

"Leif," I cautioned, glancing over at Tommy. While outside of the palace walls we'd admitted my true identity, having it revealed inside the city made fear curl in my stomach.

The bartender looked up, eyebrow raised. "If you think for one minute hearing you two were behind the Henchman shenanigans surprises me in any way, you must think I'm dumber than I look."

I stared at Tommy, shocked at his candor. "What?"

Leif chimed in. "We've actually spread the word that you're the Hidden Henchman. It's been an asset for recruiting. Your people loved you already, Lana, but now that they know you helped so many throughout Brookmere, it only emphasized the kind of Fae you are." Leif chuckled. "All of Andras's hard work trying to bad-mouth you backfired even more as your hidden identity spread across the land. It's been entertaining to watch."

Tommy snorted, interjecting again from the bar. "They probably wouldn't be so impressed if they knew their princess ran amuck in here every year for her birthday. Costing me tables and booze."

I rose, walking over to Tommy before placing my hands on my hips. "I paid for all my damages. Plus, you always got generous tips from me."

"Generous heaps of crazy, you mean," he countered. His gaze had softened though, lips twitching in the faintest smile.

"Tell you what," I said, picking up a handful of nuts from the bowl on the bar top and popping one into my mouth. "You continue risking your neck and helping with our cause and I'll fund the tavern for a year."

This time Tommy laughed. "You know what? You have yourself a deal."

Ian glanced at him. "You were going to do it anyway, weren't you."

Tommy winked—actually winked—at Ian. "You both may be a pain in the ass, but you're my pains in the ass. Queen Illiana's preferred pub wouldn't be too bad of a reputation either."

I laughed along with the others before Tommy abruptly stopped and cleared his throat. "Get back to work."

Leif saluted and ran back behind the bar, bringing out a sheet of parchment. He laid it out on one of the tables and my jaw dropped. On it was a sketch of Ellevail with various markings everywhere including a chart containing times and notes.

Amazing didn't even begin to describe the work before me. The intricacies and intimate details of not only the map itself, but of the other information it contained.

"I've been in and out for weeks, watching and recording their movements. The ones farther away from the castle are more erratic. Their motions twitchier and more uncontrollable. The dark ones around the perimeter of the city and inside the castle are the ones to worry about though. Our theory is those who were forced, fight the darkness harder and have the jerkier movements, while those who willingly turned are sharper and appear more 'normal'."

"That's right. We learned that as well," I nodded.

"Leif." Ian ran his fingers over the map. "This is incredible. These details will be invaluable for our attack. You should have considered a career in the guard."

Leif's cheeks flushed as he bowed his head. "The others are on their way?"

I nodded. "They'll be in Eomer Forest until we come back with information and decide where we'll breach."

"I'd say…" Leif pointed at the front gates. "Right through the front. I can rally a few who will cause a distraction to pull the guards away from the city gates."

"It'd certainly make a statement," Ian mused. "Walking straight through the front entrance. Bold move."

"If we plan it for shift change at dusk, it'll be even more chaotic, and you'll be able to get almost all the way to the secondary gates at the palace in the confusion." Leif rubbed his neck and then nodded as if double-checking his statement. "Meanwhile, I can head back into the palace and try to gather anyone willing to fight from the inside and meet you once you're through."

"Now I know why all the drops were so successful. You're a strategist," I complimented.

"Perhaps. It's come in handy for us a time or two. It'll help now."

"This is good, Leif. A solid plan." Ian's face turned somber. "What happened after we escaped?"

Leif inhaled. "They brought me to Andras for questioning, but he didn't care. He was so excited, he laughed in my face, saying you all got rid of the weak link. They threw me in the dungeons and left me for a few days. Then a guard came." He looked at Ian. "The one who approached us after the standoff with Andras and"—his eyes flicked to me with a depth of sadness in them—"and our queen fell."

Ian frowned, nodding slowly. "Right, I remember."

"His name is Valmik. He brought me food for about a week, and we talked. I told him my idea of the fake dark one marks, and he convinced one of the guards close to Casimir to let the guards handle turning people. There were a few who went beyond what was asked of them." Leif sighed. "Sacrificed their lives, essentially, to prove we were serious. Then we pretended they'd infected me, and I was released. Other guards, loyal to you and your family, Lana, have been impersonating dark ones as well. I try to meet up with them once a week to gather any relevant information."

I couldn't help but shiver as my throat clogged with emotions thinking about those who gave up everything on a whim. On just a hope that this insane plan would work. We would honor them after we won this war. Leif pointed to a few numbers crossed out and changing along the bottom of the map. "This is the number of dark ones combined with guards loyal to Andras that Valmik and his crew believe are in play."

"One hundred forty-two?" Lana said, eyebrows raised.

"Less than I thought," Ian murmured.

"The number has gone down significantly in the past week or so. Andras recently sent a large number of them out of Ellevail, but we didn't hear where they went."

222

I frowned. "That's never good."

Leif shrugged. "The point is, if we start this fight, that's how many we have to contend with, plus Andras and Casimir. You think we can?"

"Yes," Ian said without hesitation. "I do."

The way they were speaking brought me so much hope that we might actually succeed. A giddy feeling swirled in my chest. Light pooled at my fingertips in a sort of excited anticipation.

Leif shoved his chair back. "What in the Fates' names is that?"

"Oh, right." I smiled, waving my hand around as light formed in an arc above my head. "I have magic now."

"Well then," Leif said, laughing. "While you never needed magic to be a queen for me, it looks like we've got another ace up our sleeve to put you back in your palace, Your Majesty."

I nodded, closing my eyes as his words and the knowledge of how much work he'd done truly hit me. "You've exponentially improved our odds of winning, Leif. I don't know how to thank you for what you risked in our absence."

He moved to kneel in front of me with a hand over his heart. "I've told you before, and I'll say it again. You see us, Lana, all of us. Not just the nobles, not just the wealthy, but you see *us*. The lesser Fae. Being in your inner circle is a privilege I will never take for granted. I saw a small chance to make a difference, and I took it. But it was because you've given us direction and hope for what we could be under your reign."

My heart burst, gratitude threatening to consume me on the spot. I swallowed, not even sure what to say as I let his words sink in. They were words Ian had said, and Kade. Storm and Corbin too. I let them soak into my soul, preparing me for the role I must play in this battle ahead. I would make a difference. But first, I needed to take back my home.

"If you ever call yourself lesser Fae again, I'll punch you

square in the jaw. My right hook has improved too. I might have learned some new moves while I've been gone," I joked, tugging on Leif's arm to stand. "But otherwise, you're right. Let's go destroy Andras and start building toward our future."

CHAPTER 21

LANA

B y the following morning, the network of whispers trickled throughout the city, and those willing to fight for the resistance filled Dukes Pub.

Carefully crafted movements by Tommy's crew gained them safe passage through the streets, while the dark ones moved about unaware on their daily patrols.

After leaving Leif yesterday morning, we returned to wait for the army in Eomer Forest, where we spent the past few hours finalizing the details of our attack with Kade and the others. Our plans hinged on him being able to play the part of a dark one. He'd serve as the distraction so that a handful of the resistance could make their way to the city walls to open the front gates for our army. Leif would already be inside the palace rallying others loyal to our cause.

Then, we'd have to get through the palace gates before taking our shot at Andras.

I prayed to the Fates this worked, and we weren't leading our people to certain death.

With our plans in place, Ian and I returned to Dukes Pub. Ian stood next to me on the bar top overlooking the tavern filled with Fae. We'd just revealed everything we knew to the rebels gathered there. Mysthaven, dark ones, Thames—they needed to know all of it. The time had finally come to take action against those who'd done wrong by our world.

"Does everyone understand their assignment?" He folded his arms across his chest. "If there are questions or uncertainties, speak up now. Once this plan is in motion, we can't stop it—there is no turning back."

Murmurs of both men and women echoed throughout the room in agreement.

A voice from the back of the room yelled, "For Brookmere." The crowd became rowdy, cheering. Their love for their kingdom clearly evident by the rising noise. Fear had no place here, not yet at least. Instead, the Fae unleashed their excitement. I knew this feeling. I'd felt it myself.

There's something about being beaten down for so long that festers inside. I spent years battling it after Andras's torture. When we started the Hidden Henchman and I knew how much of an impact I'd made on my people, things changed. The excitement of proving Andras wrong, overcoming those feelings of worthlessness—all of it culminated with the knowledge that I was fighting back.

The Fae gathered here had the same energy about them. The smile spreading over my face wasn't just for me. It was for them as well.

I held up my hand to silence their celebration and waited for quiet to fill the room. "My people, this fight is not just about Ellevail, or Brookmere, or a crown stolen from its rightful queen in violent betrayal." All eyes were on me, but for the first time, I wasn't afraid to display the confidence of a queen. Instead, I allowed the knowledge that these were my people to lead and my title as the true queen to resonate within me. "No, this is for our world, for our very way of life. For all people, both in this kingdom and in Mysthaven. This is for Atheria. For our home."

I could sense Ian standing with pride beside me, his hand

gently placed on the small of my back in encouragement. My words once again brought a chorus of cheers.

Standing straighter, I placed my hand over my heart. "I will not ask you to fight this alone. I will stand by your side. I will fight beside you. Never again will we let evil walk this earth and threaten to destroy us. We are stronger than any darkness, and together, with your help, we will conquer evil for good."

"For Atheria!" a man shouted to the left of me, and the others responded the same.

My heart pounded as loud as the cheers surrounding me. This was truly what being the leader of Brookmere entailed. At least, the Brookmere I envisioned. Protecting and helping those who couldn't defend themselves. Standing up for justice and equity for all people. Greed had no place in our world, especially the kingdom I would lead after this was over. Lesser Fae or nobility, all would have a chance to be treated with fairness and respect.

"We move out in five minutes," Ian bellowed over the raucous crowd.

The Fae shouted out once more before talking among themselves. Some moved to fill a waterskin or grab something quick to eat from bowls of fruit strewn on tables.

While an excited energy thrummed close to the surface, I couldn't help but want to simultaneously throw up.

"You okay, Lan?" Ian asked as he helped me down off the bar.

Grabbing his hand, I jumped to the tavern floor. "I'm fine —nervous, but fine."

Ian held me in an embrace for a moment. "It's normal to feel that way before a battle." A twinkle sparkled in his eye though. He was born for this moment. He thrived in an environment pitting him against others. Fates, he was raised like that as a guard. He knew my insecurities though. He had been there too many times when I thought I would fail. "Just remember *who* you are fighting for. *What* you are fighting for, and you can't go wrong." He chuckled. "You know, everything you just said."

"For freedom," I whispered, and Ian responded with nothing but a smile.

An hour later, I crept down a side alley after overseeing the groups of fighters leaving Dukes Pub. Using the timed rotations from Leif, we moved in small groups toward the main city gates. We had one goal: take down as many dark ones as possible as our army flooded Ellevail to storm the palace.

It may have been a gamble to move in small groups, but the less time Andras had to coordinate a response, the better off we would be. I held Apollo in my hand. If I had the opportunity to release the darkness from anyone infected, I would. But if I couldn't… Well, I'd resigned myself to the fact that this was war. I would do what I must to protect my kingdom.

Two others traveled with Ian and me as we made our way toward the city center and closer to the gates. An eerie sense of foreboding hovered around us as the sun climbed higher in the sky. Sweat formed on the small of my back, dampening my tunic.

Clashing metal shifted my attention, and my heart stopped. Another group must have already encountered dark ones in the street, but the noise would draw too much attention. We needed to move.

We paused at the intersection; I knew Millie's Café should be on the next street over. Ian poked his head around to check our surroundings. "Two dark ones are coming—no, three. Get ready."

Slowly, each of the Fae with us withdrew their swords and

lined themselves up in a row. I followed suit and was last in line, farthest away from the corner. My cloak covered my hair, not wanting to give away my identity just yet.

"Three, two—" Ian whispered.

Before he could get to one, the group of dark ones rounded the corner and yelped in surprise. Ian sliced his sword through the stomach of the first dark one. The others leapt back but quickly regained their footing, bracing themselves for the fight.

Two on four, this should be easy.

The two other Fae with us possessed earth magic and sent vines shooting up from the ground, wrapping up the legs of the dark ones and securing them in place despite their feeble attempts to escape. Their bodies twitched in protest as the thorns pierced their skin, drawing blood the harder they fought.

Tommy's fighters were ruthless. Exactly what we needed.

"You'll never win." The smaller dark one grimaced. "We're too strong. There are too many of us."

"We'll see about that." I approached the two, Apollo in hand, and proceeded to draw blood from one's arm. The darkened liquid dripped down to his wrist from the cut as he yelled in pain. The inky mist leaving his body sent my hope soaring. His body slumped forward in relief. Ian refused to take any chances and struck him in the back of his head, knocking him out cold. He still lived though, free from the darkness. Hopefully when he awoke he would merely have a killer headache.

The other dark one still fought. Harder and harder he tried to escape, when a caw from the air distracted my companions, and their vines lost some of their grip. It gave the dark one just enough of an opportunity to grab his dagger and cut away the rest of the vines.

"Focus," Ian hissed at our fighters.

This dark one was stronger than his unconscious friend, so

I stepped back, putting some space between my opponent and me. Ian circled around, and soon we had him cornered. There was nowhere for him to go.

His eyes bulged, and despite the defeat swirling in them, he lunged forward, trying to stab Ian with his blade. He didn't stand a chance as Ian rammed his sword clean through his chest, and he fell to the ground.

"That was a close one," I murmured to Ian, who looked none too pleased.

He turned to our companions. "Don't make the same mistake again. You may bear witness to any number of untold creatures in this world during these battles. Do not let them distract you from your mission. Your life may depend on it."

They eyed each other warily, before nodding, mumbling apologies under their breath, and proceeded down the street. Ian and I followed closely behind.

Soon, we approached the large town square, normally used as a bustling marketplace filled with joyous laughter, but not today. The winds swirled around us, hot and angry. When we first arrived, Ellevail felt too still. Today, nature seemed agitated with a vengeance, enraged by the interlopers in our capital.

A rumbling over the ground stopped me in my tracks, and a cloud of shadows loomed ahead, distracting me from our mission. The sound of Fae running refocused my attention on the task at hand. I forced myself to move toward the commotion. Ian remained at my side as we navigated the last few streets and faced the gathering group of dark ones.

Ian pulled us under a nearby window box filled with wilting red roses.

As we settled ourselves in the flower bed beneath, I felt Kade's shadows swirl up my leg before he came into view on a small platform in the middle of the square.

"You're here. We missed you. Stay hidden, we will protect you."

"I missed you too." It took every bit of determination to

keep my light within me and not allow it to greet the shadows. If our plan were to work, they needed to behave and stay hidden.

As quickly as they came, the shadows left me, continuing to entice the dark ones, inching them closer to where Kade stood. He commanded everyone's attention from his platform.

His mussed hair fluttered in the wind as his darkened eyes searched the crowd of dark ones who answered his call.

"Step forward, my brothers in darkness," he bellowed to the group of evil beings. "Closer, I have a message for you from our leader." The dark ones crowded even closer to the platform. Their bodies twitching in a wave amongst the sea of evil. "Thames has sent me to you. It is time to take all of Brookmere. It is rightfully ours. Come join me as the soldiers of Atheria. Your master has commanded it."

Dark ones continued to flood the area, striding toward the square with their eyes fixated on Kade. They seemed entranced by his calling. His shadows pushed them forward, moving them as if rounding up cattle for slaughter. While I knew Kade allowed the darkness to surface in order to play the part of faithful servant, there was still a part of me desperate to run to him and let our magic mix together to squash the darkness back to the depths of where he hid it.

"The remaining Fae against us must turn or die. They have no right to this kingdom. They mean to hold us back, to destroy us. We must restore Atheria to its rightful ruler."

Kade clenched his hand at his side as he spoke, his eyes shifting back and forth from grey to black. My poor mate. He hated the darkness inside of him, yet he willingly accepted his role to help start our battle.

Letting the darkness within him creep to the surface, even momentarily, was a huge risk, but one that we had to take. My presence was nonnegotiable since I was the only one capable of banishing the darkness. It already took so much to bring him back to the here and now, but I was confident in my ability do so. My magic practically begged to be released, to save him. I wish there had been another clear way to accomplish our siege.

But we'd gone over so many strategies. No others were plausible.

Kade had been given a mission by Thames. He needed to capture me and bring me back to Mysthaven. If any dark ones were connected to Thames, it would look like Kade was still fulfilling his mission. Still controllable.

The minutes crept by, but a shift in the winds made me take notice. Approximately fifty dark ones now stood in the town square, and Kade's shadows grew exponentially. The clouds of shadows grew from the ground up, crawling to cover the dark ones entirely.

"Are you ready to fight for your leader?" Kade shouted as he stepped down off the platform and walked toward the group. Sweat beaded on his brow; the physical toll it took to only allow the darkness to simmer at the surface and not fully take control was exorbitant.

"Yes," the dark ones shouted their answers. "We will fight."

Kade smiled, the sinister smile that sent goose bumps up my spine.

Ian whispered in my ear, "He really is terrifying when he looks like that."

I didn't bother responding and kept my eyes fixated on Kade as he walked through the crowd, greeting the dark ones as if they were friends.

I wanted to vomit.

The shadows finally reached the top of each of the dark ones, now entirely out of view, and I couldn't help but hold my breath.

In an instant, the shadows responded to Kade's command and cracked the necks of every single dark one. Their bodies fell to the ground with a loud *thud*.

The shadows dissipated, returning to Kade's side, but my stomach dropped when I finally saw his face again.

His eyes were blacker than night. The darkness within him was feeding off the mass amount of death he'd just inflicted.

"Kade!" I jumped up, running to him, my light eager to touch him once more and rid that evil from his body. "I'm here."

His shadows immediately extended toward me and swirled around us. I could hear Ian shouting from behind me, but I ignored him. I needed to rescue Kade from his own mind.

I leapt into his arms, touching any part of his body I could, and called upon my light magic to flow into him. It was so easy with his shadows there, waiting for me. As simple as breathing in and out.

"You are okay," I reminded him. "I'm here. Come back to me."

My light glowed around both of us, and slowly, Kade's eyes returned to their stormy grey as relief filled his gaze.

"You will always be my savior, Illiana." Kade wrapped me in a tight embrace. "You have saved me in so many ways, so many times."

Looking up at him, I smiled and stood on my tiptoes, softly placing my lips against his. "I'd save you a thousand more times if it means I get to have you as my partner. I am forever yours, Kade Blackthorn. We are stronger than the darkness within us."

CHAPTER 22
LANA

The distraction worked perfectly.

Not only had Kade eliminated a large portion of the dark ones remaining in Ellevail, but our army now easily marched through the city.

Now, we stood outside the final gates enclosing the palace. It wasn't often growing up that my parents closed these gates. But now? They were locked, covered in chains. Bushes of thorny shrubs lined the perimeter of the wall, daring anyone to risk its wrath if they tried to climb in. Andras could try all he wanted to keep us out, but he would not succeed.

I would return to my home through its front door and reclaim it as its rightful heir. There would be no sneaking in through the back or hiding in the shadows.

We split our forces between the front and the back of the palace. Storm, Jax, Corbin, and Raya took half of the army around to the other side, while Ian, Kade, and I remained out front. Leif had already returned to the palace, tricking the guards with his fake tattoo to let him through. Hopefully he'd had enough time to rally those who remained loyal to me and prepare them for the fight ahead. It was a risky move, but he was determined to gather as many allies as possible.

As our army lined up, Ian soared above Ellevail, surveying the scene from the sky and preparing to report back on his findings. He disappeared from our sight for several long minutes, no doubt alerting Storm, Raya, Corbin, and Jax of what lay ahead.

The evening rays of sunshine slowly dipped below the horizon, and despite the summer heat, an icy breeze swept through the air.

Assessing the entrance to the palace filled me with sorrow. My family prided ourselves on our gardens; the landscape surrounding my home was always warm and inviting. Lush and vibrant, Fae traveled from across the kingdom to witness its beauty. But now? Now it appeared dark and uninviting. It had lost all its vibrance and what remained was a threatening feeling. A place I wouldn't want to be caught in the dark.

Except that was exactly what was happening.

Storm's fire magic would certainly be useful right now to just burn all these thorny terrors to ash, but it didn't matter. Fates only knew what they were dealing with. Storm's group would have to enter through the kitchens and work their way up from the lower level of the palace.

There were only so many places for Andras to hide.

Ian's hawk form appeared once more and circled above us for several minutes before he descended, landing a few feet away. Running his hands through his golden hair, he jogged toward us. "The dark ones are stationed at all the guard posts and remain hidden along the walls of the perimeter. They're waiting for us."

My heartbeat quickened. "We will not go down without a fight." The magic now coursing through my veins clamored to be released, but I would wait. I'd hold on to my secret as long as I could, not wanting Andras to have time to further prepare. He would underestimate me just like he always had. "The earth Fae can bring down the gate with their magic."

Kade chuckled. "A wonderful thought, my queen." His

shadows pooled at his feet. "But I think my shadows can unlock those chains quicker than the earth Fae. We can conserve their magic for the battle."

Ian nodded in agreement. "We want them to hold onto as much of their energy as possible. We likely have a long night ahead of us." He paused. "Are you sure this is how you want to do this? We could sneak in through our hidden entrances, just like we used to."

I shook my head. "This is my home—our home. It ends tonight."

Ian bowed his head. "As you wish it, Your Highness."

Rolling my eyes, I shoved him in the shoulder before he threw me a wink. "Guards are lined most heavily around the throne room from what I could see through the windows," Ian said. "That should be our goal."

I nodded. "On your orders, Captain." I smiled at my best friend. My rock. He went to step away to voice our plan, but I leaned forward, grabbing his arm before crushing him in a hug. "Let's win back our home."

"I love you, Lan," Ian whispered, squeezing me back just as hard as I did him.

"I love you."

He pulled away and turned toward our forces. "We march for the throne room," Ian shouted. "The dark ones are likely stronger there, but we'll meet them the entire trek through the palace. Work together and stay alert."

The instructions passed among the front lines of soldiers, on and on toward the back.

Chants rose up, battle cries filled with vengeance echoing throughout Ellevail. Our army stood tall, weapons at the ready.

Kalliah appeared by my side, panting. "Just in time," she said, drawing her blade from a sheath at her side.

"What are you doing here, Kalliah?" I gasped. "I thought you were staying at Dukes Pub to help with the injured."

Kalliah chuffed. "There is no way I am letting my best friend fight this battle on her own. This is my home too, and besides now that I know Leif is alive and well, I refuse to be without him any longer."

I hugged my friend hard. Kalliah had been with me through so much and was one of the only friends I ever had until now. That was, until I found my mate and those from Mysthaven I now loved like family. She was right though, and as much as I wanted everyone to be safe and away from this fight, they had as much right to be here as I did. "Together, then."

She nodded once before standing beside me, dagger in hand.

Kade's shadows slithered up my leg and formed their protective armor around my chest. It felt like home, and the light within me purred in response. With my shadow armor in place, Kade sent ribbons of shadows toward the chained gates. They glided silently along the grass and up the pathway until reaching their destination.

One by one the locks holding the chains in place were released and landed soundlessly on the ground.

"Fates, if you ever heard my call, now would be a really great time to listen," I prayed. "Please protect my friends, my people. Our world depends on it."

Even with the chill in the air, a warmth skittered across my arms. The wind danced around me, into my hair, before leaving again to blow across the rest of us. Nature's embrace, its encouragement. It had to be. I inhaled, readying myself to lead and fight for my kingdom, no matter the cost.

The gates to the palace creaked open and I shouted, holding Apollo above my head, backed by the voices of an army a hundred strong. We marched up the remaining hill. A rallying cry sounded, and the clang of metal on metal finally filled the air. The dark ones rushed toward our group of Fae and attacked with a fervor unlike anything I had ever seen before.

Leif was right. These dark ones were strong, faster. Much more like the group we'd encountered in Eomer Forest before the marriage trials.

Earth Fae sent vines to wrap around the legs of the dark ones, tripping them over rocks protruding from the ground. Torrents of wind whipped around us as the air Fae attempted to knock the dark ones off balance. But with each attack, they countered, sending rocks and vines of their own flying.

Everyone around me used their magic in ways I had only dreamed of. The sheer magnitude of what these Fae pulled off when working together astounded me. My light flickered inside of me, pleading for release, but I kept it locked away. For now.

I ran to help one of our soldiers laying on the ground, overtaken by a dark one.

"Don't expect mercy from me," the dark one seethed as he inched the dagger closer to the soldier's throat. "Your death is my victory."

"Not today, asshole." I stabbed the dark one in the back. An inky mist left his body, but no sense of relief graced his expression as he tipped to the side, rolling once down the hill. Unadulterated anger lined every wrinkle.

There wasn't time to think about what it all meant. There were more people who needed saving and more evil to kill.

It didn't take long to dispose of the dark ones in the courtyard, due to the sheer numbers we possessed in our army. The fighting ceased, but the lawn now looked like a sea of dead bodies. Some of which were our own. I closed my eyes, swallowing before setting my sights on the palace doors up the winding hill. Their burial would be another day. Once Ellevail was ours, they would be honored.

"Come on, Little Rebel," Kade called. "Let's go take back your throne."

Vengeance lapped at my mind, surging, fueling my need to win, knowing we were close. "Let's go."

Before entering the palace, Ian and Kade instructed our remaining forces to form groups and search the outer hallways and rooms while we focused on a direct route to the throne room.

Walking up the entrance stairs, my pace slowed, breathing in the scent of where I grew up. It didn't smell the same. It didn't feel the same.

"Andras," I bellowed in the hall as I finally made my way into the grand foyer. "Come out, you coward."

"Come on, Lan," Ian urged. "We need to keep moving."

We ran down the halls, getting closer to the back of the palace. We could hear fighting, so the others must be getting close to joining us.

Rounding the corner before the halls closest to my room, a scream caused my heart to stutter.

Kalliah ran toward the fight on the stairs. Leif looked up, noticing her, and the sight of her charged his movements. He slammed his blade into the dark one's neck, pushing him forward and tossing his body down the stairs. He didn't even look behind him to see where the enemy landed, choosing instead to sprint toward Kalliah.

Leif dropped his sword, grabbed her by the face, and kissed her deeply. She jumped, wrapping her legs around his waist and kissing him back, scolding him and confessing her feelings all at once. It was almost like the two of them forgot they were in the middle of a battle.

"Save it for later, you two," I yelled, as five more dark ones descended the stairs. "We're not done here yet."

Kade rolled his eyes as he sent torrents of shadows up the stairs and ended the lives of the first three. Corbin and Storm, who had come running after the dark ones down the stairs, quickly disposed of the other two.

"Finally decided to show up, then," Ian said to Storm.

Storm snorted. "Just needed to take a nice little stroll through the gardens first. It was getting a bit boring waiting for you lot."

Kalliah and Leif returned to my side, holding hands and grinning.

"Ian thinks they're holed up in the throne room. We go there next," I insisted.

We moved as a unit down the corridors, carefully making our way closer to our destination. Corbin, Leif, and Ian had been working together for years. I had some time with all of them too, but the way we were able to move together, watching each other's backs and eliminating anyone coming into our path with ease and precision astounded me.

For as much as I'd cursed the Fates growing up, I couldn't help but wonder if they'd created every moment of my past to lead me to these people. To guide me to right now.

Moments before we reached the entrance to the throne room, the doors slammed open and Casimir appeared with a group of dark ones, ready to fight.

The evil expression on his face sent chills down my spine, his cackling laugh filling the air. Gems glittered on gloves adorning his hands, and he began siphoning magic from a dark one next to him. "Get them," he yelled to the others as the dark one he'd drained slumped to the floor.

"Not today, Casimir," I shouted back.

These dark ones were unreasonably strong. Their magic clearly amplified in some way. As one approached me, I noticed a gem of his own sewed onto his shirt. Casimir was siphoning magic from those who had fallen into all the living dark ones, creating a more powerful army. I shuddered at what that kind of power might accomplish. Just another reason for this to end now.

Ian and Storm fought back-to-back battling three dark ones, while Kade and his shadows took on two more.

Kalliah and Leif engaged with a dark one behind me. My

sole focus, however, was on Casimir. He would die by my hand for everything he did to Ian and for his role in perpetuating the darkness and evil growing in our lands.

Casimir sneered, a hint of fear flickering on his features as if he realized how outnumbered he was and that his dark ones were being overpowered. His face turned ashen. The others were so engrossed in their battles, they didn't realize he was going to try to run.

Turning away from us, he sprinted down the hall, and I alerted the others, "He's going to escape!"

Corbin, who stood closest to me, took off after Casimir while I followed in pursuit.

"Come back here and fight me, Casimir," I shouted down the hall.

Casimir glanced back at us, but instead of fear, his resolve returned, and a smile spread over his face. A second later, pounding feet joined the chase, and more dark ones appeared from a staff door hidden in the wall behind him.

"Attack," he laughed.

"Go," Kade shouted from behind me, his shadows lashing out toward the new attackers, buying Corbin and me time to get around them.

We couldn't let him get away, but Casimir skirted down another hallway. I'd never been so annoyed at how big our palace was until now. Corbin ran faster than me, speeding ahead to round the corner. I was out of breath but remained focused on my target. I couldn't stop until we caught Casimir.

A dark one lunged at my side, as I dodged his attack, barely rounding the corner without careening into the wall.

An anguished cry filled the air. I regained my footing before stopping short, staring in horror as my weary muscles tensed.

Casimir stood in front of a fresh wave of dark ones.

He looked me in the eye with a wickedly triumphant smile

as he yanked his sword from where it gleamed straight through Corbin's chest.

CHAPTER 23

LANA

The battle around me disappeared from my senses as my chest constricted.

My heart dropped, stealing my breath with it as I watched Corbin's body fall to the ground at Casimir's feet.

"No!" I screamed. A dark one jabbed a sword at me and I spun, slashing him across the throat before shoving his body out of my way to get to my friend.

"You're okay, you're okay," I chanted over and over as shock took hold of me. I couldn't accept what logic told me. I wouldn't accept it as true.

Casimir tilted his head back, laughing gleefully. The light inside me pulled taught, forcing me to stop before reaching Corbin's body.

He's not moving. Fates, he's not moving. He's—

My knees shook.

Move. This time it wasn't my own mind thinking the words. It was my light. *Move now. Kill. Casimir is ours.*

My focus pulled away from Corbin and shifted to Casimir. My magic swelled with power, halting the pain just long enough to push me forward.

Casimir stuck out his hand and crooked his fingers, beckoning me. He didn't know my secret though.

But he would.

The light flooded my body, filling every part of me.

I screamed, the raw anguish bursting from my throat as I sprinted toward him and threw my hands onto Casimir's chest.

I let everything out, feeling the light obediently pour from my body. Every part of my magic flowed from my hands into Casimir.

As it flared from me, his eyes widened. "What? What is this?" He tried to take a step back, to push me away, but my light was stronger. It had hooked itself into him, crawling through every part of his vile body.

He screamed, unable to move. Unable to escape.

Nothing could stop me, my light growing brighter, even more intense than I'd seen it before. I vaguely heard voices calling my name, but nothing mattered in this moment other than eliminating Casimir and saving Corbin.

The torrent of magic rushing from my palms burned, and I shouted against the pain, until Casimir's entire body was shrouded in my light.

Let go now, my light whispered in a soft, soothing voice.

I obeyed, stumbling back as the energy encasing Casimir inflated once, like a breath, before disappearing, exposing his dead body on the palace floor.

Shivering, I looked around and noticed all of the dark ones on the ground. Dead.

I knew I should feel shocked, or at the very least, some sort of guilt. Instead, all I had was a hollow ache in my chest.

I fell to my knees and crawled to Corbin's body.

I reached him, my vision blurring with tears, and brought my hands to his chest. "Corbin," I urged. "Open your eyes." I shook him. "Come on, wake up."

Panic rose in my throat, and I cried his name louder, shaking him like I could somehow bring him back.

"Lana." Kade's breath brushed against my ear as his shadows and arms wrapped around me from behind. A few dark strands lifted to Corbin's neck, resting on his pulse. *This is good. The shadows will give us hope.*

Kade sighed in defeat. "Sweetheart," he murmured in my ear. "He's gone, my love."

"No." I shook my head as if keeping the words from my ears would make them less true.

"He's gone, Lana." Kade's shadows rushed around me, ardently attempting to bring me comfort.

"No," I said louder as my body trembled. "He can't be."

Kade's hands covered mine, gently pulling them away from where I clutched Corbin's shirt. "I'm so sorry."

I let out an anguished cry, and though Kade held my hands in his, I leaned forward, lying my head on Corbin's chest.

"Please," I begged. "Please, I can't lose anyone else."

Kade stroked my hair, and I turned my head toward him. "I didn't get to say goodbye," I whispered. "I never get to say goodbye."

The fighting around us must have ended, because I didn't hear the sound of clanging blades anymore.

It didn't matter though. I couldn't look away from my friend's face. The friend who consistently lifted me up with respect. The friend who'd built me the garden of my dreams simply because I mentioned wanting to experiment with flowers. A person who believed in me unconditionally, no matter how unworthy I felt.

I brushed some of his sweat-slicked hair back with shaking hands. Leif fell to the floor in front of me, shock on his face as he tilted his head back, looking to the ceiling and crying out.

Ian slumped down next, kneeling as he reached out to

touch Corbin's neck like he needed to feel for himself that he was gone.

"Get Maria," he shouted, turning like there was a servant around to give orders to. "She's here, someone get the healer."

His hand trembled above Corbin's neck.

"Ian," I choked out.

Our eyes met for only a second before Ian shook his head like he didn't believe me. "Someone get a healer!" he screamed, his voice cracking on the word "healer."

Leif brought a hand to Ian's shoulder. "He's gone, Ian."

Ian looked at me again, devastation draining his face of color. I pulled my hands from Kade, throwing myself on Corbin.

"I'm sorry, I'm so sorry," I said under my breath.

Ian moved his hand onto Corbin's head and closed his eyes, letting his own tears fall.

The silence only lasted a few moments.

"Ian." Storm's voice was rough, strained. "I'm sorry, but we've got to keep fighting. Andras—"

Ian trembled, inhaling sharply. His pained eyes met mine briefly again before he turned away. He brushed his face on his shoulder and nodded, rising to his feet. "Storm's right." Ian cleared his throat. "We have to find Andras before he tries to escape. This ends now."

I stared at the two of them, hating that they were right and that we would have to wait to grieve Corbin's death.

Kade helped me to my feet before addressing everyone. "We finish this. Corbin will not have died in vain."

"We can't leave him here," I said.

"I'll move his body to a safe location," Leif choked out through his own pain, settling on the floor beside Corbin and taking his hand. "Go. Go quickly and finish this."

I nodded, looking over Corbin's too still form, and silently appealed to my light to take away some of the pain threatening to pull me under. But it remained in a state of recovery. The blast of light killing Casimir had drained the majority of my magical abilities.

I had no idea how long it would take them to come back.

Kade cupped my face in his hands. "I'm with you."

I inhaled a deep breath, the need for revenge taking over as my body quaked with fury. "We find him. We capture him. His death will not be quick," I instructed those around me. Their faces said everything.

We were all in agreement.

Andras's hands may not have taken our friend, but his actions did. For that and every other atrocity he'd brought upon us, his time ended now.

We ran back toward the throne room, where we thought Andras would be hiding.

Kade's shadows whipped around us, flying forward, searching for the coward. We ran harder, faster, not passing any guards or dark ones, until we turned down the corridor where my parents' room had been.

A group of twenty guards stood outside their doors.

Andras had fled to *their* rooms. He'd been living here in this palace, where my parents should be.

My light ignited once more, raging inside of me, and gained some semblance of energy, driving my desire for vengeance.

"He's mine," I hissed out.

Ian called my name, but I ignored him. The others followed closely behind. Kade's shadows understood exactly what I needed as they parted the guards for me, forcing them to the side in a wave of shadowy mist.

I bolted between them as the sound of fighting started behind me. I slammed into the locked door, banging on it for a second before holding my hands out. Guided by pure instinct, I poured my magic into the handle, forcing it to unlock. The doors swung open, and I barged into the room.

Andras was dressing himself in his magical gem-covered

robe. The one I recognized from the clearing. He turned, grinning at me. "I knew you'd come. You never could stay out of trouble."

I drew Apollo from where it rested at my thigh. There would be no mercy, no trying to get the darkness out of him. There would only be death.

After every person I loved got a chance to inflict their own punishment on his evil soul.

"I suggest you not underestimate me."

He tilted his head back, cackling, before releasing a gust of wind that drove his own dagger swiftly and forcefully toward my chest. I jerked to the side, but the blade skimmed over the shadow armor protecting my shoulders.

"Still as weak as ever."

I forced my magic to stay hidden, wanting to use it to my advantage to surprise him and drink in the shock on his face right before I captured him.

"Is that all you've got?" I taunted. "Lame insults and a blade not even able to penetrate armor?"

He hovered a hand over one of the crystals and disappeared. I turned, whipping my head around, finally realizing he'd materialized behind me. I ducked away from his outstretched hands reaching toward my neck.

A flicker of annoyance contoured his features. He pulled out another blade, spinning it in his fingers so fast it blurred.

I might be forced to call my magic earlier than I wanted.

His gaze settled on me as he jabbed forward. I blocked the first two hits, only to have him catch me in the side with his fist, just above where the armor stopped.

I wheezed but held my ground, keeping his blade from my chest.

My arms shook, and another stone on his magical robe flared. He shoved me harder, his strength impossibly formidable. My light coiled inside of me, recharged enough and desperate to be set free. Andras was using someone else's Fae strength, stolen and siphoned by Casimir, no doubt.

He slid forward and knocked me to the floor as my shaking arms desperately tried to keep him at bay.

"Your mother wasn't even this pathetic when she died," he gritted out. "She fought her hardest, but she was no match for me. Queen of Brookmere, ha! More like queen of nothing."

"Liar," I screamed, my light thrashing inside of me. I contained my magic, letting it continue to grow for the right moment.

"Bested by a mere advisor."

I screamed against the pain. I couldn't hold him back much longer.

"Scream all you like. The melody of it has soothed me to sleep for years." He licked his lips, and in a rush of pure rage for everything he'd done to me, I let my light out.

The magic blasted from me, sending Andras flying backward as it surrounded his body with its power.

His eyes widened in shock as I jumped to my feet, wielding my dagger again.

"How does it feel knowing you spent years trying to get this magic out of me and never succeeded? You're the pathetic one. The weak one." I held up my palm as a ball of light swirled in my hand like one of Storm's fireballs.

"It's not possible," he snarled.

Instead of responding, I rushed toward him, flinging the ball of light in his direction. He flinched as Apollo glowed and I struck my mark, slicing his leg. A thin wisp of darkness slithered out, but nothing of substance. It reminded me too much of how Kade's darkness wouldn't come out.

Andras countered my attack slower, lacking the strength he'd displayed a few moments before.

"Guess your stolen magic doesn't last too long, does it?" I slashed out again, trying to cut him with my blade, only for him to dodge my attack.

"You will regret your undeserved confidence."

Shadows raced into the room and rushed around Andras.

"No, he's mine," I shouted.

Kade strode into the room, letting his shadows fall away as he circled us.

"Someone is in trouble." Andras shook his finger at Kade. "If you think he hasn't figured out you've gone rogue, you're just as dumb as she is."

"*Someone* certainly feels powerful being Thames's lapdog," Kade huffed, leaning against the dresser.

A sadness gripped me as I looked at Kade here in my parents' room, knowing we'd never all be together, that they wouldn't see what the two of us had accomplished. It quickly morphed into fury as I glared at Andras. His grin exposing his complete lack of remorse.

His actions, bending my parents' will with his mind magic, torturing me, torturing Ian, poisoning my father, killing my mother. All of his actions hurt those I loved. He was the reason for all their deaths. For taking them from me, never allowing them to see me with my mate or to watch me grow into the queen they'd raised me to be. It was all because of *him*.

My breaths came heavy, heaving through me as I channeled my rage, my heartbreak, my *grief* into this moment.

"I'm not going to kill you yet," I gulped down a breath, steadying my voice. "You will face worse than death."

"Bold words for a woman who is losing." Andras charged me, and though Kade stiffened, he didn't interfere. My lips tugged into a smirk as all of my focus homed in on Andras's movements.

He gave himself away more than he realized, his eyes traveling in the direction he planned to move. Using that to my advantage, I blocked two of his attacks before kneeing him in the groin. He grunted, and his hesitation allowed me to stab him in the side. Right where he'd stabbed me all those years ago. Another small burst of darkness hissed out of him.

"Who is losing now?" I asked, shoving the blade deeper.

I leashed my anger the moment I felt his slick blood on my hand. I didn't want him dead yet. No, I had a much better idea. One where we would all get out the hate for him that we needed to release.

I glanced at Kade. "Could you make sure he doesn't move?"

Kade walked lazily over to me, his eyes raking over me as desire thickened the air between us. He always did love when I wielded my blades so furiously. "What would you have me do with him, Little Rebel?" Pride made his voice swell.

I smiled at him before staring into Andras's pained face. His glare remained, but the arrogant facade cracked, and a slight trace of fear widened his gaze.

"Take him to his favorite place," I instructed. "The dungeons."

CHAPTER 24
LANA

I stood in front of the palace gates, taking in the crowds of Fae growing with each minute.

My people needed to be addressed, they deserved answers.

I may have rallied the rebels in Dukes Pub, but this would serve as the first time I addressed Ellevail on my own. No guidance from my mother or father. Just me.

My lip trembled as my body tensed. The thoughts of unworthiness, of not being ready—they weren't gone, they just lingered at the back of my mind.

I was stronger than those dark thoughts, but I could feel them there. If I succumbed, if I allowed them a voice, they could easily draw me under.

But there wasn't time for that, and I couldn't afford to go backward.

"Breathe," Kade whispered beside me. "Just breathe, Illiana."

His shadows caressed the back of my neck. My chest loosened, warming at his voice, his touch.

I am Illiana Dresden, and I am stronger than the darkness within me.

Ian jogged up the pathway, nodding. "The nobles are coming." His face betrayed his slight disgust. "Most were in their homes, drinking and eating as if there hadn't been evil taking over the city."

"They'll listen or they'll lose their standing," I said harshly. While I'd be diplomatic, the time for acting as if they were untouchable simply because magic burned stronger in their veins ended now.

This marked the start of our new kingdom.

From the upper area of Ellevail, the nobles strode forward, observing the other Fae gathered in front of me, making their way to the front of the group like they belonged there. Entitled assholes.

They better get used to mingling more, or this will be a very uncomfortable life for them.

I spotted Storm, moving forward through the crowds. He bowed his head as he approached.

"I swear if you bow one more time, I'll throw my magic at your head," I whispered under my breath.

He smirked. "I have to show you respect, whether you like it or not. Everyone is watching." He glanced over his shoulder. "This is all the Fae we could find in the streets. Tommy and some of the others helped on their end of town as well."

"You're up, Lan." Ian nudged my shoulder with his.

I sucked in a sharp breath and took a step forward. The murmurs of the crowd faded, silencing as they waited for me to speak.

"I know many of you believe I fled after the trials," I started. "That I ran away when Brookmere needed me most." Swallowing down my anxiety, I stood straighter. "This is not the case. I was taken against my will, though I know now it was for my own protection. Since I left, I've been gathering information on the darkness spreading across our land. Andras lied to you. He manipulated his role as advisor and used his mind magic against our king and queen. He murdered them."

Kade flinched next to me, but what I spoke was the truth. If it hadn't been for Andras, my father wouldn't have been ill and been faced with the decision to die rather than allow his magic to be stolen by Andras in his quest for power. Andras killed my father—not Kade.

"He is not the mastermind though. A thousand years ago, our ancestors trapped a Fae named Thames in a void between our worlds. Brookmere stood beside a kingdom called Mysthaven, both kingdoms making up our true world, Atheria."

Gasps spread through the crowd as voices picked up. I raised my hands and they all fell silent. "Thames is the one behind Andras's rise to power. We have captured Andras, and he will be held accountable for his crimes. However, Thames is still out there with one goal: to take over and destroy our world. He will spread the darkness you've seen taking over our neighbors and lands and use it for his own gain."

I inhaled. "A brave group of Fae has been working inside the city walls to try to overthrow Andras. It is because of them we were able to succeed in capturing him." Kade's shadows curled along my palm as if holding my hand. "Now a greater battle is upon us. A war not just for our kingdom but for our world.

"We've been gathering those willing to fight for our home. Those who will stand against Thames to defeat him once and for all, but we need more of you. We need to be one people, standing together in the face of evil."

"Why should we believe you?" A noble toward the front of the group sneered.

Kade's shadows tensed by my side, but Ian was the first to question the man.

"Why should any of us allow you to stand here alongside those loyal?" Ian growled. "Tell me, when Andras forced people to become infected with darkness, where were you? Drinking? Gorging yourself in the comfort of your homes?"

The noble brought a hand to his chest. "We believed the advisor as we should have."

"Wrong," I snarled. I shifted, laying a hand on Ian's shoulder to tell him I could do this. "There's a reason the lesser Fae were targeted and you were left alone. You go along with whoever gives you the most power. I'm telling you now, that ends today."

The noble's lip curled.

"We've lived for too long ranking people based on the strength of their magic, but I have seen an entire army of lesser Fae build forges, homes, and take back a castle from a man sated with stolen power. I have worked alongside Fae who showed more loyalty and heroism than an entire arena of nobles."

I stared the man up and down, letting my anger shine.

"From now on, Atheria will be different. Fae will be judged by their contributions, by their character, *not* by the amount of magic coursing through their veins."

Rage-filled shouts came from the nobles.

"Those of you who are too good to lift a sword and fight, despite having powerful magic, will find that Atheria will not be welcoming of you once we win."

"You can't threaten us." Another noble standing beside the first leered.

"I am your queen," I said.

"You haven't been crowned," someone else shouted.

Tommy shoved forward. "Mathias," he yelled. "You've been a coward since childhood, and that's the crown you're speaking to. You can show some respect, or I'll let your wife know about the women you meet in my pub every Friday night when you tell her you're working at the palace." A grin spread over Tommy's face as the noble went ghastly white. "Oops."

He stammered, his nose wrinkling as his face reddened in unmitigated rage.

"Illiana is our queen," a voice from the lesser Fae section sounded. "The rightful queen. Speaking against her is treason, especially when she's saved us from Andras and the likes of the dark ones."

"Once we win, if you wish to put forth the name of a new queen, we can discuss it," I gave a small nod to the Fae who'd spoken on my behalf. "But right now, this is my blood right. I am the heir, and I will not let this kingdom fall."

A noblewoman shoved forward, moving to the front of the nobles. "Do not think they speak for all of us," she shouted, but blinked rapidly as if remembering herself when we made eye contact. She curtseyed. "I apologize, Your Majesty." She paused before looking up at me again, worrying her lip between her teeth as if hoping she hadn't overstepped.

"Keena," a deep, powerful voice shouted, and the woman fell backward, yanked from behind. "What do you think you're doing?"

She tugged her arm free. "I am doing what is right. You hoard your powers like you matter, yet you do nothing when it counts. I watched friends disappear to the darkness for years and you turned a blind eye every time."

"They weren't friends, they were lessers," the man seethed in her face.

She raised her hand as if she wanted to smack him, but was stopped by another, lunging to grab her wrist. "Enough, Keena! You're embarrassing your family."

"No, you're the embarrassment," she shouted. The two men hung onto her arms, but she turned to look at me anyway. "There are those of us who would fight alongside of you, Your Majesty. Do not let these cowards speak for all of us in the upper districts simply because they're the loudest."

Her eyes flittered between my friends and then Storm stalked forward, wrapping a hand around Keena's waist,removing the others from her. He positioned her behind him. "What kind of men belittle a woman speaking to her queen? Or lay hands on someone answering a call to protect our world?"

He backed up, glancing once at Keena before giving her space to stand on her own again. He didn't move farther than arm's reach from her.

She raised her chin. "Frankie." She looked at a noble standing closer to the lesser Fae than the others. "We've spoken about this. Marc, you too. Gloria." One by one she called out various names and they stepped toward her. "We have wanted to make a difference for our friends, our people. If we don't use the gifts given to us by nature, there may not be an Ellevail to save. An Atheria—" She looked to me and I nodded. I was sure saying a new name was strange. "An Atheria to save," she said confidently.

"Listen to Keena," I pleaded. "We can win this together. We can rise up as one and stand for good against an army, a tyrant who believes only in evil. If we don't, we'll lose everything."

A few nobles stepped forward and bowed alongside Keena. The lesser Fae shouted, "We will fight!"

I looked out over the crowd. It may not be all the nobles, but it was a start. "We will work in the coming days to prepare for the battle ahead. If you need aid in this time, the palace doors are open. Any of *my* advisors"—I swept a hand behind me at my friends, standing tall and proud—" will assist how they can. In the meantime, thank you for believing in Brookmere. For believing in me. I will not let you down."

I smiled, lowering my head slightly toward the crowd, and took a step back.

Voices sprang up again, discussions breaking out among others. I looked over at Keena and approached, noticing Storm standing fairly close still. "It takes courage to speak against your family." I smiled. "Especially publicly."

"I've been speaking against my family for years." She grinned. "This time, I just so happened to have a queen's support."

"I know you all may feel like you don't have the fighting skills to—"

Keena lunged sideways, sliding Storm's sword out of its sheath at his side, holding it up in a ready position before extending her hand and blasting him with a gust of air. I gaped at her, and Storm flinched as his body shifted a few steps backward, his hair tugging from his loose bun. He stared wide-eyed at the blade, then the woman holding it, before cocking an eyebrow at her.

She shrugged. "We've practiced some for fun. I enjoy being underestimated."

I laughed, unable to help myself. "I think we'll get along well, Keena. If you need help with the nobles or obtaining weapons, let me know."

"Thank you, Your Majesty." She flipped the sword around, holding it by the blade with the hilt toward Storm. "Might want to be cautious of who you let touch that blade in the future."

With that, she turned, leaving down a walkway toward the group that had stepped forward during her speech.

I looked at Storm, whose dark eyes trailed her, and shook my head. "Maybe you can train with Ian if your skills are so poor that a noble bested you."

He looked at me and narrowed his eyes. "I'm, I'll—" He cleared his throat. "Someone needs me." With that, he turned on his heel and walked away.

Kade's shadows wrapped around my arms and as I turned, he embraced me. "You never cease to amaze me, Little Rebel."

I looked into his eyes, feeling hopeful. My body ached with fatigue, and I knew we still had to deal with Andras. I had to face him one more time, but seeing at least some of the nobles stand up, knowing I'd laid down my expectations for what our world would be lifted some of the weight off me.

It was one step closer to the world I dreamed of ruling.

"You better keep up," I said. "I'll need a king by my side."

He smiled, leaning down and kissing me gently, though his tongue swept into my mouth like he possessed me. Fates, I suppose he did.

"You don't *need* a king, Illiana," he whispered against my lips. "But I will stand by your side in whatever way you'll have me. I'm yours."

"Mine," I echoed, and for a brief moment, I closed my eyes and let Kade hold me before facing the next steps for the final battle looming ahead.

CHAPTER 25
IAN

I stared at the bloody blade in my hands.

They trembled as I clutched Corbin's sword and my eyes welled with tears.

Fuck.

This was my first moment alone since his death. I hated that I'd never see him again. I sucked in a sharp breath that felt more like a dagger to the chest than a breath of air.

I turned the weapon over in my palm. I'd gifted it to him years ago, when we first agreed to be a part of the Hidden Henchman. The fact that he still fought with it to this day filled me with a profound sense of admiration, yet cracked my heart in two at the same time.

Corbin had been the first one on board with the Hidden Henchman. I watched him for months and walked away each time in awe of his loyalty to the crown. Where some gossiped, Corbin didn't just ignore the comments, he put people in their place for speaking ill of the royal family. He spoke highly of the king and queen, and especially of Lana.

He'd seen right away her love for her people.

I'd trained him first, befriending him to get to know him, and he never wavered. Not once. Corbin was always himself.

There were never masks or fake niceties to contend with. What he portrayed to the world was truly who he was.

And Casimir had snuffed him out.

I winced as a wave of pain and regret clawed at me. Had I ever expressed how much he meant to me? How grateful I was to him for his friendship and all that he did for us?

The blade fell from my hands, clattering against the marble floor. I rubbed the heels of my palms against my eyes, leaning forward as I let go of the emotions desperate to be free and grieved my friend.

The door to my chambers clicked open and closed quietly. I didn't look up or even try to gather myself.

As the footsteps shuffled closer, this newly formed bond inside of me tightened.

I finally lifted my head, and Raya reached out, placing a hand on my shoulder before she sat next to me.

Her touch calmed the agony in my chest enough so I could breathe again.

I inhaled deeply before wiping my eyes.

"I'm so sorry, Ian," she whispered. "He was a good man."

I nodded. "A great man."

"What can I do?" Raya asked, tentatively running her hand in a circle on my back.

I closed my eyes, simultaneously so grateful for her presence while also wanting to rage. To punch something.

Instead, I clenched my hands into fists. "It should have been me."

She didn't say anything, just continued rubbing slow, reassuring circles on me.

"I should have kept up with Lana. I should have been the one who got to Casimir first."

"So he could have stabbed you instead?" Raya asked plainly.

"No, but maybe I would have caught the movement faster, or moved out of the way more quickly—"

"Was Corbin a poor fighter?"

I looked over at her, my brows furrowing at the question. "No, he was better than half the guards, but I'm the one who should have been leading. I'm the captain and he's dead because of me." My body slid to the ground and my head hung low.

Raya shifted to the floor and kneeled in front of me, taking my hands in hers. "He is dead because of Casimir. Corbin was a strong fighter—you're the one who trained him. Fates, I saw him through your eyes during your escape from the dungeon. If it had been you chasing after Casimir, you would be dead instead. He died a warrior's death. Do not let your guilt take away from his valor."

I shook my head. "I wish it was that easy."

"I understand, Ian," she said squeezing my hands.

I met her gaze, soft and filled with compassion in a way so unlike anything I'd experienced with her. Or maybe this was who she was when she let her guard down.

"After Dargan used me to betray my friends, after everything that happened, I broke," she said, her gaze dropping to the floor. "The guilt consumed me. I couldn't help but think that if I had been stronger, if I had done something differently, then the people I love wouldn't have been in danger. Storm wouldn't have been tortured." Her shoulders heaved, and I reached down, tilting her chin up and wiping a tear that had escaped.

"I still struggle. It's why I've been distant with everyone." She pulled back away from my touch. "I don't think I deserve these incredible friendships. Much less"—her voice broke as she whispered—"a mate."

She cleared her throat, meeting my gaze. "My point is, don't let guilt destroy you. This was not your fault."

"So it's okay for you to feel guilty? But no one else?"

She didn't answer, looking away. I gently caressed her

chin, turning her face back to look at me. "I'll try to forgive myself if you will too."

"Ian—"

I rubbed my thumb over her beautiful lips.

"Ian, I just came to check on you," she whispered, leaning away from my touch. "I should go."

I shook my head. "You asked what you could do, did you not?"

She swallowed and I moved my hand from her chin and down her neck. "It's okay to tell me if you think we're going to make this work. That we're going to stop fighting it and give us a chance. Give in to the mating bond."

My fingers tingled touching her delicate skin, and she closed her eyes, slowly exhaling a breath. She was perfect.

Fucking perfect.

"You can give me everything, Raya. I don't know what tomorrow or, Fates, the next hour will bring, but I don't want to live this life pretending you are not my mate. I want you."

"Why?" she asked after a quick breath. "I'm not someone who deserves a mate. So why?"

I smiled, continuing to brush my thumb over her soft brown skin, transfixed by the way it erupted with goose bumps. "You stayed with me in the dungeon." If she needed an explanation before she agreed to our bond, I'd bare my entire soul. "You showed me that you could easily pull away, but you stayed. You shielded my mind, and when it came time to escape, you didn't leave. You experienced it all with me. Seeing every thought, all the pain. It didn't make you run. In my weakest moments, some of the worst of my life, you endured it alongside me before you even knew anything about me."

"You wanted nothing to do with me when we met in person." Her lips twitched. I studied her face, unable to hide my smile at the thought that I could continue to study her.

Learn everything about her, what each facial expression meant. Forever. She was mine.

"I didn't know how to handle you seeing me so vulnerable. Lana's been the only other person who ever saw so much of me before. I hated knowing someone who might be my enemy saw my struggles."

"And now?" she breathed out, flicking her gaze to my lips, leaning forward just slightly.

My smile spread. "Now?" Cocking an eyebrow, I squeezed my hand at her neck and leaned forward too, lowering my voice. "I will give you every part of me—pain, guilt, joy. You name it and it's yours, Raya."

I pulled her forward, crashing my lips into hers as if I needed them to breathe.

She hesitated, stiffening for only a moment, before wrapping her arms around my neck and returning my kiss with an unguarded passion. The bond inside of me, inside of us, connecting and strengthening with every passing moment.

My hand moved to cup the back of her neck, tilting it to expose her enough to trail kisses down her silky skin. She arched into my touch, moaning into my ear. "Ian, are you sure you want to do this now, after everything that happened today?"

Stopping, I returned my gaze directly to hers. "I have never been more sure of anything in my entire life."

Raya smirked, then tackled me to the ground, straddling me before leaning forward and kissing me once more. She ran her hands through my disheveled hair, and every part of my body tingled at her touch.

I raked my hands up her chest and cupped her breast as she gasped into my mouth. "Show me what you've got."

Grabbing her black tunic, I lifted it up and over her head, longing to see and feel every inch of her. I stared, drinking in how beautiful she looked. "You are perfect."

A small smirk tilted the side of her lips, and fuck me, I needed her closer.

Without breaking our kiss, I sat up and grabbed her body, picking her up by her ass. She wrapped her legs around my waist, as I stood, carrying us both. I returned my mouth to hers, using the momentum of rocking to my feet to swing us backward until we landed against the wall. A framed map of Ellevail, clattered to the floor from the force.

We stood breathless for a moment, and I savored the feel of her beneath my hands. She trembled briefly before she let go of my waist and stood flat against the wall. Raya moved quickly, ripping my shirt so hard, I lost two buttons in the process of getting it off.

I couldn't care less.

"Pants, now," she commanded, as she hastily rid herself of hers.

I grabbed her hands, stopping her as she tried to shimmy her pants down her thighs "My sweet mate, I am in charge here." I grinned, nipping at her bottom lip once as I brought her hands over her head and against the wall. "So you *will* do as I say, or you'll be punished. Do you understand?"

A glimmer of excitement shone in her eye. "Yes, Captain. What are my orders?"

Fates above, I might be in love.

"Stay still, and don't move." I gave her a knowing look, and she nodded and left her hands resting above her head. "Good girl."

A soft whimper escaped her lips. My cock hardened at the delicious sound.

Sliding my hands slowly, I trailed down her arms, over her breasts, and down her stomach. I grazed my fingers over almost every inch of her before reaching down her thigh and slowly sliding her pants all the way to the floor.

Raya arched away from the wall, still leaving her hands above her head. I grinned up at her as her eyes flashed with heavy desire. Trailing kisses up her legs, I took my time rising to my knees.

"Spread your legs," I commanded as I positioned myself closer.

She obeyed, opening herself up to me. "Yes, Captain."

The time for soft and delicate would be saved for another day. This moment was desperate and wanting. I couldn't wait any longer.

The first taste of her sent shivers down my spine. It was intoxicating, and I wanted to get drunk off her. I lapped against her with long, smooth strokes of my tongue.

"More," Raya panted.

I grabbed her leg, throwing it over my shoulder and positioning myself further and deeper within her. She was so wet for me, so perfect with the way her hips moved against my mouth, and I loved every fucking second of it.

"Is this all for me?" I asked, looking up at her.

She stared at me, squirming and breathing heavily. "Yes," she said in a breathy exhale. "Fates, yes."

I reached two fingers up toward her lips. "Suck."

Her mouth parted and she moaned as she ran her tongue over my fingers.

After a moment, I pulled them back, moving them to her entrance. "So wet, so perfect. You're mine, aren't you, Raya."

Before she could respond, I pushed both fingers inside of her. As much as I wanted this hard and fast, foreplay was my favorite part. After the tension between us from her fighting this bond, watching her squirm and writhe until she begged seemed a fitting way to spend my time.

Raya gasped. I looked up to watch her, and she began massaging her breasts, flicking her nipples as my fingers began a steady rhythm inside of her. She knew what she wanted and wasn't shy about taking her pleasure. Fuck, she was a sight to behold.

The taste and feel of her all at the same time was

exquisite. I added a third finger, slowly easing into her as she cursed and bucked against my mouth.

"That's it. Come for me, Raya."

I could feel the tension inside of her, eager to be released. With a few more flicks of my tongue on her clit and my fingers pumping inside of her, she screamed my name.

My cock nearly exploded out of my pants, it was so damn hard. I'd enjoyed myself plenty of times before this, but nothing had come close to turning me on as much as tasting Raya and watching her come undone.

"Good fucking girl," I murmured into her as I stood to kiss her once more. "Do you know how good you taste?"

"Show me."

Kissing her this time was a sloppy, desperate thing. Her tongue stroking mine sent my head spinning.

"More," Raya practically begged. "I need you inside of me, Ian."

Discarding my pants, I stroked myself, ready to feel her come while I was inside of her. She moved forward, reaching for me. "Now, what did I say about not following the rules? Back against the wall."

She gave a sheepish grin, but the blush coloring her cheeks told me she liked it. She liked being taken care of, and I would make it my life's mission to care for her. "Are you going to punish me now, Captain?"

"You did bring your hands down, sweetheart." I licked my lips watching her eyes darken. "Turn around."

Her eyebrow raised, but she followed my command. I grabbed her ass, massaging it, before spanking her once. Moaning into the wall, she stuck her butt out for easier access, "Again."

"Shh," I said while I happily obliged.

The head of my cock rubbed against her entrance, absolutely dripping with desire, and I coated it, readying myself.

I leaned forward, biting gently at the side of her neck. "Hold on tight, darling."

Gently, I inched myself inside of her before pulling out and thrusting until I was deeply seated within her.

Placing my hand against the wall, I set a punishing pace. Her head leaned back against my shoulder, as I breathed in the scent of her, kissing her anywhere I could.

"Harder," she moaned.

I chuckled, running one hand over her hips and up to play with her nipple. "Getting greedy now, are we?"

"If this is what this feels like with you, I will be begging for the rest of our lives for more."

I gave her what she asked for, thrusting harder as sweat dripped down my back, and I felt her walls tightening around my cock. This time, she wouldn't be finishing alone. "Do not come," I whispered.

She made a sound of protest.

"Do not come, until I tell you to. You'll wait for me."

Three more hard, deep thrusts was all it took. "Now, Raya," I commanded. "Come for me."

I hurtled us both into oblivion, riding out our orgasms together. I rested my head against the back of her neck. Her damp skin matched my own as we stood there panting.

Slowly, as if sliding out of the best dream of my life, she turned to face me and wrapped her arms around my neck. She tilted her head up, leaning in, and kissed me softly. "I could live a thousand years, and this moment will always be my favorite." She placed her head against my chest as we attempted to regain our composure.

I stroked a hand over her hair and kissed the top of her head. "A thousand years will never be long enough for all I have planned for you."

CHAPTER 26
LANA

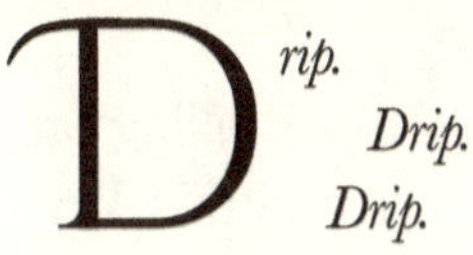

Even after all these years, the dripping never stopped. Hearing the splatter of the water droplets on the cool stone still sent shivers up my spine.

The memories of the dungeon, of this particular cell and the horrors committed against Ian and me would never be forgotten. The pain would remain etched into every fiber of my being. The walls permanently soiled with what had been done here.

Every panic attack. Every nightmare. Every moment of self-doubt. They all stemmed from the torture I'd received in this very cell.

None of it had mattered in the end though. The words of a hate-filled, cruel man meant nothing now. I worked harder every day, overcame every obstacle, and in the end, even got my own fucking magic.

Andras would never win now, and he would never see the light of day again.

He stood chained against the wall, arms above his head.

Despite the blood dripping from his ear and the black eye, he still laughed, eying each of us with arrogance despite his precarious position.

"Play all you want, Princess," Andras spat. "Thames will be here soon to stop this farce, and then you will truly understand what pain and suffering is. What I did to you will look like child's play."

As much as I wanted to let my emotions take control, I knew I couldn't let him see that part of me. He knew all too well I had let feelings rule my decision-making in the past. He would never get a reaction out of me ever again.

I leaned coolly against the bars of the cell. "Ah, well, you see, there's just one problem with that little plan. You'd have to be alive in order for Thames to save you, and I don't intend on letting you breathe for that much longer."

Andras sneered at us, his tattered purple robes falling off his shoulder. "I have served faithfully for years, and that kind of loyalty means something. I will be rescued and you will be *nothing*." His shouts echoed in the dungeon as he pulled against the chains at his wrist, but he couldn't go far.

Ian unlocked the cell door, allowing it to creak open. He paused, closing his eyes once. I wanted to reach for him, but with Andras watching our every move, I didn't want to give him the satisfaction of seeing any of us hesitate.

He said nothing as he stepped inside. Kade followed close behind, his shadows remaining ready just in case Andras got out of hand. The rest of our friends stayed outside, waiting. We were all exhausted from the battle, yet still we found the energy to care for the wounded and reestablish a chain of command. We'd worked until the middle of the night before starting to go our separate ways. Kade and I put people we trusted into place to start securing the palace and searching it to ensure the dark ones were gone. We all needed respite. Time to sleep. Time to heal.

Yet every one of them remained here by my side now, in the early morning hours.

With careful steps, I moved toward Kade and faced Andras. "Perhaps if you answer some of our questions, we will make your death a little less… How should I put this? Drawn out? Painful? Take your pick." Crossing my arms over my chest, Apollo practically hummed in its sheath, beckoning me to use it, as if the darkness called to it. But I wouldn't use it just yet.

"Like I would tell you anything." Andras sneered.

I nodded toward Ian, and he walloped Andras in his side. He must have knocked the air out of his lungs, because the coward was already gasping.

I waited a moment, picking at some dirt under my nail. "Ready to begin, then? What is Thames's weapon?"

Andras paused for a split second, barely enough time to register the confusion crossing his expression. "If by weapon you mean me, or Kade, or his army of dark ones, then there you have it. We were created by him, for him."

"Again, Ian," I commanded to my friend, who smashed his fist into Andras's side once more. I swore I heard a rib crack. "Now, Andras, didn't your mother ever tell you it was in poor form to lie? Let's try this again. What is hidden at Firestone?"

Andras couldn't mask the confusion this time. I hadn't imagined it a moment ago. "If Thames had a weapon, I would certainly know about it. I think you're making up lies, girl."

Kade stepped forward and swung at the pitiful royal advisor, splitting his lip. Blood, dark and thick, dripped slowly down his chin. "Your queen asked you a question."

I stepped forward and put my hand on Kade's shoulder, smiling. "It's all right Kade, he doesn't know. Clearly, he's not all that useful to Thames, not even knowing about this big secret weapon." I sauntered back to the edge of the cell.

Andras pulled against the chains as if he could get to me. "I *am* important."

Turning back to face him, I wrinkled my nose, not bothering to hide the disgust that came any time I thought of this man. "Not important enough, it seems." Placing my hands on my hips, admiring the scene before me. Oh, how the tables had turned.

Andras didn't falter. He remained strong in his conviction, raising his chin in a pathetic attempt at defiance. I heard my friends snicker outside of the cell. They would have their moment too.

"This is what's going to happen. Every single one of my friends will exact whatever punishment they deem fit for the crimes you committed against them. I will sit here and watch. Then, when they are done and have had their fill, I will end your miserable excuse for a life."

Andras cackled, but Kade's shadows gagged him before he could produce another sound. I continued, despite the adrenaline threatening to take over. My hands shook from the overwhelming amount of emotions running alongside it, so I hid them behind my back and moved toward Andras. I wanted him to know our threats were real.

"I will win this war against Thames. I will officially take my place on the throne, and my first proclamation as queen will be to erase every single bit of your existence. Your name, your title, your picture—all are unworthy of remembering. Not one person will ever utter your name again. Your legacy will die." My confidence returning, I flipped Apollo in my hand, still coated in Andras's dried blood from earlier. I hadn't even bothered cleaning it.

I turned to face my friends. "Who's first?"

Stepping to the side of the cell, I left the area open for the others to come forward. Lucien appeared from the darkness and weaved his way through my legs before settling at my feet.

I sighed, grateful to see him safe and knelt, stroking a hand over his scales. "Good to see you too, Luci."

Ian strode forward slowly, deliberately toward Andras. Lucien growled, chuffing a billow of smoke as if signaling Ian to begin.

My best friend stared at Andras and narrowed his eyes. Kade pulled his shadows back, giving Ian his moment.

This time he didn't hold back. He punched Andras's jaw so hard, a tooth flew from his mouth and Andras screamed. "This is for every moment of our lives you tried to destroy. You thought you could break us, that you could break her. But you were wrong. We only came back stronger."

He punched him again right on his cheek, and Andras's neck cracked as his head flew to the side. "Your ability to make us think, or see, or feel anything that isn't real is gone. We may never have been able to convince anyone of your wrongdoings before, but the truth will be revealed." Ian spat on Andras's feet. "I hope the Fates have a special kind of hell to put you through."

Andras glared at Ian and tried to wipe the blood off his mouth with his shoulder but only managed to smear it more across his face.

Ian walked backward and joined me against the wall. Reaching out, I squeezed his hand in solidarity. He squeezed mine back and whispered in my direction, "That felt really fucking good."

Kalliah started to step forward, but Raya moved in front of her, placing a hand on her arm before taking the lead, approaching the injured advisor. Ian tensed beside me.

Raya eyed Andras up and down and grunted in disgust. "I've heard many stories about you and what you did to Illiana. What you did to Ian. The problem with powerful men is they don't ever understand when their power has come to an end. Even now, you're still fighting it. Pathetic." She moved closer and struck Andras on the opposite side of his face, leaving an imprint of her ring in his skin. She shook out the pain in her hand. "That was for touching what does not belong to you. For daring to harm *my mate*."

My head whipped in Ian's direction, shocked to hear her speak the words aloud. Ian groaned and pushed himself off the wall, grabbing Raya by the arm and spinning her around. He threaded his fingers between her braids at the nape of her neck and pulled her close. "Powerful women are my weakness."

Raya smiled playfully. "Women?"

Ian crashed his lips to hers, and when he finally came up for air, he reassured her. "Woman. Only one. Only you, darling."

I grinned, turning my attention to Kade. "Did you know?" I mouthed. He shrugged, then winked at me. Even here in this cold dungeon, my heart swelled with joy knowing they would be together.

Jax made a gagging noise. "Gross. I'd rather the blood than all that." He flourished his hands in the air at Ian and Raya, who remained clasped together in each other's arms.

"Jax, you do know you're a terrible liar, right?" Kalliah entered completely into the cell from the doorway. She unsheathed the dagger clipped to her belt and twirled it in her palm.

Kalliah may be quieter, more reserved, but she had a mean streak, and if anyone crossed her or harmed those she cared about…well, I was scared for them. Andras had no idea what was coming his way. So, in part, I was not surprised that she grabbed her blade instead of using her fist.

She moved toward Andras with conviction and stabbed him in the side, exactly where he had stabbed me.

He screamed, bellowing out an angry cry that he clearly hadn't wanted to give up. Hatred consumed his eyes, but mine ran deeper.

"This is for my friends. For the ones you thought you

could break, but I will savor knowing you did absolutely nothing to change who they are today. Your darkness did nothing to change them." She wiped the blood from the blade on his shirt before turning to Ian and me, giving us a knowing glance.

Quietly, she returned to the outside of the cell, where Leif welcomed her back into his arms. He looked toward me and shook his head, indicating he didn't want time with Andras.

Jax stepped forward and partially shifted, his hand turning into the deadly claws he used so well. He swiped Andras's robe to pieces, displaying his bare chest to me. Then, with a wicked gleam in his eyes he slashed his claws across Andras's chest. The once proud advisor cried out again. Jax bowed his head before returning to the edge of the cell to stand beside Kalliah and Leif. "I don't want to waste words on a corpse."

Andras spat from the chains, "Is that the best you've got? A couple of feeble punches and a stabbing? It'll take more than that to kill me. You're all weak."

Kade snapped his shadows forward, wrapping them around Andras's neck and squeezing. He stalked forward slowly, materializing his shadow blade in his hand while assessing Andras from head to toe, utter disdain filling his features. "I won't bother wasting too much time on you either," he said, holding up his blade. "Kalliah so kindly stabbed you where I would have, so instead, I'll just leave you with this." Kade drew his sword down Andras' right arm, then his left, while the advisor screamed. "Know that you will die for nothing. Thames will be destroyed."

Andras coughed up blood as unhinged laughter sputtered out of him. "Who will destroy Thames?" He choked. "You?"

"No." Kade's lips turned up in a smile. "My queen."

As Kade made room for me, I took my place, Apollo at the ready. "They saved the best for last. For out of everyone here, you caused me the most trauma, the most pain. Now you are mine."

Andras cackled as the blood, so dark it looked black, dripped down the shredded remains of his shirt. "You think you can win? You think I'm scared of you?"

Even with the cool air flowing through the dungeons, sweat began to form on my back, on my palms. Something I'd wished to happen for so many years was just moments away.

"You should be." Slowly I started making tiny cuts up and down his arms, and small swirls of darkened mist seeped from the wounds. "Tell me, will you be so brave when the darkness is drained out of you?" I whispered.

Andras smirked. "You can't purge the darkness out of someone when it has become a part of their being. This power has coursed through my veins for years and years. No dagger or magic will ever be able to rid me of who I am. No dagger can eliminate darkness this deep without death. If you were hoping for that, you lose."

Catching my breath, my eyes wandered to Kade's. His words were most likely meant to hurt us. Despite the fear at what it meant if he told the truth, I refused to analyze it here. This wasn't the time nor the place to delve into those thoughts and feelings.

Instead, it was time to end this. Time to rest with the people I loved and walk away from this cell, physically and mentally, forever.

"Ah, there's the doubt creeping in," he needled. "It's always there. It's who you are." He snorted, his movements to escape slowing down now. "Princess, you will live with my marks forever. My death will not end the torment I'll impose for the rest of your pathetic life." He spit a bloodied glob at my face.

Lucien roared, and the room heated, on the verge of unbearable. The fire from his snout threatened all of us. How the rest of my friends stayed so calm, I will never know. I wiped the spit from my face and flicked it right back to him.

"I will live despite my heartbreak. Despite the torment you

have caused. I will live remembering my loved ones who've been lost by your hand. But I will *live*. You? You will die. You will be nothing. Your name will be nothing. Not even a memory."

Gathering all of my strength, I slammed Apollo directly into Andras's heart and the darkness living inside of him for so long exploded outward. Using the blade didn't drain me like I thought it would. Instead, the magic inside of it seemed to beckon my light, fueling it instead of using it.

The room temporarily turned so dark, it swallowed us whole, but the dagger glowed through it all. I pushed harder and harder, letting my light flow into the blade until the smoke cleared and Andras's body slumped forward, as he breathed his last breath.

"And it's *queen*, you worthless piece of shit."

CHAPTER 27

LANA

"Little Rebel," Kade whispered, his voice wrapped around me along with his shadows, which were trailing down my arms.

I blinked, trying to wake up. My body felt like a thousand pounds. After dealing with Andras and releasing all of the vengeance I'd been holding on to for so many years, the adrenaline had faded. My mind immediately turned to Corbin, another loss I'd carry forever.

Once I'd made it outside my chamber doors, my knees gave out and Kade carried me to my bed. I didn't even remember falling asleep.

The dim light of the setting sun illuminated my bedroom chambers. "How long was I asleep?" I asked, stretching my arms above my head as I tried to move despite how heavy everything weighed on me.

Kade wrapped his arm around my waist, turning me to face him. His soft smile grew as he looked me over. "A few hours. You needed to rest."

My lip trembled as Kade looked at me like I was something precious. "Andras is dead, so why don't I feel better?"

His blood would be on my hands forever, and while the world would be a better place without him, I couldn't describe the strange mix of emotions flooding my body.

Kade pulled me closer, and I let my emotions take over, crying into his chest. He let them flow, running his hands over the back of my head, massaging my neck. "It feels better for a brief moment, but people like that—their deaths don't magically erase the pain they've inflicted. We have to do that part ourselves. We have to be stronger than the scars they left behind."

My head nuzzled into his side, letting his comforting presence soothe our bond and my heart. This pulsing light inside of me containing Kade's soul alongside my own thrummed with contentment until I could breathe again.

"Thank you for helping me destroy him."

Kade lifted my chin, kissing my lips gently. "I promised you he would be dead when you were ready."

A knock sounded from the main entryway.

"It's Storm," Kade advised, rising from the bed and heading out of my bedroom.

A moment later he returned, Storm trailing behind.

Adjusting the pillows on the bed allowed me to sit up as Kade crawled over back to his spot.

He has a spot. I smiled briefly at how normal it all felt. Kade had a place that was his in my bed.

"How are you, Lana?" Storm asked, approaching my other side. He laid his hand on my shoulder and squeezed.

"I'll be all right. You?"

He nodded once.

I noticed a small satchel in his hands and inclined my head toward it. "What's that?"

He cleared his throat. "We spoke once about you receiving your warrior markings."

My lips parted as my gaze jumped to the tattoos on his

arm. I remembered how beautiful I thought they were when I first noticed them. Back when he told me their meaning—that Mysthaven Guardians get them after their first kill to remind them that, even when justified, taking a life leaves a mark.

"I thought if you were ready, you'd allow me to perform it," he added.

"He's done all of ours," Kade said from my side, running a hand down my arm in comfort.

"Only if you want them," Storm reassured. "The choice is yours."

I smiled at him but hesitated, thinking about what the sentiment meant to me now. I'd killed an untold number of dark ones as well as many of the king's men inside his study before Thames was released.

That list now included Casimir and Andras. The thought of having those deaths marked on more than just my conscience made me pause.

"If I may." Storm apparently sensed my reluctance and sat on the side of my bed. "I had an idea."

Glancing up at him, I met his gaze.

"Our tradition started a long time ago, in a land where brutality reigned. It made sense for us in Mysthaven because many times we had to dig deep to hold on to our humanity, especially when the dark ones spread and Dargan's commands became more vile." Storm unzipped the pouch, letting me see inside to a pot of black ink and some sharpened tools. "You've never succumbed to your own version of the darkness within, even with what you've endured, Lana. I wonder if you might start a new tradition. One where we honor those you fight for. Your marking can remind you of your strength. The cost of creating the world you'll rule, even if it's for the better."

My heart beat faster as I thought about Storm's idea. The beautiful meaning would allow me to honor the tradition of my friends while making it something of my own too.

"I—" Reaching forward, I gripped Storm's arm. "I would love that. Thank you."

He bowed his head and rose. "I can set up everything here."

Kade tugged on my arm, pulling me toward him so he could cup my face. He kissed my lips, then rose. He didn't say anything, but it didn't matter. I felt his pride and his love for me. His shadows lingered by my side as he ushered me up off the other side of the bed.

He straightened the sheets to give Storm a flat space to work. "Where would you like it?"

I bit my lip, thinking for a moment. "My back?"

He nodded and flipped two pillows around, moving me to the edge of the bed. "Lie here on your stomach."

I reached over to the nightstand, grabbing the journal so I could continue reading while he worked. I supported the book in front of me with a throw pillow. Kade's shadows surrounded me as I removed my shirt before laying on the bed.

As Storm continued preparing his tools, Kade sat in my reading chair nestled against the wall, just a few feet away. I opened the journal and found my spot. The first mention of Apollo. I would understand everything there was to know about this blade gifted to me from a line of queens. I glanced at Kade, earning a smile.

"This will hurt, but I'll make it as quick as I can," Storm offered reassuringly.

"I can handle pain."

Kade leaned forward, brushing my cheek gently, as Storm began to work.

As the instrument touched my skin, a piercing sting radiated across my back, but after a few minutes, it numbed. My magic kicked into gear and gave me a reprieve from the initial shock of the needle's touch. While the discomfort lingered, I swallowed it, letting the pain remind me of those who'd died for this cause.

Taking a deep breath, my focus returned to the journal. The entry was from Queen Daniella, Evelyn's daughter and my great-great-grandmother. Too many of my family's line had met early deaths. Over the thousand-year time period between Evelyn and me, there were four women. All with powerful magic and all pouring their beautiful magic into the weapon I now carried.

How Evelyn continued our line without her mate made my stomach turn though. I didn't know if I could have done it.

From the hand of Queen Daniella:

One of the merchants in town for the Festival of Blessings gathered a crowd today in the market. He spoke about an orb with the ability to hold a water wielder's magic inside of it until the user required it.

The idea is fascinating that magic can be stored.

Mother mentioned that a sorceress created something similar for Jasper in order to trap Thames. She used the same concept to put her magic into her dagger.

I still can't believe what the sorceress went through. If the words weren't written and recorded here, I would never have known of her bravery or of the sacrifice she made for our kingdom. I don't know if I will be able to make choices so selfless.

Right now, things are in order. Though there have been one or two reports of Fae going mad with an infection, it's been handled easily. Brookmere is thriving. We recently expanded to a new city, Broham, out on the coast.

But with the words of my mother's prophecy—that Thames could only be contained until a stronger power came along to defeat him—I know this bliss and safety will not remain.

The merchant's idea sparked one of my own. A Fae with unique magic to banish darkness must be coming. She will be strong, no doubt, but what if we could help her? What if she not only fights with her power, and my mother's, but with the power of generations to come?

I plan to seek out the merchant tomorrow during the festival. My mother gave everything to Brookmere, and to Atheria, as we were once called. If I can find a way to contribute, I will do it too.

I ran my fingers over the ink marking the page. So many women in this line had worked together to lead us to this moment. Flipping the page, I smiled at Daniella's obvious tenacity. Sure enough another entry referenced the day after the festival.

From the hand of Queen Daniella:

Fates above, I've got it. The merchant—quite handsome a Fae, actually—wants to visit me again, but that's beside the matter at hand. The merchant said he merely poured his power into an object of his choosing. He told me to think of it as if I was channeling healing power toward a wound.

The object would be the conduit, maintaining the power within it until I wanted to use it. He called the water out of the orb he had and then showed me how he put it back in. It's truly a remarkable feat.

When I returned to my chambers, I noticed my mother's dagger on the nightstand where I always left it. I may not have a sorceress to guide me, but the way the merchant explained it to me should work. Wouldn't her own dagger make a wonderful conduit for each generation to store some power for the one who will defeat evil for good?

I'm going to try it.

I continued reading as the time ticked by. Hours passed into the night while Storm worked diligently. Kade flipped through a book he'd pulled from my nightstand. Every few minutes he'd stroke a tendril of shadows down my arm or touch my face gently, like he was reminding himself I was still here, but he didn't interrupt my reading.

A few entries later.

From the hand of Queen Daniella:

It worked. My heart is still pounding in my chest at what I've accomplished. I channeled some of my air magic into the dagger, and a faint glow surrounded it, warming in my hand. The merchant's orb had a faint blue light to it. This, though, was beautiful. A bright white light. The dagger flared almost as if it remembered something. Perhaps my mother's magic. Either way, I will do this whenever I can, infusing it with my magic. I'll capture the details here for the next heir to continue the tradition.

The one to save us will have power given to her freely for the good of all our people.

The words weren't new to us, but it confirmed everything. The next page gave a detailed account of where she held onto the blade, where she channeled her magic into it, what it looked like, and how long she did it.

I lifted my head to Kade. "Can you grab my dagger?"

He stood, grabbing it from the table before returning. "What's going on in that beautiful head of yours?"

I ran my hand over the blade, my light magic causing it to glow like it always did. "Can I try to cut the darkness out of you again?"

His face sobered and he nodded once. "Of course. Found anything useful in the journal?"

"Nothing more than an understanding of the power held within the blade. I'd like to try to push my magic into where the journal says the others stored theirs. Maybe it would be more powerful."

"I'm at your disposal." He bowed his head.

"Hold on, I'm almost done. For fuck's sake," Storm grumbled under his breath. "Give me a minute and you can go about stabbing him all you like."

Laughing, we let Storm finish.

When the sharp tools stopped prodding me, Storm leaned back in his chair. "Take a look."

He swallowed, almost nervously, straightening slightly as I rose. His eyes remained trained on the design on my back instead of on me.

"Nervous?" I asked playfully as I turned to look in the mirror, while I held my hands against my chest.

I gasped.

"Storm." My voice came out awe struck as I stared at the intricate design. Gorgeous blooms ran along the back of my shoulder. My design wasn't at all like theirs. Instead, Storm had created something that would forever be mine. It was simple yet refined.

"There are seven flowers," he explained, pointing out each one. "Your mother and father, the king and queen, Elisabeth, Hale, and Corbin."

I couldn't say a word as my chest tightened. Tears pooled in my eyes, daring to tip over the edge.

"Your markings are a reminder of who you fight for. Your love is as strong as your light." He finally met my gaze in the mirror. "My queen."

I turned, Kade's shadows quickly cocooned my bare chest as I wrapped Storm in a hug. My heart carried the death of each person with me daily, but this, to have them marked into my skin, to remind me of what our victory would cost, of who died to allow us to live… It was more meaningful than I could voice.

"You did well, brother," Kade said, patting Storm's shoulder.

Storm pulled away, grinning. "All right, I get it. I'm incredible."

I laughed through the tears still streaming down my face and grabbed my shirt to relieve Kade's shadows of their duty to keep me covered. I glanced over at the dagger lying on the bed as if it called to me.

"Let's keep fighting this darkness," I said. "Kade?"

Kade held out his arm, and I lifted the blade, touching my forefinger to the spot immediately under the handle, where Queen Daniella referenced holding it to infuse her magic into the weapon. Pressing down on Kade's forearm, I made a small gash and closed my eyes while directing my light into the dagger.

The dagger pulsed in my hand, and I opened my eyes to find it glowing in my palm.

Hope flared in my chest, and I smiled, meeting Kade's eyes. Holding my breath in anticipation, my gaze returned to Kade's arm only to let out a sharp exhale a moment later.

A few small wisps of darkness curled out and away from his wound, but nothing to the extent we saw with Ian.

My heart sank. A desperation festered, growing more each time we failed. What was I missing?

Angrily, I threw my blade across the room, groaning and covering my face with my hands.

You can't purge the darkness out of someone when it has become a part of their being. No dagger can eliminate darkness this deep without death.

Andras's words bounced around my mind, echoing to the point of overwhelming me. But he didn't know about how many generations of my line had powered the blade.

"Hey." Kade's thumb brushed against my cheek. "We will figure this out."

I forced myself to meet his gaze.

The gentleness in his eyes wavered. "We should discuss the prophecy, combined with what Andras said—"

"No." I stepped away. "They're not connected."

Kade sighed. "At some point we have to face what will

happen if we can't get rid of my darkness. Thames can't survive."

I slammed my hands against his chest. "I said no."

"Lana." Kade's tone turned clinical, detached.

"There is a way in the journal. I will keep reading and this won't be an issue."

"Who do you think the sacrifice is about?" Storm asked.

I whirled on him, glaring. "I don't know, but we don't need to worry about it right now."

"When it comes time to face Thames, we need to be prepared," Kade said, tugging me back to his chest.

Collapsing into him, my forehead rested against the solid muscle beneath his tunic. "The sacrifice isn't one of us. It's not. It can't be."

Kade hugged me tight. "Well, I refuse to let it be you."

Looking up at him, I responded, "You don't think I feel the same?"

The love reflecting in his eyes as he took me in calmed my anxious nerves slightly. He leaned down, kissing me gently. "Of course you do."

His body jerked suddenly.

"Kade?" I frowned as he took a step away from me. "Storm, do you see this?"

Storm looked up from cleaning his tools, his skin losing all color as Kade's body jerked once more.

A grey mist, lighter than his shadows, swirled around his feet, climbing rapidly up his body.

No.

My mind froze as it immediately took me back to that heartbreaking moment in Dargan's study when Thames appeared, trapping Kade.

"Get back," Kade ordered, fear flickering in his eyes.

I didn't listen, instead stepping closer toward him as my heart pounded in my ears. "What's happening?"

"I don't know," Kade said. He flung his shadows out, but

as they tried to wrap around the mist, they were swallowed up too.

"Lana," he breathed out heavily. "Don't do anything crazy, please—"

Before either of us could react, Kade was gone.

Disappeared without a trace.

I fell to my knees and screamed.

CHAPTER 28

LANA

I didn't bother knocking before barging into Ian's room, just down the hall from my own.

"Lana," Storm shouted from behind me, but I refused to stop.

"Ian," I yelled. "Come quick."

The room was dark, except for the three candles burning on his dresser. The curtains hid whatever sunlight was left of the day. I could barely see where I was going and tripped over clothes and weapons scattered across the floor, stubbing my toe on the hilt of a sword.

"Tits and daggers!" I hopped on one foot, trying to ignore the pain throbbing in my big toe.

"Not one moment of peace around here," Raya grumbled from somewhere underneath the sound of rustling of covers.

I felt around for the edge of the curtains and flung them open, illuminating a groggy Ian alongside Raya.

"Ian, Raya, we don't have time," I said, not even having a moment to process that Raya had clearly accepted Ian's role as her mate. "You have to get up." I moved to the edge of the bed and threw a shoe strewn on the ground directly at Ian's head. "Kade's gone."

Raya immediately shot up, holding the covers over her chest. "What did you say?" she whispered. "I know you didn't say what I think you just did."

Storm finally entered the room with us. "For fuck's sake." He quickly turned around as he caught Raya covering herself with the sheets.

My patience wore thin knowing how much planning we had to do. I twisted my hands together. Gathering everyone took time away from figuring out how to find Kade.

"Kade's been taken, and we don't know what happened. I am…" I stumbled and leaned forward on the edge of the bed. "Freaking out." Ian snapped forward, lunging across the bed to take my hand in his as I stared between the two of them. "Get dressed, we're meeting in the library in ten minutes to come up with a plan."

Ian and Raya gave each other a look, and I stood there waiting for them to move, becoming frustrated when they didn't immediately get out of bed.

"What are you waiting for?" I shouted, throwing my hands in the air.

"We're coming, Lan. Don't worry," Ian assured me. He pulled the covers off, wrapping himself in another bedsheet before coming to my side. He gripped my shoulder. "Take a deep breath."

I obeyed, not bothering to hide my trembling.

"Again," he said calmly. His eyes flicked over to Raya, who I saw rise and move toward her clothes in my periphery.

"We'll figure this out," he said sternly, as if he had no doubts. "We're right behind you."

I nodded. While my body relaxed slightly, this disaster still had to be dealt with immediately, and I turned, fleeing the walls of the room. I had to do something. I couldn't stand still. "Stay with them and meet me in the library," I called over my shoulder to Storm, who couldn't quite figure out where to go.

I turned down the hall and made my way to Kalliah's

room. I prayed she was there and not in Leif's chambers, because it would take too many precious minutes to get to the other wing of the castle where the rest of the staff were housed. It was time I didn't have to waste. Nothing was more important than finding Kade and returning him to my side.

I struggled to possess the cool, calm demeanor and confidence Ian always had in times of trouble. My thoughts spiraled as I hurried down the hall. I could only presume Thames was behind this disappearance, and all I could think about was Kade in that monster's grasp. The darkness Thames forced into him, or stirred in him, taking over against Kade's will. His black eyes and haunting laugh swallowing him before my light could bring him back.

My heart stuttered and I rubbed my chest. The moment I thought he was safe, he was ripped from my arms once more. How many times would I have to endure this feeling?

Shaking my head, I steeled my nerves and continued down the silent halls. The tattoo on my back ached from the rawness of the skin, but it was a pain I would gladly endure. It anchored me to the present when my heart threatened to run to Mysthaven, no matter the consequence.

I decided there would be another tattoo joining this one soon enough. When Thames was dead, it would be forever marked on my body as a reminder never to let evil take over our lands again.

To treasure the bonds we hold dearest.

A reminder that I would destroy anyone who threatened those I loved—especially my mate.

The back staircase used by the palace staff twisted and turned but eventually popped me out three doors down from Kalliah's room. I twisted the handle and shoved my body into the door but bounced back. Jiggling the handle, I tried once more. The door didn't budge; it was locked. Unusual for Kalliah.

I pounded on the wooden frame. "Kalliah," I shouted.

"Leif, open up." When no one answered, I knocked harder, more insistent. "Come on, this is serious. Open the door."

I heard heavy footsteps thudding toward me, which were clearly not Kalliah's. The door creaked open and Jax peeked his head through the slim opening.

"Yes, Lana?" He smirked, standing shirtless before me. "You needed something?"

I was momentarily speechless, unprepared to find Jax here and in this state of dress, but it didn't matter. I blinked rapidly, shaking my head. "Look, I don't know what's going on in there, but Kade's gone. I need you all."

Jax's face fell. "What?"

"Get Kalliah and Leif and meet us in the library in ten minutes." I turned to walk away and stopped. "Or sooner." I paused, closing my eyes. "Please."

"What do you mean, 'gone'?" His normal bravado completely vanished.

"Gone." I flared my hands at him. "Poof, disappeared."

If I had to explain myself any further right now, I may actually combust. My light flowed inside of me, heating my hands and causing the force to gather in my chest as if searching for a way out.

We will find them and destroy the one who hurt them.

I held my breath, mentally pushing down my light magic to a more manageable corner for now. Going back to being erratic wouldn't help any of us.

Jax's eyes widened, taking in my struggle. "Say no more, we're on our way." He turned and yelled into the room. "Kalliah! Leif! Grab me a shirt and meet us in the library."

Jax followed me down the hall, not waiting for Kalliah and Leif or his shirt, even though we both heard them immediately scramble inside the bedroom. I gave Jax a side-eye and stifled a smirk, latching on to a respite of distraction now that we were moving toward doing something again. He shrugged in response to my silent query before a devilish grin escaped that he couldn't hide.

Ten minutes later, with everyone finally clothed, we all assembled in the library. This was my father's personal library and study. He came here often to think and reflect on whatever troubled him. Growing up, if he had some sort of life lesson to teach me, he would bring me here. I ran my hands over the section of the bookshelf he'd deemed mine. It housed some of my favorites, but it was also where he'd leave books he wanted me to read. I swallowed down the fresh grief rolling through me. I missed him so damn much.

Ian stood behind Raya, sitting in a chair next to the unlit fireplace, while the rest of my friends gathered randomly throughout the room, clearly uncomfortable with the knowledge of Kade's disappearance.

"Okay, so walk us through this one more time," Ian said.

I heaved an exasperated sigh as I paced in front of the couches by the window overlooking my mother's favorite gardens. Storm jumped in. "I was giving Lana a tattoo and then a dark shadow-like mist overtook him. They didn't look exactly like his shadows. They looked like—" He paused, and his wary eyes met mine. "They looked like the mist Thames controlled back in Mysthaven. A second later Kade was just gone."

The bond between Kade and me pulled taught, like if we took one wrong move, it would snap into a thousand pieces. I rubbed my arms as if it could calm the ache of being away from him. "I don't care what we do. We must get him back. It has to be Thames. It's the only reasonable explanation."

The others sat in silence, staring at me with what looked like pity on their faces. "Lana—" Storm started.

Turning to face him directly, I knew deep in my bones I wasn't going to like the words he would say next. Little did he know I wouldn't go down without a fight.

"I know you want to immediately go find Kade, but we have to think this through. We have to be smart."

Tears fell down my cheeks, unable to hold in any more of the emotions wracking my body. "I don't want to be smart. I just got him back, and now I've lost him again."

Ian left Raya's side and wrapped me in an embrace. He kissed my forehead and let me listen to his heartbeat, like we had done so many times before. "Just breathe, Lana." He rubbed my back as I tried to calm myself. "Listen to what he has to say."

I felt Ian nod toward Storm as if saying *continue*.

"We can't get anywhere near Thames right now. We won't win. The darkness is still there. We need to put our emotions aside and focus on figuring out how to destroy whatever this weapon is. If we can get rid of the weapon, then we can get rid of Thames."

"He could be dead by then," I snapped, pushing myself out of Ian's grasp.

Storm stepped toward me and grabbed my shoulders. "I know. Don't forget I love him too."

I swallowed down some of the anger seeing Storm's devastation. We survived by leaning on each other the first time we lost him, we could do it again.

"This is a huge risk, but it's one that we have to take." Storm reached down and held my hands firmly in his. "We have to be smarter than Thames so we don't lose all of us."

He was right and, in a way, it's what hurt the most. Evelyn and the prophecy made it clear that unless we eliminated all the darkness, Thames would continue to live. There would be no defeating him. If he did have Kade, we weren't ready to face him right now.

It didn't make the pain of losing Kade—again—any easier. I snorted thinking back to standing in my room as he disappeared. He'd begged me not to do something rash. Luckily, Storm listened better than I did.

"But we don't even know anything about this so-called weapon," Kalliah added bluntly, with her hands on her hips. A signature Kalliah move for when she was annoyed.

The library door creaked open slowly, making us all turn in surprise, especially when it opened to reveal Cassandra and Vivienne standing on the other side.

My fears morphed quickly into anger. An unreasonable bout of hatred swelled in me, and I knew my magic played a role in it. "What are you doing here?"

The two entered the room without a care in the world, like they were meant to be here.

"Where have you been?"

"It appears you need our help," Cassandra announced coolly, seating herself on a settee to my right. "So here we are."

Now they decide to show up? I was so tired of these seers just coming and going as they pleased and not giving us any real direction. What good was their power, their magic, if they couldn't even help the ones who needed it most?

"You didn't even say goodbye to us when we left the Knotted Willow. What makes you think we need your help now?" Fury laced my tone, and my hands began to shake. There were too many emotions swirling inside of me in too short a period of time.

Vivienne walked over to me, her features calm and clear. "The Fates had a different plan for our arrival."

"Well if the fucking Fates could decide on what they wanted, it would be really fucking nice," I screamed, unable to control myself. My skin glowed as my magic tried to break free, extending out of me almost like Kade's shadows. "I've had enough of their meddling."

I stood there, trying to regain some composure as my carefully built facade intended for diplomacy crumbled around me.

"By all means," Cassandra drawled. "Throw a temper tantrum. That will be extremely helpful."

"What good is your magic if you speak in riddles? Why don't you ever stay? You claimed to care about Kade, and he's gone. Again. You weren't here and we lost Corbin."

"Do you think I don't know loss?" Cassandra rose, walking toward me. "Do you think I haven't felt my soul ripping apart for a thousand years because of what I did to my mate?" She shook her finger in my face, and Storm moved toward me. "I lost my sister, the only friends I ever had, and my mate. He may be evil, but you speak of cruelty? Imagine your soul bound to Thames." She pulled back, brushing her hands down her dress. "I understand the loss you feel, Illiana. But we walk a delicate line. One wrong move and we lose this world forever."

I swallowed, allowing her words to hit as she intended. Knowing how entwined my being was with Kade's, I didn't know how she still stood after a thousand years without her mate. His destructive choices didn't eliminate their bond. I couldn't even imagine the torment that must cause her.

I bowed my head in submission. The light inside me slithered away, reducing to a more manageable simmer as I took a deep breath.

"Illiana, darling." Vivienne's voice floated in my ear, more soothing than I'd ever heard her speak before. "I've watched you grow up over the years, and you have become a breathtaking woman. But when the Fates speak, we must do as they say. It's how their magic works. We cannot go against it, or it can have dire consequences. I know none of this helps you, and you believe we are out to purposefully make things harder." She pushed a strand of hair out of my eyes. "You aren't the only one hurting. We must follow what the Fates have foretold if we have any hope of saving this world."

Lucien trotted through the door, immediately making his

way to my side and nuzzling my leg. He always knew when I needed strength. I reached down, scratching under his chin.

"We know where the troops are," Vivienne casually stated.

All our heads snapped to look at her.

"And?" Jax asked.

"Thames has called all of his dark ones to Firestone."

"Why?" I asked, my brow furrowing at the same time Ian asked, "What is Firestone?"

Jax and Raya exchanged a look before groaning in unison.

"Why do we keep getting dragged to the worst places in our world?" Jax whined.

"How are you an elite Guardian when you're scared of everywhere, Jax?" Kalliah snorted. "Are you really a big bad warrior, or are you just a scaredy cat?"

Jax stuck out his tongue at Kalliah. "You loved my cat last—"

Storm cleared his throat. "Firestone is a volcano," he interrupted, answering Ian's question.

Ian's eyes widened. "Well, that's a first. I should probably stop assuming things in books are make believe."

"If he's calling troops there, do we think the weapon might be there?" I asked out loud as I processed the revelations.

Cassandra nodded. "It's our assumption. The dark ones you captured weren't clear why they were going, they just knew they'd been called back."

"When did this happen?"

"It's why we were late. We were pushed in another direction from Ellevail."

I stared at the two women, my eyes darting back and forth between them. I had to accept there was much I'd never know about them, but one thing I needed to remember was not to underestimate them.

"How are we possibly going to get to Firestone?" Raya asked. "That is days of riding at best. At worst, a week or more depending on if we encounter any trouble along the way."

Ian frowned and paced back and forth. Storm ran his hand along the side of his face, both men looking like their brains were going a hundred miles per hour trying to figure out any way to get there faster.

"I could fly there and scope it out. It would only take me a few days," Ian suggested. "I would just need some sort of map to get me through Mysthaven."

"You've never even been to Mysthaven," Raya reminded him. "It's a terrible idea. You don't know what you are getting yourself into. If anyone were to shift and travel to determine what's there, it would be Jax. But even then, it would take him too long to get there."

I raked my hand through my hair, trying to run through scenarios in my head. We didn't know if we had days or weeks to travel, spy, and return home to plan. If there was no other way, then we didn't have a choice. We couldn't enter this battle blind, fighting some mysterious weapon, and hope to face Thames, and live to tell the tale.

I inhaled, closing my eyes as I held by breath for a few seconds, then released it. *Focus.* We would make it work.

Cassandra coughed, focusing my attention back on her. "Illiana, all you need to do is ask that pet of yours. I'm sure he'd be happy to oblige."

What?

We all looked at each other, confused. How could Lucien help us? He was a pugron for Fates' sake.

Lucien snorted, a column of smoke spewing from his snout. He looked up at me, his barbed tail trailing back and forth over the carpet, wagging as it ripped into the material every time a barb caught another string.

A grin slowly spread as he sat at attention, as if waiting for orders.

CHAPTER 29
KADE

The memories of what I'd done the last time I roamed Mysthaven stormed through my mind, unrelenting as the guilt festered inside of me.

Being here again made all of it too real. I wasn't ready to face it. I breathed through my nose, clenching my jaw as I tried to push the memories aside.

"Do pay attention. It's rude to ignore your king," Thames ordered as he casually sat in an ornate gold-trimmed chair, the seat covered in onyx velvet. He swirled an amber liquid in his glass before taking another sip. "We have much to accomplish."

I knew I needed to pay attention, but my head swam with an unrelenting grogginess, my vision blurring in and out. A hot breeze swept over my body, already slick with sweat. The heat in the room made it impossible to think clearly, but I needed to focus.

"Where are we?" I stared at Thames sitting across from me, surprised I remained unharmed. I wiped the sweat from my brow and noticed a glass of water on a table next to me. Reaching for the liquid, I hesitated as soon as it rested in my hand.

"I would drink up," Thames said, steepling his fingers in front of his face. "Pulling you here from across Atheria isn't the easiest thing for your body, powerful or not."

I frowned, glancing at the liquid again. Would he try to poison me? Was this a trap? I smelled the glass, unable to detect anything suspicious. I would have to deal with the consequences later if my assumption turned out to be incorrect, because if I didn't get something down my throat, I may combust. Swallowing the cool liquid in large gulps, I instantly felt relief.

"Where are we?" I asked again.

A smirk spread across Thames's lips. "Firestone, of course. Where else would we be as the end draws near?" He stood and sauntered over to a railing I hadn't noticed before. He looked pleased as he peered down, examining something below. "Yes, the weapon is almost complete."

The longer I sat here, the more my senses returned to full capacity, even if they did so sluggishly. Far too slowly for this situation.

Thames turned away from the balcony's edge, a firelight glow dancing over his face. "Feeling better?"

I hesitated, unsure of what the fuck was happening.

He cocked an eyebrow but didn't make a move.

I nodded once.

"Come, come," he said as he waved his hand for me to join him at the railing.

Thames acted as if I hadn't completely disobeyed his orders. I hadn't brought Lana to him—fuck, I hadn't bothered returning to him at all. Every one of my senses urged me to proceed with caution, but if Thames was willing to talk, I would play along.

Carefully, I rose, feeling for my shadows within me, in case we needed a quick escape. Concern furrowed my brows. They felt distant.

We're here. Pay attention. Survive.

I shook my head, clearing the last bit of fog, and moved to Thames's side. "Tell me more."

Before he uttered a word, my jaw dropped as I took in what he had been looking at. I glanced over my shoulder, realizing we were standing in a room carved into the side of the volcano. The walls were rough, without any pattern to how the hollow cave-like room was constructed. A slender staircase made up of uneven rocks snaked downward toward an opening in the center of the volcano. Molten lava bubbled in a large pool beneath us.

Thames's eyes glistened with glee, as he placed his hands on the railing, surveying everything. "It's here." He whisked his hand before him. "It's all here."

I took a deep breath and allowed myself a moment to process what he'd laid out before me. "The volcano is the weapon?" I whispered, desperate for it not to be true.

"I have been feeding the darkness into the volcano for years now. Your father's inconsistent help with this task irked me to no end. No matter, you are here now and together we will finish this."

It was incomprehensible. Using the volcano as the weapon seemed impossible, but for a Fae who had been trapped for a thousand years, I wouldn't put anything past him.

"How does it work?" I turned to face him, pretending to be captivated, in awe of his power and capabilities.

A bell rang in the distance, and footsteps echoed below. "I too have learned a thing or two about *sacrificial* magic over the years," Thames spat. "My mate was particularly skilled in that area of sorcery, and while she may have thought I wasn't paying attention, I was." The smile spreading over his face appeared eerier than usual as the glow from the lava danced over the curves of his face.

He nodded downward, shifting our focus away from the stairs and small pools to a much larger pit of lava. A line of Fae stepped through a wide opening opposite the end of the staircase. A Guardian stood, arms crossed, at the edge of the molten pool, tapping his fingers on his forearm as he waited for the Fae to approach. When they made it a few feet from the ledge, the guardian waved his hand, beckoning the first Fae forward while simultaneously drawing a dagger from his side.

"Do you accept your fate and pledge yourself to the darkness?" the Guardian asked as he handed the dagger to the woman.

She bowed her head and clutched the dagger, slicing across the palm of her hand. "I pledge myself to the darkness."

The blood from her palm dripped into the lava below, sizzling. Black smoke swirled into the air, reminding me of what the darkness looked like when Lana banished it from Ian's body, and exactly what had exploded out of Andras at his death.

The hair on my arms rose as I watched the woman hand back the dagger and step off the ledge, directly into the pool of lava. Her body erupted in flames before completely disappearing from sight.

I inhaled sharply as a chill crawled over me. Her scream lasted a mere second, echoing around the walls of the cavernous volcano before it died.

Thames breathed in deeply, his eyes rolling back in his head as if in ecstasy at the sight of the death. "You see, for those who accept the darkness willingly, it's embedded into their body. Into their essence. It overtakes all rational thinking almost as soon as they accept me. Those who sacrifice themselves willingly fuel my weapon."

"How does their sacrifice translate into a weapon?" I forcefully tried to keep the rising bile down, swallowing the foul liquid before it could crawl up my throat. Thames was marching the people of Mysthaven to their death and relishing it. A line of willing participants continued funneling in, despite seeing the path only led to death.

"When the volcano is at full capacity, we let it erupt. With the power I've funneled into it, it will explode, releasing my magic with it, and we will cover the entire world with my darkness, the magic I have harnessed for a thousand years. It will be so strong, we won't need to infect the Fae directly with daggers or other weapons." He chuckled under his breath. "No, they will simply breathe, and it will enter their system. I will be able to control them all and Atheria will be mine." His knuckles whitened as he gripped the railing.

I staggered on my feet as the world stopped around me. Thames would destroy everything good, everything kind and beautiful remaining in Atheria. The entire world as we knew it would be gone. Lana's light wouldn't matter if he infected her, but even if she stayed safe from her clear immunity to the darkness, she'd be wholly alone.

Focusing my gaze on the dark ones sacrificing themselves, I lifted my chin. I needed more information to formulate a plan. I refused to leave Lana alone for one second in this world. While my shadows may have been in agreement, they rolled in agitation.

We will find a way.

I kept my face neutral. If I had any hope of defeating Thames, I needed to play along. Make him believe I would follow his every command.

Stepping back from the railing, I bowed, hoping he would ignore my momentary hesitation if I showed him some reverence. "My king, it's a genius plan, but what happens to those who are disloyal? Those who do not accept it willingly?"

Thames ushered me toward him, placing a hand around my shoulders and pointing down to the line of Fae. A few appeared through the opening, this time with chains around their ankles, unable to move more than a few inches at a time.

Their sluggish movements made it look as if they were under some sort of spell.

"Their death is still a sacrifice, even if it is not to the darkness itself. A sacrifice of magic is better than no sacrifice at all." He watched me carefully as he spoke. Then he leaned in and whispered in my ear, "Besides, what better way to deal with traitors? Hm?"

The Guardian below reached for the first man in chains and, without any warning or hesitation, threw him over the side. His horrific screams still echoed throughout the chamber as his charred body sunk into the molten pool. It had to be torture burning alive.

"Sacrifice. Is that what all of this comes down to?" I asked, swallowing my disgust.

Thames's entire face twitched. The calm facade he wore faltered. "You don't even know the meaning of sacrifice." Thames's lip curled. "I was forced to live a thousand years in the void, in utter darkness. My *mate*"—spit flew from his mouth—"thought she could rid Atheria of me. She was mistaken. Now the world will pay for her transgressions."

Thames paced back toward his chair, grabbing his glass and swallowing the remaining liquid. A decanter sat on a small table a few feet away, and I snatched it, moving toward him to refill his drink. It might keep him talking if he thought of me as a loyal guardian.

He shoved the glass toward me, shaking it in his hand. My shadows tightened inside of me suddenly, and a glimmer of evil twinkled in his eyes. Once his cup had been refilled, he took another large gulp and I took a few steps away, putting space between us.

"She betrayed me all those years ago."

Thames stalked toward me. He continued to approach, forcing me to keep retreating until, without realizing, my back was to the volcano wall. I tried to call upon my shadows, but they didn't come.

Fuck, there was something in that drink. I knew better than this. He did this to us once before and I had been so stupid for believing he wouldn't do it again.

"But you know who else has betrayed me?" Thames whispered. "*You.*"

I jerked against him as our bodies practically touched. Fuck. *Fuck.*

I tried to focus on the tie to Lana, the bond filling me with light. My shadows twitched in response but wouldn't come forward. They were there inside me, fighting to break through whatever barrier Thames had poisoned me with.

His power was terrifying, and if I didn't find a way to stop him, Lana would be his next target. He snapped his fingers and my body lifted off the floor, slamming into the wall as his mist secured my wrists and ankles in iron grips against the volcano.

"Thames, what are you doing?" I tried to remain calm, but the growing pit in my stomach filled every part of me with dread. "I can help you."

"Did you know my own mate poisoned me?" Thames lifted his glass in front of his face, staring at the liquid. "It's how she made me weak enough to unleash her sacrificial sorcery and trap me in that miserable void." He took a sip and sneered in disgust. "Did you really think, after living through her deception, *you* could betray me, and I wouldn't find out?" Thames roared so loud I flinched. "I sent you on a mission and you didn't return. You killed my soldiers and weakened my army."

"I had to regain her trust," I argued. "She would never come willingly with me if she didn't believe I was hers," I said, trying anything to keep him talking while I prayed to the Fates that whatever this poison was would wear off quickly enough for me to call upon my shadows and get us out of here. I had to find a way to return to Illiana.

Thames snickered. "Ah, ah, Kade, you're *lying.* My

darkness is everywhere. It lives and breathes with me. It lives and breathes here." He shoved a finger to my chest and let his eyes roam up and down with a gaze of utter repulsion. "There's nothing you can hide from me. You *want* your mate bond. You *love* her. Pathetic. It made you weak, so I will have to kill her myself."

"If you touch one hair on her head, I swear death will seem like a *gift*." I pulled against the chains holding me back, but it was useless. I couldn't move. My shadows hadn't returned, even though they fought aggressively within me for purchase.

Without any magic, I was completely vulnerable to anything Thames wanted to do to me. But worse, I couldn't get free of these damn chains to protect Lana.

"You know," he murmured as he returned to his seat slowly, "I was going to kill her after using you, but how wonderful would it be to kill her in front of you. Her and that bitch Cassandra. I will watch that bond break as she dies, and you will know then, there's no way to escape your fate."

Thames collapsed into his chair, laughing to himself. "I like this plan. Get comfortable," he snapped. "You're going to be here until you die. You are my most prized possession after all, the one that has been fueled by the darkness the longest. Since the day of your birth, you have been infected with my will. You are the last and final piece I need to complete my weapon."

"I will never go willingly," I grunted. "It will be for nothing."

Sipping his amber liquid, Thames looked calm and relaxed. "The amount of darkness living inside of you is more than enough, whether you're willing or not. You alone would, most likely, be enough. The rest are merely my insurance."

He sickened me. Sweat dampened my skin as the lava surged with each Fae continuing to sacrifice themselves below us. Suddenly, I stopped jerking against the restraints, instead trying to dig inside of myself to release my magic from Thames's hold.

"It's useless," he said with a laugh. "You will be fed into the volcano, and the world will be covered in darkness. I will be king to people devoted to *me*. There is no sacrifice that can save Atheria this time. You'll lose everything, and I will be untouchable against the Fates themselves."

CHAPTER 30
IAN

"I don't understand how Lucien has magical abilities that are supposed to help us," Lana said, hands resting on her hips as she paced around her private garden.

Still midsummer, the massive rows of hedges still protected us from any outside view despite their decayed state. Though the garden lay deadened like nature and life in Ellevail currently, it had been the only truly private place we could think of. The palace and most of Ellevail remained in a state of chaos as staff and Fae we trusted restored order.

Still, I didn't miss the pained expression on Lana's face when we assembled here and she took in the sight. She'd immediately wrapped her arms around herself, trying to hold it together. This had been her special place with Corbin, a world they'd created together. Seeing it destroyed after losing him pained me. I could only imagine how it made her feel.

"I told you the pugron understood us," I murmured, shrugging while trying to distract her from our surroundings. "You were the one who didn't listen."

Her gaze snapped to mine and she narrowed her eyes, even though her lips quirked ever so slightly. It was the closest thing to a smile I could ask for at the moment.

"Understanding us and possessing some kind of magic are two very different things."

I crossed my arms, watching her intently as she paced again. Strands of her hair whispered in the breeze, falling disheveled from her loose braid, and the dark circles under her eyes had deepened through the night.

A few hours had passed since we left the library, just as confused as when we entered. When Vivienne and Cassandra left us, they indicated we needed to meet them here at daybreak. We took that time to set up shifts for our people to bury the dead and begin cleaning up Andras's mess of our capital. With all our stomachs rumbling, we needed to take a moment to regroup.

Kalliah managed to wrangle up breakfast. Now most of us sat along the stone benches in silence, eating various fruits and sweet breads. Storm stood stoically, tracking all of Lana's movements, watching her as if he thought she might disappear next.

Storm and I only had a few moments to talk in between the chaos. Both of us were in full agreement on one thing—convincing Lana of our plan would be tricky because it required her to stay behind. But it was the *only* way.

Vivienne and Cassandra claimed Lucien was the key to helping us. The shock of that statement lasted all of two seconds before I remembered how often he'd randomly appeared throughout the palace.

The problem now would be ensuring Lana remained here while we made our way to Firestone. There was no other choice. Heading to Mysthaven could *not* include her. In the end, she would be the one to defeat Thames, and right now, she wasn't ready for that. If we did anything to risk her life or chance Thames getting to her too soon, everything would be over.

Lana stopped pacing to stretch but immediately winced as she twisted her back.

Storm stepped forward, stopping her motions. "Your tattoo is still healing, be gentle with your movements. You don't want to cause any more friction than necessary for at least one more day."

"Okay, okay," she sighed. "I'm just tired and so damn worried."

Storm nodded. "I know. Me too."

"Lana." I stared at her, determined to convince her as soon as possible to go along with staying behind. "I know you're dealing with so much right now. You're concerned about Kade, you want to help with figuring out the weapon, but we can't risk potentially running into Thames while we gather more details." I sipped at the tart juice in my cup before swirling it around. I took any distraction for a break from having this conversation with the one woman who might stab me for demanding she sit anything out.

Well, except my mate. I glanced toward Raya, who gave me a small encouraging nod before looking at Lana. The fierce glare she wore appeared weaponized to kill. "Besides, you just won your home back. You're needed to start rebuilding and to provide some stability for your people here. You are their queen. How would it look if you left again?"

"So you want me to send all of you off to destroy a weapon we know nothing about while I sit here?"

I tilted my head, raising an eyebrow.

Her shoulders slumped. "I hate this," she sighed as she collapsed onto a bench, resting her head in her hands. "Logically, I understand, but emotionally? I don't want you all to do something risky while I remain here, helpless."

Storm backed away and leaned against a hedge row next to Leif, while Kalliah approached to sit next to Lana. "Your feelings are understandable, Lana, but you are the only queen here. Let us be there for you, and for Brook— Atheria in other ways. We're all here, able and willing to do anything to ensure we come out of this the victors. While this may be our home, and you may be our queen, you are first and foremost our friend. It's that friendship, that love, that we fight for."

Lana smiled and placed her hand on Kalliah's, resting both on top of her leg. They sat there for a moment, leaning into each other,sharing further unspoken feelings, when we heard rustling.

Vivienne and Cassandra appeared between the hedges; their matching lavender gowns flowing behind them. They looked so content together.

"Judging from the look on Lana's face, I'm assuming you convinced her to stay behind?" Cassandra asked, her voice low and full of hope.

Lana scowled at Cassandra before softening her gaze when she looked at Vivienne.

Lucien pranced around a hedge into the garden and strode toward Lana's feet. He nuzzled into her dark brown leather shoes, then rested his head comfortably on top of them. His tail wagged slightly as he took in the surrounding courtyard.

The sound of a sharp intake of air in front of me returned my attention to the seers. Vivienne stood preternaturally still. Her eyes had turned milky white.

"Lana—" I ushered her over to my side for safety, and Lucien growled as she moved him out of the way. Worry laced her expression as she stared at Vivenne.

With Vivienne's head tilted back, she spoke. "Sacred magic twisted and scorned, all so he can be reborn. Fire, fire set it free. Fire, fire, the world will be." Her head snapped forward, as the words hung in the air and the color returned to her eyes.

Cassandra reached for Vivienne, holding her arm.

"I'm all right," Vivienne said softly, but stumbled the moment she tried to take a step.

Cassandra didn't let go of her sister but looked to me. "We must forge ahead. Time is of the essence."

"What was that?" I asked, nodding to Vivienne.

The seers glanced at each other. "We've been getting glimpses, flashes of things, but nothing consistent. Fate is at a breaking point now. Everything that's happened is converging into a final showdown. Each choice that is made reforges Fate's path."

"So we could ruin everything with one wrong move?" Jax asked.

Cassandra's gaze softened, surprising since most of her time here had been spent snapping at everyone. "We are trying to ensure that doesn't happen."

"How can Lucien help us?" Lana asked, shifting the conversation back to the task at hand.

"Lucien is a pugron." Cassandra bent down and called him over to her. Lucien lifted his head before snorting out smoke and lying back down in front of Lana, ignoring the seer. Cassandra let out a disgruntled *hmpf*. "These creatures always did love Evelyn the best. She had quite a way with animals. No matter how hard I tried, I never had the touch she possessed."

"That actually makes a lot of sense," Lana thought out loud, clearly reconciling all the information we knew about Evelyn and everything that had happened in the Southern Forests. "If Evelyn could command the strox and the razorven, a pugron would've been easy, I'd imagine."

Genuine smiles graced Cassandra's and Vivienne's lips as they simultaneously moved closer to Lana.

"Tell us what you know of a pugron's powers, my dear," Vivienne said.

Everyone waited for Lana to respond. She frowned, looking down at Lucien for a moment. "Well, I'm not exactly sure. It's always been a mystery to all of us. I mean, he breathes fire, but he also moves about the castle in ways I've never understood."

"He came to me many times when I was in the dungeon,"

I offered my previous thoughts aloud. "He appeared out of nowhere and would vanish into thin air."

"Yes, that is a pugron's major ability." Vivienne smiled. "Lucien is a portal keeper."

Jax snorted. "A what? A portal keeper? Come on, is that real?"

Cassandra and Vivienne were unamused by Jax's disbelief. "Yes," they snapped in unison.

Jax quickly shut his mouth.

"Pugrons can create portals to anywhere they, or anyone in their familial line, have been before," Vivienne continued. "All you have to do is ask and I believe he will take you to the volcano."

"That would mean that Lucien is either a thousand years old—" My mind whirled at the insane possibility.

Lana cut me off. "Or pugrons in Lucien's line were here before the world split in two." She reached down and scratched behind his ears. "How old are you, sweet thing?"

"Old," Cassandra chuckled. "Pugrons live extremely long lives for such little creatures. It is likely his parents were here with Evelyn."

Honestly, it just seemed insane, but after everything…was it really? Who knew what we should and could believe anymore.

"So all we have to do is ask little Luci here to make us a portal and it can take us to Firestone?" Jax asked incredulously. "That's it?"

Vivienne straightened her gown. "I would suggest Illiana ask, he is loyal to her. If you ask, he may incinerate you."

Lana stuck out her tongue at Jax in a move so unqueen-like for such a serious situation, it reassured me that the Lana I knew and loved was still in there. We hadn't lost her yet to the anguish of being separated from Kade.

She glanced at me, then to Storm. "I'm assuming you

both have ideas on who should undertake a portal jump to Firestone?"

Storm's lip twitched as he crossed his arms. "Perhaps."

"Out with it, then."

"Jax and Ian," Storm answered immediately.

Lana's eyes narrowed, but I didn't miss the slight furrow in her brow. She was surprised. "Because?"

"We're shifters," I answered for him. Storm nodded. He was a damn good leader, and I appreciated his quick thinking. It rivaled my own, and I was grateful to have an equal navigating these circumstances. "Meaning we can physically retreat faster than all of you. We also possess the ability to be stealthier in our animal forms. We can get in and out, hopefully without being noticed."

"Just the two of you alone?" Lana asked.

Raya flipped her sword around in her hand like she was bored. "I've gotten pretty good at my babysitting duties with you, Your Majesty." She winked at Lana, and though it wasn't directed at me, my heart skipped a beat at her beauty. Since she'd accepted our bond and stopped punishing herself for what happened in Mysthaven, she'd been lighter despite the challenges and dark path that lay ahead.

"I don't like this." Lana wrung her hands together. "You've never even been to Mysthaven, Ian." She stepped toward me and whispered, "What if you don't come back? I'm barely hanging on right now. If I lose you too…"

My fingers found hers, and I interlaced them. "It's a risk we have to take. This is for our world's survival."

"He won't be going alone," Raya added. "He'll have Jax and Lucien. They'll get the information we need and report back in no time."

"I can't believe you're not worried about me too." Jax crossed his arms and rolled his eyes.

"Have you always been this needy?" Lana retorted.

He grinned. "For my queen's attention? I haven't had a queen in a long time, so I'm going to say yes."

I let Jax's humor soak into the tension-filled atmosphere. It allowed me a moment to hide my own fears. I couldn't show Lana or Raya how worried I was. What if we didn't succeed? Not only in finding whatever this weapon was but in getting the information we'd need to destroy it. We couldn't lose this war, but right now, there were too many outliers. If we didn't find a way to eliminate this threat or destroy the darkness in Kade, defeating Thames wouldn't matter at all because it wouldn't be possible. Beyond that, Lana would never recover. I didn't know how many more losses she could take and still maintain her sanity.

Losing her mate? That wasn't even on the table.

I'd had less time with Raya than she and Kade, and already I knew if either of us lost the other, there'd be no place for us here. It wasn't just a deep-rooted feeling; it was as if accepting the bond intertwined our souls together. There was no longer one without the other.

I couldn't help but flick my gaze to Cassandra. Knowing this feeling, I wasn't sure how *she* continued functioning. Especially for a thousand years.

"Well, since that's settled," Jax said, rising to join me next to Lana. "How does one travel through a portal?" Jax's expression shifted and filled with mischief. "Can I continue to use it after this? Or is it a one-time thing?"

Cassandra rolled her eyes. "For you? Fates help anyone if Lucien lets you bounce around our world on a whim."

Jax winked at the seer, eliciting a sharp, brisk chuckle. The first I think we'd heard from her in weeks.

Lana worried her lip between her teeth, her gaze floating between Lucien and Vivienne. "You believe this is the right move?" she asked her. "That I stay, and they go through a portal like this?" Her gaze turned icy when she looked over at Cassandra. "Because if I send my friends into this unknown portal and they come back harmed—or worse, dead—I will not hesitate to banish you from this kingdom, or the next."

I held my breath, unsure of how Cassandra would respond. Vivienne seemed to be the tolerant one, but the more Lana pushed Cassandra, the moodier she became.

Instead of reacting, both sisters shook their heads. "The Fates have spoken; it is their will," Vivienne said solemnly. "We would not lead you astray, not as we approach the final hour. The portal is safe."

Cassandra sighed. "As for what they find, we can't make promises."

Lana's jaw twitched as she clenched it. I shifted my position, resting my hand between her shoulder blades. She relaxed slightly.

"You believe this is right?" she asked me much less angrily than the tone she took with the seers.

I nodded. "We'll learn about the weapon and come right back to discuss how to destroy it."

She looked into my eyes, searching for hesitation. She wouldn't find any. Fear or not, this *was* the right decision.

"Lucien," Lana finally called, kneeling on the ground as he trotted up to her legs. "I don't begin to understand how your power works, but will you please use your extremely cool portal powers to help my friends?" Lucien sat up straighter, wagging his dangerously sharp tail. "I will forever be in your debt." She tickled her fingers under his chin.

The little pugron nodded his head in clear understanding and rubbed his smooshed face into Lana's hand, demanding more scratches. "I'll take that as a yes," Lana giggled. "Good boy."

Feeling eyes on me, I lifted my gaze to meet Raya's. A faint tinge of color rose to her cheeks as she teasingly mouthed, "Be a good boy."

I laughed, ignoring the others as I crossed the space between us, cupping her face in my hands.

"I'll be a *very* good boy so I can get back to showing you who is in charge." I wrapped my hand around her neck, bringing her lips to mine for a kiss that was over far too soon.

Lucien breathed a stream of fire from his mouth, and we both startled at the flames. He spun in a circle and then lifted his chin. The area in front of him turned hazy as a cloud formed, swirling, shiny and black.

He glanced back at me and then looked at the portal again. It grew in size, until it appeared as if I could walk through easily. He stopped, padding backward, and smoke hissed out of his nostrils.

"Well, that's our cue." Jax walked fearlessly toward the portal, but as he reached Lucien's side, he looked back toward Leif and Kalliah, still seated on one of the stone benches. "Take care of our girl, Leif. I'll be back as soon as I can."

"I'm *not* your girl," Kalliah huffed, despite the blush coloring her cheeks. "How many times do we have to go over this?"

"Just keep telling yourself that, sweetheart." Jax threw her a wink anyway and waited for me.

I squeezed Raya's hand and left her side, moving quickly to give Lana a hug, "We'll be back as soon as we can. Try not to get in any trouble while we're gone."

"Be careful. Don't do anything stupid, please?" Lana's voice quivered. She was trying to stay strong. I'd seen it so many times before.

"See you soon, Lan."

Jax and I gave each other one quick look and then stepped into the portal.

Fates, I prayed we didn't die.

CHAPTER 31
IAN

Stepping into the portal, we were immediately surrounded by deep glittering colors, swirling together in a vortex.

My stomach dropped as a falling sensation made my insides feel like they were coming out of my body. A band of magic propelled us forward. I couldn't be sure how long we were in the portal, but it felt like mere moments before we stumbled out face first on the other side.

Well, Jax and I stumbled. Lucien trotted past us with a look of exasperation as he waited for us to regain our composure.

"That was the freakiest thing I've ever done," Jax mumbled as he brushed the dirt off his pants.

Nodding, I blinked, then shook my head in an effort to right myself. "I honestly couldn't agree more."

By the looks of the puffs of smoke in the distance, I'd guess Lucien's portal landed us on the outskirts of Firestone.

The jagged landscape provided a stark contrast to anywhere I'd ever seen before. The earth looked dead, cracked and forgotten. Though an eerie sense of beauty lingered here, it was the opposite of Brookmere in almost every way.

"How is this the same world as Brookmere?" I asked, stepping around a deep red tree whose sap oozed like blood down its bark.

Jax snorted. "I'm partial to Brookmere's beauty myself now."

I narrowed my gaze at the wistful expression he wore at the comment.

"Because, well…you know, all that green."

This time Lucien huffed from beside us, smoke puffing between our legs where we stood.

"Right, not the beauty of one of my best friends. The greenery." I nodded, hiding my eye roll as I straightened and faced the direction of the volcano. "Ready?" I asked both of them.

"Let's do this." Jax cracked his neck twice before shifting into his panther form. He leapt forward, sprinting toward the volcano without a second glance toward Lucien or me.

The pugron let out a plume of smoke from his snout and ran off behind Jax, trying to keep up with his stubby legs. Snorting, I shook off the laugh at the sight and looked to the sky. Inhaling, I shifted into my hawk form, taking off into the cloudless sky.

Soaring over the land, I could hardly comprehend the landscape before me. I remembered the Mysthaven crew discussing the differences in our lands, but seeing it in person was something else entirely.

Even from above, the land held the same haunting look. Where were the lush rolling hills? The forests? Wildflower groves? All I saw was shrubs that looked like they would draw blood if you got too close, poking through dry dirt.

I wondered where Raya wanted to be after all of this ended. If she enjoyed Brookmere or preferred Mysthaven's climate and landscape. The bond thrummed inside of my chest.

My preference will be wherever she is.

The thought hit me hard, almost sending me plummeting from the sky. The bond was so much more than a deep well of love.

It was a reforging of what it meant to be home.

My wings wavered as the scent of sulfur permeated my senses, pulling me from thoughts of Raya. The heavy aroma clouded the air, burning my nostrils. The closer I flew to the volcano, the stronger it became.

In our shifted forms, it took no time at all for us to reach the base of the volcano. I passed by Jax and Lucien, splitting from their side, and continued to fly over the area to get a better view.

Indistinct noises echoed as I soared above the opening, where a line of Fae stood just a few feet away from where Jax and Lucien now hid. They shuffled forward in a queue, waiting to enter the volcano itself. Beyond them, though, my stomach bottomed out at the sight. There were hundreds, if not thousands of them waiting. I continued in a loop, noticing a vast area of tents set up. Thames's army strode around, and a small fight between soldiers even broke out around a campfire. An oily sensation I now recognized as the darkness skated over my skin.

This had to be Thames's army, including all of the dark ones called here from Ellevail.

"Are you okay?" Raya's voice caressed my mind, and I let out an audible breath, even in hawk form.

The reassurance of her presence, even in my mind, kept me from spiraling into defeatist thoughts. *His army is massive. How could he possibly recruit this many people?*

"Most were probably forced."

My muscles tensed automatically in disgust, and my wings stiffened.

"Be careful."

While I hated that she had reasons for her fear, her concern bolstered the protective obsession she was slowly becoming. *Worried for me, mate?*

"You wish," she huffed.

As I flew back toward Jax and Lucien, I tried to get a final estimate of the army's size. I didn't know how we could possibly defeat all of them. We had to find a way somehow. Right now, we needed to focus on the task at hand: finding the weapon. We'd face the army itself soon enough.

Will you stay? I asked Raya.

I felt a comforting warmth radiate through my mind and spread into my chest. *"Always."*

Do you think you can get into Jax's mind?

She paused. *"I haven't ever done it except with you. Though…"* She paused. *"The seers made a comment that the mate bond could make our magic stronger. So I can try."*

Tell him I'm taking one more loop and to stay where he is, I said. *Please.*

Raya left my mind and our connection ended. I hated it. When this was over, I had quite a few things I wanted to try with our bond. Experimenting with what we could feel in our minds was at the top of my list.

I felt her again before I heard her. *"It worked,"* she said breathlessly. *"I did it."*

Grinning internally, I tried to allow her to feel my pride. *Good girl.*

She scoffed but this time, stayed.

I soared farther around the volcano to glimpse the Fae side I'd passed in my first loop. A screech escaped me as an immense fear rattled through my entire body. Along this side of the volcano, massive cages rattled, the sound echoing in a small trench. Inside, huge beasts thrashed back and forth.

Raya? I asked breathlessly in my mind. *Can you see this?*

"Fates, it's the voidlings."

Voidlings?

Tension radiated from her presence, even though it was only inside my mind. *"Poisonous creatures contained to the void when the mist still existed. They're deadly."*

I used my keen eyesight to observe as much as I could of the monsters. One opened its mouth, snapping at a guard standing feet away from its cage. My shudder ruffled the feathers on my wings as I stared in horror at its three rows of razor-sharp teeth and impossibly thick, snake-like tongue. The beast's scaly exterior shifted from blue to black as they moved.

And they're poisonous? I muttered in my mind. *Just what we need.*

"I'll tell Cassandra immediately. We need to start working on an antidote if Thames has them for his army."

Finishing my last loop around the perimeter, I dove toward the ground to join Jax and Lucien again. I was thankful for my hawk sight since it didn't take long for me to spot them hiding beside some brush. Jax remained in his panther form until he spotted me.

By the time I landed a few feet away, he had shifted back into his Fae form. "Took you long enough," he joked.

How was he ever left in charge of anything?

"Yeah, well, perks of a being able to fly, I can see everything. There are thousands of dark ones on the other side of the volcano." I let out a breath, putting my hands on my hips to stretch slightly. "Plus, something called voidlings? About thirty cages, filled with them."

Jax's face slackened and lost almost all of its color. "Voidlings? How do you know that?"

I tapped the side of my head. "Raya saw it and told me."

"I knew hoping they'd simply disappeared with the void would be too good to be true," Jax said, running a hand through his hair. "Of course they're Thames's pets now. Can't just settle for thousands of dark ones, had to go and add the poisonous voidlings into the battle too."

Lucien let out a growl, and our attention shifted to the pathway a few feet from us. Immediately, we dropped, crouching behind the thorny green bush. Two dark ones marched past, patrolling the area, and we waited for them to move away before we continued our conversation.

"We need to keep moving and get back. Any ideas on how to get inside?" I asked. "I've never even seen a volcano before, let alone tried to enter one."

Jax shook off the concern about the beasts and cracked his knuckles, then indicated for me to follow. "Rumor has it there are several entry points built into the foundation of the outer walls. How or why, we were never told. Even as one of the elite, I was never privy to that information." He pointed to the base of the volcano just a few hundred yards away. "Let's try over there first."

I surveyed our surroundings, ensuring all remained quiet, then gave him a nod. "Lead the way."

Silently, we moved along the fractured ground, hiding behind sickly looking wind-sculpted white trees to avoid detection. As we got closer, the air thickened, the humidity rising. Sweat beaded on our brows, and my tunic stuck to my body.

"Is it always this hot?" I muttered, shaking my shirt, peeling it from my skin.

Jax shook his head. "I mean, it is a volcano, but no, it's not normally like this."

Lucien took a step as the ground cracked beneath his feet. With a small leap, he escaped a fissure appearing in the ground, revealing a fiery-looking substance.

Jax inhaled sharply. "That can't be good. We need to move faster."

I agreed, watching the ground at our feet as well as our surroundings now. Creeping a few more feet, Jax finally reached a small opening to the volcano. "We're here." Lucien shook his entire body, barbed tail knocking into the rocky mountainside, clearly relieved not to be lingering around the outskirts anymore.

We stared at a small opening, dark and narrow, with heat radiating outward. I wiped my brow against my tunic. Jax nodded forward, about to continue, but I reached out and grabbed him by the shoulder. "Look, if something happens to me, you have to make sure you get back to Lana."

"Ian." Raya reappeared hesitantly in my mind.

I have no intention of not making it back to you. Just a precaution.

I didn't even want to think about what could happen. The thought of leaving Raya behind made my skin crawl, but Lana losing someone else made me sick. Nevertheless, this was war, and the possibility had to be discussed. "Do not play the hero. If it's a choice between me or escape, you choose escape. One of us must live to be able to fight another day."

Jax chuckled. "If you think Raya would let me live after leaving you behind, you're a greater fool than me."

"Accurate," Raya added.

"Jax," I said sternly. "I need you to promise. The information gets to Lana, no matter what."

He looked at me skeptically before rolling his eyes. "Can't she see any information we find out anyway?" He pointed to my head.

"Tell that idiot I can only see what you do."

"She said she can only see what I see," I relayed.

"Fucking mates," Jax sighed. "All right, you got it. I will risk certain death returning home without you, should you fall. It's not going to come to that though. This is a simple reconnaissance mission. We've got this."

"Careful," I grumbled. "We don't need to tempt the Fates." Despite cursing them for years with Lana, too many things had come together, making it impossible to deny their influence. A shiver ran down my spine. "Let's go."

As I waited for Jax to shimmy through the crack, the sweet notes of Raya's voice whispered in my head.

"Stay alert."

We'll be back before you know it, I replied.

Once Jax disappeared into the volcano, it didn't take me long to make my way through the entrance. The hard rock scraped against my back as I pressed through to enter and stand next to Jax.

I exhaled forcefully, taking in the enormity of the volcano. Huge walls of stone cascaded upward in a vortex, almost making it impossible to notice anything else.

A soft glow cast toward us from a pathway to our left, the ground littered with fresh footsteps in the dirt. "Only one way to go," Jax said quietly.

We stuck to the edge of the pathway, trying to stay in the shadows as much as possible to conceal ourselves along with the footprints we left behind. The dirt transitioned to stone eventually, and the pathway bent sharply on an incline. The random sounds of rumblings deep down beneath the Earth's surface accompanied by the distant sound of marching footsteps echoed in the chamber. They seemed far enough away that we wouldn't immediately run into anyone, and I was grateful as we made our way forward.

We climbed up the spiraling path, not meeting another soul along the way. There was only one way forward, with no additional rooms or trails diverging from it. If someone did come, we'd have to kill them quickly, or the sound would echo. Besides, there was nowhere to hide.

Lucien trotted behind us, but his expression didn't inspire any sort of confidence. His snorts, normally arrogant and unbothered, came out short as he panted in the humid air.

Ten minutes later, we finally heard a deep, gritty voice coming from down the hall. Jax put up his hand and we slowed our speed.

Inching forward, we edged along the spiral pathway. Jax peeked his head around a bend in the corner, turning to me and indicating it was safe to continue. We remained silent as we rounded the corner. An opening lay ahead, and my patience wore thin as we had yet to discover anything. Agitation was a living, breathing entity crawling through my veins. At least I knew Raya was still with us, her steady presence strong in my mind.

By this point, the sweat dripping down my back was a constant flow, soaking every piece of clothing. I shifted my shoulders, attempting to find any sort of comfort. My palms were slick, not just from the heat but from my anxious nerves as well. It didn't matter how many battles I'd fought or missions I'd completed, any time I got close to my intended target, adrenaline coursed through my veins. I spread my fingers wide and gripped them into fists again before shaking out my hands.

A heavy *clunk* of chains rattling against stone burst around us as a lone voice roared in pain. Jax froze, shoulders flinching upward, and our gazes met, knowing we'd both come to the same conclusion. Deep down in my gut, I knew that voice.

Kade was in the chamber ahead, and it didn't sound good.

I gripped Jax's shoulder. If Kade was here, chances were Thames was too.

"Careful," I mouthed. Jax nodded once, stretching his shoulders out.

Our reconnaissance mission had suddenly turned into a rescue effort.

I took the lead, stepping ahead of Jax and sliding forward. We pressed our backs to the wall. I tilted forward, leaning just far enough to peer into the room. My stomach dropped at the sight before me.

Kade's body was chained to the stone wall, his shadows nowhere in sight. His head hung low, and his tunic stuck to his chest, ripped to shreds. Blood stained the torn garment, but also, thick, long lines of burns were etched across his chest as if fire itself had whipped his body.

Fuck, this was bad.

Jax raised his eyes expectantly and mouthed to me, "See anything?"

I nodded but knew I needed more information. Kade's body had taken too much of my attention. Jax moved back a few steps, walking to the other side of the pathway, and crept forward to investigate the room as well.

I peeked around the corner once more and noticed another figure in the room. A man sat in a regal-looking chair, a terrifyingly calm expression on his face as he glared at Kade. He twirled a black whip in his hand.

I jerked back, looking at Jax. "Thames?" I mouthed my question.

All he did was nod once.

"It's useless," Thames laughed. "Submitting to me now will allow you to end your suffering. If you don't, every minute will be painful until I throw you into the pit and let the world erupt. Then I will be untouchable by even the Fates themselves."

Kade didn't lift his head to acknowledge Thames.

"Though…" Thames grinned. "I do enjoy this form of entertainment as I wait for the others to finish up. Not much longer now."

Kade remained unresponsive.

Absolute dread drowned my rationale momentarily. Jax appeared just as horrified.

That was probably the worst possible thing we could've heard. If Thames thought it wouldn't be long until his plans were ready, we were royally screwed. He was waiting for the volcano to erupt? But why? Was that the weapon?

Can you hear? I asked Raya.

"Every word."

Scuffling behind us snapped both our gazes down the pathway as the shadow of a person approached.

Jax and I both lunged back toward where we'd come, moving to silence the Fae, but before we could take him out, he shouted, "What are you doing here?" Footsteps thudded; he hadn't been alone.

We didn't think. We just ran. Lucien wheezed spurts of fire as he cleared our path.

"Shift!" I shouted as I began the transformation into my hawk form, just as two dark ones skidded to a halt in front of us.

We ripped past them, and Jax ran his clawed hands across each of their necks before completely shifting into his panther form. He grabbed Lucien around the neck with his mouth and threw him up onto his back.

A pugron riding a panther in a volcano? On any other day, I would have appreciated this ridiculous scene, but we needed to get out, and fast. It would be a tavern story for the ages if we lived to tell the tale.

As we traveled farther down the path, shouts rang out from somewhere else in the cavern. We made it to the opening, slipping through and running around the outside of the volcano.

The sounds of dark ones gathering, barking orders at each other carried into the fields around us.

We had to get out of here—now. There would be no rescue mission today. No more opportunities to find out more about whatever weapon Thames had inside the volcano.

But at least we knew where Thames was.

And Kade.

Raya remained with me, quiet and somehow masking whatever she was feeling. Perhaps she did it on purpose to help me focus.

We fled farther, trying to find a safe enough spot to portal back to Brookmere.

My heart pounded as my mind filled with deep sadness. We couldn't save Kade yet, as much as I'd wanted to, and I had to be the one to tell Lana what happened. I didn't know why his shadows weren't helping him like usual, or why he couldn't heal himself at all while chained against the wall.

Jax let out a pained growl and shifted back to his human form. I did the same, landing on both feet.

Bloodied marks ran along the base of Jax's back, like Lucien had sunk his barbed tail into his skin. "You are the most badass little guy, but fuck, did you have to hold on to my flesh like your own personal reins?" He winced as Lucien jumped from his back, creating a portal in the open area while appearing completely unbothered by Jax's pain. We quickly stepped through and escaped this miserable place.

We fell out of the portal, thrown off balance just as we were the first time, landing in the middle of Lana's chambers. Lucien popped out of the portal beside us, exhausted and panting, but on all fours. The portal closed quickly.

Lana, Kalliah, Raya, and both seers were seated in her sitting area. Our friends jumped to their feet, while the seers watched us with unreadable expressions.

"What happened?" Lana demanded, as Kalliah examined Jax while Raya came to my side, helping me up. "Tell us everything."

Jax frowned and wiped the sweat off his face. "It's bad."

Lana's gaze shifted rapidly between Jax and me. I grabbed a glass of water off one of her tables and gulped it down, the liquid not only cooling my throat but helping my body recover slightly from the intense heat.

I set it down and reached for Lana. "Kade's at Firestone. He's with Thames."

She brought a hand to her chest and rubbed. "And the weapon?"

"I think…" I frowned, running my hand over my neck. "I think the volcano's the weapon." I hesitated for a second. "He's going to feed Kade into the volcano and let it erupt."

CHAPTER 32
LANA

Despite knowing in my gut that Thames had kidnapped Kade, hearing it stated didn't make the confirmation any easier to accept.

I wrapped my arms around my stomach as if I could hold myself together. If Thames had Kade in the volcano, which was the weapon we needed to destroy, how would we win?

We hadn't agreed on much, but not meeting Thames until the darkness was eliminated seemed the most important, the one thing we all knew for sure.

"Okay," I said a few times to myself under my breath.

"One step at a time. Just like before. We think, we plan, we execute. We don't rush so we avoid making mistakes." Storm's hands rested on my shoulders, giving me strength as I closed my eyes.

I stepped out of his touch and turned, facing the room so I could take in each of my friends. Kalliah tended to an injury on Jax's back, while Raya and Ian sat side by side on the couch, whispering to each other.

Storm didn't take his eyes off me though, tracking my every move. My anger at the seers would be enough to distract me, so I avoided looking toward where they stood in the corner of the room.

Instead, I paced in front of my fireplace.

"How is the weapon the volcano?" I questioned. "Or does it only work if Kade is thrown in somehow?"

Ian sighed, leaning his arms forward onto his legs. "I don't know."

"It'd be safest to destroy the whole thing," Jax surmised, turning his head to face Kalliah. "I know you love me, but you needn't worry, beautiful. I'm already healing."

Kalliah smacked the back of his head before retreating to one of my chaises. She crossed her arms, rolling her eyes at Jax, who merely grinned at her.

"How do you destroy a volcano?" I ran a hand up my arm to ground myself and not allow my panic to rise at the impossibility of it. I'd never even seen a volcano. "Describe it," I said, not bothering to direct my command to Ian or Jax specifically. "What does it look like? Where is Kade in relation to it?"

Jax leaned back against the side of the couch. "It's a fairly large monstrosity. It took Ian a few minutes to fly around the perimeter to gather the size of the army."

"Which is massive," Ian said, running a hand over his face. "A few thousand at least camped at the base of the east side of the volcano."

Storm grunted. "He's been busy for years. I'm surprised it's only that."

"Oh, and don't forget the voidlings," Jax added.

I shuddered. Raya had told us immediately about Thames keeping the beasts locked away with his army.

"We're working on creating the antidotes," Vivienne said. "We'll have as much as we can before the battle."

I closed my eyes, rubbing the bridge of my nose at just how much we had to accomplish in such a short period of time.

"There are tunnels inside of it, pathways," Ian continued "One entry has a line of dark ones that look like they're being tossed into the pit of fire inside of it."

"Lava," Jax said. "It's called lava. We avoid it or it will kill us. Burning death." He shuddered. "No thank you."

"Right," Ian continued. "Kade is…" He paused, giving Jax a side-eye glance. "There. We overheard Thames say that he'd throw Kade into the lava and the volcano would erupt. That no one could stop him."

"So he needs Kade to die *in* the volcano for it to erupt. Meaning the eruption is the weapon?" I tried to process all of the information, but I didn't understand. "There's no weapon we have that could take out what sounds like a mountain." I stopped pacing and stretched my neck.

If I don't think this through, Kade will die. I'll lose him forever.

My breath hitched and my light stirred, rising in response to my anxiety.

Instead of fueling it, it warmed my chest, where I felt the connection to Kade most, soothing it.

Focus.

"Nothing is as it appears at first glance," Vivienne said from the side of the room.

I lifted my gaze to her. She smiled at me, waiting, like she thought the statement gave me an answer.

She raised her eyebrows when I remained quiet. "How many times do you need a prophecy to tell you that light is what defeats darkness? You have light within you, Illiana."

I clenched my fist. "Do you think the Fates could do us a favor and give us something concrete instead of measly breadcrumbs that take more time to decode than we have?"

Cassandra tsked. "Every single choice you make can change the course of fate."

The seer's eyes had been filled with hatred since the last time we saw her. Before Thames escaped, she'd cared for Kade, she was kind to me.

Since then, she'd taken on a stern demeanor. It was almost as if she was a different person entirely. For a brief moment, the flicker in her eyes just now betrayed her. I stared at her and watched the cold, indifferent mask slip back into place.

But I'd seen it, a crack that gave her away.

I took a step forward, and as I reached for her, she stepped back, turning away from me. "The Fates don't give us carte blanche to see all there is. They give us what they want us to know at the time. They want to see who is worthy. They want to see how *we* respond. We are not here to steer fate; we are here to guide you along the way. Do not think that we are omnipresent."

I lowered my head. "I apologize."

I didn't know why Cassandra was freezing everyone out, but she must have a reason. Perhaps the Fates were testing her, or she feared Thames. Regardless, I didn't have time to wonder about her intentions.

"Do you have any suggestions?" I asked, rubbing my arms, attempting to reel in my anger.

Cassandra and Vivienne exchanged a look.

"Child, you are right," Vivienne said softly. "You can't meet Thames before the end."

I ran my fingers through my hair. "So either we need to get Kade out and destroy an entire volcano without being detected or find a way to call Thames away to give us more freedom to do what we must."

"I can attempt getting into someone's mind," Raya suggested. "Maybe try to find a dark one to tell Thames you're attacking somewhere? Or within his reach—anything to get him to leave."

I stared at her. "I thought you couldn't enter anyone's mind but Ian's?"

She gave me a small smile. "Apparently there's something to the mate bonds that makes your magic stronger. I was able to talk to Jax when they were in Firestone."

Jax laid his head back on the couch. "Freakiest moment of my life, hearing Raya in my damn head."

Cassandra scoffed. "That's just a fraction of what you could do if you trained your magic now that you're bonded," she said as if it was common knowledge. She looked out the windowed doors leading to my garden.

"They didn't have the knowledge we did from before Thames was trapped," Vivienne reminded her sister.

Cassandra softened, but only for Vivienne. "You're right," she whispered.

The others continued talking, thinking through ideas for destroying the volcano, but I was processing everything Cassandra revealed to Raya.

The mate bond made our magic stronger? Maybe it wasn't only my light that drew Kade out of his darkness but the bond between us. Perhaps both of us needed to work together to purge the darkness from him. I closed my eyes, breathing in a few times, continuing to push down any emotion not helping me focus on freeing Kade. On destroying the volcano and ensuring Thames rotted away forever once I killed him.

Refocusing, I thought back to the moments when I felt most connected to my magic. Most of the times when it exploded out of me or burst out in a show of strength were when our magic entwined together, calling to each other. Kade was a part of my soul.

Those of us in this room didn't need to destroy the volcano.

Kade and I did.

Nothing is as it appears at first glance.

"Let's try it," I said. The others stopped talking and stared at me. "Raya, let's try it. We find someone in Mount Legion who can convince Thames—"

"No," Cassandra interrupted.

I frowned at her and noticed her hands clutching the chair in front of her, knuckles white.

She saw my stare and quickly let go, stretching her hands. One by one, she looked at each person before straightening her spine impossibly tall. "There is one way to guarantee he won't be there."

We stayed quiet, even as Vivienne gripped Cassandra's shoulder as if to stop her.

"He'll come for me if he thinks he has a chance to take me," she said. Her hardened voice matched the cold facade she now masked herself with. "You'll have to work quickly, but I will draw Thames out and you—" She stared at me. "You will free Kade and destroy the volcano."

CHAPTER 33
KADE

After so many hours chained against the walls of the volcano, I'd lost feeling in my hands.

My head slumped forward as blood dripped down my arms from my wrists. Even though my tunic was a deep navy blue, dark stains seeped all the way down my shirt. At least, the thin parts of it remaining.

My skin stretched taut where Thames used the lava from the volcano in whip-like devices. Pain unlike anything I'd ever felt before ripped through me as each fiery lash burned into me. I'd been whipped a hundred times before, but never with lava. The stench of burning skin made me want to vomit.

My healing magic returned slower than I needed but enough so that I healed the most debilitating injuries. The poisonous drink Thames gave me still lingered in my system. The small amount of shadows that had revived inside of me were focused solely on containing the darkness Thames desperately tried to control. He hadn't succeeded. I'd held on to the glow in my chest that was Lana and used my shadows to smother the darkness.

I wouldn't give in, not again.

I needed to find a way to break free from this prison and

return to my family. Being forced to listen to hundreds of dark ones sacrifice their life to fuel this weapon sent chills down my spine. While most may have done so willingly, the screams of those fighting their deaths were even worse. So much pointless death. Hours of pain-filled cries were almost enough for me to give in and allow the darkness out, if only to keep from feeling such anguish at the senseless loss of life.

I fought the temptation though. With Lana and me accepting the mate bond, I leaned into our connection. It alone gave me the strength to hold on, minute by minute.

Can you snuff it out completely? I thought toward my shadows, knowing I didn't need to clarify what I meant.

I felt the dread when they answered. *No.*

Didn't hurt to ask.

I'd been a pawn in Thames's game for longer than I realized. He'd used my father to create the perfect dark one. A monster greater than all the others.

Because that was what it all came down to. Thames had created me, the darkness inside of me, for almost my entire life. For so long I'd lived with this unknown evil, and the moment I'd started to feel a reprieve from his grasp, like I had an actual chance of ridding myself of his toxicity, the floor crumbled beneath me.

My hopes had soared when Lana discovered she could cut the darkness out of Fae with her dagger. After our failed attempts though, it seemed futile to keep trying. Especially given what Cassandra and the final prophecy indicated. I wasn't ready to think yet about the consequences of this unbreakable darkness. I thought about how Evelyn and Jasper had to sacrifice everything just to *trap* Thames, and part of me knew I wouldn't be so lucky that I'd get to keep Lana without a sacrifice of our own.

Fates, I swore I wouldn't leave her, but all our choices were leading us too close to that point. The one where in order for Lana to succeed, we'd need to ensure I was gone.

I looked across the room to where Thames sat in his stupidly ostentatious onyx chair, deep in thought. He leaned his head back, his fingers moving in front of him along with the sounds of the screaming. He swirled his fingers as if conducting a symphony, clearly basking in the sounds of dying dark ones. His weapon grew stronger with each passing moment, scream by scream.

I gritted my teeth, trying to redirect more of my magic toward keeping the darkness contained. This volcano would not be where I died. I would see Lana again. See her rose-gold hair shimmer in the morning's light, feel it twisted through my fingers, with her neck exposed to my lips.

I could barely contain the moan as I thought about Lana and the last time I claimed her as mine. I would survive this and get back to her and enjoy every second at her side. Even if it was only for a short amount of time.

"What are you complaining about now?" Thames asked, rising and sauntering toward me. "I thought I told you to keep quiet if you wanted a quick and painless death. Not that I think you deserve it, considering your betrayal."

I huffed out a dry laugh. "I was just thinking about Lana and how you underestimate her at every turn." A sly smile graced my lips as I struggled to lift my head to face Thames. "She will come for you."

Thames cackled and sent a torrent of air across my body, forcing me even farther back against the wall. My skin pressed into the sharp rocks, gouging me and creating more wounds while opening the dried ones up again. "I'm counting on it."

He turned his back to me, making his way to his chair, but stopped suddenly mid-stride. Thames clutched his chest as he drew in a sharp breath. "Cassandra?" he whispered.

Confused, I listened closer, and after a few moments I heard a faint voice in the distance. Or was it in my mind? I couldn't tell.

"Thames, come to me," Cassandra crooned. "Come to me so we may speak. It has been a thousand years, my mate."

The initial shock left Thames's face, and instead, it contorted to unadulterated fury. He screamed, unleashing his whip toward a dark one teetering on the volcano's edge, killing him instantly as he fell to the molten lava.

"How fucking dare she ask me to meet her after all this time," he spit. "*She. Betrayed. Me.*" His shout was so loud, the volcano tremored under the force of his rage. He paced around the room, speaking to himself. "I hate that woman. I hate her so fucking much for what she did to me. She imprisoned me for a thousand years. I could have given her the world. I could have given her *everything*. And how does she repay me? A life in the void."

Thames was unhinged on a good day, but in mere moments, he spiraled in a way I didn't anticipate. He growled, still holding a hand to his chest.

He clawed at the same spot I felt Lana. It dawned on me the pain he must be in, and I couldn't help but smile. Being away from Lana was torment, but knowing he'd been trapped without his mate for a thousand years, on top of the betrayal, tasted like sweet justice.

Thames grabbed his glass, throwing it against the wall in a rage. The splintered pieces pierced my skin, now sensitive with so many wounds.

"Thames—" I started, unsure of how to use this to my advantage but willing to try anything.

Thames didn't pay the slightest attention to me. He continued on his tirade as he paced around the room, tugging at his hair, rubbing at his chest. He looked deranged.

"I want to hate her. I should hate her." He ran his hands through his hair. "But resisting the bond is futile. Ever since I've been released back into this world, I've been dying to be near her to satisfy this ridiculous pull."

I tugged at my bindings, wondering if I could maneuver

while he remained distracted. I still didn't have all my strength back, but whatever Thames had poisoned me with was finally beginning to wear off and I could feel my shadows strengthening.

"Please, Thames," Cassandra begged once more. "I was wrong. Let's finish this together."

Thames whipped his head to me. "Do you hear her? Can you hear that bitch's voice calling to me?"

"Yes." I didn't need to say anything else. Just a simple confirmation of the voice I heard. I wasn't sure what Lana and the others had planned, but I hoped it was good. It had to be for this to work in our favor.

Thames yelled and a grin stretched across his face. "She's seen my power and knows the only way to survive is by my side." He tilted his head back, staring at the ceiling and laughed. "Oh, you'll be punished, my burdensome mate." He winced again, this time practically ripping at his robes, like something crawled over him. "I'm coming, Cassie. I'm coming. But you won't be ready for what I have in store for your betrayal."

Thames ran out of the cavern like a man possessed, leaving me alone in the room.

Anxious to take advantage of the moment, I strained, calling my shadows to free me from these chains. A few weak streams of shadows appeared at my feet, but not enough to pick the locks.

They were hesitant to fully pull away from the darkness.

Understanding their reluctance, I continued looking around at the chains, at the walls, thinking of what I could do to escape.

With nothing standing out immediately, I rested my head against the rock. I focused instead on conserving my energy, biding my time for a few moments as more of my powers returned me to full strength.

Determination settled into my bones, and where ten

minutes ago I thought death would be my only friend, I had now remembered who I was and what I had to live for. I *would* see Lana, Jax, Storm, Raya, and even fucking Ian again.

Lifting my head up, I hung there, ready, memorizing every detail of this cavern as I etched it into my brain.

A soft crackle of energy pulsed next to me, and Lucien appeared on the floor out of nowhere, trotting confidently into the room through some strange black glittering substance.

I laughed, seeing him of all things. "What the hell are you doing here, little pugron?"

He snorted out a plume of smoke toward my feet. Perhaps Thames wasn't the only one losing his mind. I must be too, because there was no way Lucien could be here.

The glittering oval pulsed, widening slightly as a torrent of commotion surged through. Storm, Raya, Ian, and Lana stumbled through the same spot, collapsing on the floor, followed closely by Jax and Kalliah.

"You're on my foot, Jax," Kalliah scolded, as the group of them jumped to their feet and scanned the room.

My jaw hung open in disbelief at the chaotic sight in front of me. "What the actual fuck."

"Kade!" Lana called out to me, and the few shadows that had returned jolted toward her, crawling up her legs and wrapping themselves around her. "You're okay," she reassured herself as she met my gaze. Her eyes checked on my own as she reached up, stroking my face. "We're going to get you down."

"I'm fine, or I will be fine," I replied, my heart pounding. "We don't have long; Thames is trying to find Cassandra. I don't know when he'll return. He's given me that same magic-dampening poison Hale used on us before. I don't have access to all of my magic, or I would have been out of here a long time ago."

Storm chuckled. "He will have a hard time finding her, but I agree we have to be quick."

Jax, Raya, and Kalliah stood guard at the entrance to the room, while Ian, Storm, and Lana inspected the locks on my wrists. I'd never seen Thames produce a key, so Fates only knew if there actually was one.

"Tits and daggers," Lana cursed. "I don't see a way to get these cuffs off of him, do you?" she asked both Storm and Ian. "Don't worry, Kade, we're going to get you down."

I grinned down at my perfect, beautifully bold mate. "I feel like the damsel in your fairy tales."

Lana cast me a stern look. "Not the time."

I shrugged, unable to stop smiling. She was here, unharmed, and with Thames gone for now, he couldn't get to her. In this moment, Lana was safe.

Ian and Storm stood there for a minute, debating what to do.

"I could try to melt them off," Storm suggested, and he reached his hand toward the iron shackle on my wrist, clasping his fingers around it. "It may get hot—"

"I heard he likes it hot," Jax whispered far too loudly from where he stood next to Kalliah.

She shoved him. "I'm going to let Leif beat the shit out of you."

"Promise?" Jax laughed, and she shoved him again.

Storm rolled his eyes but otherwise ignored them. "Hold on."

He gripped the chains and concentrated his fire power on the rivets holding together the shackles, melting them instead of the chain as a whole. The heat burned my flesh, but once they fell to the ground, I felt immediate relief, keen to rub the aching skin. Storm did the same thing on the other side and eventually, both of my hands were free.

Blood rushed back into my fingers, which tingled as they reacclimated to being held at a normal angle. Lana threw her arms around me, and I couldn't help but breathe in the very scent of her. My entire body relaxed against her, the tightness in my chest eased as our bond settled. "Hi," I whispered against her hair.

"You said you'd never leave me again, liar" she murmured in my ear.

My throat tightened with emotion, but I pushed aside the thoughts from earlier. I'd deal with them later. Right now, she stood before me, and I never wanted to let her go. "Let's get out of here so I can grovel and worship you properly."

Jax gagged. "Ugh, come on, guys. Get a room." He winked at Kalliah before coming over to me and clapping me on the shoulder. Ian moved to replace Jax as lookout and gave Kalliah a look I could only imagine meaning *really?*

Storm peeked over the edge of the railing, and his eyes widened in shock. "What in the Fates' names is happening down there?"

Reality set back in as the momentary happiness we all felt at reuniting dissolved. My face turned grim, and I released Lana from my grasp. "That's the weapon. Those dark ones are sacrificing their blood and their magic to fuel the volcano. Whenever he deems it ready, it will erupt, and darkness will spread across the entire world, infecting anyone it touches. No longer will it have to be injected into their bodies; it can be breathed in."

"Fuck," Ian and Storm said in unison.

Lana looked like she was about to lose herself, but then something flashed across her face and determination set in. "Let's put this mate bond to good use, Kade. I have an idea."

CHAPTER 34

KADE

Hell if I knew how to destroy a volcano without making it erupt.

If we triggered anything, we'd be giving Thames exactly what he wanted. He'd made it sound like he didn't actually *need* me but *wanted* me to ensure his victory. The volcano erupting in any way could still give him what he wanted.

Lana rubbed her fingers against her forehead. "Vivienne kept reminding me my light could defeat all darkness." She peered over the ledge at the dark ones screaming into the pit. Then she tilted her head up, looking around. "Ian, do you think there are other openings closer to the top like this one? If we can get higher, I can try to use my light somehow without worrying about dark ones catching on to us."

"On it," he said, jumping and shifting in less than a minute before quietly flying upward. With the growing smoke and hissing sounds from the bodies, along with the screaming, no one below was any the wiser of our presence.

Ian took longer than I thought he would have, but when he returned in his Fae form, his entire body was covered in sweat. "There's another ledge farther toward the top. There's a network of tunnels throughout the volcano, and I think I've found one that will work."

"We need to hurry," I said. My skin crawled in anxious anticipation of Thames's return. I didn't know what Cassandra was doing or how long she could stall him, but we didn't have an unlimited amount of time. Lana still had to do whatever she thought would work with her light, and something told me she'd need every spare second to crush this volcano.

We ran up a narrow, steep path. I scraped my shoulders along rocks more than once, cursing this damned place the entire time. Lana stumbled, and I unleashed my shadows, catching her and allowing them to wrap around her. They needed her. For the first time since taking Thames's power-stifling poison, my magic surged forward, no doubt a side effect of being around Lana. As we ran, I let my shadows touch her and sure enough, they thrummed back to life.

We finally arrived at the ledge near the top of the volcano, allowing us a better view of just how wide the colossal mountain was.

The lava I'd seen from my chains was red and fiery-looking, but on the other side of the pool, a strange hue of black bubbled. It was as if the darkness devoured the lava there. Though liquid, and still churning like the red side, the growing black lava radiated a vile, oppressive evil. It filled me with absolute dread.

"What do you need from us, Lana?" I asked.

She bit her lip as she shifted back and forth on her feet, staring at the pit beneath us. "I'm going to try to tell my magic what I want and see if it can snuff out the darkness. Then I'll have to find a way to bring this place down."

"I'll use my shadows to help tear it down when you're ready," I said, confident I could aid her somehow. I glanced over at the others, waiting off to the side. "Maybe Lucien should portal the rest of you home first, in case something doesn't go our way."

"Absolutely not," Ian said, clenching his fists. "We're in this together."

Lana just shook her head. "Kade is right. If something happens, we need you to finish this war. Our people will need leaders."

"No," Storm said with a sense of finality I knew wouldn't waver. "The only one who can finish this is you, Lana. We're staying."

Storm stared at Lana with conviction, turning toward me next. "We're not separating. We're destroying the volcano and going back to Ellevail to prepare for Thames."

I nodded. "Okay," I conceded. "We'll guard the tunnel and buy her time."

The others pulled their weapons, ready to take on any threat once Lana started wielding her magic. I reached forward, pulling her in for a kiss, just because I could. "You can do this." No matter what happened here today, I was so fucking proud of Lana and all she'd overcome.

She smiled, then turned to face the lava far below. Her body glowed, light rising to the surface of her being, radiating outward and illuminating the space around us. She looked down at her hands briefly before aiming them down toward the blackened portion of the lava. Light poured from her in an endless stream, cascading down in a breathtaking torrent of pure white.

Her hands trembled the closer her magic got to the pool of lava. Wisps of darkness writhed against the light before sizzling in a smoky evaporation from the surface.

The screams of the dark ones sacrificing themselves ceased as Lana's light flooded the cavernous volcano. I glanced over the edge as the head guard frantically looked around, searching for the source of the light, while the others stood with slackened jaws.

"Be ready for anything," I told the others.

The guard's gaze locked on Lana and he shouted, pointing upward. I didn't hear what he said but knew they'd be coming.

Lana's arms shook and she stumbled, almost falling to one knee as her light went out. I sheathed my sword and ran over to her.

"It's not working. I'm not strong enough," she said through gritted teeth.

"You are the strongest Fae I know, Lana. You can do this." I brought my hands to her sides, gripping her hips as I steadied her.

Let us go to her, my shadows begged.

"Let me help," I whispered in her ear, obeying their wishes.

Lana turned her focus to me, glancing over her shoulder. A spark lit up her eyes. "Just like in the forest, but we channel all of it, every bit of our power into the center of this volcano."

Nodding, I grabbed her hand, smiling. "I believe I did tell you my shadows destroy when we first met."

She laughed and I took her hands in mine, facing her. "Are you ready?" My palms were sweating as the heat in the room became unbearable. It didn't matter, we were on the precipice of greatness, all because of her.

Lana smiled, as she tightened her hands around mine, our bodies facing each other. "Do your worst, Kade Blackthorn."

Dropping every reservation, every snide comment, hate-filled glare, I let my shadows free, allowing them to cascade out and over all of the surrounding area. A stream of them wrapped around Lana's body, waiting for her magic to appear.

Come out, my love. We've missed you.

Lana's light pooled above our joined hands in a small sphere, almost timid.

"Come on, I know you can do this," Lana coaxed her

magic. I could see the strain on her face, the desperation for more of her light to appear. "We are enough," she whispered.

Be with us. Join us. We are your home. We will protect you.

"Relax, Little Rebel. Your magic is a part of you." I let go of her hands and pushed a strand of loose hair behind her ear, as we stood above the pool of magma. "It does not define you. Your magic merely accentuates the already powerful person you are, both inside and out."

Lana let out a breath and rolled her shoulders back, reaching her hands up to the ceiling.

"Together," I encouraged, cupping her face and allowing our magic to intertwine. My shadows swirled around her, and the light emanating from her palms grew brighter. The shadows crawled up her slowly, reverently, as they weaved themselves between the strands of her light.

A shout behind us almost distracted me, but I didn't take my eyes off Lana. I had to trust our friends to hold their own so we could finish this.

I watched, transfixed as our magic swirled, colliding together with a hungry power. The voices of my shadows and Lana's light blended together. The vortex of all that was good in this world, with all that I was forced to be—the darkness forced upon me—combined in a torrent of magic. Her arms fell, but the vortex of power continued upward. I reached for her, needing to be close, and pulled her close to me, enveloping her in my arms. The touch between us jolted our magic, acting as kindling, fueling our abilities to a burning point. My skin screamed. We could only hold on for so much longer before we would reach the point of no return.

"Now, Illiana," I shouted over the noise of pure power bellowing through the cavernous volcano. Whatever our magic was doing, we had to let it go and let it detonate. "Give it everything you've got and let go."

She looked up at me, fear lacing her widened eyes. She

looked so afraid, but she never had to be that way with me. There was nothing I wouldn't do to keep her safe.

"Don't be scared. One more push," I said, wiping her eyes.

"I love you," she said, right before she closed her eyes and proceeded to unleash her magic completely.

The light and shadows boomed, forming a tornado of magic, drawing out all of the evil from the center of the volcano and wrapping it tightly in a vortex of magic.

It was a sight to behold.

Despite the mission at hand, my soul felt at home watching our power working together, feeding off of one another. My heart knew love, pure and powerful, and if I died right now, I would die knowing this was what love felt like. This was the power of our bond.

Of us.

I clutched her tighter. "I love you too."

Funneling the last remnants of my energy, I released every shadow within me and fell away from the ledge, pulling Lana with me as we toppled backward. Our tornado of shadow and light plummeted into the core of the volcano, and everything exploded.

The ground shook, pieces of stone cracked around us, while the walls crumbled apart. The same mist we'd seen previously floated into the air, evaporating quickly, unable to be used against anyone or anything.

"We did it!" she screamed both in excitement and fear.

I grabbed Lana, covering her from the flying debris she didn't notice in her victory. The volcano was imploding, and we had to get out before we were crushed in the aftermath.

"Quick, to Lucien and the others," I shouted over the falling rocks, but Lucien was already at Lana's feet.

"Storm," I called, seeing him closest. He held an arm over his head and yanked Jax's collar with his other hand.

A boulder-sized rock smashed to the ground, blocking

Storm and Jax from us just as more rained down around them. A woman's scream pierced the air, and Lana's body went rigid next to me.

"Kalliah," she yelled.

I gripped her arm, trying to keep her from diving into the falling debris, but she yanked harder than I expected. Climbing over the rocks crashing around us, she skidded to a halt as Kalliah's body came into view, strewn across the floor.

We found Jax kneeling beside her, brushing the hair out of her face before checking her body for any other wounds.

Blood trickled down Kalliah's scalp and Lana shouted, charging forward. A shake of the ground reverberated through the cavern, tilting us sideways.

Another round of rocks fell, thankfully smaller this time, but Lana wasn't paying attention, and I had to grip her around the waist to pull her away from Kalliah.

Jax jerked his head up, making eye contact with me, then Lana. "I've got her," he shouted, above the growing noise of chaos. "Lana, you've got to move. Go."

"Listen to him," I begged her. A whisper of my shadows sparked in desperation, despite their depleted state.

Storm shouted our names.

"Over here," I responded. "Where's Lucien?"

A light flared from the far side of the chamber.

"The little beast is with Ian, Raya and me," he answered.

We didn't have long. Another quake in the ground threw me into motion. "Jax will need help," Lana argued.

I turned my head, looking behind me, and saw Jax lifting Kalliah.

He looked at us, frustration etching his face. "I swear on my life we're right behind you, but you need to go," Jax insisted.

"He's got her."

I dragged Lana away, considering throwing her over my

shoulder as panic welled at the sight in front of me. Rocks fell faster—we had mere moments until this place was rubble.

Thankfully, she stopped fighting me as I laced our fingers together. We jumped into the colorful portal just as crashing rock landed behind us.

Lucien's bark sounded as if the pugron was angry at our near-death escape. I wrapped myself around Lana's body as we traveled through the swirling portal, and I took the brunt of the fall as we landed on a stone floor.

Beside me, Jax and Kalliah appeared, then Lucien, who seemed frazzled, tipping over as soon as the portal closed behind him.

I listened for Lana's breathing, letting it calm me, knowing we were safe.

"Are you okay?" I asked her as we unraveled ourselves from the ground.

She sat up and pushed the hair out of her face, nodding before shoving herself off me. "Kalliah." Her voice cracked, and she crawled toward where Jax was holding her in his lap. She rested her hand on her friend's arm, eyes wide.

Jax's face scrunched up, and I saw the blood streaming down the side of his own face. Something had hit him too, but there was no sign he had any awareness of it. His full attention was on Kalliah.

"Come on, wildcat," he said, rocking her. "Wake up." He raised his head. "Someone get a healer!"

Footsteps echoed down a corridor, and I looked around, seeing that Lucien had portaled us to the foyer of the palace. "Kalliah." Leif ran to us, gaze completely focused on her lying in Jax's arms. Vivienne appeared close behind him. Leif skidded to a halt before Kalliah, kneeling in front of her and Jax.

"What happened?"

"She was hit as the volcano collapsed," Jax said, his eyes

glassy. Vivienne slowly approached. "I lifted her up, I don't know if something else is wrong, I just had to get her out."

"You did well," Vivienne cooed, turning to look over her shoulder. "We'll get a healer."

I cautiously reached for Lana. "Give them some space," I whispered, taking her hand and holding on. A shiver ran over my spine, and I held on to her tightly. Right now, touching her was best, selfishly. I couldn't let go of her hand, lacing our fingers together to reassure me that she was here. That *I* was here.

"Is Cassandra back?" Lana asked, only to be met with Vivienne's concerned stare as she shook her head.

The doors burst open not a second later as Cassandra ran through them. Dirt covered her body, sticks and grass protruding from her disheveled hair. Her clothing was torn and in shambles, a stark contrast to her usually put-together look. She stopped in front of us, reaching for me, and I grabbed her arm to steady her.

"Glad to see you alive and well, my boy," she panted. Her eyes, initially warm, shifted almost instantly, turning cold.

"Cassandra?" I asked. Worry sat like ice in my veins.

She waved me off as Vivienne came to her side, taking her from me. "You're all right," she said, rubbing her sister's arms.

Cassandra nodded, and Vivienne wasted no time. "Good, you have work to do."

Before she could retort, she followed Viviene's gaze to Kalliah. Without hesitation, she approached her, resting a hand on her forehead, closing her eyes.

Her knees buckled, but Storm was there, grasping the sorceress to keep her from crashing to the floor.

"I'm fine, I'm fine," she argued, but Storm didn't let go. She didn't move from his hold either.

"Kalliah?" Leif's pained whisper had us all holding our breath.

The fae's eyes fluttered open, followed by a sharp inhale.

"Fates," Jax sighed, tugged her toward him, and she curled into his chest, wrapping her arms around him. Leif slumped forward, and I didn't miss Jax tugging him to Kalliah's back as he whispered not just to Kalliah but to Leif as well.

Lana let out a relieved breath, and I let her fall into me.

We'd made it out.

Destroyed the weapon.

Even battered, we'd accomplished something momentous.

Cassandra cleared her throat, tired eyes filling with worry as she glanced first at me, then to Lana. My heart dropped.

"He knows," she said, her voice trembling with a subtle hint of fear. "Thames knows what we've done. He's coming for us all."

CHAPTER 35

LANA

"Send any remaining riders we have," I commanded, standing at the front of the war room table.

The rest sat around the table off the throne room, normally reserved for advisors and the king. In fact, I'd only ever been in this room once before when I was a small girl. To be sitting here now, as queen, even though I hadn't been crowned yet, readying myself for war, was surreal.

What would my father say if he were here? Would he be proud of my choices? I couldn't help but wonder what decisions he would have made had he been the one standing in my place right now.

"We need all the help we can get, and there may still be Fae out there willing to fight for us," I added.

Earlier, we'd sent a few riders out to the closer cities, but we hadn't covered all the land, hence the orders to push harder and search farther.

Together, we decided to try to cut off Thames at the border, to gather our forces between Firestone and Ellevail in an effort to keep the battle away from those not fighting.

We'd sent word to the Knotted Willow hours ago to give

the women and children an option to come to Ellevail to be farther away from the battle if they wished.

I looked at the guard I rattled off orders to. "For those who are willing to fight, you tell them to meet us at the border. At the midway point between Demarva and the Southern Forest."

The guard nodded and proceeded out the door, prepared to fulfill my command. Ian had vouched for him when I asked for someone we could trust. He had been present at the death of my mother and fought against Andras. I paused, and I couldn't help but smile at the realization that I'd kept my promise, and not a moment of my time had been wasted thinking of him.

My mind spun, desperate to ensure I'd thought of everything we needed to face Thames, all while my stomach churned knowing how much danger we'd face on the road ahead.

I rested my hands on the table in front of me, looking around at the tired faces of my friends. We'd been running through plans and divvying up final tasks for hours. The sun's golden rays sank lower in the large glass windows as dusk approached. Our best estimate was we only had a week, if that, before Thames made his move, and there was no time to waste.

"We also need Tommy and the other rebels to prepare our people. I'm not sure what will happen in the final battle, but I want their homes fortified, protected as much as possible. Let's prepare for the worst-case scenario."

All of us sat around the table with our map laid out in the center. Pins marked every town where we'd completed a Hidden Henchman drop, those who'd already pledged their allegiance, and the ones we could still check in on for additional forces.

"Do you think we have the numbers to defeat him?" Storm asked. Ian and Jax had been the only ones to see the force gathered at Firestone, so the room was quiet waiting for an answer.

Ian frowned. "I'm not sure if any number would be enough. We don't know how many dark ones remain. While we may have put a dent in his army with the aftermath destruction of Firestone and eliminated his ability to infect others as planned, I don't dare underestimate what he will do."

"Thames has waited a thousand years for this," Kade mused. "He won't give up easily. He can control the darkness inside of the dark ones—they are utterly his." He reached for my hand. "I think I am only spared because of my connection to Lana." He leaned down, kissing my knuckles, then brushing his thumb across them, as if he were sealing in the gesture.

"We need to be done with this guy. He's cramping my style," Jax grumbled as he reached for some bread and cheese laid out on a table behind him. "I really miss Opal's mead and my own obnoxiously big bed."

I shot him a dirty look, my eyes narrowed.

"Uh, not that your beds aren't great, Your Most Royalness," Jax explained. "It's just that, there's nothing like your own bed, am I right?" His gaze darted toward Kalliah and Leif, a crease appearing faintly between his brows before resting his arms across his chest and examining the map once more.

Raya sighed. "You are insufferable, Jax." She scooted closer to Ian, who slung his arm around her shoulders. "But really, Opal's mead is some of the best. Maybe I could take you there one night for, you know, uh…" Raya blushed as she squirmed in her seat. Her eyes darted around the room, realizing we were all watching. "Just to get to know each other more."

Ian chuckled, "Raya, are you asking me out on a date?"

"I mean, I'm not *not* asking you out…"

Ian pulled her in and kissed the top of her head. "I'd love to."

I rubbed my neck, stretching it from side to side. My chest tightened. The waiting in this final stage before we fought Thames might kill me. But at the same time, I loved watching what we'd built here. What two kingdoms joining together meant. How incredible it could be if we were able to pull this off.

Three knocks on the door echoed in the room, and we all turned to see who wished to enter. "Come in," I called.

A teenage boy, maybe around sixteen years old, stumbled into the room, shoved from behind by a noble wearing flamboyant orange robes. I frowned, addressing the noble while the boy caught his breath. "How can I help you?"

The noble sneered. "This *child* has important information and took his damn time around the palace. He claims he couldn't find you. Clearly he doesn't understand how important it is to get deliveries to his queen in a timely manner." The noble shoved the boy's arm again and mumbled, "Lesser Fae," under his breath like a curse.

I cleared my throat. "You'll refrain from touching him again, or I'll toss you out of the palace altogether. Did you not hear me when I spoke about equality among our people?"

The noble's jaw dropped. "His failures reflect poorly on Ellevail, Your Majesty."

I raised an eyebrow, allowing my disapproval to hang in the air until the noble shifted uncomfortably. "Well if that's all, this young man has the message, not you. Your services are no longer needed."

He opened his mouth to protest, but Kade's shadows shoved him out and slammed the door.

Jax snorted. "How long until you think they learn their pedestal is gone?"

Leif snickered, nodding. "Nice one." The two of them fist-bumped, and I didn't miss Kalliah rolling her eyes, despite the twitch of her lips into a faint smile.

I waved the boy closer to me. "You were looking for me?" I asked, giving him an encouraging smile.

"Yes, Your Majesty. This letter arrived from a carrier about twenty minutes ago. Normally Mr. Corbin would take care of it, but…" He paused, collecting himself before taking a deep breath, and handing me the letter. "But since I am now the most senior stable boy, I decided to bring it to you myself. I would have gotten it to you sooner, but, well, I got lost. I am so sorry, my queen. It won't happen again." His bottom lip quivered, and he hung his head low.

I couldn't help but smile, even as my heart ached, the pain still fresh from losing Corbin. "What's your name?"

"Justin, Your Majesty. Justin Greenleaf."

"Well, Mr. Greenleaf, thank you for your due diligence in getting me this letter as quickly as you were able. Corbin would be so proud of you for your commitment to your job."

I pushed through the ache at using Corbin's name, holding my smile as my eyes misted.

Justin's lips curved upward in a shy smile, and I could physically see the relief flow through his body, his shoulders relaxing as he realized he wasn't getting in trouble. "Thank you, Your Majesty. I will learn the palace layout better immediately. It won't happen again."

"You do have big shoes to fill." I swallowed the lump rising in my throat. "Corbin was the best when it came to caring for the animals in this kingdom. He was compassionate and courageous, and a dear friend. I know if you studied under him, you will exceed every expectation anyone could have for a protege of his."

Kade looked over at me, pride evident on his face. He nodded, mouthing to me, "Well done."

Justin bowed low again. "I promise to do my very best,

Your Majesty. I won't let you down." He left the war room with his head held high.

"That was kind of you, Lan," Ian said. "He'll remember you took time to listen to him instead of taking the noble's word as law."

I took a moment to reflect on the interaction. It was nice, yes, but to me it was more than that. "I know my parents never meant to treat me poorly, but they always handled me like I would break. I didn't have magic then, and everything they did was to protect me, but I just can't help but think about where we might be if they had any sort of faith in me. If they'd believed I could handle the truth about what we're facing as I got older.

"Some of our most loyal, caring, and attentive Fae are the ones who have seemingly the smallest role to play. I never want anyone in my kingdom to feel like the work they do doesn't matter. Everyone is important. Everyone deserves to be treated equally with kindness and respect. Even the Fae with the littlest drop of magic in their blood will be rewarded for their loyalty and generosity. We have a long way to go to win this war, but I want us to start building the kingdom we dream of now.

"While I know I won't make everyone happy with every single decision I make, I will always choose to make choices that are in the best interest of my people. I will be a queen of and for the people of Brookmere."

"That's my girl." Kade beamed.

I was proud of myself too.

Looking down at the tattered letter, I opened it. Another city answered our call to fight. They'd meet us at the border in a few days' time. My hand trembled as I held the paper. Ian and Corbin had done well during their initial visits, traveling to the locations the Hidden Henchman had assisted to rally an army. Now even our riders who were unfamiliar with what our group had done for Brookmere were calling Fae to arms and being well received.

I moved the marker on the map, another burst of hope flooding the air around us.

Ian rose, walking toward me with a satisfied smile when a cacophony of cawing rattled the windows.

A few screams rose from outside of the room and we jumped from our seats.

No, no, Thames couldn't be here yet. *Please.*

My heart raced as I ran to the window to see what was happening outside.

"What in the Fates is that?" Storm asked, his face turning ashen.

A massive group of strox flew through the sky, their battle cries filling the air while pure pandemonium ensued on the palace grounds below. There had to be at least a hundred.

Guards and staff scattered, running and screaming as the massive birds circled ahead.

"Come on, we've got to get outside, now," I shouted, running out the main war room doors.

I didn't wait to see if the others followed, continuing urgently to get outside. No one, besides those in this room, knew these beasts weren't going to harm them, that they were loyal to me and my line. At least I hoped that was the case and there hadn't been some chance that Thames got to the beasts in the woods as well.

Regardless, I wouldn't let anyone—fae or strox—be hurt on my watch at their appearance.

Sprinting through the halls and down the stairs, the sound of footsteps trailed behind as the rest of my friends followed my direction.

I burst through the palace garden doors, squinting against the sun to see the beasts fly overhead. "They're heading toward the back of the palace," I shouted, continuing to run toward the incoming army of strox.

I stared in awe as their numbers hovered above the arena, waiting. The very same arena where we'd battled them not too long ago.

Though cries in the air echoed with fear, nature gave the impression it was pleased by the strox's presence as we ran toward them. There wasn't a single cloud in the dimming sky as the beasts circled above.

I ran upward, taking the steps to the royal dais two at a time, and as I crested the landing, I stared at the arena below. I gasped at the overgrown, devastated sight of the once magnificent structure. Andras had left it in shambles, allowing the remnants of our fight to remain. A stark reminder to those who opposed him versus those who had claimed victory that day.

I shivered before moving to the edge, one I'd stood at what seemed like a lifetime ago.

The few Fae brave enough to follow outside screamed, pointing to the sky. Royal guards rushed out in droves, preparing their weapons as their battalion leaders barked orders, pointing up at the beasts.

"Ian," I turned, yelling for him behind me. "I need you to tell the guards' leaders not to shoot—that will be the fastest way to stop them. Tell them not to hurt the strox."

Ian nodded as he jumped over the ledge of the dais and ran toward the rows of guards.

I grabbed Raya's arm. "Go with him. Maybe you can use your mind magic to try to get some of them to listen. They're scared and might react without thinking."

Without hesitation, she took off, catching up to Ian and joining him as they waved their arms to get the attention of the soldiers.

Storm, Kade, Jax, Kalliah, Leif, and I all continued down the steps into the arena. The strox were beginning to land, cawing into the evening sky. The ground shook as they dove down in groups.

A few guards poured in through the tunnels the contenders had used to enter during the marriage trials.

Chaos swarmed around us between the cries and sharp orders. A heady fear permeated the tension-filled space.

A few Fae appeared along the outskirts of the arena, where they'd watched the marriage trials not long ago, standing huddled together in small groups as they stared at the growing number of ancient birds.

Behind us, I could see over the back of the arena toward the palace, where staff that had been outside ran toward safety or hid behind bushes—anything to save themselves from the beasts.

"Lana, watch out," Kade shouted as a royal guard threw a javelin at a strox that had already landed on the arena ground. The weapon passed right over my head as Kade's shadows yanked me back to avoid being hurt. The javelin hit the strox in one of his wings, and the bird let out a pained yelp.

Whipping myself around, I searched for the guard responsible. It took me a minute to spot him a few feet away looking mighty impressed with himself and calling to others to follow his lead.

"You," I seethed. "Throw one more weapon at the strox and I will feed you to them for dinner. Do you understand?"

The guard appeared perplexed, shock paling his face. "Your Majesty, they'll attack. There's too many."

"Do not harm them," I yelled.

The guard bowed his head in shame. "I apologize, Your Majesty."

"Tell your comrades now. No one attacks. Go."

It couldn't hurt to have the guards spreading the word among themselves while Ian and Raya tried to get to the leaders as well.

The guard ran toward a group of Fae working on loading a flaming ball into a catapult.

I finally made it onto the arena floor, and the sight took

my breath away. There were so many strox, more than I thought even existed. I felt Apollo hum in its sheath, alive with power as if this was where we were meant to be, alongside the ancient birds.

"Jax," I called over my shoulder. "Go with Leif and Kalliah to block the tunnel entrance. The more people running in, the harder it will be to maintain order."

"On it," he shouted, tugging Kalliah and Leif behind him.

Kade and Storm remained by my side, Kade's shadows trailing behind me as I slowly approached the beautiful yet frightening beasts.

A few guards called my name, running down the stairs we'd descended from. "I've got them," Storm said, turning to approach them.

The strox who had been shot jolted forward toward the guards with the catapult, and I ran. If this one attacked, there would be no convincing the guards to stop.

I skidded to a halt in front of the strox, holding up my hands in front of him.

While Evelyn had assured me they wouldn't harm me and they'd even helped Jax hunt in the woods, the sheer number of them overwhelmed me, making me freeze.

My heart pounded, and even though the sun was setting, it glowed brighter, pulsing as if encouraging me with its rays illuminating the field.

Cautiously, I skirted around the edge of the arena, maintaining eye contact with the injured strox. Its gaze followed me instead of attacking, allowing me to guide its attention away from the catapult. While the injured strox fixated on me, the other beasts all positioned their bodies to face the dais. I glanced over my shoulder and looked toward it from this angle. The once pristine white marble pillars were now cracked, fissures flowing down. One of the front pillars had crumbled completely.

Suddenly, the sound of beating wings and beasts slamming

to the ground ceased. The guards' shouting died down, and a calm silence descended over the arena. I still held up my hands toward the wounded strox, though it had calmed significantly and stood side by side with the others.

Emotions flooded me as I stood on the field. The last time I was here, my mother was alive. I'd seen my parents together for the last time without even realizing it. Then I'd run into battle, not knowing if I'd live to see another day, yet pushing myself toward the fight without magic anyway. Swallowing down the fear of what was happening in my home in order to defend it. While the same was true today, I knew this time, my death wouldn't be at these beasts' hands.

This time, I had the power to prevent the battle between beast and man.

I lowered my hands, watching some of the guards and staff come out of hiding and move slowly into the open. Seeing people here, knowing the dais stood behind me where I'd watched my trials alongside my parents, where I'd watched Kade and Ian, my breath hitched. Grief, love, anger, all of it welled inside and coursed through my body.

A vice tightened around my chest. How had so much happened in such a short amount of time? My voice caught in my throat as tears streamed down my face. It took me several moments to gather myself before standing tall in front of the strox.

Kade's shadows whispered at my feet, and the light inside of me warmed at their touch.

He let me stand tall before them, on my own, just as he always did. Waiting beside me in case I needed him but allowing me to do what I had to.

One of the strox in the front took a step forward, slowly, almost reverently. As I met its black-eyed gaze, I knew why they'd come.

"Have you come to aid us?" I asked.

The strox raised and lowered its head once.

I touched my fingers to my lips, in awe of what the strox's help could provide and that they'd come without being called. They'd come to defend our home. Their home.

I reached forward, touching my hand to the creature's beak.

"Thank you," I whispered, goose bumps lining my arms.

Despite the misunderstandings, the trouble they'd faced before from us, they were willing to fight for what was right. Willing to fight for us.

I stroked my hand gently over the strox's beak, curling my fingers around its face before I looked up into the beast's eyes. Hoping I'd conveyed my gratitude, I scanned as many of them as I could, making eye contact with each.

The strox in front of me stepped back, away from my touch, and dipped his head, bending forward before lowering his beak to the ground.

One by one, the rows of strox behind him followed his lead and bowed before me.

Bowed before Evelyn's line in a time when we needed them desperately.

Bowed before a queen.

CHAPTER 36
LANA

Silence hung in the air.

The chaos of the strox taking over the arena had vanished as the magnificent creatures remained bent to the crown. The royal guards stood frozen in place, jaws open in shock at the sight. One guard rubbed his eyes as if it were a dream.

Kade's shadows remained pooled at my feet, and I sensed him approaching from behind. He stepped around me, facing me as he too got down on bended knee. "Your Majesty."

"Are you crazy? Get up." I grabbed his hand and tried pulling him to me. The strox along the front line raised their heads slightly, eying the two of us carefully. "You do realize you are a king, right?"

Kade smiled but shook his head.

Movement rustled in the silence, and I looked up only to be rendered speechless as goose bumps prickled the back of my neck.

The Fae in the arena, every single one of them, dropped to their knees as well, followed by the royal guards. Fists over their hearts as they bowed their heads. I watched awestruck, my heart palpitating in a nervous rhythm. I glanced toward

Ian to see his reaction but found him kneeling as well, a smile plastered across his face.

All my friends bowed alongside the rest of the Fae gathered here. My lip quivered as a resolve, unwavering and steady, beat in my chest. I wished those I'd lost could be here to see this. Not the bowed heads, but the people coming together as one in the face of danger.

"Do you remember what I said to you after the festival?" Kade's voice floated to my ears. "Look around, Lana. You've brought not just me but an army of Fae, your friends, the guard, your kingdom, and even the damn strox to their knees. You will lead us to victory. It was the role you were born to play, a queen not sitting idly by anyone's side but leading this world. Our world." He reached for my hand, kissing my palm. "Besides, every good king knows it's really the queen who rules the land." He chuckled, grinning up at me.

I let out my own laugh and tugged on his hand. "Please," I whispered, so nervous for what this all meant. "Stand with me."

He rose, followed by the strox and everyone else. He intertwined our fingers together as we faced our people.

I signaled to the Royal Guard, waving for them to approach. Those farther away ran closer, gathering with those already awaiting instructions. Ian and the others funneled people closer to the dais. Despite watching the strox bow before me, they remained cautious as they skirted around the edge of the arena, putting as much room as possible between them and the battle birds.

The guards settled into formation to my left, still tense and breathing heavily, but present. I allowed them a moment to catch their breath before giving them my set of commands.

"The strox are on our side. They will not harm you if you do not harm them. They are loyal to me." I paused, allowing the information to settle. Once satisfied the initial shock had worn off, I continued. "We have a powerful ally, and they will join us in our fight against Thames. Rest. Sleep, if you can. We leave at dawn for the border. Ready your weapons—the time for battle has come." My chest tightened as the words left my mouth.

So it begins.

"All hail Queen Illiana," a voice rang out from the guards. Others followed, chanting in unison before they marched away to prepare for our early departure.

My friends made their way toward Kade and me as the reality of what we were about to do set in. I had given the command; the decision had been made. Tomorrow we would leave to find Thames and battle for Atheria.

"So, uhm." Jax cocked an eyebrow, his focus solely on the strox. He crossed and uncrossed his arms, restless watching the birds. "What are we supposed to do with all of them?"

My breath caught as a weight solidified in my chest. "Corbin would have known what to do. He had a way with animals unlike any Fae I've ever seen. You would have thought that was his actual magic."

"He had a way with everyone," Ian chimed in, remembering his friend. "Trust me. You thought I was the playboy? You have no idea."

Raya playfully smacked his chest, and he kissed the side of her head before sobering. "He would've figured out how to care for them and loved it." Ian pursed his lips, holding Raya tighter to his side.

I could tell Ian was trying to keep himself together. He always relied on Corbin as a confidant, especially when it came to Hidden Henchman activities. The bond between them had been special, and I prayed we could end this so my friends could grieve. So we all could.

"What do you think they eat?" Jax mused, his sole focus on the strox.

Kalliah rolled her eyes, standing with her hands on her hips next to Ian. "Why are you always talking about food?"

"What?" Jax put up his hands in confusion. "I mean, they've got to eat at some point, and I don't want any of us to become a late-night snack. We need them at their fullest potential." He eyed the creatures warily one more time. "You know, I'd just like to state for the record, I don't think I'm the most qualified for dinner duty."

"Chicken," I muttered under my breath.

Jax winked at me. "They answer to you, Your Majesty. Not your favorite general, Jax Wilder."

"Did you actually get promoted?" Raya snorted.

Jax dramatically let his jaw drop. "Excuse me? It's a very busy time for Her Royal Highness. It's at the top of her to do list, already a done deal."

I laughed, realizing just how far Jax had burrowed into my heart. His levity, his playfulness. He'd been through so much too, but he didn't let it change him.

Storm stepped forward. "Come on, Kade. Let's go before Jax promotes himself to a prince or some shit. We'll go figure out what to do with the strox."

Kade looked slightly dejected but resigned himself to join Storm. He pinched my chin between his finger and thumb. "I'm in awe of you," he said, quickly planting a kiss on my cheek before making his way to the arena steps and huddling to devise a plan.

"Be good to my ferocious friends," I yelled as they walked away.

Kade and Storm turned and bowed in jest. "As Your Majesty commands." Storm smiled.

I didn't want Kade anywhere else but by my side, but if he had to be with anyone, I was glad it was Storm. The bond between us tightened, my chest expanding to enclose the enormity of my feelings. It begged to remain close to him, not just from desire, but from the unknown of what still lay ahead. At the forefront of that fear was the knowledge that the prophecy had yet to be fulfilled. The darkness in Kade still remained.

Bickering beside me brought me back from my concerns.

"Is there a duty you do think you're qualified for?" Kalliah asked with a slight smirk.

Mischief glimmered in Jax's eyes. "I'm going to get some dinner for us, but save me a spot in your room tonight, Kalliah. I can show you exactly what I'm most qualified to perform." He winked and disappeared quickly back toward the castle.

"You can't be trusted alone in that kitchen, Jax," Leif shouted, running after him. "I'll come with you to make sure you don't break anything, or Lucinda will have my neck. I refuse to be fired because of your incompetence."

Kalliah sighed, letting her head fall back. "Because Leif is the person who never pisses Lucinda off." She shot me a look that I couldn't decipher as exasperated or happy, but she ran to catch up with Jax and Leif. "Meet you in your room in an hour, Lana."

Ian and I couldn't help but laugh. I was beyond pleased my best friend had found the love of not just one but two men.

"I promise I won't fire you," I said, crossing my fingers over my heart. "Or Leif." I narrowed my eyes. "And apparently, not Jax either."

Draped across the chaise, I shoved the last bite of biscuit smothered in jam into my mouth. Despite how unladylike it may have been, I licked the sticky sweet substance from my fingers.

Ian and Kalliah sat across from each other in front of the unlit fireplace, inhaling the last pieces of their dessert.

"My compliments to the chef." I nodded toward Kalliah, savoring every last bite of the sweet bread.

"You know, for as ridiculous as Leif is sometimes, he really is a fantastic baker." Kalliah wiped her hands on a nearby napkin. "He may have taught me a thing or two over the years." She leaned forward, whispering, "The secret is honey in the dough, but don't you ever tell him I shared his family secret. I'll deny it until the day I die."

I giggled. "Your secret is safe with me."

"Besides," she added, "pretty sure the only reason Lucinda hasn't given him the boot from the kitchen is because no one else knows how he does it."

I laughed. "Lucinda deserves a raise, I think."

Ian walked toward the window closest to where I lay on the chaise, distracted by something. He looked out at the garden and took a deep breath. "Once tomorrow starts, there's no going back."

My shoulders slumped forward as the nervous energy for our path ahead returned. I wanted to spare the people I loved from the road we traveled.

Kalliah moved to sit next to me, squeezing onto the chaise, and Ian turned to face us. "We have fought our entire lives to survive, but this will be the hardest battle yet. I just—" Ian paused, running his fingers through his loose hair. "I need you both to know how much I love and admire you. It has been a privilege to be your friend for all these years."

It felt like all I did was cry lately. The burden of the kingdom, the grief that had come with this fight—they were constant companions whose only outlet seemed to be through tears. I didn't know how else to respond though. Even Kalliah looked like she was ready to burst into tears, a rarity when it came to her.

Kalliah stood and moved next to Ian, grabbing his hand and laying her head on his shoulder. "The privilege has been all mine." She sighed then stood, still holding Ian's arm. "You two took me in and trusted me with your deepest secrets. You made me feel like I belonged somewhere for the first time in my life. Like I had a place, not just in this palace but in this world. Even when the other maids would make fun of me for having lesser magic, you never once let me believe a word they said. Your kindness changed my life. Your friendship has given me more than I ever dreamed of having."

My chest expanded, bursting with the love and connection I had in these two people, my oldest friends. "I love you both so much," I said, my voice wavering as I walked toward them. "Through thick and thin, you two were always the ones who kept me from breaking. Without the two of you, I would be nothing more than pieces of a Fae disguised as a princess."

I reached out, wrapping them both in an embrace.

These were my rocks. I would not have survived years of torture and deceit if I hadn't had these two friends by my side. I owed them everything.

Kalliah pulled away first. "Well on that mushy note, if this is our last night before war, I'm going to find my man."

Ian grimaced, but I couldn't help but giggle. "Don't you mean *men*?"

With a completely deadpan expression, Kalliah picked up her belongings, and turned to me before reaching the door. "I don't have the slightest clue what you're talking about."

She left before we could tease her any further. "It took Leif, what, three years to get her to admit she liked him?" I asked Ian. "How long do you think Jax will have to wait?"

"At least half that," Ian said, walking to the almost empty plate and popping the last biscuit in his mouth. "Come on," he said before swallowing. "Let's go outside for a moment and get some air."

I nodded, following behind a misty-eyed Ian. I knew if I said something about his show of emotions, he'd make his usual comment that his eyes had simply been watery from the dry air.

He opened my balcony door, and we stepped out onto the veranda. We'd stood in this spot so many times before, pouring out our hearts to each other.

I leaned my elbows on the marble railing overlooking my garden. My once beautiful escape lay dead and dreary beneath us. I closed my eyes, gripping my hands together as I thought about how I'd tend to it alone now. Without Corbin. I inhaled a sharp breath as the pain in my chest became almost unbearable.

"This is really it," I murmured, "the final battle of good and evil."

Ian let out a breath. "Remember everything I taught you. All the training we did was for this. Unknowingly, we've been preparing you for this your entire life."

Gripping the cool marble railing in my hand, I could feel the light magic inside of me dancing in anticipation, pleading to be let free. It seeped outward, giving the area a small glow. Ian glanced down and smiled at me. "Fates, Lan. Of course once you gained magic it'd be as beautiful as it is powerful."

I tried to laugh, but it came out strained, emotions clogging my throat.

"I just hope it will be enough," I whispered. "I hope I will be enough."

"Illiana Dresden," Ian spoke in his captain voice. "You have survived more heartbreak and anguish than any Fae should have to suffer. You were tortured for years. Your parents couldn't help you because they were under Andras's spell. Fates, they weren't even your biological parents. You never even had a chance to know your birth parents. Yet you stand here today, a survivor. Not once did you let any of those things break you. Andras's torture alone would have made even the strongest of soldiers crumble. I would know," he added with a whisper. "But you stood tall. You fought back."

"I—"

Ian held up his hand. "No, let me finish. Lan, you did all of that without magic. Look at you now. You don't just have magic, you have one-of-a-kind, never-seen-before light magic. Something so rare and so unique, of course it would be your power. You have always been enough, and there is not one doubt in my mind you will fulfill these Fates' awful prophecies and save us all. You just have to believe in yourself as much as every single one of us believes in you."

I pulled away and threw my arms around Ian, unable to stop the sobs as I clutched onto him. "I could never have done this without you. I love you, more than I can ever say. It wasn't because of myself that I survived. It was because of you." I lifted my head and looked into the eyes of my best friend. "I was nothing without your support. Thank you for loving me, for reminding me what's real, for enduring the nightmares together." I couldn't continue, couldn't get any other words out.

Ian hugged me tightly again. We didn't move, just stood there, savoring the comfort we brought each other. Though my heart sagged, heavy with worry, it also strengthened because of this man. I'd cried at the loss of all my parents, believing I had no family left, but Ian? Ian was my family.

"You helped me not only survive, but you created the beginning of this crazy family we've assembled. The one we've chosen for ourselves."

He laughed, his breath catching as he sucked it in, wiping his eyes. "Fuck, this group is insane."

We laughed together for another few minutes, reminiscing about the past.

"Whatever happens, know that you have made my life better by being in it," I said.

Ian kissed the top of my head as we stared out into my garden below.

A familiar tug drew my attention away from Ian and back to my chambers.

Kade coughed, leaning against the doorframe. "If you two are done having your moment, Raya is looking for you, Captain," he said. "And I need Lana. Alone."

CHAPTER 37

LANA

Ian didn't need to be told twice.

He slid away from me, giving me one last loving smile.

The energy radiating off Kade's body oozed desire with a dangerous undercurrent I couldn't name. As much as I loved Ian, in no way did he need to be present for anything that was about to transpire.

Looking between us, Ian smiled. "I'll just see myself out, then."

We walked back into my room, and Ian gathered his belongings as quickly as possible before heading to the door. "Goodnight, Lan. Kade." He dipped his head and shut the door.

Kade immediately scooped me into his arms, carrying me like some damsel toward my bed. "It has been too long since I've felt you naked and writhing beneath me, Little Rebel."

Giggling, I feigned shock. "Whatever shall we do?"

Kade's shadows shut the door to my bed chamber, and he playfully threw me on the bed. I bounced once as he proceeded to crawl toward me. "I can think of quite a few things to do to you."

As his body loomed over mine, I grabbed his shirt and pulled him close to me, desperate to feel his lips on mine.

"If this is the last night we are alive," Kade murmured between kisses, "I will spend every minute of it with you."

Running my hands up and down his back, I felt his muscles rippling with anticipation as his shadows filled the room, blocking us from the outside world. The light magic inside of me hummed with excitement, trickling out of my hands and swirling alongside Kade's shadows.

I groaned as Kade's lips roamed from my mouth down my neck in slow, luxurious kisses. The fire in my core ignited, ready and waiting for him. "I will never get enough of this," I breathed, my voice quivering with an ungodly need.

He reached for the edge of my shirt and ran his hand across my stomach, tracing my body up toward my chest. Teasing me with the calloused tips of his fingers, he caressed my breast, his thumb rolling over the tip of my nipple. A jolt of pleasure deep in my belly twisted, taking me higher until I didn't think I would be able to breathe without him inside of me.

"Get me out of these clothes," I demanded. "Now."

Kade chuckled as he continued to tease my nipple with his fingers. "Is that a royal order?"

"Kade."

His mouth crashed into mine, and he rolled me on top of him, adjusting my legs and settling them on either side of his hips. My head fell back, and I moaned unabashedly as his hard length pressed against my clit through my pants in exactly the right spot.

Danger danced across his features, the darkness in his eyes stuttering in and out as he lost control, even before plunging into me, but it didn't scare me. I would gladly accept any and all danger this man would give me. I knew now that no amount of darkness inside of him would take him away. Kade was mine.

Pulling back, I made my way off of Kade's body and the bed, standing beside him.

"Where do you think you're going?" he growled playfully. "I had you exactly where I wanted you."

"Good things come to those who wait, sir." I took another step back. "Now sit there and watch."

Kade's brow lifted, but he shifted back against the pillow, lying propped up on one elbow as he stared at my body with lust.

Shadows danced at my feet, yearning for attention and wanting in on the action.

"Tsk, tsk." I tousled my hair. "You will have to wait your turn too."

Kade rolled his eyes at his shadows, but his attention never left my body, allowing his gaze to roam up and down.

Slow and seductive. That was what I wanted this dance to be for Kade. Edging him in the best possible way. Grabbing the hem of my shirt, I lifted it higher, slipping it over my head, swinging my hips and losing myself in the moment. I let go of my fears, of my insecurities, and any feeling of unworthiness I'd clung to for so long.

Swaying to a beat in my own head, I ran my hands over my body, moving down toward my pants. I drank in the sight of Kade's cock straining against his pants as he observed my movements. I grinned when he planted his hands on the bed, gripping the sheets as if he barely contained himself from reaching out to me.

"Not yet," I purred, shaking my finger at him. "I've still got clothes to remove." I lifted my foot and placed it on the edge of the bed. Reaching down, I exaggerated my every movement, removing my slipper from my foot, pulling myself back up before doing the same with the other.

"You're so fucking beautiful."

Kade's shadows took matters into their own hands and untied the string holding my pants up so they fell to my ankles.

"Naughty shadows." The light inside of me poured out of my palms quickly, mixing with the shadows. Pure unadulterated happiness filled every crevice of my body as my magic sang alongside Kade's.

I swore our magics themselves were mates too with how they acted.

Unable to control himself anymore, Kade threw off his shirt and removed his pants. "You can't expect me to sit here watching you and not do something about it," he groaned, falling back onto the bed. Kade stroked his cock as I continued to stand before him, wrapped in shadows and light, swaying to the rhythm of our magic.

"I am done waiting for you, Little Rebel," Kade growled as he rubbed his palm over the tip of his member. "Get over here now, so I can bury myself inside of you."

Tying my hair in a low bun, I made my way back on the bed and straddled Kade. He wrapped a hand around the back of my neck, pulling me to him, his thumb stroking against my pulse point. I expected rough desperation behind Kade's kiss. Instead, our lips grazed each other, soft and tenderly. Hands exploring thoroughly as if both of us knew the other needed to touch every inch and memorize this moment.

This time felt like so much more. Despite the raw hunger throbbing inside of me, our movements weren't hurried. This wasn't anything but genuine love between the two of us, yearning, delicious passion that we allowed to consume us slowly. Fates, I'd allow Kade's love to consume me for eternity.

Unable to resist him any further, I lowered myself onto his ready cock inch by inch, moaning into his ear.

"Fates, you're so fucking wet for me," Kade groaned.

I shifted to pull back, craving to set us on a rhythm that would take him deeper, but he grasped my hips, stilling me.

"Ah, ah," he grinned up at me. "It's my turn now."

His shadows slipped around my wrists, tugging them together behind my back, pulling me until I arched slightly.

Another slid up the back of my neck and into my hair, tugging it ever so slightly.

Kade and his shadows held me in place as his lust-filled gaze devoured me. I whimpered, squirming around his length, needing it deeper.

"You look so beautiful tied up in my shadows." Kade sat up, taking one of my nipples in his mouth and biting.

I cried out, shifting my hips.

He didn't let me pull him any deeper. I felt his smile against my skin as he tenderly licked my other nipple. "I think I could get used to this sight."

"Please," I begged. My body had devolved into a quivering mess. The only thing that would make it better just out of my reach.

Kade pulled out, lying back down on the bed as his hands gripped my waist. Before I could beg again, he plunged into me. "So pretty when you beg," he praised. His hands caressed over my hips, trailed by more of his shadows, both entwining with my light and touching me. My body rested fully in Kade's control, as he slammed into me again and again. Stroke after stroke, the pleasure inside of me built until I was gasping for breath, body tightening, chasing the high only he brought me to. Kade rubbed my clit with his thumb in slow circles, igniting another fire inside of me.

"More, Kade," I pleaded as I writhed on top of him.

He obeyed willingly. "Such a good fucking girl." *Thrust.* "You're mine." *Thrust.* "You'll always be mine." He repeated the phrase through his own moans of pleasure.

His shadows tightened in my hair as Kade drove me higher until my orgasm hit in rolling waves. I screamed his name as I trembled in the aftershocks.

Breathless and glowing, I shivered with contentment as both of our magics buzzed with excitement, ready for more. We were all far from satiated.

His shadows loosened, letting go of me with tender

caresses. I brought my forehead to Kade's as I caught my breath before he kissed me once more. "The Fates did one thing right," he whispered, running his tongue slowly over mine. "They brought me to you. I will never be able to thank you enough for saving me from myself. For letting me be *me*. For seeing beyond my past, what I was forced to do. You accepted every dark part of me with open arms and looked at me as if I still shone bright. You never turned your back on me, on us. You are my salvation, Lana."

My heart burst with the love I had for this man. I ran the tips of my fingers up and down his arm, and goose bumps appeared in a trail. "For you, my love—my mate—there is no mountain I wouldn't climb. No darkness I wouldn't face to stand by your side. There is only me and you."

A hungry look flashed in Kade's eyes, and he shifted, rolling on top of me before leaning me back onto the bed. Taking a moment to readjust himself, he pushed a strand of hair that fell across my face behind my ear.

"Whether in this world or the next, Little Rebel, you will always be mine."

This time when he leaned down to kiss me, our tongues swirled in a bewitching harmony I knew I'd never come back from.

He propped himself up with his hand next to my head as he began moving with slow and steady strokes inside of me. Our gazes locked on each other, memorizing every second of our time together.

Tears formed in my eyes, as neither of us looked away. Seconds turned to minutes, and any concept of time erased itself from the room altogether. Moonlight shone across the bed, illuminating Kade's body in all of its warrior glory. I ran my hands along the lines of his tattoos, along the scars of his chest. I closed my eyes as the pleasure slowly built inside of me again. A deep crescendo of love and desire, waiting to be set free.

I let out a small cry as my body teetered on the edge of something more than anything we'd crashed through before. Emotions ravaged me as Kade's breathing shallowed. When the tears formed in his eyes too, I lost every shred of my own control.

"Together," he rasped. "Together."

"Kade, I'm so close."

"I know, love, just a little bit longer."

Biting my lip, I held on for as long as I could, but with two more beautifully deep, sensual thrusts, he threw me over the edge and there was no coming back. My entire body convulsed in the most mind-altering orgasm I'd ever had. I cried out, watching him, feeling him everywhere. My mind and heart completely connected to this man before me as the bond in my chest broke and reforged into something unfathomable. Kade found his release, and together we rode out our orgasms in bliss.

All the broken pieces of self-doubt, of ever feeling not good enough, thoughts of not being worthy of love were shattered by this man. There was no part of me that remained untouched, that remained less than. Not just because of him, but because his love gave me the space to also love myself.

Kade grabbed a small cloth from the bedside table and meticulously wiped away all evidence of our time together, placing kisses on different places of my body as he did.

A few minutes later, we lay curled up under the blankets while he stroked my hair with my head nestled on his chest. "Lana, we need to talk about the prophecy and what it might mean."

I stopped breathing, the high of what we'd just experienced together crashing around me as panic set in. "No. No, it is not an option I'm willing to consider."

Kade pulled my chin up to look straight into his eyes. "We have to consider it. The Fates have foretold the darkness has to be gone for Thames to be destroyed. We can't dismiss it. We need to prepare for what happens if we meet him and the darkness is still with me."

"I refuse," I said more firmly. "Losing you is not an option I will entertain ever. I will not spend our last night discussing it." I placed my head back on his chest and scooted my body as close to him as possible, wrapping around him like just that action alone could somehow keep me here.

Kade sighed, "We can't escape this forever. We're out of time."

"Forever can start tomorrow." A tear threatened to escape, but I refused to let it fall. I would not give it voice or allow it to take hold. This would be something that presented itself tomorrow. After all, we still had to figure out how to get the darkness out of half this world. Whatever we did would work on Kade too.

I would not let fear destroy the most amazing night I'd ever had. The intimate connection between us wasn't common, it was otherworldly, and that had to mean something. This bond between us was unbreakable, and I wouldn't ruin this perfect moment by talking about any prophecy, much less one that could be interpreted as taking Kade away from this world.

Kade must have realized he'd lost this battle, because he wrapped his other arm around me, pulling me in closer, and said, "Sleep, Illiana. Replenish your magic." He kissed the top of my head. "You will need every ounce of energy you have to win this war."

"I will win this war with you by my side, Kade," I said, allowing his presence to soothe me as I drifted to sleep. I closed my eyes and prayed to the Fates they were wrong.

CHAPTER 38
KADE

The void gaped open between our two kingdoms as if it might swallow both sides whole.

I stared out at the dead land I'd crossed over so many times in the past few years, standing empty, fulfilling its name more now than it ever had before.

We'd arrived only a few hours ago after a hard ride, stopping only once on our way to the border. The morale among our army was better than I thought it would be, especially with an army of strox bringing up the rear. Those with us consisted of more untrained Fae than warriors, and still they rode confidently toward this battle.

We'd allowed for an extra day of rest once we arrived here. At least, we hoped, based on our estimates as to when Thames would arrive. We'd have to start scouting frequently to find a more exact timeline for when to expect Thames. Cassandra could only tell us it would be soon.

The breeze blew gently around me, swirling through the camp and alleviating the blistering heat we'd traveled through all day. The wind stirred my shadows, and I couldn't help the dry huff of laughter escaping my lips. I'd swear Lana was a goddess, not a mere Fae from the way nature responded to her and the people she loved.

"Fates, I hope you're with us," I whispered to the breeze as it wrapped around me once before it flitted away.

Onyx nudged me with his wet nose, and I reached up absentmindedly to brush my hand over his mane. "It all comes down to this, old friend."

He neighed, bumping his nose into my shoulder.

Closing my eyes, I released a few shadows from where they trapped the darkness, hoping against rational thought that perhaps being around Lana had destroyed it altogether. The evil inside me opened its eye, waking. I was in control now, too surrounded by Lana's light for it to overtake me, but the fact of the matter was it still remained.

As quickly as my chest constricted, it relaxed as Lana's presence drew closer. I breathed deeply, taking in the soothing calm she brought me.

"Jax's group should be back soon with the last batch of weapons from The Knotted Willow," she said.

I murmured in acknowledgement, tugging her back until she rested against my chest. We stood quietly as we stared out across the barren land before us.

I caressed her shoulder with one hand, while I held her against me with the other.

Behind us, Fae moved about the camp, speaking in low voices among themselves. The closer we got to the border, the quieter the group became. I couldn't blame them.

Though a few reassuring breezes swirled around us, a heavy tension lay thick in the air. The weight of what was to come bled into everything around us.

Hooves padded the ground, approaching from the east. Jax led a group of riders, and some of the anxiousness at being separated from everyone eased. I needed to know that even if something happened to me, Lana would be protected by others who loved her. Those who would ensure she succeeded, whatever it took.

Six Fae rode behind Jax, straight to the center of camp, bags hanging from the sides of all the horses.

"If you don't already have something to fight with, grab one here. Take one you're able to hold and wield without tiring yourself completely. Work with another Fae if you need to practice how the weapon feels and moves with your body," he shouted. "Spread the word to everyone arriving, there's plenty for us all."

He helped the others gather the various swords, scythes, bows, and daggers in the center of camp before striding toward us.

"Thank you," Lana told him.

He flung his arm around her, effectively taking her from my grasp. "Anything for my queeny." Jax eyed me over Lana's shoulder. "Ready?"

I nodded. Jax, Storm, and Raya had all kept an obnoxiously close eye on me, either worried Thames would drag me away again or that the darkness would creep up to overpower me. I knew Storm especially wondered how this was going to play out, but he saw more than most.

Ian and Raya walked forward after finishing their own tasks among our army. "I'm going to fly," he said. "I'll see where they are. Figure out how much time we have."

"We're sure they're coming this way?" Kalliah asked, trailed by Leif.

"Can't you feel it in the air?" Raya looked skyward. "I think the Fates themselves are holding their breath."

The Fates themselves. Fuck, they had better be on Lana's side.

She has us. She will survive.

My shadows remained confident. Though they were as burdened as me, their unwavering conviction that Lana would remain alive in the end hadn't faltered.

No matter what, she would live.

Me? Neither my shadows nor I held confidence in that.

"Be quick," Lana told Ian. Her voice remained calm, but she twisted her hands together in front of her.

The captain shifted and took to the skies, soaring higher into the distance until disappearing from our sight.

"There's at least two more groups arriving according to rumors among the army," Storm said. "One is a large contingent from Larkslary, the other from Starhaven."

I cocked an eyebrow at Storm.

Lana chuckled. "You learned the city names fast. Perhaps I'll make that Colonel Storm title official. Maybe even before we dub Jax General Wilder."

Jax scoffed as he stared out across the void. "Rude, Your Majesty."

He may be playful, but I'd trust the man with my life. He scanned the horizon, his eyes shifting to those of his panther, using his superior eyesight to catch anything we might miss otherwise.

"I merely read a map," Storm said, but I knew him. He thrived on competence and how meticulous he was when it came to battle. I had no doubt he had memorized every city the first time we pulled up a map. "I'll keep an eye out on the perimeter." He tilted his head, indicating he wanted me to follow.

I stroked a finger down Lana's face. "I'll be right back."

We moved away from the group, and Storm crossed his arms, turning to me as soon as we were out of earshot of the others. "Do you have a plan?"

"For the battle?" I smirked. "Win." I shot him the most arrogant grin I could muster.

"You know what I mean," he snapped before inhaling. He hung his head, shoulders dipping. "To get rid of the darkness still inside of you, Kade."

"Lana and I will figure it out." I gripped his shoulder,

refusing to acknowledge my own fears in order to convince him. He needed to focus like the rest of us. "We will."

He narrowed his eyes, searching for the lie. So I made sure he didn't find it. "If you need my help—"

I took him by surprise, cutting him off and hugging him. He stiffened before hugging me back. Pulling away, I patted his shoulder. "You've always been there for me, and then you protected her when I couldn't," I said. "You're the first person I'd go to if we needed anything."

He slugged me loosely. "None of this mushy stuff. Save that for Jax. I'll return to the front once everyone is settled."

I nodded, watching the closest thing I had to a brother walk toward the back of camp. A few guards approached with questions, needing assistance, and I busied myself aiding our warriors. Some of the younger Fae needed help remembering their groupings. We'd hastily tried to mix the skilled and unskilled warriors as best we could, saving a few exceptional warriors for the middle to push their groups forward after the initial battle began.

Before I knew it, a hawk cried out above us, and I jogged back to the edge of the void where Lana waited.

"An hour," Ian said immediately after landing. "They're on the move quickly. We've got an hour. Tops."

The havoc that ensued as word spread through our camp to ready for battle was exactly what I'd expect it would be.

Fear wormed its way into our army, which would only grow once they saw Thames face to face. They needed a distraction. Ian and I suggested each battalion leader speak to their groups, encouraging them, but experienced soldiers were few and far between in this army.

Andras allowed so many of the guard to turn or be forced

to turn, that those who remained loyal and alive amounted to a smaller number than we'd hoped.

The people needed Lana.

She inspired them, encouraged them. I sent out my shadows, feeling for her. It only took a moment.

Jogging toward the tents, I found her putting her armor on.

"Let me help," I said, staring at my mate as if the world revolved around her. Then again, *my* world revolved around her.

She wore a fitted all-black outfit providing her the ability to move freely while also protecting her as much as possible from any initial strikes on her body.

"Where did this come from?" I asked, trying not to let my gaze linger on how well it fit her.

She looked over her shoulder at me, fastening the thicker armored vest around her chest. "Brookmere has an excellent group of Fae who design clothes, armor, and more. Perhaps you should visit when this is all over."

I growled, tugging her body close to mine and reaching my fingers around to help her lace up the leathers along her arms. "Oh, I will be doing more than just visiting, my queen."

She laughed, her face lighting up for only a moment before she laid a hand on my chest.

"You'll need to save your energy, Kade," she said. "No shadow armor."

I brushed my knuckle over her nose. "I'll give you shadow armor if I want."

She gripped my arm, a small hint of fear flashing in her eyes. "Please," she whispered. "Please don't do anything stupid."

Reaching my hand up to cup her cheek, I rested my forehead to hers. "That's my line."

We lingered for a moment, but it ended too quickly. "Your people need to hear from you. They're anxious."

She nodded, sheathing Apollo on her thigh, opposite a longer sword at her hip.

We walked in silence toward the front of the camp. The Fae stood shoulder to shoulder, some with heads high, some glancing nervously around them. Lana raised her chin, taking in the sight of her people. "Fae of Atheria," she said, her voice amplified outward on the winds. "I know you're scared. That's okay. There can be no bravery without fear." She looked out, taking in the army that gathered at her request.

The vast number of Fae who believed in the message flooding across Brookmere to rally against the darkness still took my breath away.

"You've heard us say what we're fighting for, what we need to do. You wouldn't be here if you hadn't. But let me remind you, we are defending our homes. Andras tried to crush Brookmere, making it weak under his control. But you prevailed. *We* prevailed."

A few shouts rose up, chanting with confidence.

"You resisted the darkness. You fought alongside us in Ellevail. You traveled hundreds of miles to join us. You've already proven yourselves to be courageous. Now Thames wants to do what Andras couldn't."

"Never," a few cried out to more cheers.

I stared at my mate, my heart and soul. She was everything I could have ever imagined for myself. I didn't deserve her or her valor. Her love was the greatest gift of my life. Standing here, taking in the way she commanded an army, the way they were as enraptured by her as I was, made me think of the legends that would be written of this moment. Stories passed down for generations about Illiana Dresden.

"He will not succeed," she shouted. "On my life, he will not succeed this day. Take the bravery you've already shown and use it. Let it build. Stand united with me. We will defend our home and each other. We are stronger than the darkness.

We are stronger together than the dark ones and evil will ever be."

Whooping and hollering rang through the crowd. Some of the army threw their magic upward, sparks bursting in the sky, cool winds sweeping among the troops and the earth rumbled, as they embraced Lana's words.

The clouds cleared overhead, and light shone down on our army. Lana looked to the sky, her eyes glassy as she basked in the sunlight, savoring its warmth. Eventually she tilted her head back down to her people, and the rays of sun caressing her skin made her look ethereal. I swallowed down the lump growing in my throat. This woman was everything.

A force.

A savior.

Mine.

"Nature is with us. If the root of our magic is with us, who could possibly stand against us?"

She drew her sword, raising it toward the sky. "For Atheria, we fight!"

Our soldiers drew their blades in unison, chanting, "For Atheria, we fight," as our battle cry.

I drew my own blade from my back and joined in.

Lana stood, chin raised, chanting along with her people.

And when her brilliant blue gaze met mine, I shouted louder, letting my pride shine through both my words and actions.

"For Atheria, we fight!"

CHAPTER 39
KADE

A thunderous echo of hatred reverberated across the void before we even saw Thames's army.

When they appeared, the sheer magnitude of the force rippled over our soldiers, and the confidence Lana had worked to build faltered. We were vastly outnumbered.

"Steady!" Lana shouted, allowing her voice to carry as it had before.

Thames's army marched forward, not halting until they were halfway through the void. The masses cheered, taunting and shouting at our troops.

The calm that always came over me before a battle settled my nerves, allowing me to take in as much detail as possible. My gaze shifted over the enemy until I caught sight of him.

Thames.

He marched in the middle of his army before raising his hands and rising off the ground. I couldn't even be sure what the core of his magic was at this point.

"Fae of Atheria, you have been deceived," his cold voice sounded around us, and there was a part of me wondering if people could hear him all throughout the land. "The darkness

I offer is not the evil you've been told it is." The grin on his face did nothing to hide the monster inside of him. "It will bring you strength. It will enhance your magic. Don't you want to know what real power feels like? Especially those of you who have been burdened under the weight of being less than for so long."

A wicked laugh left his mouth.

"We will not cower before you or betray our world," Lana shouted back at him. "Not one of these Fae is less than. It's *you* who hold that distinct honor."

He tilted his head back, laughing harder. "Ah, you of all people know what it's like to be powerless, Illiana Dresden." His voice slithered across his dark ones, across the entire void, directly toward us. "To be worthless." He tsked. "Pathetic."

I kept my eyes on Thames while moving my hand toward my mate. His words echoed the ones Andras had tortured Lana with years ago. Words that were meant to make her cower in fear.

This time? His words did nothing to cause her pause. Instead, I saw her lips twitch upward from the corner of my eye.

"How easy it would be for you, if your words meant anything to me, Thames. Unlike you, I've already proven my worth. Can you say the same?"

"Maybe let's not taunt the evil being that couldn't be killed and was trapped instead, yeah?" Jax hissed.

"Let her rile him," I responded. "He's more likely to make a mistake."

Thames rose higher in the air, his grey mist seeping out over the front lines of his army. "Why don't we find out, *child*."

Thames raised his hand up to the sky and a swarm of voidlings launched from behind him, flying toward our army.

Our people shouted, never having seen the beasts. Before I could give an order, the strox cawed from behind us, rising in response to the new, winged threat.

I watched in awe as the battle beasts flew over our army and made their way directly toward the voidlings. The creatures met far above us in a flurry of wings, roars, and screeching.

Shouts from the ground ripped my attention from the skies as charging dark ones came into view through Thames's grey mist, ready to engage.

"For Atheria," Ian shouted as our own soldiers surged forward in response.

The final battle for Atheria had begun.

Lana used her sword instead of her light, cutting down dark ones like she was born to do it. Fates, she *was* born for this.

"Keep count," Storm shouted at me, shoving me sideways as he jumped and plowed his blade through the neck of a dark one to my left. "I swear to the Fates themselves if you exaggerate your kills this time, I'll take all the coin left in Mount Legion as my winnings."

"You're on," I shouted, materializing my shadow sword alongside my other blade.

Though I fought the soldiers before me, my attention moved back and forth between them and Thames. He stood, gleefully watching the battle, but not engaging himself.

What is he waiting for? my shadows asked.

I didn't know how to answer them because I had the same question.

A sharp sensation stabbed into my leg, brushing by me as it scraped the skin. I jerked around, catching the end of Lucien's tail swishing away from my leg. He trotted through the battle, breathing fire at dark ones as he went.

"Fucking pugron," I muttered, unable to stop a smile at the thought of Lana's pet being just as headstrong as her.

I slaughtered three more dark ones before turning to see a shimmering portal appear and Jax's panther form jumping through. He popped out behind the group of dark ones around him, shifting back so only his claws remained and driving them through their chests. He laughed, looking down at the pugron.

"Damn it, Luci, brilliant execution." He shook off the partial-shift and picked up a sword from the ground, twirling it before starting his attack on the next group.

Storm shot fire forward toward a battalion approaching on our right. A whooping cry rang behind us as the noblewoman Keena sprinted toward it, throwing her hands out and fueling Storm's fire as it blew forward, covering two entire lines of soldiers. They screamed, flailing, engulfed in magic.

Storm whipped around, staring open-mouthed at the woman.

"Damn, I didn't know that would work so perfectly. Carry on." She winked toward my now sputtering friend and ran off toward another group of Fae.

"I can't tell if he's intrigued or angry," Lana chuckled as she watched Storm chase after the woman.

"Both," I confirmed.

She grinned at me. "Definitely both."

I looked at Lana, checking her over for injuries and found nothing substantial. Despite fighting by her side and knowing she could hold her own, there was an uneasy feeling growing that I couldn't quite shake. The bond between us ached in my chest knowing what might happen today.

We'd either walk away with a free Atheria or we'd die. I couldn't stomach the thought of Lana not existing. I had to physically battle the desperation rising inside of me in order to focus. I couldn't make a mistake. Not now.

Screams and agonized shrieks echoed toward us from the edge of the battle. Dark ones *and* our Fae ran farther into the fray.

We braced ourselves, unsure of what to expect from the sudden panic when a stampede of razorven came into view.

Lana ran, shoving through to get to them as I chased after her.

"It's okay," she shouted to our army. "Hold! Hold your positions."

She stopped in front of the razorven, watching them. Sure enough, they ran right to her side as if awaiting instructions.

"Kade."

Cassandra's voice was soft, brushing against my ear, even though she wasn't standing anywhere near me. I turned, looking around the battlefield until I saw her next to Vivienne toward the back by a few strox standing proudly, protecting the seers.

She waved a hand in the air, beckoning me. "Lana," I said hesitantly, not wanting to break her concentration with the creatures.

"We fight Thames and his army of dark ones," Lana addressed the beasts. "Our soldiers will fight alongside you. The dark ones are yours to do with as you please." She shouted to our people nearby to spread the word that the razorven were with us, just like the strox.

I shook my head. Mystical creatures emerging to fight alongside the love of my life? It wasn't something I could have dreamt up myself.

Lana turned toward me, smiling.

"Cassandra's calling us," I said loudly, shouting over the noise of the battle around us.

She nodded, and we raced to the back, while she encouraged the army along the way, praising their work against the odds.

We stopped before the seers, and Cassandra cupped Lana's face. Her eyes were almost white, but not quite. I didn't know if she was having a vision or merely trying to take in as much of the battle as she could. The softness she displayed toward Lana now reminded me of the woman who healed me growing up.

"You can't forget the prophecy," she said to Lana. While moving her hand to Lana's shoulder, she reached her other toward me.

"Banish all ties to darkness with light, if any remains, so will this blight," she whispered. "There is an entire army of dark ones with his evil embedded in them. He will win if that darkness remains."

Lana's frantic gaze darted between Vivienne and Cassandra.

"You will need everything you have if you want to banish it," Vivienne said. She stared straight at Lana until her face softened.

She whirled to face me. "The most powerful our magic has ever been was in the volcano. We obliterated not just the darkness, but the volcano itself." Her voice trembled with excitement. "If we tried it again, if we channeled our magic together, we might be able to draw the darkness out of his army, just as we did the lava."

I nodded slowly at first, understanding seeping into me as every word she said settled, making sense.

Cassandra dropped her hands and heaved a sigh of relief. "Conserve your energy and build the momentum together."

The seer stepped back, chanting under her breath before she circled her arms in a wide arc around us. A shimmering, almost translucent dome appeared above us and she opened her eyes. "It feels good to use my sorcery again," she said. "This will offer some protection. If Thames figures out what you're doing, he'll come directly for you. He won't want to keep playing around if you have a chance of bringing him down. I don't know what he knows of the final prophecy. I'd like to think nothing, but I wouldn't take a chance."

"Once we destroy the darkness, it should make the battle much easier," Lana said, glancing over her shoulder at the fight still waging.

"Do not underestimate hatred," Vivienne cautioned. "Though some are with Thames by force, others chose evil. Getting rid of the darkness does not automatically mean his army will be nothing."

"Hurry," Cassandra urged. "We'll help others as we can while making sure you have time to fulfill your destiny." She laced her fingers together before cracking them. "Care to watch me work like old times, Vivi?"

"Show-off," Vivienne muttered, but the two walked off toward the very back rows of our army.

Lana smiled, glancing up and around at the glittering dome still encasing us. "Kade," she said, excitement building in her voice. "This is what we were missing."

I frowned, unsure of what she meant.

"I've tried to merely cut the darkness out like I did with Ian. But it's not enough with how deep it lies embedded in your body."

She took my hands, eyes glistening, with a brilliant hope shining through both her gaze and her words.

"When we do this, once our magic explodes, I'll grab the dagger and use it on you. Our magic should be at its peak. We didn't even include the dagger when we banished the darkness out of Firestone. Imagine the power it will contain with both of our magics infusing into it? It was created to destroy the darkness for good, but it will take everything we have together to do it."

I let out a disbelieving breath of air. "You're a genius, Little Rebel." I pulled her in, claiming her lips for far too short a kiss. "A genius."

We moved forward, finding a spot less occupied with our troops. The dome moved along with us, unable to block out the cries filling the air from the war. I tried not to think about how many were fighting and falling.

Lana reached out her hand, taking mine in her own. Her

light flared, and shadows twisted from my palm around hers. This time her light crept over my skin too. There was no need to coax it out of her, it lay ready.

"Let's rid Atheria of his darkness once and for all." She grinned up at me. "Then destroy *him*."

CHAPTER 40

LANA

As our palms connected, a tingle of energy shot upward, coating my body with magic.

Everything came down to these few moments. Ridding this land of the darkness, pulling it out of Kade, then destroying Thames. Our prophecies had led us to this moment, together.

The pit in my stomach, since failing to eradicate Kade's darkness, lessened for the first time after hearing the final prophecy.

Light is stronger than dark. It'd been woven into every prophecy, every journal entry from my ancestors, every fiber of this very world.

Light was what would drive out the darkness, defeating it once and for all.

I looked around as our magic slowly built inside of us. Where would we channel it to?

The volcano had been easy; there was a clear target, but this wasn't the same. There wasn't an obvious answer.

"Where," I murmured, still glancing around as Kade's shadows danced along my skin, calling more of my light forward. Power welled up, strong and resolute. This time as I urged it to respond, it did so willingly.

I glanced out at the dark ones. "The darkness is not residing in one single place, it's everywhere. The prophecy is clear, *all* of it has to be destroyed," I continued, talking to myself.

"Including any he may have hidden away." Kade's eyes flashed black before turning back to their grey.

"Are you all right?" I gasped, touching his cheek.

His smile reassured me. "I've been using my shadows to lock away the darkness for so long that releasing them allows it to come to the surface." He unlocked one of our intertwined hands and brought it to my neck, stroking his thumb along my collarbone. "The darkness isn't as present when you're here, Lana. Focus. Don't worry about me."

I closed my eyes and basked in his touch, letting it attempt to soothe my fears while strengthening me at the same time.

"We need to find a way to spread our power everywhere, touch everything." I paused, thinking. "Touching."

I stared at the ground, then my dagger, then back to Kade. "The earth," I whispered.

Even with the dome around us, wind rustled the grass beneath our feet, the sun pulsed as its rays brightened. Just as it had done before, when I'd been on the right track with the strox. A gift from nature, a confirmation. "Let's try to funnel our magic into the earth, so that everything touching it can be infused with light. If we're right and it can cover Atheria…" I exhaled slowly, sending a prayer to the Fates that I was right about this.

Kade's lips parted as his eyes widened. "Into the earth," he repeated.

Slowly, he moved his hand from where it rested on my neck and we kneeled, lowering our hands to the ground. Kade laid his over mine, and my light, charged with his shadows, formed a cocoon around us.

A furious roar bellowed in the distance, and I turned my head. The fighting near us parted as our army shrank back, pushed from beyond by a force stronger than themselves.

"Protect your queen," a shout rang out. Tommy charged toward us, turning and standing in front of the ground where Kade and I kneeled.

Fear may have etched Tommy's features, but he gathered his group of rebels, and they bravely swarmed to block us from Thames's renewed attack.

Another roar echoed into the world as a dark mist circled around Cassandra's enclosure. Thames knew what we were doing, and he was pissed.

"She said the dome wouldn't last long." My voice shook as I dug my hands more firmly into the ground. "Cassandra can only give us so much."

"Together, Lana." Kade met my gaze.

I trembled with anticipation. Everything I'd become had led to this. My light, foretold for a thousand years, was our only advantage, and it was time to unleash it on our world.

Closing my eyes, I focused all my attention on the ground beneath my fingers. The sounds of the battle, all the screams faded into the background until it was me, Kade, my light, and his shadows. His breathing, his very heartbeat perfectly in sync with my own.

I inhaled a steady, calming breath as I wrapped my magic around my hands like a coil.

We're ready, my light reassured me, speaking confidently, fueled with the love I felt in my soul.

We were one, my magic and me. The light an extension of me. My body shook at the force of the magic gathering inside. I clung to it, letting it well up despite my trembling.

"I'm here, Little Rebel," Kade's voice caressed over me, but I kept my eyes closed, focusing both of our energy into one solid torrent of power. I dropped every doubt, every fear I had, and let the light reign supreme.

My magic plunged into the depths of the earth as a scream escaped my body. Staying connected with its power, I held on, letting everything flow through me to pour outward with purpose into the earth. I felt it then, a pulse of energy scattering in the depths of the soil, gliding through Atheria along the feet of everyone here in the battle, and outward even still.

Kade's shadows circled the light, reinforcing it like vines coiling together to carry the charge across all of Atheria. My arms shook, my body pushed to the brink of its limits, but still I didn't let go of the power. Not yet.

I groaned under the weight of it all, feeling Kade's grip tighten around me. He grunted, as if feeling the heaviness of our power extending itself to its limit.

Apollo burned at my thigh, and I forced one hand from the ground, pulling the white dagger from its sheath. I channeled every last ounce of my magic, Kade's shadows, every ounce of *myself* into the blade.

I directed my love for my parents, the king and queen. The pride I felt being theirs and knowing they loved me like I was their own.

I channeled the love I had for my birth parents, knowing they died with a fierce devotion to each other, and to me.

I poured my dreams from childhood; though there had been trauma and torture, there had also been a love most only dreamt of having. Something unconditional from the start. A love that never asked for anything in return. Love given freely and genuinely from my best friend. I thought of Ian, of his strength, of his absolute, unwavering belief in me.

"You're doing it, Lana." Kade's voice brushed over me in a strained whisper.

I tilted my head back, squeezing the blade harder as I pictured the friendships that came after Ian. Of Kalliah and her spirit, of Leif and his humor. A tear escaped as I thought of Corbin and how he'd made me feel worthwhile every damn time we spoke.

My chest constricted, the toll of holding myself together to accomplish this goal reaching a breaking point. I let the pain come, adding it to my thoughts and emotions I used to fuel my magic, because at the root of that pain was love, light itself.

More faces came to mind, boosting my heart to give more and more of myself. Raya, how much she'd suffered, and most importantly, how she'd endured it all through the love of her friends. My best friend's mate.

Jax with his ability to make everyone smile.

Storm, who had been my shield and support when we'd both lost Kade.

Apollo grew hotter as it glowed so bright, I saw it even behind my closed eyes.

Hale's devotion. Vivienne's perseverance. Cassandra's sacrifice for the world.

I opened my eyes, and they immediately connected with Kade's storm-grey ones as he leaned back to see my face. His face was red, strained and weary, and yet his gaze still softened as I watched and admired his perseverance. Sweat beaded on his forehead, and I knew he was giving me everything he had.

Kade.

Last but far from least, I poured every emotion this man had awakened in me forward. I would give every drop of magic to the world if it meant allowing him a moment of peace. He saw me when I had no magic to offer our world, when he believed he needed someone powerful to help him defeat his father, and chose me anyway. He thought I was worthy, loveable, powerful even without magic. He saw the queen I could be before I did, and he stood beside me. He allowed me to learn, to grow, and to fight my battles head-on, knowing he was always standing there alongside me.

"I love you," I whispered.

With a quivering hand, I expressed what I'd known my

entire life into the dagger, letting it flow alongside the love and warmth I'd already spilled into it.

"I am Illiana Dresden," I cried, my body weak but holding on. My voice surprised me with its steadiness as I inhaled slowly, lifting the dagger above my head. I focused all of the magic into Apollo the way the journal had instructed, running my fingers over the center and pouring the last remaining bit of light directly into it. "I am stronger than the darkness within me."

I plunged the dagger forcefully into the ground, unleashing a devastating scream.

The earth rippled, almost tearing me away from the dagger, but I held on tight, not breaking the connection. Kade wrapped his body around mine, holding on to me with everything he had as light overpowered our world, blasting out in a brilliant, blinding white.

It was all there. For this moment in time, the world existed only in a white nothingness.

As quickly as it flashed into existence it retreated, back into the dagger itself, and I yanked it from the ground. I grabbed Kade and cut a deep gash along his arm, aiming true to rid the darkness from him and Atheria completely. He flinched but remained strong as a faint line of black oozed out of the wound.

I cried out as pure joy radiated from the bond, outward.

It worked. We'd done it.

There was no time to continue watching what we'd both hoped for so long as the glittering protection encasing us crumbled.

I jumped up, turning and staring in horrified awe as Fae stumbled to their knees around us. Intertwined with our army, the dark ones fell. Some vomiting, some sobbing. Shouting and pained wails momentarily replaced the sounds of combat.

Some Fae appeared furious, looking around with frustration before they charged our soldiers to continue the fight. They lashed out at our army, determined to finish what Thames had started.

Fates, Vivienne had been right. Eliminating the darkness didn't end the battle. It merely took out all of Thames's ties to this world.

While we'd succeeded, it wasn't the end. We'd made Thames vulnerable, and now we needed to end him.

A thunderous *thud* sounded, shaking the earth itself. My eyes widened as I looked up, seeing the strox screech victoriously at the voidlings falling from the sky. Their bodies scattered, dead and unmoving on the ground, strewn about the battlefield. My light had destroyed the evil creatures along with the darkness.

"Kade," I said frantically, resheathing Apollo at my thigh and grabbing my sword. "It's not over yet."

I faced him, ready to run to Thames with him by my side. Our gazes collided, and he gave me a small sympathetic smile. "Now it's just a fight among regular Fae. You took their darkness."

"We did it." I grinned. "We need to help the others." I glanced down at his arm and nodded toward it. "How do you feel? It must be so freeing to finally be rid of that evil living inside of you after so long."

I reached for his arm, but he pulled it back.

Dread snaked around my heart, building in me so quickly, it almost knocked me to my knees. "Kade?"

The sky turned grey and storm clouds rolled in from Mysthaven's side of the border. The tides were turning, but now I wasn't quite sure in whose favor.

He shook his head just once. "No, Little Rebel. You purged the darkness from our world, it just didn't work on me."

CHAPTER 41
LANA

The wind whipped through the mayhem, angry, as the sky morphed from grey to black.

Lightning flashed briefly, illuminating the sky. Nature fought just as fiercely as we did, furious at the way the battle unfolded.

Thunder boomed again, rattling my blood-soaked armor.

A loud, eerie cackle carried above the storm. "You think you can destroy the darkness?" Thames's voice shouted, as lightning flashed across the sky once more. I looked across the field at the man who was the reason for all of this. His eyes gleamed with the mania of a madman as he stood on the edge of the void, watching Kade and me with malevolent glee. He clasped his hands in front of his chest. "The darkest of them all still stands beside you. My prized possession."

After draining my magic, my mind moved slowly, processing what Thames said.

No. No, I wouldn't accept this outcome.

"It doesn't matter." I stumbled forward, gripping my sword. "If I can rid the darkness from an entire army, I can save him too." Running my fingers over Apollo at the sheath on my thigh to reassure me of its presence, I glanced around me. "You underestimate the lengths I would go to protect my mate."

Some of the dark ones who were turned against their will, now free, fled the battlefield. Yet others in Thames's army fought back against the torment they'd endured, switching sides.

Those still loyal to Thames, however, didn't back down. They continued their fight on the bloodied battlegrounds.

The momentary elation from our perceived success quickly crumbled. Our forces were exhausted. Even though the dark ones had lost their magical boost from the darkness, they were still unyielding in their need to kill. Those who fought for Thames knew if he won, they would be rewarded for their undying loyalty. At least I'm sure that was what they believed. It was exactly the sick and twisted mind games Andras played his entire miserable life. It would seem he learned from the best.

Thames stood among his people as they fought around him, watching, waiting for me to make a move. He knew, just like I did, it would come down to us in the end. He was perfectly content to let his army die while biding his time for my final move. I hated the bloodshed and death. So many innocent lives lost for nothing more than this Fae's greed to dominate a world.

"You've given your heart to a monster, and while he lives, you'll never be rid of me." Thames's laughter echoed as loud as the thunder rolling over us. "You failed."

Kade grunted as he sent his shadows to destroy the few dark ones closest to us, buying us time as Thames was pushed back by the force. His magic was as weak as mine, exhausted from the fight and the enormous amount of energy we'd just expended eliminating the darkness.

Kade turned to me, panting and desperate, "Lana—"

The look in his eyes held a resignation I would not accept. "No," I cried.

"Lana," Kade yelled, and my eyes widened in shock when his pupils flashed black. He raked his hands through his hair. "We can't escape this any longer. Your light, while it holds the darkness within me at bay, doesn't work on me like it does with everyone else." He paused. "We've tried everything. You can't save me."

I couldn't form a response, the words lingering on my tongue unable to be spoken. The truth I refused to believe for so long had finally left his lips.

You can't save me.

"I can try again." Adjusting my grip on the dagger, I moved closer to Kade. "It will work this time. It has to work."

Utter delusion overtook every rational thought. I reached to grab his arm, but instead, he tugged me closer to him. Kade rested his forehead against mine as he held me against his body. "Lana, it's time," he whispered. "A willing sacrifice of life," he said, repeating the damned prophecy. "I am willing. I will not let myself be the reason Thames remains alive."

"No!" I screamed at him again, slamming a fist against his chest. "I refuse to lose you. After everything we've been through." My voice cracked, and a sob wailed out of me as the overwhelming burden of his words suffocated me. "We are so close. It can't end like this." Tears streamed down my face.

Cassandra battled a dark one a few yards away, and after taking down her opponent, ran to us. She looked at Kade, who nodded at her. An unspoken acknowledgment that ripped through me as I realized this wasn't a shock to her.

"You knew," I screamed.

Cassandra grabbed my arm. "Time runs short."

I shoved her off, turning my blade on her instead. "You will not take him from me."

Her own eyes filled with tears. "I can't make this easier for either of you, but I can buy you as much time as I can to say your goodbyes."

Cassandra stepped away, but Kade moved toward her, pulling her into an embrace. "Thank you for everything. For all of those years when you were the only one looking out for me, healing me, protecting me. I owe you my life."

She smiled. "No, Kade, I owe you mine. I have lived a thousand years separated from my sister. Until you, it was a lonely existence. You were the son I never had." She kissed his cheek, patting it once before pulling away. "Be strong."

Kade nodded once, and Cassandra ran, leaving us behind. "Thames," she yelled, her voice loud and filled with a millennium of rage. "You're mine."

Thames drew his sword and readied himself for Cassandra's attack, but I couldn't watch.

My heart pounded in my chest so painfully I wanted to fall to my knees. I'd rather die than live one day without him.

Sweat and blood dripped down in rivulets, touching every part of my body. Kade's shadows swirled at my feet, snaking up my legs, calling to my light as it rose to the surface, exhausted but responding to the love from its shadows.

It's time.

I didn't know if it was the shadows or my light telling me, or both.

"We can't give up," I whispered.

Kade took my hand, the one holding Apollo, and pulled me back to him. "We've tried every way to get this darkness out of me, and it hasn't worked. I am the last piece of it; the last connection to Thames. When I am gone, you can destroy him."

He lifted my chin with his other hand and kissed me, sending every ounce of love through his touch. Filling the empty well of sadness heaving in my chest with a devotion so pure, it obliterated everything.

When he broke the kiss, he rested his forehead against mine, stroking his thumb across my cheek. "You have to kill me, Lana. With your dagger, with your light, let my darkness explode. It's the only way."

My body trembled. "You're my mate, my love. I can't be asked to do this. It defies everything we are made to feel." The world turned black around the edges, and I couldn't catch my breath. Panic and rage fought for dominance, and I threw the damn dagger on the ground at our feet. "You're my soul, Kade. I can't, I can't."

Panic won, rising in my throat. What Kade asked of me, what the fucking Fates asked of us, was unthinkable. It may be one thing to banish your mate to the void, never to be seen again, but to kill—no, murder—your mate… Never.

I fell to my knees, and Kade joined me on the ground. "I give my life, so you can live, Illiana." Kade kissed me again. "Deep down, I've always known I would have to sacrifice something, and as the prophecies continued, it became clearer it would be me. Every part of this story, of Thames's reign has been built on giving up the impossible. This is what great magic is built on. This is the only kind of magic powerful enough to defeat the darkness for good. Evelyn and Jasper knew it. Cassandra knew it." He stroked his thumb again over my tear-streaked face as he sucked in a sharp breath. "I know it."

Kade reached for Apollo, placing the dagger in my hand, and wrapped his fingers around mine.

"I love you too much to let you fail now," he said softly.

This was exactly how my father had died, yet now I was the one ending the life of someone who didn't deserve it.

"You've endured suffering your entire life. You've given enough," I argued, Kade blurring in front of my eyes. I quickly wiped them on my shoulders. I didn't want to miss a moment of my time with him. He had spent his life beaten and infused with darkness. Spent his life with a power-hungry father who'd killed his mother. I touched his mother's necklace hidden beneath my armor. It would be the only piece I'd have to remember him by, and it shattered me in ways I couldn't even begin to fathom.

We were never even given a chance by the Fates. They let us lead our tortured lives, finally granted us utter happiness, only to rip it out from underneath us.

"I did suffer, but then I met you." He smiled at me, despite his own tears gathered in his eyes. "You walked through the forest and met Storm and me"—he stumbled over his words, emotions raging in torment across his face—"and I swear my shadows wanted you then. They've always known. I wasn't much further behind them."

This couldn't be happening. I whimpered, leaning into his hand on my face.

"I loved you before I understood what was happening. And loving you…" He paused, kissing my forehead. "Loving you saved me. It made every horrible moment in my life worth it because it led me to having you. My mate. My life. My love."

"It's not fair." I trembled, only remaining upright by Kade's strength now.

"I know," he said. "Words cannot express how grateful I am to say that I was given this time with you. To be able to love you, to hold you, even if it was just for this tiny blip of time."

I threw my arms around him, my body shaking as my tears soaked his shirt.

"Even the Fates can't keep me from you," he said, stroking my hair. "Death can't keep me from finding you, on this side of the world or in the afterlife. My heart is connected to yours, and it will beat for you until we are whole once more."

Bellowing screams sounded close by and thunder boomed, shaking the ground.

"Now, Lana," Kade said, holding me back to look at me. "We can't wait any longer."

Gripping the dagger, I cursed, roaring as I let it rest in my palm. "I love you, Kade Blackthorn. This is not the end of us. Mark my words. I'll rip the Fates apart to get to you again."

He laughed, a tear streaking down his face as he took me in. His gaze warming me, showing exactly how much he loved me. I would never live a moment wondering how my mate felt. Not a single moment.

"I have no doubts, Little Rebel."

We kneeled before each other, staring into each other's eyes. Kade stayed stronger than I did, but the slight waver in his hand told another story as I placed the tip of the dagger at his heart. He wrapped both of his hands around mine and leaned forward. He placed one last kiss upon my lips and his shadows cocooned around our hands, solidifying our grip on the dagger's hilt.

Apollo hummed, glowing as we said our final goodbye. My light spilled into it, raging as angry and broken as I was while it met Kade's shadows one last time.

All it took was one forceful motion, one thrust to slice through Kade's shirt and pierce his heart.

His face contorted with pain that he immediately tried to mask. His eyes fluttered, face strained in agony, but he didn't look away. I refused to as well, watching the brilliance of his grey eyes fade.

"I love you, I love you, I love you," I repeated over and over.

Blood leaked from his wound, and he hunched over, into my arms. Delicately, I laid him on the ground, the dagger still stuck in his chest. His shadows, waning, retreated inside of him.

We'll miss you.

I forced my light to fuel the dagger, feeling the pain of our bond shattering.

With his dying breath, Kade whispered, "From now until forever, Illiana Dresden, I love you."

The earth shook. Thunder roared. And Kade took his last breath.

I screamed before throwing my body on top of his.

A burst of darkness exploded outward, shrouding everything in the vicinity in what looked like the darkest night.

Kade's lifeless body lay unmoving beneath me. The darkness dissipated, evaporating from existence, all while I screamed in agony as my soul ripped in two.

I couldn't breathe, couldn't move as the scream died on my lips.

Killing Kade may have destroyed the darkness, but it came at the cost of my soul. My heart shattered into a million pieces, never to be whole again.

CHAPTER 42

IAN

I lunged, twisting as I drew my blade across the neck of a dark one.

Or, just an enemy at this point.

Lana destroyed the darkness in Thames's army. My chest burst with pride for her, for all she'd accomplished. For all she'd endured to get to this moment.

It had been shocking to see the amount of darkness seeping out of so many people on the battlefield.

Only, that alone didn't stop the army from fighting us.

"Ian!" Raya shouted behind me, and I turned quickly, finishing my opponent.

I ran to her, the closeness allowing the building tension in my chest to ease. I'd lost sight of her when the storm rolled in. Though the skies didn't dump rain on us, the clouds shrouding us made it difficult to see.

Her eyes appeared glossy, and when I took her elbow, she shook her head in the direction of two enemies battling each other in front of us.

She wobbled but then looked over to the right, freezing again.

I watched in awe as one of the soldiers turned around,

slashing right through the man who had been following him. The other managed to thrust his own blade into the neck of his attacker, and both collapsed to the ground, dead.

"You're terrifying," I told her. "Terrifyingly brilliant."

She laughed. "I decided to push my magic since this bond supposedly makes us stronger. I can't do it for as long as I hoped though."

I gripped her cheeks in my hand and kissed her fiercely. "Fates, woman, I love you. You can puppet me around for practice as much as you'd like when we finish this."

"Don't tempt me with a good time."

I kissed her again, not caring we were in the middle of a war. How had I not believed in mates before this? Before her?

"I will be honored to tempt you for the rest of my damn life," I murmured, my lips still stealing kisses between words.

A battle cry behind me stole my attention from the gorgeous woman beside me. An annoyance my attacker would soon pay for. I spun, fighting back-to-back with Raya.

Thames's army, though significantly less than it had been, still boasted larger numbers than I wished. This was far from over. Thames's taunting echoed around us as he called to Lana and Kade.

His minions ran forward, a fresh wave approaching. I wanted to go to Thames directly and take out years of anguish on behalf of Lana; Andras had been his lackey after all.

But I knew that Lana would have to be the one to defeat him with her light.

So instead, I clenched my sword and continued destroying his army one by one.

Cassandra's voice shouted above the storm, calling for Thames. I saw her white hair billowing behind her as she fought with her own mate. I shivered, not wanting to think about how long she would be able to last.

Lucien barreled through the army, breathing fire at a group of soldiers cornering Ryland.

He was a better swordsman than I was, but right now it was eight on one, and even the best swordsmen had little hope of beating those odds.

"Go," Raya shouted as she charged into another fray. "Help him."

Ryland saw me as I destroyed any who crossed my path on my way to him. He barely looked fatigued, standing there, smiling. "Captain." He tilted his head as he continued swinging.

Fucking showman.

The more men and women we took down, the more confident I became. We had to be making a difference, making some kind of dent in what was left of Thames's army.

But it would be up to Lana to finish this. I stepped back as I felled the last of the group Ryland battled. I needed to find Lana.

A streak of black whipped by my line of sight. Jax's panther jumped by me, ripping the throat out of a soldier before he shifted back. He left his claws out, swiping at the chest of another and gutting him instantly. He glanced back at me. "Bet you wish you got that partial-shift down now, huh?"

I narrowed my eyes, looking up as strox crashed down on Thames's army overhead. I grinned wickedly at Jax and shifted my arms into wings.

Fuck yes, I didn't think that would work.

I rode a gust of air under my wings to bring me into the group of enemies stalking toward Jax from behind before dropping into the center of them and unleashing hell.

When I'd taken down three, Jax finally appeared again. "Not bad, Stronholm. Perhaps I'll allow you a place under my future command."

A scream behind him seized our attention. Kalliah lay on

the ground, one of Thames's men standing above her, holding his sword over his head to strike.

Jax's figure blurred in front of me, moving faster than I could fathom, but he wasn't going to make it in time.

Though he was a few yards in front of me, I still ran. I couldn't lose someone else—not Kalliah, not anyone.

Jax shifted and leapt farther than what should have been possible, front paws outstretched as he dove, not at the soldier but to cover Kalliah.

The blade came down and he roared, falling to the ground on top of her.

A blade shot through the gut of the soldier that wounded Jax.

Leif stood on the other side of it. "Fuck you," he seethed, kicking the man back and turning to face Jax and Kalliah.

Jax shifted back to his Fae form, and when I made it over, I froze. He lay bloodied in Kalliah's lap, his left hand missing.

Leif stood motionless, in shock, but Kalliah moved fast. She adjusted, moving to lay Jax's head gently on the ground before tearing at her pants, ripping the cloth.

"You stupid, stupid man," Kalliah cried. "Why would you do that?"

Jax groaned. "If it's a limb or your life, I'm choosing your life every time."

Kalliah brushed a hand over Jax's forehead. "Ian, help me staunch the blood so his healing can kick in."

Raya's voice shouted in pain from behind us, and I spun toward the noise.

"Never mind, go," Kalliah ordered.

I hesitated, but she wouldn't let me stay indecisive.

"Go, we'll take care of him."

She stroked Jax's head, whispering reassuring words as Leif turned, guarding both of them. "I've got them," he said.

My confidence wavered before crashing into a rock in my

gut. Why did it feel like this was all suddenly spiraling out of control?

I ran toward Raya's voice and saw her battling fearlessly, killing dark ones without hesitation. But their numbers were too great for her to fight alone.

Before I took another step to help her, darkness enveloped us. Shouts of terror and cries rose, even louder than the sounds of battle as everything disappeared from my sight.

"Raya!" I yelled, but my voice was only one of many crying out.

What in the Fates?

I couldn't even see my hand in front of my own face.

I stayed still, unmoving until the darkness faded, allowing me to see again. I twisted around, trying to regain my bearings.

Then I heard it. An agonized scream I recognized all too well.

It was only then that I saw her. Lana, holding her dagger lodged in Kade's chest, screaming a sound I would never unhear for as long as I lived.

CHAPTER 43
LANA

A numbing cold spread through my body as I lay on top of my mate.

Gone.

Kade was dead.

I hadn't let go of the stupid fucking dagger yet. I couldn't.

Letting go meant it was finished.

Illiana.

The light, still depleted from purging the darkness from the world—from Kade—writhed inside of me.

My eyelids were heavy as I lay my head on Kade's chest.

I could lie here with him. Go with him. Follow to where he swore he'd wait for me.

Perhaps I should.

Wind whipped through my hair, chilling me to the core.

"No," I said out loud, though my voice came out strangled and hoarse.

Again, the sensation came, crawling over me.

"Leave me alone," I hissed at the wind around me.

My body stopped drowning in pain the third time the wind whipped through my hair. Enough that I lifted my head from Kade's body, the motion painful, as if I was ripping out my soul.

When I looked up, time had slowed. The battle continued, but for this short blink of existence, I saw everything.

The noise of my breath exhaling echoed too loudly in my ears. My hair blew across my damp face. Despite how broken it was, my heart still beat. Slow. Alone.

Ian fought, facing in my direction as if he meant to make his way toward me. Raya was close behind, the pain etched on her face unbearable to see.

Another breeze caressed my face as I noticed Storm running toward me, fire haloing his entire body as he barreled through the army.

Storm. He'd be devastated.

I blinked again, my hand twitching slightly on Kade's chest while one still clutched Apollo.

Beyond Storm, Kalliah sat on the ground, Jax lying with his head in her lap, as Leif fought a dark one next to them. Jax was strangely still as Kalliah moved above him, unbothered by the oncoming attacks Leif faced protecting them. Fates, I couldn't tell what was wrong.

Finally, my gaze found Thames. Cassandra moved around him, commanding his full attention. Maybe we'd distracted him when Kade's darkness exploded outward, but right now, wrath defined every line on his face, except his motions were sloppy. Like fear had finally crept in. With Kade dead, he had no more ties to Atheria.

He was vulnerable.

With Kade dead.

Another wail escaped me as I looked back down at him.

Move, my light said, breaking through its own sadness. *It's time to make his death mean something. Move.*

I brushed the hair blowing in the wind from his face.

A low cry came from over my shoulder, and I looked over

to see a strox. The animal lowered its head to Kade's leg, then inched closer.

It bumped my shoulder.

The beasts had been born of pain long ago. It wasn't only Kade and I who had to sacrifice. So many others had to as well in this war against Thames.

The first feelings, other than this overwhelming heartache, churned in my body as I faced what I must do. The world came back into focus. My breathing, ragged and growing heavier, was the first thing I registered. Each breath pulled in rage and pushed down the agony I would have to face after this.

After Thames died.

His evil forced me to lose my mate.

He was to blame.

His time was done.

I called on my light for a strength I didn't think possible and roared as I yanked the blade from Kade's chest. I rose to my feet, my sole focus homed in on where Thames battled Cassandra across the field. Though unsteady at first, I straightened, allowing the only remaining shards of my soul to fortify around an unyielding fury.

The strox nudged me again, and I faced the beast. It lowered before me, and I finally understood. It would carry me to our target.

I took one step, then another. Reaching down, I lifted my discarded sword in my hand after sheathing Apollo and approached the strox. Climbing over its side, I touched the bird's warm neck, as if it could infuse me with the strength. I needed to finish this.

"Take me to Thames," I said, shocked that my voice came out as strong as it did.

The bird took off, soaring upward, and I pressed my knees to its sides. "Across the battlefield first," I ordered.

Though we had more fighting among us—those who'd

turned back, our own soldiers, strox, and razorven—Thames's army had been built over years. Thames had turned countless others in his short time free from the void, even with so many sacrificed to Firestone. My people needed hope, and though I felt none with half my soul gone, it wasn't about me right now. It was about Atheria.

The strox flew close over the battle, and I raised my sword high in the air. "The darkness has been destroyed. Finish this fight. For our homeland, for each other. Thames will regret the day he challenged us."

I dropped low, circling to the cheers of my people before squeezing the strox again.

"We end this," I said, empty but determined to get my revenge before I broke.

This time, the strox took me straight toward the man responsible for all the loss and pain in my life.

I held out my sword, urging the strox to dive faster toward Thames.

Cassandra spun away, not looking at me at all but making way for me all the same, as she elegantly shifted away from her battle.

I screamed, bearing my sword down from atop the strox. Thames grinned, throwing his hand out and knocking the strox off course. I jumped off quickly, allowing the bird to regain its bearings.

Fae attacked the strox before it could make it back to me, but I landed on my feet, my knee only grazing the ground before I rose, standing before Thames.

"Ah, the great prophesized queen comes to face me at last," he said. His arrogance from even a few minutes before had lessened.

"Your mate too strong for you?" I said, clutching my dagger and sprinting toward him, unwilling to let him live a moment longer. I whipped my sword forward as he dodged out of reach.

His chilling laugh raised goose bumps on my arms. "At least mine lives."

I screamed, readying my sword before him as my light flared. I couldn't let my emotion lead this fight. Not this time.

Inhaling sharply through my nose, I recentered myself. As Thames laughed, I sliced my sword at his neck, bringing my dagger into the path he'd be forced to retreat to. He dodged the sword to his neck, but my dagger slammed home into his thigh.

He cried out as a small bit of darkness seeped out of him from the wound.

"You think that pathetic cut can kill *me*?" he asked.

"Maybe not," I grunted, blocking his sword. "But I hope it's torture feeling it in your skin."

Thames pulled back, rising on a cloud of his darkness. Thunder rumbled through the sky.

"You have no idea the power I've collected," he said, his voice taking on an echo-like hollowness. "You are nothing, and you will be squashed like the pathetic royal you are."

I heaved, my body's exhaustion catching up to me the longer this took. "You're wrong."

I called forth my light. *We can do this. We have to finish it.*

My light responded, growing despite how much energy we'd spent. Apollo glowed in my hand, and I felt energy shifting from the dagger into me. Apparently, it wasn't merely good for channeling into. It could be used to fortify myself as well.

I threw a ball of my magic toward the bottom of the darkness Thames perched himself on, and a hole burst through it.

Thames shouted, flinging a shot of fire toward me. I rolled out of the way but screamed as a second shot skated over my arm, burning away the sleeve of my tunic.

He has magic from centuries of kings, my light warned. I responded, *Our magic was foretold to destroy him. We will not falter.*

Staggering to my feet, I charged forward. I couldn't allow him to wield his magic from afar, I needed to return to hand-to-hand combat. He'd had centuries to perfect his control of his magic even if he was trapped for a thousand years, but he was vulnerable now that his evil was dying.

Thames watched me as if I was a mere amusement. He aimed his hands toward the ground, and pieces of debris and dirt rose high before flying toward me.

I cried out, throwing my hands up and trying to use my light as a shield. It cocooned around me, and the debris turned to dust as soon as it passed through the light's barrier.

I lowered my hands and saw the first flicker of doubt cross Thames's face.

Smiling, I held my head high. "I am Illiana Dresden," I shouted as I ran toward him. "I am stronger than any darkness." Channeling my light into the base of his evil, I unleashed all I could, forcing him to return to the ground.

The darkened mist he'd elevated himself on shrank until he crashed back down. He screamed viciously, directing all of his anger and hatred toward me.

My light flickered. I was running out of power, my stores severely depleted. All I felt was fear, but I couldn't let it get the best of me. I refused to let it overpower me. I had come too far, *we* had come too far to be stopped now. If my magic needed to rest, I'd finish this with my blades. Just how I'd lived my entire life, fighting for every inch, without magic.

Exactly like Ian trained me to do.

I barreled forward, fighting through exhaustion. While Thames's strength didn't show signs of waning at all, failure wasn't an option for me.

His blade met mine, but he sent a lash of fire wrapping around my hand. I screamed as my skin blistered, but I didn't let go of my weapon.

Time stilled, slowing strangely as the wind brushed against

me. Only this time, when nature caressed me, it carried a whisper.

Cassandra.

"Illiana."

This was her magic.

I looked to where the wind directed me and saw her and Vivienne kneeling on the ground next to Kade.

My heart stuttered through the pain seeing Kade lying there.

Time returned to normal, and Thames pulled back, parrying again, his attacks deliberate and strong. I blocked a blow that would've killed me, and my arms shook as Thames's thin face sneered in mine. I winced as my hand flared in agony from the burns Thames had inflicted.

"Kade's darkness needed to be destroyed, but he wasn't the final tie to Thames," Cassandra whispered on the wind. *"I am. His mate."*

I stumbled back a step. Thames didn't fall forward like I'd hoped, but we both raised our weapons again and continued this battle that felt unwinnable. I had to find a weakness and exploit it.

"When I'm gone, finish this, Illiana. Then live."

The breeze died instantly, and in its place Cassandra's cry filled the air, heartbreak lacing every second of the wailing sound.

Thames whipped his body around, distracted by the agonized scream, but I didn't waste the moment she'd gifted to me. This precious opportunity to end Thames once and for all. I stepped forward, flinging the last traces of my light I could muster directly into the center of Apollo. Straight into the place where every woman in my line had channeled their energy. I called on their magic to help me, fusing it with my light as I stabbed it into Thames's back. Light pulsed, shining around us.

He gasped, falling forward. I removed the dagger, kicking Thames so he lost his balance, forcing him to the ground. He rolled over in surprise, but I pounced, stabbing him in his heart.

His eyes widened, taking me in. I snarled at him, letting my hatred show on every line of my face. "You will never be anything more than the evil mentioned in storybooks. Not a king, not all-powerful." I twisted the blade harder, deeper into the flesh and bone of the evil plaguing our lands. An unintelligible sound escaped from his lips as blood gushed from them.

My hands shook, but I didn't stop pouring my light into the blade. The thrill of seeing the monster beneath me, at my mercy, sent a rush through me, giving me what I needed to see this through.

"Bested by a queen and her mate, who sacrificed everything and *won*."

Thunder boomed, and the winds whipped around us, as I removed the blade and stabbed it into Thames's chest one more time.

His darkness, his very essence exploded out of him, decimating the ground around us.

His eyes widened even further in shock, but it only lasted seconds before his face fell flat.

Thames had been defeated. Atheria was free.

At last, it was finally over.

CHAPTER 44
LANA

A ripple of cosmic energy radiated from where Thames lay dead, blasting outward, sending everyone in the vicinity to the ground.

I landed on my back, the wind knocked out of me, gasping for air. The earth shook, trembling for a moment as the aftershocks slowly died down.

I felt numb. My body unable to handle anymore, physically or mentally. The emotional devastation I ignored to finish this war burned at my throat, coming back in full force. My broken soul shattered to a point that even Thames's death couldn't bring a smile to my face.

I'd completed my purpose, and now? I had nothing left to give.

The fog of darkness retreated slowly, along with the storm clouds, thunder, and lightning. Slivers of sunshine peeked through the waning clouds, warming my slick skin. I rolled to my stomach as the ground shuddered again. Bracing my hands on either side of my body, I gasped.

The land between our worlds, which was once void of life, shook, dirt and decay splitting away as greenery rose triumphantly from the cracks. The rift repaired itself and suddenly, faster than should have been possible. Atheria was finally whole.

Fae cheered around me, their celebratory cries filling the air. A pack of strox circled above before they flew south toward their home in the forests. Their help had been invaluable to win this war, taking out more legions of men than I'd even realized. Perhaps they'd return once they mourned their own losses.

Despite the magnitude of our win, none of the victories today could heal the most broken part of me.

Kade was dead.

Would anyone truly understand what we sacrificed so they could live? I prayed they never did, for their sakes. The price had been too high. But I was a queen, and alongside my king, we chose to willingly suffer so they could flourish. It was what we did as rulers.

Sacrifice.

It was what should be done.

But it didn't help the torment now.

I rose to my hands and knees, shaking, knowing I wouldn't be able to stand yet. Grief, exhaustion, all of it weighed too heavily on my body.

I gulped down a full breath and set my sights to where I'd left Kade's body. Vivienne hovered over both him and Cassandra, who lay still beside him. I choked back the endless stream of tears. How much more death would we face? Would *I* face?

The others had to be okay. Please, Fates above, please don't have taken anyone else from me.

Forcing myself up on my elbows, I crawled across the distance toward the body of my mate and Cassandra.

I knew Cassandra said she had to die, but hearing Vivienne's wails as I approached was agonizing.

I continued to crawl, knowing the true heroes of this battle lay dead in front of me. I sobbed, choking on bile rising in my throat. I needed to be with Kade. I had to get to him, to hold him one more time.

Making it to his body was pure torture. What these two incredible Fae did for our world would be written into the history books of our time, never to be forgotten. Vivienne looked unharmed, yet just as broken as me.

Her kind eyes, even in her own grief, found mine.

"I'm sorry," I whispered. I looked at Cassandra, her hand clutching Kade's arm where a deep cut bled between her fingers. Even in his death, she clearly tried to heal him, the Fae who took care of the boy who needed love when he received none.

Forcefully, I dragged my gaze to Kade, letting my eyes rest on his beautiful face.

I clutched Apollo in my hand. Heaving my body up, despite the exhaustion. My magic barely responded, but I had it in me to try one last time.

For Kade.

I took a few deep breaths. "Please," I whispered, glancing up at the clouds. "Please help me. Give me the strength to save him."

I reached, deep inside of me, giving my light the little energy I had remaining. "We can do this."

My light responded, surging even though I knew I'd have nothing left if this didn't work. Still, we refused to give up.

I placed my hands atop his chest, closing my eyes and channeling every pure, powerful thought of love and life into him. I gritted my teeth against the drain on my body as both my heart and my light joined together to help Kade.

"Illiana," Vivienne said, speaking my name softly. It sounded like pity. I wouldn't accept this end, and I certainly had no time for pity.

The light shone bright in my hands, pulsing a few times over Kade's chest before dying out.

I gasped, slumping forward. I reached my hand up to his

neck. "It worked, it worked, it worked," I chanted, willing it into existence.

But there was nothing.

No breathing. No pulse, not even a faint one.

"No," I howled, looking back to the sky. "How could you? I did everything you needed me to do. Thames is gone." My voice was hoarse, weak, but I kept screaming. "Give him back."

Pulling myself on top of him, I managed to lay my chest atop his body, desperate to be close to him before I had to return to those around me and don the crown of queen once more. I didn't even know if I could lead my people right now. The thought of walking away from Kade's body caused my last remaining rationality to completely dissolve from my mind.

"I miss you already," I whispered as tears streamed down my face. "I miss you so damn much. I don't want to do this without you."

"Sweet child," Vivienne said, her warm hands somehow steady as they brushed my tears away. "You did so well."

"I don't want to stay here without him," I admitted.

"Lana?" A strangled sound interrupted us, and Storm fell to his knees beside me. I couldn't even lift my head from Kade's chest to comfort him as he brushed a hand across his friend's forehead. "No," he whispered, laying his head atop Kade's.

I let out an unintelligible sob.

Footsteps approached, shuffling toward us, and I glanced over to find the horrified faces of my friends. Raya fell to the ground and howled Kade's name. Jax stumbled, falling beside her. I sucked in a sharp breath at the soaked bandages around his arm. Besides his bloody form, the others looked worn and dirty but unscathed.

Ian approached and gasped, looking between me and Kade's body. Dropping to his knees he reached for me.

"Lan, oh Lan," he murmured, stroking my hair. "I'm so sorry."

"I killed him," I said, my voice almost inaudible. "He sacrificed himself because I couldn't find a way to destroy his darkness. So I had to—"

I raised my head, wanting to see Kade's face despite how painful I knew it would be. Storm rose and reached for my hand. "I'm so sorry."

Vivienne inhaled a shaky breath, eyes turning white. "A gift for the one who suffered through strife, a choice for her blood, a life for a life."

My gaze shifted back to her. "What?"

Her eyes cleared, and she smiled at me as one single tear fell from her face. "A thousand years is long enough to spend separated from my sister." Vivienne reached forward, cupping my face gently. "Watching you become who you were meant to be has been a privilege, my queen."

I swallowed, not sure what the seer meant. She ran her fingers through her sister's hair before placing her hand next to Cassandra's on Kade's arm. She took a deep breath before making eye contact with me. "Live well, Illiana."

Vivienne's hand shimmered, emitting a white light. My eyes widened as the seer trembled. A moment later, her figure went limp, and I lunged forward to catch her falling body.

I didn't understand what was happening as the life visibly drained from her.

"W-what? Why?" I stammered.

I looked at Ian, whose surprise and confusion mirrored mine.

Cradling Vivienne's head and laying her on the ground, I heaved a breath. "What was the point? Why would she die?"

I pulled my hand back, touching Kade's chest again as my mind swirled in torment watching another person go.

His chest dipped beneath the weight of me, and I yanked my hand back.

His chest dipped?

I ran my hands over him, trying to see if it was my imagination.

A nearly invisible wisp of shadow curled around my wrist, and I gasped.

Kade's eyelids fluttered, and he spoke, his voice barely audible. "I knew a certain dagger-wielding princess would be the death of me."

My heart stopped, my body frozen as I stared into the grey eyes of my mate. "Kade?"

He tried chuckling, but it turned into a cough. "I'm here, Little Rebel." He reached up, cupping my cheek and taking me in. He closed his eyes and reopened them, like he didn't quite believe he was here again. "Turns out Vivienne had one last sacrifice of her own to fulfill."

"You're alive?" I stared in disbelief, my body unable to move. He winced, trying to sit up, but before he could, I flung myself into his arms, burying my face in his neck.

I bawled until I practically lost my voice as Kade held me.

"Fucking Fates." Storm's choked up voice was joined by the sound of Raya crying.

Jax, of course, laughed. "I'm putting in for an extended vacation," he said. "I need a break from this shit."

Kade chuffed but didn't let go of me.

I squeezed him harder, murmuring against his skin. "How?"

His hand circled the back of my neck, pressing me against his skin. "Vivienne changed places with me somehow, sacrificing herself as well. Cassandra gave me the last pieces of her magic. It wasn't enough until Vivienne channeled whatever she had left into me. I swear I heard their voices pleading to the Fates themselves, but I don't quite understand the rest."

My lip quivered. For years, I'd been furious at Vivienne for reciting the prophecy, but she gave her life so quickly for his.

She and her sister. Not only did they save our world, but they gave me a gift I'd never be able to repay.

"Two thousand thirty-one," Storm said, punching Kade's arm. "Fuck you."

Kade laughed, but still didn't release me. "Two thousand seventy-three." He replied. "Guess we still have time for you to catch up."

I couldn't see his face, not with my own buried in Kade's neck, but I heard Storm's hoarse laugh.

Tears streamed down my face as my body convulsed. "Never leave me again, Kade Blackthorn. Do you understand me? Never again."

"Never again," he vowed. "I swear it. Not even in death."

***

Ian, Raya, and Storm instructed the Royal Guards who were left to take all those still loyal to Thames to a holding area.

Once his darkness exploded across the field, enough of his army yielded that our forces were able to secure victory.

The dark ones may have lost all the evil within them, but there were those few who refused to admit defeat. Some fled, a fact I'm sure would be an issue later. But for those we captured, we'd have to figure out what to do with them in the coming days. Which included where we housed prisoners—Mount Legion or Ellevail?

A Fae lunged forward, hissing at me. "We'll never pledge our loyalty to you." The guard wrapped his hands in vines so he couldn't escape, but he still fought to free himself. We were stronger, and he was vastly outnumbered. It reminded me that just because we'd won the war, it didn't mean everything would immediately become peaceful.

Ian and Storm dragged the man away, while Raya followed close behind. "Shut up or I'll find a razorven to feed you to," she threatened, flicking her hair over her shoulder before giving us a mischievous grin.

"Fates, I love when you're feisty," Ian groaned.

"And they thought *we* were bad." I leaned toward Kade, still soaking in his presence after believing I'd lost him.

He snorted before nuzzling his nose against my neck. "We'll have to step it up."

Kade held my hand as we surveyed the land. Dead bodies littered the ground from both sides of the fight. Their deaths felt bloody on my hands. They were my citizens, my people. Even the dark ones. How many had turned because they felt they had no other choice?

I would never take for granted the sacrifice they made to fight for our world, but the longer I stared across the aftermath of our battle, the more the adrenaline pumping through me waned.

Kade leaned over. "Breathe, Illiana."

I obeyed, inhaling deeply, allowing the crisp air to fill my lungs.

"Their lives were not lost in vain," he said. "We will build a land all Fae will be proud to live in."

I watched the Fae from both Brookmere and Mysthaven working together so seamlessly, I stopped being able to tell who came from which side of the void. The injured were being attended to by those who had any healing abilities, while others collected weapons from the fallen. I knew Kalliah and Leif were coordinating a final meal from our supplies and handling preparations for everyone to depart back to their homes.

Out of the corner of my eye, I caught them in an embrace. I couldn't help but smile, and walked toward them. Fates, they deserved to have a chance.

Jax stumbled forward from where he was helping pack up camp, rubbing at the blood-soaked bandages on his wrist. My stomach dropped when I saw what had happened during the battle. I knew it had been unrealistic to think everyone would make it out unscathed, but Jax was vibrant, full of life. How would he fight without a hand? How would he shift?

"He will relearn what he needs to and bounce back fine," Kade whispered in my ear, kissing the side of my head.

I glanced up at him. "Can you read my thoughts now?"

He grinned. The sight took my breath away. "You wear your emotions on your sleeve. And"—he knocked his finger underneath my chin—"I know you."

Leif pulled away from Kalliah and took purposeful strides toward Jax, putting his arm around his shoulder, steadying him. Kalliah joined him, wrapping her arm around his waist to help support the shifter. "Come on, let's go find a healer to help clean you up. I think you've let enough people go before you at this point."

Jax whimpered, "Wait, before we go…" He pouted. "Do you think you could love a cat with three paws?"

Kalliah jabbed his side. "For the last time, we are not in love."

Leif ruffled Jax's hair. "She'll come around. Don't worry."

I didn't miss the blush coloring Kalliah's cheeks as she glanced around and saw we were watching. I raised an eyebrow playfully, and her blush deepened before shaking her head and walking him toward the healer's tent.

Those three would be trouble.

A group of Fae approached, ones that I recognized from our initial gathering at The Knotted Willow. "Your Majesty." They lowered themselves in a bow, pausing before returning to their full height.

"Yes?" I stepped forward. "Are you injured? Do you need assistance?"

The Fae in front shook his head. "We await your orders. What shall we do now? Where do you need us to go?"

I smiled softly. "Your bravery is commendable, and I

cannot personally thank you enough for fighting for Brookmere."

"The honor was ours, Your Majesty." He bowed his head again.

"Tend to your injuries, eat a good meal, and then return to your homes. Repair what has been broken. Rejoice with your loved ones. We are free from the evil plaguing our land. You deserve to celebrate our victory."

The group of men bowed once more. "As Your Majesty commands it."

They walked away, clapping each other on their backs. One of them even jumped into the air, hollering in excitement.

A line began to form as others followed the lead of the first group. One by one, those I'd battled beside thanked me for their victory.

I trembled, overcome with emotions knowing that what Kade said was right. This was the start of a new land. Nobles and lesser Fae stood together, waiting, talking among themselves, and working together to pack up camp and share a meal together.

Each time someone thanked me, I responded, "The victory is yours."

Because none of this would have happened without Fae from the entire land answering the call.

Close to an hour passed as I stood with Kade by my side, greeting anyone who wished to speak to me.

We tensed when one Fae threw himself at my feet. "Throw me in the dungeon and toss away the key," he cried. "I did not want to do it, but he threatened to kill my entire family if I didn't allow his darkness inside of me. I do not deserve to live for what I did to our kingdom."

I kneeled in front of him, as a few gasps came from the line behind him.

"Look me in the eyes, please." I ensured his gaze met mine

before I continued. "What happened to you was not your fault. You were forced into something you didn't ask for."

The man lowered his head, but I pressed a hand to his heart. "When the evil left you, you stayed. You fought. You braved the darkness, and I am proud to have battled this war beside you."

He opened and closed his mouth, struggling to find words.

I held out my hand, standing with him. "Go return to your family. I'm sure they're worried about you."

Though he left visibly upset, his shoulders weren't as slumped as they had been before.

Kade's shadows whispered across my cheek and through my hair, begging me to turn to my mate.

"We love you."

I couldn't help but giggle—his shadows always were the most vocal with me, but as I let the little pieces of my light out, they wrapped together in complete harmony.

"We love you too. Let's go home."

CHAPTER 45
LANA

A week had passed since the battle at the void, though it felt like no time at all.

Between getting back to Ellevail and devising a plan for how to move forward as Atheria instead of Brookmere and Mysthaven, discussing the prisoners of war, setting up teams to help rebuild, and planning for a memorial service, we were all run ragged.

Today though…today we planned to honor those who had fallen during the battle. Not just our final one, but the entire time Thames had infiltrated the minds of both the innocent and the evil people already lurking in our world.

After all, this had taken years of planning, years of seeping into the minds and bodies of our people. Those who fell deserved to be recognized, and we all needed to say goodbye so we could move on. Together. I readied myself to enter the arena, brushing my palms over the front of my dress. Kalliah swatted my hands away and made a few final adjustments to my outfit.

"Are you ready?" she asked me, stepping back and admiring her work.

"I'm not sure I could ever be ready." I clenched my jaw

shut, hoping I had the right words to heal our kingdom. I reached for her hand and squeezed it. "But I know with my friends by my side, I can make it through this day." I took a deep breath. Thousands across the land were grieving the loss of their friends and family. I knew the chances of holding myself together without falling into a puddle of emotions would be next to impossible. Today, I would be a queen grieving alongside her people. Just as I had fought beside them.

I lifted the skirts of my dress and ascended the stairs to the dais overlooking the arena.

The same arena I'd stood in a few months ago, dreading having to pick between eight Fae who fought for my hand to be the King of Brookmere. If only I knew how all of our lives would be irrevocably changed forever at the start of my marriage trials.

I lifted my chin, holding my head high, remembering how proud I was of all we'd accomplished.

I wore my mother's tiara, passed down from generations of queens. The amethyst stones nestled into the silver metal, reflecting the purple of Brookmere. It complemented my emerald dress, covered in lace appliques. The back of the dress dipped low enough to display my tattoo from Storm.

Apollo still rested on my thigh, hidden beneath the layers of my skirts. The dagger gave me the strength to move forward, and it served as a reminder of the terrible things that had passed. A reminder of the cost for the freedom we'd obtained, but it also served as a tangible reminder of my own strength. I could protect myself and my people, now and always.

Behind me, seated in the back of the two rows of chairs, sat the few royal advisors we had left from my father's reign, not corrupted by Andras. Each one had pledged their loyalty to me upon my return. In front of them sat Ian, Storm, Jax, Leif, and Raya. The advisors sat behind them because little did they know we'd be creating a new group of advisors. Ones with ties to Brookmere and Mysthaven, as well as some lesser Fae, and perhaps a noblewoman who'd stood up for what was right. Keena wasn't seated there today, but she would find herself in our midst soon enough.

My eyes landed on the place where my light had already strayed. Kade stood waiting for me so we could approach the podium together.

He wore a black crown upon his head, and his shadows danced at his feet. Smiling, he reached for my hand, which I gladly accepted.

This was my first official event as queen, and even though we hadn't had time for a coronation yet, I was assured by everyone the formalities would follow shortly. All we had to do was figure out who would rule over all of Atheria.

Still, despite being in Brookmere, it only felt right to address the people with Kade by my side.

"Thank you for doing this with me," I said, leaning in to him.

He kissed my cheek, turning his head slightly to whisper in my ear. "If you think I'm ruling anywhere without you by my side, you are sorely mistaken. Besides, I do look good in the crown you made me. It's like Mysthaven's but better."

I laughed, basking in his smile as we walked the rest of the way to the podium, and he bowed slightly as I took my place.

I looked out and noticed not a single seat sat empty in the arena. The earth Fae had worked hard to restore the area to something beautiful but made a few changes to accommodate today's event. Keeping it for everyone's use and for gatherings among our people had been the easiest decision of the hundreds I'd had to make.

This time, the arena boasted rows and rows of benches lining every inch of the ground to make room for as many citizens as possible. They'd also taken down the division between nobles and lesser Fae, allowing everyone to be seated together.

No clear divide of class. It was everything I'd ever dreamed of. Even some citizens of Mysthaven had made the trip to be with us today, and they appear to have been welcomed with open arms. Beyond their style of clothing, it was hard to tell them apart.

"Whenever you're ready," Kade whispered as he took two steps back, allowing me to have this moment with my people.

I motioned for him to join me, but he shook his head almost imperceptibly. "I will rule with you, Little Rebel, but it's you who led these people."

I swallowed my retort once I saw the stubborn look in his eyes, so I placed my hands on the podium.

My heart pounded in my chest, and tears already formed as I looked down at a giant slab of marble forming a semicircle around the base of the dais. The monument was engraved with the names of those who had fallen protecting our kingdom, etched in a deep purple with gold filigree. No expense was spared in the creation of this memorial. I wanted their names to be remembered forever.

The first two were my parents, Fallon and Sebastian, followed by King Alister and Queen Roxana. Cassandra, Vivienne, Elisabeth, Corbin, and Hale. All of their names were directly below the podium, so any time I addressed our people, I would stand on the strength of those I loved.

I took a deep breath and spoke; my voice carried on the winds to the farthest corner of the arena.

"Good morning, my fellow citizens of Atheria. We are gathered here today to pay tribute to those who selflessly sacrificed their lives to protect our kingdom. These men and women are true heroes, and without them, we wouldn't be here today. We honor each and every Fae who perished during the Battle of the Void. The loss of each of their lives is a tragedy, but we will be forever grateful for them standing by their kingdom in such a perilous time."

The crowd clapped. Yet when I looked out, I saw many Fae with tears streaming down their faces. While we were able to recover many of the bodies of the fallen, not all were able to be returned to their families. Today was even more important for those families who could not perform a proper burial and say their final goodbye.

"As many of you know, the Battle of the Void was merely a culmination of years spent fighting the darkness. Many of you felt as though you fought alone on the borders. Some of you in Mysthaven battled tyranny even longer. These losses started long before this final battle. So today, we honor not only the brave warriors who fought at the void but all of those who gave their lives in the name of freedom. Those who stood against the darkness. Those taken against their will. It is for the past and present that we honor those no longer with us."

I looked over to Kade, who nodded with a smile.

"We will hold a moment of silence to pay tribute to those who lost their lives."

I bowed my head and remembered all of my family and friends who'd perished so we could live. I let myself feel the weight of the goodbyes I never got to say. The years of friendship and love, taken and gone in an instant.

Tears fell in large droplets on the surface of the podium, but I didn't hold back. I wouldn't show my people an emotionless queen today.

Then I thought of those I didn't know, my loyal citizens who chose to fight. I'd been working tirelessly to meet with any living family member of those who'd perished. I went to their homes, wanting to personally express my gratitude for not only what their loved ones did but the sacrifices they too had made. I offered each family monetary compensation to try to help offset their expenses. Money would never erase the loss of their loved ones, but it could provide one less stressor while they figured out their new normal. Almost every single family said, "Give it to the next family, there are others who need it more." I made sure to leave coins hidden somewhere in their home for them to find later.

Word about the Hidden Henchman spread, and it seemed anyone we spoke to had more stories about the goods and, more so, the hope our role had inspired in a time when the border villages needed it most.

I let myself feel it all before inhaling slowly. There would always be parts of me missing, but I smiled, knowing that somewhere, they were all watching over us. Or maybe they were on their next adventure. I'm sure the Fates had more in store for the next life.

When the moment passed, I took a handkerchief from my dress pocket and dabbed my eyes.

I continued, my voice stronger now. "Let this be a reminder to all of us that there is nothing that can't be accomplished through friendship and compassion. We would not have succeeded without all Fae: nobles, those with lesser magics—every single Fae played a role in our victory. Moving forward, this will be the standard: to work together regardless of class. Respect for all.

"We may not all agree, but we are capable of sharing, discussing, and finding a way forward. Greed and ultimate power have no place here in Atheria. Should there ever be a time when disagreements need to be settled, we will hold a weekly forum to mediate such requests. Never again do I wish to see our kingdom falter. It's when we are divided that things fall apart."

Tear-stained faces watched me, and I tried to make eye contact with as many people as I could.

"Atheria is a kingdom that can and must work together. We are better together. While I, as your queen, may not have every single answer to how our kingdom will be run now that Brookmere and Mysthaven are united once more, I promise you, I will work every day to keep both sides of our kingdom prosperous." I motioned for Kade to join me by my side. This time he obeyed.

"King Kade Blackthorn has also assured me that as the rightful ruler of Mysthaven, we will secure peace and harmony among our people. Together, King Blackthorn and I will restore Atheria to its former glory."

The crowd stood on their feet and cheered, chanting and hollering.

My friends behind me joined in, screaming and clapping.

I held Kade's hand, and my light shone, extending out of me and blanketing the arena with a beautiful golden glow. I couldn't contain it as it danced and shimmered in the sun's rays, basking in hope for the future.

I waved to the crowd as my friends stood on either side of me. Finally, I closed my eyes and thanked nature silently.

Placing my hand over my heart, I smiled at my kingdom. "May nature guide you."

EPILOGUE

LANA, SIX MONTHS LATER

I brushed my fingers over the grey roses lining my garden. Corbin had been right, they had come back to life, blooming even after Ellevail had fallen in my absence. With evil gone from the world—and with what I suspected was the remnants of my dear friend's magic—it took barely any effort at all to get the place exactly as he'd created it.

After gathering a few more flowers to complete my bouquet, I stared up at the sun, letting it warm my face.

The past few months hadn't been easy, but they'd been some of the best of my entire life.

I shifted my deep blue dress, cursing the layers of tulle as I kicked my feet, struggling to lift my skirts while holding the flowers.

"I swear, will there ever come a time when you aren't looking like you're desperate for my help?" Kalliah said from the bottom of the stairs.

I grinned. "Where would be the fun in that?"

"Come on," she sighed. "Half your hair is out already."

We climbed the stairs together and entered my chambers. With my garden behind here, I couldn't face taking up residence in any other part of the castle. So, at the demand of my more elderly advisors, my rooms were slightly reimagined to accommodate a queenlier space.

That also made room for my king, who stayed true to his word and refused to leave Ellevail for any extended length of time.

I sat at my vanity while Kalliah took out pins and rearranged my hair, braiding the top and then gathering the rest to the side to drape down my shoulder.

A knock sounded at my door, and I called for whomever it was to enter.

Ian stepped into my room, carrying a tray of baked goods.

"I stole these but also spread a rumor in the kitchen that it was Leif. Lucinda is going to lose it," he laughed.

"Leif is an advisor now, he can't still be afraid of her," I said, reaching for a chocolate croissant.

Kalliah snorted. "Yep, still afraid. He's even got Jax running from her."

"Oh? Does he now?" I teased, grinning at her in the mirror. "Where are your men at the moment?"

Ian laughed as Kalliah blushed. "Not my men."

"Right. Jax was a flirt since I met him, yet you simply glance at him and he bows at your feet. One would think you're the queen in his eyes. And don't get me started on Leif."

Kalliah scoffed.

"Do they play nicely together?" Ian teased, falling onto one of the chaises with biscuits in both hands as he propped up his feet.

"You would think that a queen and the Commander of Atheria's forces would have a little decorum," Kalliah huffed. "A miniscule amount at least."

Ian and I said, "No," in unison and laughed.

"Technically, I haven't been crowned queen yet," I argued.

Kalliah pinched my shoulder. "We're getting ready for your coronation. I'd say you're queen."

My coronation. One I'd be doing alongside Kade. We'd assembled representatives from both Brookmere and Mysthaven, and in the month-long summit, the thing most readily agreed upon was that we'd both rule.

It wasn't an issue, luckily, since according to Kade, once the political nonsense was over, we'd be having a wedding, something he claimed to be vital.

I bit my lip, remembering how I'd all but tackled him in a secluded hallway after that meeting, allowing him to put his shadows to very good use.

Another knock echoed in my chamber, and Ian jumped up. Raya and Storm both entered, dressed in stunning outfits for the occasion.

Ian swept Raya into a hug, pinning her to the wall next to the door as he kissed her.

"For fuck's sake, you two," Storm grumbled as he dodged out of the way. He straightened the collar of his black tunic.

"Don't you look dashing." I smiled at him as Kalliah pinned the last piece of my hair up.

Raya wore a gold dress, shimmering every time she moved, which was often considering Ian couldn't keep his hands off her.

Storm wore a blue sash over his jacket, fiddling with it. "I don't understand why there's so many layers to this damn thing."

I walked toward him, flipping a part of the sash that had twisted at his shoulder. "You're the Duke of Mysthaven." I grinned. "Titled and everything now. You represent half of the kingdom. You're going to have to dress the part for official events."

He rolled his eyes. "As my queen commands it," he added, sounding irritated except for the small smile he gave me.

Jax stumbled in the room, followed closely by Leif. He ran in and kissed Kalliah on the cheek before diving for the tray of food. "Fates, I'm starving. Lana, if I'm going to be here, we need to talk about the lack of fresh apples in my room."

Leif, smiling and shaking his head at Jax, kissed Kalliah's other cheek before walking farther into the room.

"You mean Kalliah's room?" I asked.

He narrowed his eyes. "Our room."

"Maybe it's not me who needs the extension to my rooms but my lady-in-waiting," I teased her, but she wouldn't meet my gaze in the mirror.

"I swear, one more word, Lan—" She paused suddenly. A deep pink rose to her cheeks. Jax stopped eating and moved to go to her, but she swatted him away. "You know what, actually, yes. It's *our* room. I'm with him." She pointed to Leif. "And him." She pointed to Jax. "They've both crawled under my skin and I happen to love them, so there's no need for anymore teasing." She sighed, brushing her hands along her dress before she nodded.

Jax jumped from the couch, undeterred this time by her shooing, and kissed her, cupping her face before pushing her body against Leif. "I have been waiting for this moment for months," he sighed, grinning.

I laughed, clearing my throat. "Honestly, Kalliah, we just wanted you to finally admit it."

She huffed, but there was no hiding her smile as her men flanked her, fussing over her in the way she deserved.

A shimmering black hole appeared by the fireplace, and Lucien jumped out of it, no longer hiding in corners when he used his magic. Kade followed a moment later.

I ran across the room, jumping into his arms. While I didn't fear his trips to Mysthaven, the bond in my chest only settled when he was close.

He rested his hands on either side of my neck, tilting my chin with his thumb as he kissed me deeply. "Fates, I missed you."

"It was two days," Jax said through a stuffed mouth.

Kade shot him a look. "You left after one because of 'urgent matters' back here."

Jax grinned and shrugged.

Lucien twirled in a circle and collapsed onto the cushioned bed Jax had made for him. He'd found someone in Mysthaven to use their magic on it so Lucien's tail didn't rip the fabric. He'd officially become the most spoiled pugron alive.

Well, the only pugron alive that we knew of right now.

Perhaps I'd have to let him run in the Southern Forest to see if there were more in Atheria. After all, he could simply portal us there. We were forever grateful for those particular abilities, allowing us to avoid wasting so much time traveling between the two palaces. Especially for Raya, Jax, and Storm, who still had duties to tend to in Mysthaven.

Kade had already made it clear he would not be residing in Mysthaven at all, hence immediately pronouncing Storm his successor and placing him in charge.

"Everything okay?" I asked my mate, adjusting the pins atop my head delicately to keep Kalliah from yelling at me for ruining her masterpiece.

He nodded. "Everything is signed, the advisors we selected are in place, and all are ready for their duke's return after the coronation."

"I still can't believe you're making me do this," Storm said. "I'm not royalty."

"Technically, you are now," Kade said, clasping his shoulder. "Think of it as payment for all the shit you put up with."

"Oh, by giving me more *shit* to deal with? Perfect." He shoved Kade playfully.

"I heard some of the former nobles were going to Mysthaven to show unity among our people," I said, reaching down on my vanity for Kade's mother's necklace.

Kade's eyes softened as he watched me put it on.

Storm cleared his throat. "Oh?"

"Keena is supposedly among them."

He stretched his neck as color spread up it. "I wouldn't know anything about that."

I hummed, taking one last look in the mirror.

A rapid knock at the door took each of us by surprise this time. "Who else is left?" I asked.

"Your Majesty," a frantic voice sounded from the other side of the door. "Your Majesty."

I opened it to a red-faced staff member. He'd been with my father for years and served as his assistant. He longed to retire, or so he said. He'd agreed to stay on until a replacement could be found. However, every person he interviewed had some shortcoming that made them unfit to fill the role. Part of me thought he'd never be able to give up his job. He was always mumbling about how the castle wouldn't run on time if it wasn't for him.

"Your Majesty." He bowed his head. "Everyone is—" He froze, quickly taking in the room filled with so many advisors. It was a sight most were used to seeing from us at this point, our casual demeanor with one another, and the fact that we gathered in my private chambers as if it were a public space. Yet they all still acted shocked each time. I had a feeling the way we ran things would take some getting used to. "Everyone is waiting. We must make our way to the throne room, or we'll be late."

"We wouldn't want that," I said, placating the kind man.

He pushed his spectacles up his nose from where they'd slipped. "Very good. Very good. Come now."

With my friends surrounding me, we made our way to the throne room. They entered first, bowing dramatically. Kade and I stood in front of the closed doors, waiting to be announced.

He took my hand, kissing my palm before wrapping it around his arm. The doors opened. "Ready, my queen?"

I nodded, and together, we entered the throne room, glass

dome sparkling above us. The roses blooming were brilliantly full, wrapping around the columns scattered throughout the grand chamber. The marble floors glistened, reflecting the starry night beautifully.

A hush fell over the crowd, and as we passed, every person dropped on one knee. A quartet played a song created as the new Atherian anthem, a blend of both kingdoms' styles.

As we made our way down the aisle, I tried hard to take in every detail before me. All of the faces of those in attendance. I wanted to just be present in this moment. Before I knew it, we'd arrived at the end, our thrones waiting to be taken.

Ian approached us, two guards carrying the ceremonial crowns behind him. One of whom had been responsible for burying my mother. Ian had promoted him, and I could already tell he planned on mentoring him for future promotions.

"What are you doing?" I asked.

"A new law was passed this morning by the council of advisors. Coronating the king and queen falls to the Commander of Atheria."

I bit my quivering lip, knowing we had come full circle, and my oldest friend would be the one to crown me as queen.

Ian shifted to the side, standing in front of Kade. "Kade Blackthorn, do you swear to serve Atheria, the united kingdoms of both Brookmere and Mysthaven, to the greatest of your ability, ensuring peace reigns in our land? Devoting yourself to the good of both kingdoms, putting your people above all others?"

"I will honor and serve," he said. "No one will be above my mate though," he whispered in my ear.

Ian shot him a look, rolling his eyes before he stepped forward as Kade kneeled. I watched as my best friend crowned my king.

He stepped in front of me next.

"Illiana Dresden." His voice cracked, and a few people in

the crowd chuckled. He cleared his throat. "Do you swear to serve Atheria, the united kingdoms of both Brookmere and Mysthaven, to the greatest of your ability, ensuring peace in our land reigns? Devoting yourself to the good of both kingdoms, putting your people above all others?" I watched tears glisten in Ian's eyes as I took a deep breath. I'd been queen in name for months now, but this official ceremony felt different, bigger. Uniting a healed land.

"I will honor and serve," I promised proudly.

I kneeled, feeling the crown settle on my head. When I rose, Ian winked. "I'm so proud of you," he murmured softly.

Ian turned, addressing the crowd. "May I present King Kade Blackthorn and Queen Illiana Dresden."

"Long live the king! Long live the queen!"

Fae clapped and cheered, but none louder than our own friends, who had become our family. As I looked out into the crowd, Kade spun in front of me.

"Long live the queen." He kneeled on the ground, bowing his head. One by one the crowd rippled, bowing in turn.

"Rise, my people. Let us celebrate." I smiled at all of them, just so happy to finally be here, finally queen.

When Kade lifted his head, he didn't move right away.

"Little Rebel." He grinned at me mischievously. "I once told you if there was the slightest chance I could win your heart, I'd get to my knees before you and claim you as mine."

I swallowed, unable to look away from those perfect stormy grey eyes.

"Will you do me the honor of allowing me to be *your* king from now until the next life, our next adventure, in all the forevers to come?"

Jax yelped, shouting a joyful cry. "What do you say, Queenie?"

I laughed, choking on my tears as I grinned down at Kade, despite them blurring my vision. I blinked them away, nodding furiously.

He rose, pulling out the most gorgeous ring. The silver band was covered in an array of amethysts and diamonds, while a single sapphire gem sat on top.

The ring slipped onto my finger perfectly, and he lifted me up. "I had another reason for going back to Mysthaven. I had to pick up my mother's ring."

I leaned back, smiling and cupping the side of his face. "Anything from you is perfect. I'll wear it proudly."

"You haven't technically given your answer yet, Little Rebel."

I swallowed back my emotions as I threw my arms around him. "Yes," I laughed.

We will marry you, my light answered too.

Kade's eyes widened, and his shadows flared. "I heard them."

I winked at him. "I knew we'd get there."

He spun me around in a circle before setting me back down and offering his hand. "Dance with me?"

"In all the forevers to come," I answered.

He put an arm around my waist, leading me forward. The string quartet started playing again as Fae cleared the floor, making way for us.

He pulled me close, spinning me around as the starry night sparkled above us. "I'm thinking Kade Dresden?"

I laughed. "You'll change your name?"

"Blackthorn means nothing to me. I belonged to you before I even met you, Little Rebel. I *will* claim you and all you are in every way possible. Including your name."

Without any regard for proper decorum, I jumped into his arms, letting him hold me against his body, and kissed him. He spun me around once before I slowly slid down, shivering in anticipation of our life to come.

My light and his shadows danced around the floor to the rhythm of the strings.

The crowd cheered.

My heart and my soul were complete.

Surrounded by the love of my kingdom, but most importantly my friends, I closed my eyes and reminded myself that I was Illiana Dresden, and I was stronger than any darkness.

The End.

Curious what happened in Kalliah's room with Jax and Leif?
Check out this Bonus Scene from Jax's POV!
Please note, this scene features multiple partners.
Download the bonus scene here:

ACKNOWLEDGMENTS

We can't believe it's time to say goodbye to these characters, this world, and our very first series together.

Writing together has been an incredible journey neither of us were truly prepared for. From a fun idea, to working together plotting, writing, marketing, learning, struggling, laughing until we cried—it all culminated in this, the finale of The Broken Prophecy Series.

The hours we've spent together creating this piece of our souls were some of the very best. We are so grateful you've joined us on this adventure, and we can't wait for the plans we have to come!

To our Alpha / Beta Readers—Katie B., Mims, Megan, Cara, Shanni, and Katie D.: We'll never be able to say thank you enough. Thank you for reading rough, unedited versions of our work and providing unbelievable insights, comments, and critiques. Thank you for not only cheering us on with your comments and reactions, but also for pushing us to be better. We love you so much. Thank you for your time and energy!

To our Little Rebels Street Team: What did we do to deserve you?! This wouldn't be the same without our unhinged chats, group videos, and fun. The time and energy you spend promoting our work is absolutely unreal. It's you who have made so many of the things we've been able to do possible! Getting to meet some of you in real life has been some of the absolute BEST times and we can't wait for all of our adventures ahead and to meet so many more of you!

To Tairn is my Dom Daddy: Thank you for letting us lure you into a group chat with a ridiculous name ... we'll never apologize for capturing you and refusing to let go. Thank you for evolving from readers to friends, to the besties we can't live without. We are so grateful to have you not just in our writing life but intertwined into EVERY aspect of our lives.

To Jessica Threet & Gabriel Michael: There is no one else for Lana & Kade (and all the characters you brought to life). Thank you for pouring your heart and talent into our audiobooks. Your passion shines in every second of your performances. We have loved getting to know you and can't wait to see where you go in your careers ... we'll be fan-girling and cheering you on always!

To Christie Stratos at Proof Positive Editing: Thank you for pouring your knowledge and talent into this series and making it the best version of our words.

To Jessica Allain at Enchanting Covers: We know we pester you *constantly* for covers, character art, sprayed edges, and so much more. We're so lucky we came across your website and are thankful to have you in our corner, bringing our covers, art, and ideas to life!

To our friends and family, who went on this wild ride of an entire trilogy with us, THANK YOU!

To Anna's parents, who watch her daughters while we travel to conventions, signings, and more ... you're saints. Thank you for supporting our dreams.

To Ray for always being so supportive and giving me the time and space to pursue this dream I didn't even know I had. I love you so much. This wouldn't be possible without you.

Last, but never least ... we want to thank you, our readers! None of this would be possible without you. Every post, share, message to us, every moment has been a surreal experience, and we are grateful for you every single day. Thank you for taking a chance on us and allowing us to grow and chase dreams we never even knew we had. You are amazing, beautiful, one-of-a-kind souls we can't live without.

This isn't goodbye, it's just so long for now. Lana, Kade, Ian, Storm, and all your favorites will always be here, waiting for you to come home to Atheria.

May nature guide you, Little Rebel.

Until next time ... Happy Reading!

WHERE TO FIND ANNA & HELEN

We're most active on Instagram & in our Facebook Reader Group! We'd love to hear from you there!

Facebook Reader Group:
Anna & Helen's Enchanted Society
https://www.facebook.com/groups/
annaandhelensenchantedsociety

Anna's Instagram:
https://www.instagram.com/authorannaapplegate/

Helen's Instagram:
https://www.instagram.com/authorhelendomico/

ABOUT THE AUTHORS

Anna Applegate is a USA Today Bestselling Author. She writes fantasy romance and lives tucked away in rural Maryland surviving on coffee, champagne, and an unchecked book addiction.

Anna is an avid reader, especially if it involves morally grey love interests. She enjoys escaping into the fictional worlds she creates - filled with strong heroines, surprise twists and turns, and "destroy the world for her" leading men.

***

Helen Domico published her first romantasy in 2024 and has no plans on stopping. Writing a book was always a bucket-list item, but when the opportunity knocked on her door to do so with one of her best friends, she couldn't say no!

When not writing, you can find Helen reading, spending time with her family, and sneaking in a glass of cabernet. Helen resides in central Maryland with her husband and two children.

***

Anna & Helen love hearing from their readers! Find them on their social media or website to connect!